W9-AHH-177

MANIA

MANIA

CRAIG
LARSEN

PINNACLE BOOKS
KENSINGTON PUBLISHING CORP.

PINNACLE BOOKS are published by

Kensington Publishing Corp.
119 West 40th Street
New York, NY 10018

ISBN-13: 978-1-61523-586-5

Printed in the United States of America

For
my brother
who has been my cornerstone
and who has blazed all my trails

Part 1

chapter 1

The murder seemed to unfold out of step with time.

It was past midnight. The air was cool, brisk. November was giving way to December, and a storm was riding into Seattle. Rain clouds had been gathering, looming low in the sky all day long. Fog lay over the waterfront like a heavy blanket, slowly stealing into the city on the back of a menacing, salt-laced breeze. Without a moon, it was a particularly dark night.

A half step behind his older brother, struggling to keep pace, Nick's face reflected his distress. Feeling ill, he had left the raucous, fumy bar in front of Sam, crashing through the doors into the night like he was trying to escape. A few blocks on, his face was sweaty, and he felt flushed, out of breath. His ears were still ringing with music from the jazz club. Oblivious to Nick's discomfort, Sam led the way to the car in silence, his back straight, his footsteps drumming a deliberate, rhythmic beat.

The shadows were so dense that Nick and Sam could barely see the edge of the deserted parking lot where they had left Sam's new BMW a few hours earlier. Nick had the vague sense that they were being watched. Neither he nor Sam, though, had any idea that, just thirty feet away from them, crouching hidden beside a rusted Dumpster, a man dressed in rags was spying on them. Waiting. Hypnotized by the echoing cadence of their footsteps.

The lights at the ferry landing flickered in the fuzzy darkness, receding behind them as the two brothers crossed Alaskan Way. In front of them, across the empty lot, a public staircase leading steeply up toward Pike Place Market disappeared into a blackness as solid as a charcoal wall. Several clubs had let out, and the stillness was broken by distant shouts. Two streets down, five or six drunken college students were squeezing into a car, loudly debating whether to head back to campus or look for an after-hours venue. The tendrils of a girl's high-pitched laughter cascaded shrilly through the night, encircling the brothers like the hair of a siren, punctuated by the metallic slam of a door. Nick hardly heard the sounds.

His fingers had found a wad of bills at the bottom of his jacket pocket. He gripped the roll, weighing it, then let it go. The paper felt grimy, dirty. Hunching against the cold, he eyed his more successful brother, aware that he must have slipped the cash into his pocket during the course of the evening. This wasn't the first time Sam had come to his aid. Without Sam, he would have been homeless. About a decade before, after their parents died, Nick had suffered a breakdown. Sam had taken him in and helped him through college. Nick wanted to be grateful. He needed the money. He barely had enough in his checking account to make rent. Resentment was welling up inside him so strongly, though, that Nick could barely restrain himself from hurling the bundle of cash at the back of his brother's head. Like a rock. Like a jagged, heavy chunk of stone.

Nick felt his teeth clench. Sam was striding gracefully next to him as though he hadn't been at all affected by the vodka. His posture was rigidly upright. Nick had never really put it into words before, not until this very second. *Sam was the more powerful of the two.* He had grown up, whereas Nick somehow still felt like an ineffectual kid. Nick's body stiffened. Struggling to catch his breath, he had to fight the sensation that Sam had gripped him around the neck and was squeezing his thumbs into his windpipe. The asphalt danced a bit beneath his feet.

A few steps farther, the small blur of movement in front of them that presaged the attack barely caught Nick's attention. The darkness seemed to change shape in front of them, that was all. Sam didn't see it. Glancing upward, trying to pull himself from his thoughts, Nick looked instinctively for the closest source of light. On the edge of the dark, empty lot, an industrial street lamp was burning overhead, its dim bulb suffocating in a swirling pool of mist.

When the shadows shifted again, Nick reached to touch his older brother lightly on the arm, stopping himself in midstep. His heart leapt. *Someone was out there, no more than twenty feet in front of them.* The wind picked up off Elliott Bay, slicing through Nick's thin jacket, blowing the tail of his shirt in front of him like a mast pennant.

Sam opened his mouth to ask Nick why he had stopped. He had time only to face his brother before a blurred, ferocious shape emerged from the darkness, rushing at them with a violence that stunned both the brothers, rooting them to the ground. Nick couldn't comprehend the speed with which they were being attacked. The whirling shape was already on top of them before it resolved itself crisply into the form of a tall, crazed man dressed in rags.

Sam was a half step in front of Nick, in the man's path. He didn't move. The wind was lifting his hair, but he stood as still as a statue, frozen with confusion. Nick didn't have time to try to warn him. The man was charging them, one hand reaching toward Sam's shoulder, the other raised above his head, brandishing a knife. Nick didn't hesitate. He leapt in front of his brother, reaching for the man's wrist. As he met the larger, stronger man, it felt as if the man was going to trample him.

Nick was aware of how greasy the man's sleeve was. The rancid smell of the man's clothing filled his nose. His unshaven chin dug sharply into his cheek. When Nick reached for his other wrist, trying to stop him, the man's fingers sunk like nails into his ribs. Why wasn't Sam helping? The man was grunting, trying to regain his footing, wrestling himself free. This was no scuffle. He was going to kill them. Nick clung to his wrist. "Sam, help," he heard himself mutter. "Sam, please." *Louder.* "Sam!"

He was drowning. The man was taller than he was. His arms were longer. His wrists felt as wide and powerful as two-by-fours. When the man finally found his balance, he pushed Nick off him and threw him to the ground. The asphalt spun toward his face with the intensity of a cyclone. Nick had the impression that he was landing on the gravelly pavement face-first, without breaking his fall.

Nick was only vaguely conscious of the violence that followed. The knife described a gleaming arc through the mist. Nick heard the sharp slice of its blade sinking into flesh. But the night had otherwise gone silent. Sam shuddered, then crumpled to the ground without a sound.

Nick couldn't breathe. He was screaming without words. *Why, Sam, why? Why didn't you protect yourself?*

Nick gathered himself. His arms and his legs shook. Had he been stabbed, too? No, he wasn't bleeding. His forehead had hit the pavement, and his ribs were stitched with pain, but he was all right. He would be next, though. The man had dispensed with Sam, and he was turning on him.

Nick slid backward on the pavement, cowering, trying to escape. The man was approaching him, raising the knife into the air.

"You and I are brothers."

The man's savage voice sent ice through Nick's veins. He wanted to ask him what he meant, but he couldn't. *How are you and I brothers? Sam is my brother.* Had he only imagined the man's words?

Nick became aware of a sudden blur of movement in the darkness just beyond the man. His heart leapt when Sam rose up improbably from the ground, pulling himself heroically to his feet behind the crazed attacker. He closed on the man like a shadow. He was going to jump him.

The last image that registered with Nick was the man's face. His skin was pocked and sallow. His nose seemed to droop over his upper lip, and it was freckled with large black pores and snaked with veins. His eyes were watery blue and bloodshot, open too wide.

Then the night went black.

When Nick opened his eyes, the blackness blanketing him didn't make sense. His legs and feet were icy cold, and he could taste the warm, slippery, briny flavor of blood in his mouth. For a split second he imagined he was lying frozen in snow. He didn't understand the sound of the foghorn behind him or the harsh feeling of gravel against his cheek. He had opened his eyes squinting, somehow expecting the glare of daylight.

Things pieced themselves back together gradually. He was in Seattle. He had been sitting in a jazz club for a couple of hours. His ears were still buzzing from the music. It had been loud, and he and Sam had had to shout to each other just to be heard.

Sam.

Nick pushed his hands against the ground, raising himself up. He had been lying facedown, his cheek pressed against something sharp. His legs had been wide apart, almost as if he had been sleeping, looking for a comfortable position in his slumber. *Where was he?* He twisted onto his side, expecting to find himself in the parking lot. Where were the voices and laughter of the college students?

"Sam?"

The air was as heavy as wet towel. He recognized the splash of water slapping against a pier and then the screech of a seagull. His body ached all over. Sharp pains shot through his ribs every time he tried to move, winding him. His cheek was throbbing. He raised his fingers to his face, understanding that he had been badly cut. A large lump had formed over his left eye.

"Sam," he said, louder.

The gigantic shadow next to him resolved itself into the hull of a ship, rising out of the fog beside a pier fifty yards away, across a stretch of black water.

Nick winced.

Abruptly, his ears rang with the sound of the man panting, running toward Sam and him out of the shadows. The man's lurid face was in front of him. Nick could see his rough skin, his cracked lips. His watery blue eyes were open wide with panic, almost as if he were the more terrified, as if he were the one being attacked, not the two brothers. The man's hands were wrapped in tattered and dirty, oily rags. The knife glinted in the weak light of the street lamp overhead. The man was going to stab Sam. He was breathing raspingly. His clothes were rustling. The sound became impossibly loud. Falling to the ground, Nick squeezed his eyes shut and raised his hands, preparing himself to be struck.

"Sam!" His voice seemed to echo in the darkness, and then the vision faded away.

The sound of a train rolling slowly over rusty rails caused Nick to open his eyes. His surroundings began to make sense to him. Where he had expected to see the flat pavement of the parking lot, he found grass on sandy soil, carefully planted bushes and trees. The huge aluminum hulls of a few aircraft were rolling eerily through the night, being ferried by train to one of the Boeing plants. He was in Elliott Bay Park. That's where he was. More than half a mile from the lot where he and his brother had been attacked. He had been lying unconscious on the running path, in the small strip of green planted between the railway tracks and the dock where cargo ships moored to take on loads of gravel.

Fighting the pain that gripped his body, Nick raised himself to his knees, then stood all the way up. His face was bloodied and bruised. He was certain that a number of his ribs had been broken. The soles of his feet felt raw and cut, and he realized that his feet were bare. Where were his shoes? He straightened his jacket on his shoulders and looked around.

It was so dark, the fog so heavy, that he could barely

see. He glanced at the black shadow of the ship moored on the pier, then began walking back toward the parking lot on Alaskan Way, becoming ever more anxious. A few steps on, he began to trot, then to run.

The swirling red lights of a police cruiser were visible from a distance, silky in the brackish mist being swept into Seattle by the approaching storm. Nick slowed down. The way the lights were shifting and dancing in the dark air, he understood that more than one cruiser had answered the call. The police had gathered in force, treating the parking lot like a crime scene. Something terrible had happened to Sam. He listened, trying to make sense of the voices squawking over police radios and the scratch of footsteps in the gravel. Confusion overwhelmed him. He wished he could recall what had happened.

Nick slid backward on the pavement as the man approached. The grit of the asphalt was sharp on his fingers. When his brother rose up behind the man, Nick's hopes rose with him in his chest. Sam wasn't going to let this happen. He would grab the man, wrestle the knife from his hand. When Sam took a step forward, though, he stumbled uncertainly on his feet, unable to find his balance. The man had stabbed him. The knife had already done its damage. The man turned around to face him.

"Look out, Sam!"

Sam seemed barely conscious. The man took his time. He gripped the knife, weighing it deliberately, tightening his filthy fingers around its handle. Bending his knees, he swiveled his hips and shoved the knife into Sam's stomach. Blood splattered Nick's face. Sam lurched forward, momentarily suspended on his toes above the man's powerful upward thrust. His face was a study not in terror but surprise. He wasn't afraid. He was stunned. He hardly seemed to react. Then he fell away from the knife. The sharp steel blade scintillated evilly in the dark night.

Nick scrambled to his knees, fighting to reach his brother.

Three squad cars were parked askew, the closest one with its doors wide open, as though it had screeched to a stop and the police officers had jumped out. An ambulance waited nearby. Several orange cones had been planted on the ground, yellow tape pulled around them. Despite the late hour, a few people had collected at the edge of the scene, gawking at the policemen. Nick hurried forward as he saw three men dressed in white picking up a large black body bag, heaving it onto a waiting stretcher. He stepped over the yellow police tape and fought through the gathering of policemen, unable to reconcile their relaxed attitude with the image of his brother's body in a zipped bag.

"Let me through!"

Someone seized him from behind. Nick tried to wrestle himself free, but the man holding him was strong. His fingers dug into Nick's biceps. Nick took in the faces of the policemen surrounding him. One of them was smiling. Another was speaking about the Seattle Seahawks, a football team. Light glinted off the brass badge pinned to an officer's uniform. The blur in front of him resolved itself into a face.

"Whoa there," the policeman said. "What's the rush, buddy?"

Several other policemen turned to look, their faces impassive. The plainclothes policeman in front of Nick—a tall, young man with a slightly pudgy face, dressed in a rumpled jacket and tie—alone appeared concerned. He held Nick by the shoulders, cataloging the cuts and bruises on his face.

"My name is Detective Adam Stolie," he said. "Hey—don't I know you?"

Nick shook his head. His throat was thick, and he couldn't seem to find his voice.

"Slow down there," the detective said. "You're Nick Wilder, aren't you? The photographer from the *Telegraph.* You're so beaten up, I almost didn't recognize you." The detective glanced behind him at one of the other policemen. "Hey, Brady," he said. "You want to come over here, give me a hand?"

A patrolman, shorter and thinner, broke free from the group of incongruously chatty policemen. Detective Stolie was studying Nick. "You want to tell me what you're doing here?"

Nick looked over at the long black bag on the stretcher. The orderlies were strapping it down with wide blue polyester straps, latching them closed with steel buckles. His eyes filled with tears.

"That's my brother," he heard himself say. "That's Sam."

He twisted to one side, trying to free himself. Stolie released his grip and let him go, and Nick fell to his knees next to the stretcher. The orderlies stopped what they were doing and took a small step backward.

"Open it up," Stolie said. Hesitating, one of the orderlies reached across Nick and unzipped the top of the bag.

Sam's eyes were open, unseeing. Nick couldn't make sense of his brother's face. It had been badly slashed. His cheek was hanging in a flap off the bone. His mouth was a bloody pulp, nearly unrecognizable. His teeth had been kicked into his throat. His hair was plastered to his forehead with a dark black, bloody scab. A gelatinous goop was oozing from his ears.

Nick hardly noticed. He was staring into Sam's open, lifeless eyes, crying uncontrollably. "What the hell are you doing?" Nick heard the wild shout. He didn't understand, though, that the voice belonged to him. "Why'd you put him in this bag?" His hands were ripping at the heavy black polyester, trying to pull his brother out from the body bag. "Can't you see? You're going to suffocate him." He turned on the orderlies, then, holding his bloody hands up toward the officers in supplication, found Detective Stolie with his eyes. "He can't breathe. Damn it, help me!" His voice rose into a scream. "You're going to kill him. Please, help me get him out of here!"

chapter 2

One month earlier, at the beginning of November, Nick had been woken up just before dawn by the buzzing of his cell phone. Despite how wintry it was outside, the building's heat was set too high, and Nick's cramped studio was hot and stuffy. He woke up disoriented, not certain what was happening. When the phone buzzed again, the dim light from its LCD screen gave shape to the dark room. Nick shielded his eyes and, raising himself onto an elbow, picked up the phone, becoming vaguely aware at the same time of the staccato rattle of the wind against the thin window panes. Recognizing the number, he settled back into bed and closed his eyes, then at last brought the phone to his ear.

"Officer Tyler."

"My man, Nicholas." The policeman sounded wide awake. No doubt he had been at the station through the night. "Sorry to wake you."

Nick ignored the apology. He was used to these calls.

"I thought you'd want to know. I'm just about to dispatch a couple of units out to Kent. You know the Peck Bridge?"

"Sure."

"There's a body there. They say it's a pretty bad sight. Something to see."

Nick was pushing himself up onto the side of his bed. "Has it gone out on the radio yet?"

"You know I always call you first, my man."

"What time is it?"

The police dispatcher didn't answer. He was laughing without mirth as he hung up the phone.

The sky was beginning to lighten into a white blanket of mist twenty-five minutes later as Nick's old white Toyota sputtered and choked to a stop near the Peck Bridge, on the outskirts of Seattle. The engine died when Nick stepped on the brake. Rather than try to restart it, he let the car roll silently to the shoulder of the two-lane road, then yanked on the emergency brake.

Outside, it was crisp and cold. There weren't any buildings along this stretch of the road. The landscape was barren and gray. The trees that lined the bank of the river had lost their leaves, and their branches looked naked and sharp. Nick walked the rest of the way to the flat, nondescript bridge. Down beneath him by the river, a team of policemen were sealing off the area, running police tape from stakes they had planted in the wet soil. Even though their light was no longer necessary, a few of them were still carrying flashlights, the lamps burning yellow holes into the thin fog. As Nick watched them, a white Channel 11 news van pulled to a stop on the bridge. The passenger window rolled down, and a heavily made-up woman leaned her head out, holding her coiffed hair carefully in place. "Sometimes I think you must drive in with the cops," she said to Nick.

Nick glanced back at her over his shoulder. On camera, the makeup made the woman look older. In person, Nick thought, she looked like a young woman with too much cream on her face. He noticed a smear of rouge in one of her eyebrows. He didn't bother saying hello. "I don't have the equipment to carry around that you do, Sheila."

"So what's it like down there? They letting the media in?"

Nick was noticing the hostile way the driver of the van was eyeing him. "I just got here. I don't know."

"Well, we'll see you down there, Nick." The window closed, and the TV van pulled forward, searching for a place to park and set up. Nick felt the woman's eyes on his back as he crossed the street.

Looking for a path down to the riverbank, he walked to the edge of the bridge, then took a step into the thick brush. The soil was muddy, and his feet sank with every step. He felt the mud seep into his shoes, then through his socks. These were his newest running shoes, his orange and black Nikes. He would have to clean them when he got back home.

The highest-ranking cop on scene was a beat officer Nick hadn't met before. They were still waiting for the homicide detectives to arrive from headquarters downtown. "What do you have?" Nick asked the cop.

The officer pointed toward the body. Nick could smell the coffee the man had been drinking a few minutes before. "As far as we can tell, she was murdered somewhere else. Her body's cold. The killer must have brought her out here to dump the body."

"Who was she?"

The cop sized him up. "You're with the *Telegraph*, right?"

Nick showed him his press card.

The cop read it and, satisfied, handed it back. "A hooker—a streetwalker from downtown. First and Second Avenue."

"Who found her?"

The cop shrugged. "A couple of kids on their way to pick up papers. You know, for their paper route."

"They still around?"

"We got 'em in a van up on the street."

"Can I ask them a few questions?"

Again, the cop shrugged. "It's a free country."

"You got a name for her yet?"

"Claire Scott, we think. She was reported missing a few days ago. Someone's on their way out to ID her now."

"You mind if I take a look?"

"Be careful not to trample anything until Homicide gets here," the cop said. "But one or two pictures won't hurt, I guess."

"Thanks."

"Just tell Benson I sent you over."

Nick was aware of the tracks his footsteps left in the muddy ground as he walked toward the body. No one stopped him as he approached. Maybe because the victim was a prostitute, Nick thought. No one cared. Aware of the damage he was causing to the crime scene, though, Nick himself stopped about fifteen feet from the body. When he could smell it. He stared at the pattern of ugly blue and purple bite marks the killer had left in the whore's yellowing skin. He raised his camera to his eye, using his telephoto lens to bring the naked corpse closer to him. The apparatus made a satisfying click as he noticed the blood matting the tuft of hairs at the woman's vagina. Nick found himself blinking as he took the camera away from his face, swallowing to keep himself from becoming sick. The killer had entered the woman with a blade.

Turning away, trying to forget the small cloud of flies buzzing above the rotting flesh, laying their larvae in the prostitute's wounds, he caught sight of another set of tracks in the muddy soil. He let his eyes follow them until they disappeared into the tall grass and nettles feeding off the river. Noticing something unusual about the footsteps, he looked back at the tracks he himself had left, deliberately comparing them. He raised his camera again and snapped a few pictures of the muddy footprints. Then he backtracked, retracing his steps away from the body.

The cop who had let him pass was busy turning Sheila back from the crime scene. Nick waited for him to explain that her crew would compromise the evidence. *But you let him through,* Sheila said, pointing toward Nick. The officer's face remained impassive. *Maybe I shouldn't have,* he said. Up at the bridge, a convoy of five or six cruisers was pulling to a stop, lights flashing, splashing the river valley with waves of electric color. *That's Homicide now,* the cop said to the TV crew. *You talk to them. As of now, the crime scene's sealed, and I'm going to have to ask you to step back. Come on now, you, too,* he said to Nick. *Step back up to the road.*

"Let me ask you something," Nick said as he approached the officer again.

The officer didn't respond directly. "Just keep walking."

"You take a look at the set of footsteps leading up to the body?"

"Yeah, sure," the officer said, irritated.

"You notice anything odd about them?"

"Like what?"

"Go take a look at them again," Nick said. "You'll see. Whoever left them wasn't wearing shoes."

"How do you know?"

"Go take a look at them again," Nick repeated.

He passed Detective Adam Stolie without saying hello. The detective had his hands full. He glanced at Nick without noticing him. A teenage boy was walking in front of him, threatening to break away from the group of policemen and to run down the embankment toward the body half hidden in the grass. Stolie grabbed him by the shoulder to restrain him.

"Yo, Daniel," the detective said. "Slow it down, would you? We don't even know it's your mom yet, okay?"

Nick stopped at the edge of the bridge. He propped his camera on the low concrete barrier to steady it, then zoomed in on the body. Ten minutes later, he was able to snap a few good pictures of the boy identifying his mother, his face drawn, destroyed.

It began to rain as Nick left the crime scene. Sheila was helping the Channel 11 crew stow the camera equipment into the back of the van. As he walked past in the direction of his car, he smiled at her, but he didn't slow down.

"You know," she said, finding her voice, "I saw you the other day. At the press conference at City Hall."

Nick was already past her. He recognized that she

was just trying to keep him there, but he stopped anyway. "Did you?" He had no recollection of her being there.

"Yeah. I was—well, I was going to ask you if you wanted to get lunch sometime—or whatever."

Nick realized that he had never really looked at her. Her makeup was so thick that it was beginning to crack like the floor of a desert. Instead, though, Nick became aware of the blush of her skin underneath. "Sure," he said. "That would be nice. Hey—I'd better get going now—I've got to get these pictures uploaded if I want them to hit the afternoon edition."

"Yeah. Sure." Sheila smiled beneath her oily mask.

Walking on, Nick flinched a little, trying to erase the image of Sheila's awkward approach from his mind.

Back at his car, he looked up at the sky as he kicked off some of the mud caked to the soles of his shoes. In the last week, the weather had turned. It had gone from late summer to autumn. The rains would get heavier soon, the nights would get longer and colder. Without the sun, the chill would never fully leave the air.

The sight of the mutilated corpse had shaken him. Unlocking his car, Nick decided to stop at the Starbucks he frequented near his apartment for a coffee before heading in to the paper. He wanted time to settle himself, and he could just as easily upload his photographs onto his laptop and send them into the office from there, using the café's wireless link. He twisted the key in the ignition and flicked on the windshield wipers, unconsciously squeezing his arms against his ribs, tightening his fingers around the plastic steering wheel as he pulled away from the curb.

Lost in his thoughts, haunted by the vision of the

corpse lying butchered in the wet grass, Nick had no way of knowing that just a few minutes later Sara Garland would fall into his life, unexpectedly, with the certain grace of a diver swooping without a splash into a deep pool of water.

chapter 3

Beyond the plate-glass windows of the Starbucks, the sky was so low and gray that street lamps were still burning at ten in the morning. A fierce wind was blowing, whipping brown and yellow leaves down the broad street, tossing heavy drops of freezing rain in handfuls against the thick window panes. The café was packed with students from the University of Washington. The line stretched nearly to the door. Nick had been lucky to snag the table in front of the gas-burning fireplace. Unsteady still, he was staring at the screen of his small computer, oblivious to the voices rising and falling around him.

When a green-eyed girl with Nordic blond hair stood in front of his table and spoke to him, Nick hardly noticed her. She was only one more of the rumpled, tired-looking students milling around the room, waiting for an empty table. The blond-haired girl put her slender ivory hand down next to his laptop and leaned closer to him.

"Is anyone sitting here?" she repeated.

His interest piqued by the smooth texture of her skin and her long, delicate fingers, Nick looked up at her. The first thought that crossed his mind was that he had never seen a more beautiful woman. The tall, svelte girl smiled at him, and Nick found himself smiling back at her, stunned by the radiance of her eyes. "No," he said, shaking his head. "No one."

"May I?" She rested a hand on the back of the chair opposite Nick, but politely waited for him to respond.

Nick shrugged.

"It's a good place to sit," she said, slipping into the chair. "Right in front of the fire."

As Nick pulled his laptop back to clear a space for her on the table, he realized that she wasn't carrying a coffee.

"I just came inside to get out of the rain," she said, reading his gaze. "I left my house this morning without my coat. It's cold out there."

"Yeah. Miserable."

Drops of water glistened in the girl's hair like tiny diamonds. She was wearing a thin white blouse, and her shoulders were wet with rain. Nick's eyes were drawn despite himself to the lace straps of her bra, visible through the sheer material.

"When I saw this place by the fire, I thought I'd grab it." She glanced out the slick window at the dark, windblown street. "I hope you don't mind."

Nick shook his head.

"Will you hold this chair for me, then?" She twisted around in her seat and checked the line in front of the counter, just as one of the servers raised his voice and announced, *Keith, your non-fat cap' is ready. Keith.* "I think I'll get a cup of coffee."

Nick was unable to take his eyes off her as she walked to the counter. A number of other heads turned as well as she walked past. She was an extraordinarily beautiful woman. Assured and elegant, flawless. Nick wondered who she was and what she did. He imagined that she was at least twenty-five—too old to be an undergraduate at the university. She had distracted him from his computer, and he was still watching her a few minutes later when the server behind the counter called her name: *Sara. Your tall low-fat latte is ready.* She smiled at him on the way back to the table, and Nick felt his face flush. Once again, he was aware of the people watching her as she walked. She moved gracefully, and she seemed nearly to be glowing in her white blouse and tight jeans.

"So your name's Sara," he said as she sat back down across from him.

She was holding her coffee up to her lips, blowing on it. "Good job, Detective. Sara Garland," she said. "And you're Nick, I take it?"

Nick felt his eyebrows rise in surprise.

"It's on your cup," Sara said, smiling lightly. Nick followed her eyes down to the cup of coffee on the table between them, where indeed the server had scrawled his name with a thick black marker.

"Yeah. Nick Wilder."

"I hope I'm not interrupting you. It looks like you're pretty busy."

Nick glanced at his laptop. The screen had long since gone black. "No. I'm glad for the break."

She looked at him critically, trying to gauge his age as he had judged hers. "You're not a student. A graduate student, maybe. Or a teacher?"

"I'm a reporter," Nick said. "With the *Seattle Telegraph.*"

"That sounds glamorous."

Nick shrugged. "Not really. It's a lot of hours, and it doesn't pay much. The truth is you've got to be a little insane to work a job like this."

"What are you working on now? Are you writing an article?"

Nick shook his head. Sara's question had brought the image of Claire Scott's corpse back into his mind. The contrast with the woman sitting in front of him was unsettling. He closed his eyes and brought his hands to his face, running his fingers through his hair, becoming aware at the same time how disheveled he was. He had left his apartment a few hours before without showering or shaving.

"Are you all right?"

Nick noted the concern in Sara's eyes. "Is it that obvious?"

"You look upset, that's all."

"I have to admit," Nick said, "I am a bit. I'm sorry. I've been with the paper for a couple of years now. I should be used to it." He was surprised by his own candor. "I've been working as a photographer. I see things sometimes. It still gets to me."

Sara was peering at him.

"I'm sorry," he repeated. "I shouldn't have said anything."

Sara dismissed his apology. "No—don't be sorry." She hesitated. "It was a body. A murder. Wasn't it?"

"Yes." Nick was taken aback. "How did you know?"

"I have a confession to make, too."

Nick waited.

"I didn't sit down here because of the fire. I was standing behind you for about two minutes before I approached the table. You were pretty absorbed in your computer."

"You saw the pictures."

Sara nodded. "I have to tell you," she said, smiling wryly. "I was pretty relieved just now when you told me you were a reporter."

Nick took a fresh look at the beautiful woman in front of him, intrigued that she would sit down with him after seeing the images on the screen of his laptop.

"You took those pictures today?"

Nick lowered his eyes.

"So you were there. Standing right there, I mean. Almost on top of her."

"Yes." *Close enough to smell her.*

"No wonder you're freaked out."

From the corner of his eye, Nick noticed Sara's gaze traveling down his legs, taking in the mud drying on his shoes.

"It scares *me*"—Sara said, shivering slightly—"and I wasn't even there. To see a body like that, it must be pretty frightening—no matter how many times you've been around crimes like that before."

"It is," Nick admitted.

"I didn't really get a good look at the pictures. But I could see how violent the crime was. The guy who did it must have been crazy."

"That's not what scares me."

Sara was silent, waiting for Nick to meet her stare, waiting for him to continue.

"It scares me more how sane he was."

Again, Sara shivered. "What do you mean?"

Nick regretted that he had let them dwell so long on the murder.

"Tell me," Sara said, prodding him.

"How the same person can be one thing at night,"

Nick said at last, "and then something else during the day."

Nick read Sara's confusion.

"The guy stabbed this woman so many times—so brutally—she was nearly unrecognizable," he explained. "This same guy, though, takes the time to gather her up and sneak her out to the bank of this river to dispose of the body. That's what scares me. That the same person can somehow reconcile the two realities."

"Because you think maybe we're all capable of doing the same thing." Sara's eyes hadn't left his face. "That's what you mean, isn't it?"

"To some degree—yeah, maybe."

"Sane during the day. Killers at night."

Once again, Nick looked down at the table.

"You think you're capable of it?"

Nick turned Sara's words over in his mind. He found himself wondering whether she was asking him a question. *The truth is you've got to be a little insane to work a job like this.* His own voice seemed to resonate in his head, and he felt his face flush.

"It still sounds pretty amazing," Sara said into the awkward silence. "Your job, I mean."

"And what about you?" Nick asked her, determined to change the subject. "What do you do? You're not a student either, are you?"

A slight darkness clouded Sara's expression. There was something overwhelmingly *light* about Sara, he realized in contrast. Her hair was silvery blond. Her eyes were translucently green. Her teeth were dazzlingly white. Her skin was ivory. Still, as radiant as she was, there was something mysterious about this woman in front of him, too, something elusive he couldn't define. "No," she said, "I'm not a student, either. Is it so obvious that I'm too old?"

Loosening up a little, Nick looked up and down her body, from the top of her head to her toes. After all, she had invited him to. "Not exactly," he said. "It's not that you look too old to be a student. You seem too focused."

"That's the last thing I am." Sara's laugh was genuine, and Nick felt himself relax even more. "Just say it, I look too old to be a student."

He refused the bait and pushed the compliment another way. "Too polished anyway."

"I'm an actress," Sara said. "Well, off and on, anyway. Off right now. That's why I'm back here in Seattle."

"You're from Seattle originally?"

"My parents live in Bellevue."

"You're staying with them?"

Sara shrugged. "For a while. Maybe I'll get my own place one of these days. Or maybe I'll just head back down to LA."

"You've got something to head down there for? A project, I mean—a movie?"

Sara shook her head. "I've been lucky enough, I guess. But I haven't pursued it as much as I should. I'm thinking maybe I'll do something else entirely. Get into business, I don't know."

Nick's cell phone vibrated, and he glanced down at its screen. Recognizing Laura Daly's personal line from the *Telegraph* building, he remembered the staff meeting this morning, the first one for the month of October, when assignments would be handed out by the editors. The senior editor would no doubt be wondering where he was. "Excuse me," Nick said. "I've got to take this." He pressed a button on his phone and raised it to his ear. "Laura?"

"Were you planning to grace us with your presence, Nick?"

"I know. I'm sorry." Nick threw a quick, embarrassed smile at Sara.

"Don't sweat it. We'll talk when you come in. Listen, you somewhere close? There's something I'd like you to do now. A couple of blocks from here. It can't wait. You got a pen?"

Nick cradled the phone against his shoulder and searched through his bag for pen and paper. After scrawling down an address, he snapped the phone shut and looked apologetically at Sara. "I've got to go."

"Oh, really? That's too bad." When Sara glanced down at her watch, Nick noticed a gold and platinum Rolex loose on her wrist, its face set with diamonds. Not exactly the watch of a struggling actress.

"I wish I didn't have to. It's work." He closed the lid of his laptop and gathered his belongings from the table, scooping them into the soft leather shoulder bag he carried as he pushed his chair back from the table.

"Well, I enjoyed meeting you, Nick."

"It was good to meet you, too," Nick said, in a hurry.

"You're not forgetting something?"

Nick stopped to make certain he had grabbed all his things from the tabletop, then looked up at Sara, meeting her friendly gaze. He wasn't certain what she was referring to, and his expression reflected his puzzlement.

"I thought maybe you were going to ask me out." Sara's tone was playful, but she dropped her eyes, bashful.

Nick ran his fingers across his unshaven cheeks as he tried to assess her sincerity. He hadn't been expecting the approach.

"I have a weakness for shy guys," Sara said, as if she were answering an unspoken question.

"I thought the pictures might have frightened you off."

Sara laughed sweetly. "The pictures are why I'm here."

Nick measured her for a few more seconds, once again intrigued by this woman. There was more to her than her pretty face, he thought. Her appearance camouflaged it at first, but then, as much as her beauty validated her, the juxtaposition served too to heighten the observation. *She was dangerous.* At last, Nick relaxed into a smile. "I suppose I could ask you out for a coffee. But we've done that already, haven't we?"

Sara met his eyes. "It'll have to be something more, then."

Repeating the innocent words in his mind, Nick felt a sudden thrill pass through him, taking his breath away. "That sounds promising."

"Give him an inch and he takes a yard. I meant dinner."

"Really?"

"You sound tentative. You don't want me to see who you are after dark?"

"Now you're just mocking me. I'm shy, that's all. You said it yourself. That's what makes me so irresistible."

"You go to work now," Sara said. "Here's my number." She reached across the table and took Nick's phone from him, tapping a few numbers onto the display and then saving the number under her name. "Give me a call. I'm free tonight, if that's not too soon."

"No," Nick said, wondering how he would be able to wait that long. "It's not too soon. I'm free tonight, too."

Sara watched him as Nick found his way through the

crowded coffee shop to the exit. It was an unguarded moment for her, and her face reflected what she felt inside. Had he turned back around, her wistful expression would have confused him. Standing behind him as she had worked up her nerve to approach him, looking over his shoulder at the photographs this self-possessed man had taken that morning at the crime scene, Sara hadn't expected to like him. Not like this. Not this much.

chapter 4

After leaving the coffee shop, Nick headed downtown. He parked his car at the *Telegraph*, then cut back a few blocks on foot to Fourth Avenue to stake out the address the senior editor had given him over the phone. The rain had let up, but a drizzle was soaking through his clothes. Across the street from his target, he took his camera from his bag, checking its settings as he killed time, brushing water off its lens, scoping out the neighborhood. A few pedestrians were wandering in and out of some of the storefronts, but for the most part this section of town was abandoned in the middle of the day. A wind whipped up for a few seconds, scattering cold raindrops in its wake. Nick turned his back to it, waiting for it to die.

The address belonged to a nondescript three-story brick building. A massage parlor occupied the second and third floors, above a rundown store selling vitamins and health supplements. A small neon sign glowed feebly in a curtained window on the second floor, spelling out MASSAGE in dusty red letters. The heavy blackout curtains in the windows had been sitting undisturbed so long they were streaked and faded. One or two had come loose from their rods and had been tacked back into place with nails.

After ten minutes, the flimsy, worn door leading up to the second floor hadn't been disturbed. Except for the glow of neon, there wasn't any sign of life upstairs. The clerk in the vitamin shop on the ground floor had spotted Nick, leaning against a street lamp half hidden by an old and rusty, junked car, and every so often the greasy-haired man would glance at him, trying to figure out what he was doing there. Nick looked up at the sky, measuring the light. It was dark, but he wasn't going to have to worry about the resolution of the photographs. He made a few adjustments to the camera's settings, then snapped a picture, examining it for shadow on the LCD screen. Satisfied, he raised the camera back to his eye and took a few pictures of the neon sign and the front door.

Some minutes later, an unmarked squad car slowed in front of the parlor before continuing down the street. Nick watched it slow again at the end of the block and come to a stop at the curb in front of a fire hydrant. The brake lights glowed bright red, seeming to streak the heavy air with their color, then went dark. All four doors swung open. Nick zoomed the camera in a few notches, then snapped several pictures of the street cops as they stepped from the car.

An unmarked white van with wired windows followed half a minute behind the cops, pulling to a stop just in front of the car. The lead officer went over to the side window and said a few words to the driver of the van, then turned to face the other three uniformed policemen. "Okay," he said. "Let's get this done." He let his eyes travel the length of the street. Nick was aware when the officer's gaze paused on him, taking him in. The policeman gave Nick a nearly imperceptible nod, then, checking his watch, led his squad toward the parlor. "Me 'n Wilkins'll do the honors upstairs. Horace, you stay out here in the street. Murphy, you take a run down the alley there and find the back of the building. Radio in when you've got the rear covered."

"You got it," one of the cops said.

The officer glanced at the sky. "Hoof it, why don't you, Murph. It looks like it's going to pour again in a few minutes here."

The cop disappeared down a narrow alley halfway down the block. Nick could hear the scrape of his footsteps echoing off its close walls, then the rattle of a metal gate in a chain-link fence.

When his radio squawked a few moments later, the officer checked his gun, then led another of the cops through the scarred, peeling door to the second floor, leaving the fourth patrolman behind them on the sidewalk. Nick took a quick snapshot of the two policemen disappearing into the building.

They were standing barely twenty feet apart on an otherwise empty street, and it didn't surprise Nick when the remaining cop addressed him. "You with the paper?"

"With the *Telegraph*," Nick replied.

"You drew the short straw, huh?"

Nick shrugged his shoulders.

"It's a pretty routine bust," the cop offered. "We don't expect any trouble."

"It's not so often you close these places down."

The cop slid his hands beneath the edges of his utility belt and squared his shoulders. "No, not so often," he conceded.

"What makes this one worth the trouble?"

The cop shook his head. "They say the girls are underage, I guess."

Nick nodded, remembering that Daly had told him the same thing on the phone. *They say they're trafficking in young girls from China.* Laura Daly had spoken the words strangely, without much feeling—like this was something that might go down every day. Her lack of emotion had surprised Nick a little, and the words stuck with him.

From upstairs, a single, truncated shriek rent the silence. The cop twisted to look up at the curtained windows. "That'll be one of the girls," he said. "Sounds like they probably caught her in mid-session." He smirked at Nick. "Shouldn't be long now."

Five minutes later, the flimsy door swung back open. Nick raised his camera to his eye. The first person into the street was an old Chinese woman dressed in a robe and slippers, her hands cuffed in front of her. She was followed closely by the lead officer. "Why don't you get over here, Horace"—he said to the cop, yanking the door all the way open—"give me a hand with this."

As the cop joined him, the officer reached back into the building to lead the next person out—one of the prostitutes. Nick snapped a picture as she stepped into the street. She was anything but underage. She was short and squat, wearing tight black pants that failed to hide her lumpy legs, a pink shirt streaked with stains. She bent her head forward as she emerged from the stairwell, covering her face with her hands in shame. Four more women followed, all of them Asian. None of them was attractive, and, like the first one out the door, not one of them was young.

Three customers stepped outside behind the prostitutes. Nick took a picture of each of the men as they stepped into the street. The first was an awkward young man with a pimply red face. The second, a tall man in a plaid shirt and jeans, looked like a construction worker. Finally, dressed in a cheap dark blue sports jacket and a pair of ill-fitting khaki pants, a stout, mustached man with a thick head of wiry hair was escorted through the doorway by the last cop. His eyes drawn to a flash of gold in the weak light, Nick zoomed in on the heavy wedding band encircling the stout man's pudgy finger and pressed down on the shutter.

The lead officer spoke a few words into his radio, and the driver swung the white van around and met them in front of the building. Nick took pictures of the police helping the prostitutes and their johns into the van. The cop had been right. It had been a routine bust. There was nothing spectacular here, but Nick figured he had captured the tawdry color Daly wanted for the spread. The van pulled away to take the offenders to the station to be booked.

About to return his camera to his shoulder bag, Nick was surprised to see the stout man in the blue sports jacket still engaged in a conversation with the lead officer. *Why hadn't they arrested him like everyone else?* Nick snapped a quick picture of the officer unlocking the handcuffs from the man's wrists, then at last continued down the street toward the *Telegraph.*

Nick was staring at his computer in the cavernous newsroom. The room was bustling with reporters. The desks were all occupied, and messengers were running down the aisles and corridors. The editors were hunched over copy, laying it out and readying it for the next edition. After turning in his pictures of the raid, Nick had caught the second half of the staff meeting late that morning. Afterward, though, he hadn't sat down to begin his new assignment. Instead, he Googled Sara Garland on his computer, and he spent the rest of the day sorting through the few images he found.

"What a beauty," Laura Daly said over Nick's shoulder.

Nick hadn't heard the senior editor approach over the din of the newsroom, and he swiveled in his chair to look up at the tall, gray-haired woman. Despite the fact that she was large boned and dressed in a predominantly masculine wardrobe, there was something unmistakably feminine about Laura Daly. She ran the paper on a shoestring, and she demanded the respect of the entire staff, from her editors down to the clerks. Nevertheless, she rarely raised her voice. She never tried to dominate at all. Instead, her authority derived from her character. She led because people wanted to follow. Nick tracked her eyes to the screen of his computer. "I met her today."

"Did you now?" Daly studied the screen. "There's something curious about her eyes. She looks like she's seen a lot."

"How much you think someone like her can earn acting?" Nick asked. "Bit parts, I mean, on a few TV shows." He was thinking of the gold and platinum Rolex on Sara's wrist.

Daly considered the question. "I have no idea. They don't earn all that much, though. A few hundred dollars—a thousand dollars—an episode if they're lucky. I don't recognize her. You?"

"No." Nick imagined that he would have remembered her if he had ever seen her on the screen, even in a small part. She was that beautiful. “Her name’s Sara,” he said. “Sara Garland.”

“Garland?” Daly let a quiet whistle sneak out through her teeth.

“You know her?”

“Not her,” Daly said. “Her dad. You work for him.”

Nick looked up at his boss, perplexed.

“Her stepfather is Jason Hamlin. That’s Jillian’s daughter. Now I say it, she even looks like Jillian, doesn’t she?”

Nick had seen Jason Hamlin in the office a few times, but never his wife. “I’ve never met Jillian.”

“Google her, too, why don’t you?” Daly chuckled dryly. “So it doesn’t really matter how much she earns acting.”

“She said she’s living with her parents in Bellevue.”

“That’s the Hamlins,” Daly confirmed. “Their house is on Lake Washington. Right on the lake, with its own pier. It’s a place Jay Gatsby would have found impressive.”

“I’m having dinner with her tonight.” Nick regretted the note of pride in his voice.

Daly pursed her lips. “That reminds me, Nick. I’ve been meaning to ask you something about your brother. Sam’s behind that biotech start-up, isn’t he? Matrix Zarcon, right? He and that fellow from Harvard—Blake Werner—started the company a couple of years ago.”

“That’s right.”

“There’s a rumor going around town the company’s knee-deep in Hamlin’s money—about to go public. You might want to ask your brother for details. With all the stem cell research floating around, there’s bound to be a controversy there. I bet it’s something we’re going to want to cover.” Daly smiled. “You might even ask Sara about it tonight. Maybe she’s heard something we can use.”

"No problem, Laura," Nick said sarcastically. "I'll work it into the conversation in between where were you born and what's your favorite color."

Laura Daly rapped her knuckles lightly on Nick's desk before moving on. "Atta boy, Nick," she said. "It gets into your bones, the newspaper, doesn't it?" She was two or three steps beyond Nick's desk when she turned back around. "Just don't forget the spill on Elliott Bay," she said, referring to the assignment she had given Nick earlier. "The EPA's saying over fifty thousand gallons of toxic sludge spilled into the bay before Hanzin Shipping caught the leak. I want to see photographs on my desk—front-page stuff for Sunday—within the week."

Nick waited until Daly had taken another few steps, then turned his attention back to the screen in front of him.

chapter 5

At four o'clock, sitting in his apartment on the edge of a threadbare sofa he had bought as a student, his cell phone in his hands, Nick was lost in a daydream. He lived north of the University of Washington, in the same cheap studio he rented during his last year in graduate school. The apartment was shabby and small, but it was all he could afford. Unaware of his surroundings, he let his eyes wander out the window, down to the parking lot three stories below. He couldn't stop thinking about Sara. Not since he had first seen her that morning. About her eyes and the ivory color of her skin and how long and delicate her fingers were. About the way her hips had swayed as she crossed the café.

Rousing himself, he glanced at the clock next to his bed, then brought up the number Sara had keyed into the phone's memory. It took a few seconds to find the courage to press the call button. Waiting through three long rings before she picked up, he almost lost his nerve. He hadn't been sleeping well for the past week, and it had been an early morning. He felt dizzy, fatigued almost. He couldn't find his voice when she answered.

"Hello?" Sara said a second time.

"Sara? It's me, Nick." He steadied himself. He didn't want to blow his chance. "From the coffee shop. From the table in front of the fireplace."

"I remember you, Nick. Even without the fireplace."

Relieved to find her receptive, Nick felt himself relax. He had been picking absently at the leather bracelet on his right wrist, and he let it go and straightened up. "I was just wondering whether you still thought dinner would be a good idea."

"I'm glad you called," Sara said. "I was hoping you would. I've been thinking about you today, too."

A wave of adrenaline passed through him without warning, upsetting his balance. He attributed it to his nerves. It took a couple beats to regain his composure.

"That's a *yes*, Nick," Sara said into the silence.

"I kind of figured that."

There was a beep on the line, and Nick took the phone from his ear to look at its LCD display. Sam was trying to call through. Nick brought the phone back to his ear, ignoring the interruption. He would call him back.

"So what are you thinking for dinner?" Sara was asking him.

"To tell you the truth, I'm not sure I can afford the dinner you expect."

"What makes you think I expect something specific?" she asked, teasing.

"I don't know." Nick didn't want to admit that he had spent the afternoon at the paper researching Sara and her family.

"Maybe I just want to spend a little time with you,

Nick—wherever we end up. And maybe I'm thinking about more than just the dinner anyway."

"You give her an inch and she takes a yard," Nick said in response to the innuendo.

Sara laughed. "Touché."

"I have something unusual in mind."

"Sounds interesting."

"I wouldn't get your hopes up." Nick laughed, realizing that his attack of nerves had passed. "I've got this assignment."

"From the paper?"

"What would you say about a trip on the ferry over to Bainbridge Island? I'm supposed to take photographs to complement this story the *Telegraph* is doing. If we go quickly enough, we could catch the five-thirty ferry, and maybe we'll get lucky and I can get a dramatic shot or two of the crossing at sunset."

"Will you pick me up?" Sara asked.

"Just tell me where you are, and I'll be there."

Nick forgot that Sam had tried to call him, and he was on his way down the concrete staircase to the parking lot when the phone rang again. "Hey, Sam," he said, raising the cell phone to his ear without slowing his step. "What's up?" His voice echoed hollowly in the stairwell.

"Nothing much," Sam said. "You sound happy."

"Do I?"

"Yeah. It sounds like you're running. Where are you?"

"I'm at home. On my way out."

"I thought maybe we could get together."

"I can't right now. Maybe tomorrow?"

"Just for a minute," Sam insisted.

Nick had reached the ground floor, and he pushed the door open and stepped outside onto the small gravel lot where his old, rusty Corolla was parked. Huge cumulus clouds had gathered in the sky, hovering just beyond the Olympic Mountains. The afternoon was fading, and the clouds were darkening at their base, like cotton balls dipped in black ink. "I really can't right now," he said. "Sorry. I'm getting into my car. I've got to go."

"I'm just around the corner," Sam said. "Wait for me. There's something I want to show you." He hung up the phone before Nick could object.

Nick was standing, restive, at the side of his old Toyota when Sam pulled into the lot in a car Nick didn't recognize. The tinted, smoky driver's-side window slid down.

"So what do you think, bro'?"

Nick wasn't sure what his brother was referring to.

"About the car," Sam explained, smiling and lifting his Ray-Bans. "Didn't you even notice?"

Nick took a step backward to take in the Arctic silver BMW. He could smell the scent of its rich new leather through the open window. He knew that Sam was doing well at Matrix Zarcon. He had started the company two years ago with an old friend of his, Blake Werner, and Nick knew that Sam was integral to the development of a new drug to treat schizophrenia. Sam was even talking of taking the company public if the drug was approved for testing by the FDA. If the company was being funded by someone like Jason Hamlin, as Daly had told him, Sam stood to make serious money. Still, Nick hadn't appreciated that his brother had cash to spend on such an expensive car.

"Would you ever have imagined me in a ride like this back in Madison?" Sam asked, content with his brother's reaction.

Nick shook his head. "It's a beautiful car, Sam. Things must be going pretty well for you and Werner."

A shadow briefly darkened his brother's face. "Didn't I tell you, bro'? Blake and I parted ways months ago."

"What?" The news surprised Nick. Blake Werner and Sam had been friends for years, and as far as he knew, the company belonged just as much to Werner as Sam. "What happened?"

"Nothing happened." Sam glossed over his unease with a smile and a shrug. "Blake didn't have faith. He wanted to move on. Anyway, it's his loss. Things keep getting better and better. With any luck, I'll be parking this in front of my own house in another few months."

"You've got to be kidding."

"Why don't you hop on in?" Sam suggested. "I'll let you drive if you want. There's actually a house for sale just north of here I'd like you to see."

Nick smiled. "Tomorrow, okay? I've got to run."

"Not even ten minutes? You should feel the way this thing handles. And I've got a busy day tomorrow."

"I'm sorry," Nick said. "I'm busy now."

Sam looked at his brother carefully for the first time since pulling into the lot. "What's up?" he asked. "You look like shit."

"Do I?"

"You've got black circles around your eyes."

"I haven't been sleeping well," Nick admitted.

"You okay?"

"I'm fine. It's been a long day."

Sam turned the key in the ignition, smothering the purr of the BMW's powerful engine. "It's not money you're worrying about, is it?"

"No." Nick was impatient. "It's nothing. Really. And I do have to go, Sam."

Ignoring Nick's anxiety, Sam stood up out of his new car. He gave his brother a quick hug, then leaned back on the hood. He glanced down at his watch—the same stainless-steel Citizen quartz that his parents had bought him as a high school graduation gift. "Take a minute, Nick. Tell me what's going on. If you need a loan, just tell me. I'm doing okay now, and you know I'd do anything for you."

Nick was overcome with a welter of emotions. Stress from being kept against his will, when Sara was waiting for him. Gratitude at Sam's generosity. And then a sudden resentment he didn't understand. "It's always money with you," he muttered. "That's your answer for everything. So long as you've got it, you're good. Without it, your life's a mess."

"What the hell would you say something like that for?"

It took Nick a few seconds to realize that Sam was simply looking at him. He had to battle the sense that his brother was in his face, grabbing him by the wrists, pinning him backward against something hard and sharp. The sensation seemed to fly away from him with the same frustrating elusiveness that a dream will escape upon waking.

"I'm sorry," he said, trying to calm himself. The words tripped off his tongue. "I didn't mean that. I know how generous you are."

Nick *did* know precisely how generous Sam was. He knew that he was forever in his older brother's debt. After their parents died—in a car accident, when Nick was seventeen years old—the two brothers had sold the house in Wisconsin and liquidated most of the family's assets. The entire fortune hadn't amounted to much—less than $55,000 each. Sam had saved his half of the inheritance. He had consulted a financial advisor, but opted just to bank it conservatively into a savings account bearing a few percent interest. After finishing his last year of high school with barely a C average, Nick, on the other hand, had blazed through his share.

Looking back, Nick wasn't sure where the money had gone. He had disappeared for nearly eighteen months. Most of that time, Nick spent backpacking in Asia and then South America. Finally, he ended up on the Pacific Coast of Costa Rica, shacked up with a Dutch girl, surfing, smoking pot, sleeping until noon—paying for both their expenses when he could barely afford his own.

Nick woke up one day by himself, flat broke, not a thing to his name except his digital camera and a silver chain he had worn as a talisman since he was a kid. He didn't have two dimes to scratch together. He knew, though, that his brother had decided to attend the University of Washington a couple of years before, and, hitchhiking and working where he could for his meals, he began heading north to Seattle to find him.

One of things Nick had learned was how to get around without money. The roadways were buzzing with people in motion. He hitched rides in the back of trucks, often with migrant workers heading north looking for work. On one long stretch of highway, he even tied himself to the undercarriage of a big rig. He walked when there was no other alternative. Once back across the border in the United States, he jumped trains like the original hobos.

Nick traversed Central America on the Pan-American Highway, all the way from Nicaragua through Mexico, without incident. Then, walking down a side street in downtown El Paso, Texas, after midnight, looking for a hostel, he was jumped by two men. Nick knew that he was being followed. The streets were so empty, however, that he had nowhere to run. He ignored the first man when he called out after him. The second man, though, caught up to him before Nick understood the danger.

Nick didn't have much the two men could steal, only a couple of dollars in his pocket. The two men took what they could. They tore the chain from his neck and pried the camera from his fingers. Then—though there was nothing to be gained by it—they beat him up pretty badly. Nick spent the next few nights on the street, forced for the first time in his life to beg. By the time he found himself on Sam's doorstep, his hair was so long that Sam barely recognized him, and his lips were so cracked he couldn't speak.

In the year and a half that he had been gone, Nick hadn't contacted Sam once. Not knowing whether his brother was dead or alive, Sam had grieved for a time, then made his peace. Nevertheless, without once asking his brother what had happened to him or to his share of their parents' small bequest, Sam had spent what remained of his savings to put Nick through college.

"I know you're only thinking about me," Nick said. He felt Sam's eyes on his face, examining him. His hands felt cold. He opened and closed his fists, trying to feel his fingertips.

Sam's face resolved itself into a grudging smile. "Don't worry about it, bro'."

"I'm just tired," Nick apologized. "I keep waking up at the same time every night. I keep having this dream—the same dream every night."

"What is it? What's going on?"

Nick shook his head. "I don't know."

"What's the dream about?"

"It's about you, Sam."

An odd look passed across his brother's face. A look of recognition, Nick thought later, not of surprise. As though his brother had caught glimpse of a ghost, but one that he was expecting to see.

"It's about the lake," Sam said. "Isn't it? You're dreaming about the day we went skating on the lake."

"Tell me what happened that day."

Sam's lips pressed together.

"I remember being on the ice with you," Nick said. "And I remember the ice breaking. You went into the water. You disappeared for thirty seconds, maybe more. I was scared to death. I skated to the edge of the hole, where the ice was broken. I remember lying down on the ice—the ice bending underneath me. The water was so cold, I didn't think you were going to make it." Nick was trying to hang on to the memory. "The thing is, I don't remember anything after that."

"Stop it," Sam said.

"It's just like that in my dream. I'm reaching into the water, looking for you. It's so cold my hands are freezing, turning blue. But in my dream, there's blood. The water turns red."

"I'm telling you, stop it," Sam said sharply.

"You climbed out of the water. That's what you told me. I lay down and put my hands in the water and found you, and you pulled yourself up. That's what happened, right, Sam?"

Sam placed a stiff hand on Nick's shoulder. He made an effort to modulate his voice. "Just stop talking about it, okay? It's a bad dream you're having. That's all."

Nick turned, freeing himself from Sam's grip. "I've

been feeling so dizzy recently," he said. "I don't know what's going on. It's been like this for a week now, every night. Ever since we had dinner last Friday."

"Maybe it's a touch of the flu," Sam said. "The weather turned last week. It's been pretty cold."

Nick smiled wanly, recovering himself. "I'm sure you're right. I'm sure it's nothing."

Sam gave his brother a gentle tap on the arm. "So where are you off to?" he said, brightening. "Why are you in such a hurry? It must be something important."

Nick's eyes brightened as well. "I met this girl," he said. "I was going to tell you."

"You like her, huh? She must be pretty special."

Nick opened his mouth to tell Sam about Sara. Sam's wolfish expression, though, silenced him.

"Are you okay, bro'?"

Nick remembered that Sara was waiting for him. "I'm fine," he resolved. "Really. But I have to go."

"You sure?"

Nick pulled away from Sam, twisting to slide through the open door into the Toyota.

"Do you want me to drive you?"

Nick inserted the key into the ignition. The engine turned over a few times, then ground to a halt. He tried a second time. Again, the cylinders sparked, then died. The battery sounded weak.

"Let me drive you," Sam said again.

Nick felt a burst of adrenaline surge through his veins. With more time, he would have taken a taxi. He couldn't have defined the feeling, but the last thing he wanted was to get into his brother's new car.

"It'll be better to show up in a car like mine anyway," Sam said. "And like this, I'll get a chance to see this girl of yours myself."

chapter 6

Impossibly, Sara was even more beautiful than Nick remembered her.

He spotted her from the passenger seat as Sam navigated his new BMW through traffic. She stood out from the crowd at the bus stop downtown where he had arranged to pick her up, tall and slender, dressed in jeans and a short, shiny leather jacket. Her long blond hair was tangled slightly in a scarf laced with a metallic wool weave. Nick was aware of the look on his brother's face when he pointed her out to him. Sam didn't say a word, but simply stared at her.

Nick pulled the latch and jumped from the car, stepping up onto the red-painted curb to greet her. When their eyes met, he could barely contain his excitement.

Sara, though, hardly seemed to notice him. She was distracted by the sight of another driver. "I thought you'd be coming alone," she said. "Who's this?"

"It's my brother, Sam."

Sara squinted, trying to get a better view into the car.

"My car broke down. Sam offered to give us a ride."

Waiting for her to turn back toward him, Nick watched, inexplicably shaken, his hands icy cold, as Sam and Sara peered at one another through the slightly tinted windshield.

Nick had been balling his hands into tight fists. It was only when he loosened his fingers that he realized how cold he was. Midnight in January in Madison, Wisconsin, the dead of a Midwestern winter. There were no streets anymore in the rural neighborhood, only gingerbread houses sagging beneath the weight of a heavy snowfall. The air was still. It was so quiet Nick could hear the muffled sound of snow dropping from branches and eaves blocks away.

I can't watch TV with you, Nick. I don't want to. Elizabeth Munroe's voice rang in his ears. *There's a dance tonight. At Visitation.*

Earlier that day, Nick had crossed the lawn separating his house from the Munroes'. Elizabeth Munroe had been waiting for him on her front porch. In his right hand, shoved into the pocket of his heavy parka, Nick was clutching a silver chain he had bought for Elizabeth the weekend before. At four o'clock, the sun was already disappearing from the low, heavy sky, throwing orange shadows across Elizabeth's face. Nick considered the seventeen-year-old girl in front of him, aware of how warm the silver chain had become in his hand. He understood that this random moment was a turning point. *I'll go with you to the dance, then,* he said.

Elizabeth's eyes dropped from Nick's. *I've already asked someone else.*

Who?

Elizabeth hesitated. *That doesn't matter, does it?*

Nick wanted to protest. He wanted to remind her that they were boyfriend and girlfriend. But he couldn't speak the words. *Is this really what you want?* he asked her weakly instead.

I've got to go, she said. *I've got to get ready.*

Nick let the silver chain slide out of his hand to the bottom of his pocket. He crossed the snow-covered lawn back to his house and lay down on his bed. Dropping onto his bed still in his school clothes, he fell asleep before dinner, ignoring the shout from his mother when it was time to eat. At ten it began to snow heavily. Nick had gotten into bed with his window wide open, and thick flakes of snow came swirling into his room, melting into the air as they met the heat.

Nick woke up in a sweat before midnight. His parents had already gone to sleep for the night, and the house was completely dark. He bundled up into his jacket and scarf and gloves, then trudged across the lawns separating his house from the Munroes' next door. The lights were still on downstairs. When he saw Elizabeth's mother cross through the foyer from the living room into the kitchen, he screwed up his courage and climbed the steps to the front door. Elizabeth's mother shielded her eyes as she peered outside to see who was ringing the bell so late. She smiled when she flicked on the light. She had always liked Nick.

"Elizabeth's not back yet," she said to him, glancing at her wristwatch. "I thought maybe she was out with you."

"No." Nick avoided her eyes.

"I don't know when she's getting back. It *is* Friday

night." She stood with the door in her hand, scrutinizing Nick. "You're welcome to come in and wait for a while if you'd like."

"That's okay." Nick tried to conceal his embarrassment.

"I'll tell her you stopped by."

Nick walked back down the steps, then crossed the lawns again, retracing his tracks. He sat down on the short set of stairs that ascended the swell in the lawn halfway between his family's house and the curb, in the shelter of two tall birch trees, hunching forward, trying to stay warm. Heavy snowflakes tumbled down toward him through the black sky, accumulating in a thin layer as powdery as baking soda. Time passed slowly, and Nick managed to forget about the cold until he loosened his fingers and then curled them back into fists, and sharp needles of pain shot through his fingertips.

Sometime after midnight, the night's silence was broken by the sound of an approaching engine. When the car was a block away, Nick recognized it as the Munroes'. Elizabeth had gotten her license the year before when she turned sixteen. Nick pushed himself forward a little on the stairs, readying himself to confront her. He had no idea what he was going to say. All night long he had been looking forward to this moment. Now that it was here, though, he was awash in confusion.

When the car crawled through the thick snow in front of Nick's house, he realized with a shock that someone was sitting with Elizabeth. She hadn't come home alone. Nick watched the car as it slid sideways to a stop. His eyes were trained on the passenger door, waiting for it to open so that he could see who it was.

The door remained shut. Inside the car, the two black silhouettes merged into one. Nick realized that

Elizabeth and her date were locked together in a kiss. He felt tears sting his eyes. He wanted to turn and to run back into his house. He remained frozen where he was, waiting.

At last, the passenger door swung open, and the dim yellow light flickered on inside. Nick's heart leapt as its glow fell across the face of the person who had been kissing Elizabeth.

He watched Sam step from the car.

"Nick?" Nick was hardly aware of the pressure of Sara's hand on his shoulder. She was shaking him, and Nick was looking back at her, into her eyes. He wasn't focusing on her, though. The voice speaking his name seemed to be coming at him from a huge distance, resonating toward him like the sound of a stone being thrown against the walls of a long, narrow tunnel. "Nick? Are you okay?"

Nick blinked a few times, then at last brought Sara into focus. The cacophony of the traffic blared in his ears. He was surprised to find himself in downtown Seattle. He had felt so deeply transported back to Madison, he was disoriented.

"Are you okay?" Sara asked again. She didn't try to hide her concern.

"Hmmm?"

"You were in a trance."

When Nick smiled, her face melted into a genuine smile, too. Nick felt her fingers, cold in the late afternoon, sliding into his own. She drew herself into him, and he could smell the clean scent of her lipstick. Once again, as he recovered himself, his excitement overwhelmed him.

"Let's just pretend your brother's not here," she said. "It's good to see you. I've been thinking about you all day. I wanted to be alone with you—so that I wouldn't feel self-conscious when I did this." The movement toward him was so graceful that Nick had the impression that it was in slow motion. Her cheeks were cool. Her lips, though, were warm. Her hands squeezed his even tighter. Unexpectedly, she stood up onto her toes and, closing her eyes, kissed him, almost furtively. Nick hesitated, and then he was kissing her back.

The dull, hollow sound of a drum beating resolved itself into the sound of Sam rapping the windshield with his knuckles. Reluctantly, Nick drew himself back from Sara, aware of his brother's impatience inside the car. A bus, Nick realized, had pulled up behind the BMW, and Sam needed to get out of its way. "We'd better go," he said.

Sara didn't let go of his hands. He had to pull away to open the front door for her. On his way into the backseat, he turned to look at the bus. The driver was looking back at him, an annoyed but envious look on his face.

"I hope this isn't out of your way," Sara was saying to Sam as Nick closed the door behind him. "It's not much fun driving downtown at rush hour."

"My name is Sam," he said, introducing himself.

"Nick told me." Sara twisted around in her seat and looked into Nick's eyes as Sam began accelerating from the curb. "You're his older brother. Sam." She flashed Nick a smile, then turned to Sam. "You didn't have to do this," she said to him flatly. "We could just as easily have walked."

"It's only a few minutes driving."

Sara's leather jacket squeaked against the new leather

of the seat as she turned back toward Nick once again. "You could almost be twins. The two of you look so much alike."

"Sam's three years older than I am," Nick offered.

"And a few inches taller," Sam said, glancing at Sara. Nick noticed his eyes widen as he faced her.

"And he drives a better car, I take it." Sara laughed playfully. The small note of mockery in her voice wasn't lost on Nick. Her hand found his knee. "Lucky I don't care about things like that. I know what I want when I see it."

In the rearview mirror, Nick was aware of the deflated look that crossed Sam's face. Sara's fingers were teasing his thigh. Stifling the confusion of pride and panic welling inside his chest, he shifted forward and took her hand in his own, shy of taunting his older brother.

The streets were crowded with traffic, but it was flowing smoothly, and they circled down to the ferry landing on the waterfront a couple of minutes later.

chapter 7

Sara took Nick's hand as they were walking up the hill from the steel and concrete ferry dock on Bainbridge Island into the small village of Winslow. It was a careless gesture, but it sent a spike of pleasure through Nick's heart. He tried not to show his surprise.

The sun was setting, and the tops of the clouds had turned a soft, golden orange. Across the flat plane of the bay, Seattle glowed, and the fading sun creased its towers with horizontal streaks of electric yellow light, like lines drawn in crayon. Nick and Sara stopped to watch the ferry as it churned the water white in its wake and began its slow glide back across to the city. A flock of seagulls gathered over the ferry, their screeches echoing up the hill. When the ferry blew its deep bass horn, in the aftermath the falling evening felt suddenly quiet.

Nick had taken a number of photographs on the crossing. The ferry had been nearly empty, and he had spent much of the half-hour ride positioning himself to get a few shots over the prow, with Bainbridge Island rising up from the water into the dramatic sunset. The slick from the toxic spill glistened like gasoline in the camera's frame, in a psychedelic swirl stretching from one side of the bay to the other.

"So what now?" Sara asked, turning away from the sweeping view.

"There's a small fish shack in town," Nick said. "It's not much to look at. It doesn't even have a name, I don't think. Maybe you know the place?"

Beneath them, the distant buzz of a car's engine broke the silence. Nick cataloged the noise but paid no attention to it.

Sara shook her head. "I don't know Bainbridge very well. When I was little, we always stayed over on the other side of the sound, on Lake Washington."

The car's engine was getting louder. The car was climbing the hill, getting closer.

"They serve caviar they bring in from Canada," Nick said. "The only caviar in Seattle I can afford. I thought maybe you'd like it."

The car switched on its high beams, carving holes into the fading light. It rounded a switchback curve too fast, its tires squealing. Nick realized how quickly it was approaching when he turned to face it. They were standing in the center of the lane, and he had to grab Sara and yank her out of the way, whipped by the car's wake. Nick got a look at the driver as he tore past: a sandy-haired man wearing a Hawaiian print shirt.

Sara broke the silence. "I don't know whether he even saw us," she said breathlessly.

"He was driving too fast."

"Well, he missed us." Sara laughed. "So why don't you lead me to your fish shack, then," she said, trying to recover the mood, "Captain Nick."

Nick held out his arm, and Sara looped her hand beneath his elbow. It didn't just feel good to Nick, it felt *right.* His skin tingled beneath Sara's fingers, and almost euphorically, he remembered the sensation of her lips unexpectedly on his, standing at the bus stop next to Sam's new car.

The small, rustic restaurant was cozy and warm, crowded to capacity, its linen-topped tables laden with plates of freshly grilled fish and frosty glasses of chilled white wine. Coming inside from the crisp evening, Sara stood close to Nick, snuggling up to him as they waited for the hostess. Nick's temper flared as they were being seated, though, when he noticed the sandy-haired man sitting with a young woman at a table next to the window.

"Don't let a man like that ruin a beautiful evening," Sara said to him a few minutes later. She touched Nick on the shoulder, and he noticed that she had poured him a glass of wine. He lifted the glass to his lips, determined to ignore the man and his date.

I should've just bought him out, the man said as the waitress set an icy plate of caviar in the center of the table between Nick and Sara. His voice bellowed through the tiny restaurant. *The opportunity arose, and I coulda had him at a good price.* Nick did his best to block the conversation out. He was aware of the way the man kept staring at Sara, though. His brow was sweaty, and he found himself barely able to control his hatred for the man.

Nick became aware of Sara's fingers on his forearm. She played with his sleeve, then ran her fingers up toward his bicep, demanding his attention. "Where did you go all of a sudden?" he heard her ask.

He shifted in his chair, taking her in. "Nowhere," he said, smiling. "I'm right here."

"So tell me something, Nick."

Once again, Nick became aware of her fingers on his arm, drawing him into her orbit.

"What did you think when you first saw me this morning?"

Nick raised his eyebrows, surprised by the question. *I thought you were the most beautiful woman I had ever seen*, he wanted to say. "You reminded me of someone," he said instead.

"An old girlfriend," she guessed.

"I was just a kid."

"She was blond, too?"

Nick shrugged.

"What was her name?"

"Elizabeth Munroe. We were neighbors, back in Wisconsin. We grew up together."

"The girl next door."

Nick acknowledged the cliché. "I was really young," he said again.

"Was there any chance you'd say no?"

Nick didn't understand the question.

"This morning. When I asked you out," Sara explained. "You hesitated for a couple of seconds before you said yes."

Nick smiled. He had paused because she had taken his breath away. "I doubt I would have been able to tell you my own name," he said.

"I thought you were pretty cool. You'd be surprised by some of the reactions I get from men."

Nick bit his tongue. He wouldn't have been surprised at all.

"So tell me about Sam—about your brother, I mean."

Despite himself, Nick felt his shoulders stiffen. *At that price, anyone woulda bought him out. The joker was desperate. In over his head.* Nick felt his eyes sweep across the small restaurant to the man in the Hawaiian shirt.

"Nick?" Sara's fingers were caressing his arm.

"What do you want to know?"

"Is he jealous of his younger brother?"

"Jealous? Sam?"

"Yeah. He strikes me as the jealous type. You look surprised. Am I wrong?"

"People usually assume it's the other way around, that's all."

"What—that you're jealous of Sam?"

Nick felt himself flush, uncertain why. He didn't want to admit to Sara that he might have reason to envy his older brother. "Sure—yeah. He's always been, well, the successful one. Ever since I can remember, he's always seemed to know what he wants and how to get it."

"That doesn't sound like something to be jealous of," Sara said. She squeezed Nick's arm, then took her hand away to take a drink of her wine. Nick swam in her regard. "I'd be jealous of you if I were him," she said. "After all, you're the one who got the girl."

After dinner, realizing they had just twenty minutes before the nine-thirty ferry back to Seattle, they hurried outside. Without warning, Sara grabbed Nick by his hands as they were crossing the gravel parking lot. She pulled him to her and kissed him. Nick drew her body against his, aware of her warmth, aware of the taste of wine on her lips. Her fingers were soft as they found the skin beneath his shirt. And then the moment was interrupted.

Nick heard footsteps on the gravel lot, and the sandy-haired man and his young blond date stepped toward them from the shadows.

The man let a whistle out through his teeth. "Young love," he said just behind them. "How nice it is." When Nick broke away from Sara, the man looked him in the eye. "You're a lucky son of a bitch to get a taste of lips as sweet as that."

The snow was melting. It was Saturday, and Nick woke up late. He had barely been able to sleep the night before, after waiting up for Elizabeth and then seeing Sam step from her car. He had drifted off that morning with the approach of dawn.

Outside his window on the third floor of the brick house, the sun was shining. Icicles had formed on the eaves, glistening like long slivers of crystal. The window was open a crack, and a breeze was blowing into the room, fresh with the leafy, grassy smell of melting snow. Before anything else, Nick became aware of the silver chain he had bought for Elizabeth around his neck. He had put it on the night before after getting home, deciding to keep it himself as a reminder of his feelings for Elizabeth. It had gotten caught underneath him during his sleep, lightly strangling him. Then the slosh of footsteps three stories beneath him entered his consciousness, followed by the echo of his name being called. He pulled himself out of bed and walked in his boxer shorts to the window. Elizabeth Munroe was outside in her backyard, looking up at the house.

Ten minutes later, Nick was standing with her beneath the low overhang of her parents' back porch. Her hands were loose on his waist. He was aware of her fingers on his skin. "I'm sorry, Nick," Elizabeth said. "You have to believe me. I'm sorry."

Nick was overcome by the depth of her emotion. He

ran his fingers through her long blond hair. "But I saw you, Liz," he said. "Last night, you went to the dance with Sam."

They had held hands before. But Nick had never been brave enough to kiss her. He liked the way she was leaning into him now. He could feel the swell of her young breasts against his chest. She lifted herself onto her toes, raising her mouth toward his. He could smell her hair.

She crushed her lips against his. His face became wet with her tears. Her fingernails dug into his back. Her hair caught in his mouth. "I'm sorry," she kept saying. "I don't want Sam. I want you."

The ambush took Nick by surprise. Sam had hidden himself behind the birch trees on the front lawn. As Nick headed back home, he leapt out and grabbed hold of Nick's jacket and slung him backward. The ground was icy, and Nick's feet slipped underneath him. His back slammed into the side of a tree. Sam grabbed him by his wrists, pinning him. The bark tore into his skin, and the shock of the sudden violence left him winded. He tried to fight back, but Sam was taller and stronger. Nick was barely able to remain on his feet. Sam's fist landed on his face. He began to fall, but his brother held him up, hitting him again and again, until Nick, at sixteen, his face bruised and bloody, collapsed to the ground, his cheeks wet with blood and tears.

When Sam leaned down toward him, Nick thought that his brother was going to pick him back up. Instead, Sam placed a knee onto his chest and pinned him, then wrapped his hands around Nick's neck. Nick looked up at him, unable to resist, unable to comprehend, as his brother dug his thumbs into his windpipe and squeezed, choking him. Strangling him. Nick panicked. It felt as if he might suffocate. Still, Sam didn't let go of him. Not until Nick began to black out. Not until Nick understood that his brother was holding his life in his hands.

"Stay away from her," Sam growled. "You hear me?" At last, he let Nick go. "Stay the hell away from her."

Nick swiveled away from Sara, moving without thinking. He was aware of the strength radiating from his arms. An exultant sense of satisfaction shot like a jolt through his body the instant his hands connected with the tweed of the sandy-haired man's jacket. His fingers tightened around the fabric until the cloth ripped. Nick pulled the man to him, then shoved him backward hard, and the man went sprawling, tumbling into his own parked car before he had time to react.

Sara's face whitened with shock. She raised a hand to her mouth as Nick leapt onto the man, yanking him up from the ground by the lapels of his jacket and shoving him against the side of his car. The parking lot was filled with the two men's raspy breathing and the scrape of their footsteps, but neither man uttered a word.

"Hey," the man's young date said. "Hey, stop. Stop!"

Nick had the man by the throat, the other hand pressed like a staple into his chest, pinning him to the side of his car. The man's windpipe felt soft in his hand. The flesh of his neck offered no resistance. Nick's teeth were clamped together, and the expression on his face didn't change even when the man began to gasp and then choke.

"Nick, please," Sara said, trying to separate the two men. Her hands were tugging Nick's shoulders. "Don't, Nick. Please, you'll kill him."

Slowly, Nick became aware of Sara's hands pulling at

him. He gave the man a final shove, then released him, allowing him to collapse. His girlfriend bent to the man's side, looking up at Nick in disbelief.

"Come on," Sara said. She led Nick into the shadows. "Let's get out of here."

They were safely on the ferry, Seattle rising up from the dark black plane of the water, before Nick understood what he had done.

When they reached the ferry landing in Seattle, Nick was certain that Sara would make her escape. His hands were still tingling with the sensation of the tweed fabric ripping beneath his fingers as he grabbed the man's jacket. His jaw hurt. Perhaps the man had taken a swing at him, Nick couldn't remember. Sara's voice was still ringing in his ears. *Don't, Nick. Please, you'll kill him.* He had frightened her. He had let the man get to him. His temper had gotten the better of him, and no doubt he had scared the hell out of Sara. As he descended the gangway to the dock, downcast, watching her feet, mesmerized by the light step of the Gucci pumps she was wearing, he prepared himself for her good-bye.

Her hand finding his as they touched solid ground came as a complete surprise. He looked into her eyes, then found himself lost once again in the warmth of her kiss. Passion coursed through him with the same intense violence the fight had caused just an hour before.

"I'm so turned on right now," Sara said. Her voice was a siren's song in his ear, soft and melodious and seductive. "I want you so much."

Nick understood that this was happening too fast. They hardly knew one another. All Sara had seen of him so far was a sullen, repressed young man, unable to bridle his fury. But even as this thought passed through his mind, Nick realized that, as elegant and refined as she was, Sara had another side, too. He had to have her. He had to make love to her right here, right now.

He leaned down, and when their mouths met, he bit her lip. His fingers dug into her flesh. He had to restrain himself from holding her so hard that he would hurt her. "I'm sorry," he said.

Sara stepped up onto her toes, pushing herself against him, finding his lips once again with her own. "No," she said. "I want you. I want you like that, too."

Nick looked around the empty parking lot. They hadn't driven to the landing, and this late in the year there were no taxis at the stand. "We'll have to walk."

"I can't wait, Nick."

"What?"

Sara broke away from him, then took him by the hand. The sound of her pumps on the pavement was nearly drowned out by the guttural roar of the ferry's huge diesel engine. Nick let himself be led across the dark parking lot. "Over there," she said. She was peering across the landing, and when the wind blew she reached up to pull a few loose strands of silvery blond hair from her mouth. "At the Two A.M. Club. We'll go into the restroom."

Looking back on that night, it wasn't the thrill of sex with Sara for the first time that Nick would remember. It wasn't the fear of discovery, either, or the knocking on the locked door after they'd been inside the restroom for ten minutes. It was the music. That's what Nick remembered. The music playing inside the club, muffled through the metal door. The Police. "I'll Be Wrapped Around Your Finger." Bob Marley. "No Woman, No Cry." The Killers. "Romeo and Juliet." Sara's skin was cool and smooth against his. Her hands undressed him. His fingers got tangled in her hair. The music played, and slowly she made love to him. So goddamned slowly. The music played, and there was no one else in the world, nothing else but Sara. Her mouth was on his body. She was naked in front of him. Tall and thin and naked inside the dirty restroom. Kissing him softly. Licking him slowly, so goddamned slowly, until the air turned into snow.

Part 2

chapter 8

The air was laden with snow.

The small lake near their house in Wisconsin had frozen over. Just after dawn, the morning still dark as night, Nick and Sam stared out the window, trying to read the low, stained sky, listening to the radio for the list of school cancellations. When Braxton Middle School was announced, Nick climbed back into bed and pulled the covers snugly around him.

Sam was three years Nick's senior, and at thirteen he was substantially older. He rousted his younger brother from bed and threw him his jeans, boots, and a sweater, bundled up in a loose but heavy wad. The buckle from his belt hit Nick sharply on the cheek, and for a couple of seconds he considered getting angry with his brother. At last, surrendering, he followed Sam into the kitchen.

Their parents had left for work already. With the roads covered in snow and ice, their father had had to leave the house at five-thirty to get to his job at the power plant, before the kids were even awake. Their mother had to leave with him if she wanted a ride. They only had the one car, a beaten-up old Chevrolet Impala.

Skating was Sam's idea. Nick wanted to run out of the house and play, but Sam slowed him down. He jerked him back by the arm and kept him inside while he made sandwiches and packed lunch bags. Then he made sure their skates were tied together by their laces and that Nick remembered his gloves. The two brothers left the house with their skates slung over the handles of their hockey sticks at eight-thirty, the sky still dark, heavy snow still falling, heading determinedly in the direction of Lake Issewa. By car it was a ten-minute drive without snow on the ground. On a day like today, the boys would be walking the better part of an hour.

Tossing their boots next to a tree, they jumped onto the thick, chalky ice, the dull blades of their cheap skates digging deep, powdery tracks into its slightly soft surface. They passed a hockey puck back and forth, shouting excitedly as they raced one another across the lake.

At eleven-thirty, the sun broke through the clouds, turning the day brilliantly, impossibly white. Nick's skates got caught in an arcing track, and he nearly lost his balance. He squinted in the blinding light, leaning on his hockey stick, raising his eyes upward. The sky hadn't turned blue. The clouds had simply thinned, and the sun lit them brightly from behind, like the shell of a lightbulb.

When Nick lowered his eyes again, he had the impression that he couldn't see. The entire landscape had become a two-dimensional plane, a blank piece of paper. Nick felt a spurt of panic. He understood even as it was happening that the emotion was irrational, but he couldn't control it. He hadn't been keeping track of time or where he was skating, and he wondered if he had gotten separated from Sam. He scanned the lake for his brother, relieved when he caught sight of him. Dressed in blue jeans and a red sweater, Sam stood starkly out from the desolate background, a solitary figure drawn on an empty canvas.

Nick's relief was short-lived. Nick noticed that they weren't alone on the lake. Clothed entirely in black, with a gray muffler wrapped around his neck and a stubbly beard as dense as a smear of charcoal, the stranger could have been a hole in the ice. There was something about him that Nick didn't like. He felt shivers run down his spine. *The man was standing out on the middle of the frozen lake without skates.* Nick watched him until he realized that the man was looking back at him. Then he turned away.

By noon, the burst of sunlight had dimmed. The boys were sitting on the stone wall edging the southern boundary of the lake, eating the sandwiches that Sam had packed for them that morning. Snow was falling again. Nick's teeth chattered a little. He had tumbled not far from where they were sitting, where the ice was so thin that he could see through its surface to the murky green water underneath, and when he had gotten up his jeans had been soaked through. He had hardly noticed while continuing to skate, but now that he was sitting unmoving, eating, Nick realized how cold he was. Still, his only thought was to finish his sandwich and to get back out on the lake again. It was Sam who suggested that they head home. He didn't like how ominous the sky was getting. The wind was whipping up, and with the snow even their shouts had become muffled, as though they were trying to make themselves heard through the fabric of a heavy, wet blanket.

"You boys live around here?"

Neither of them had heard the stranger approach, and they both swiveled their heads toward the man dressed in black at the same time.

"You have any more of them sandwiches?" the stranger asked when neither responded to his first question.

Something was wrong about the man. He was dressed in an elegant coat, and the scarf around his neck was as soft as cashmere. He was wearing black leather gloves, nothing like the nylon and polyester ones men like their father would wear. The man's face, though, was a ravaged mess. His hair was shaggy and greasy, and his skin was drawn. His eyelids were swollen above his brown, empty eyes. He gave off a strange mixture of scents: the rich smell of expensive wool and leather, then the raw, sour smell of cheap whisky. Nick understood without being able to articulate the observation that the man was wearing stolen clothes.

"We only made enough for ourselves," Sam said.

"You live around here?" the man asked a second time. He looked up from the boys to survey the landscape, as though he might be looking for a house nearby. Nick realized how menacing the sky had become and how hard the wind was blowing. His legs were all at once icy cold. His lips had become purple, and his teeth chattered loudly.

"Just over there, by that road," Sam lied.

The man continued looking past the brothers. "I don't see no road," he said at last.

"It's hard to see in the snow," Sam said.

The stranger's countenance changed. Nick realized that his eyes had become the eyes of a predator. When he took a step toward them, Sam leapt from the wall onto the ice. The dark sheet cracked beneath his weight.

"Come on, Nick!"

Nick understood that he was supposed to be scared. Still, he held onto the remains of his sandwich in his gloved hand as he pushed off the wall to join his brother. He hadn't appreciated yet that they were going to have to run. He became aware of the half-eaten pieces of bread and bologna from Sam's sandwich scattered at his brother's feet.

"You boys don't have to be skerred," the man said. He was moving toward them now, and there was no mistaking the intent in his dead eyes. Nick was too young to put the danger into words, but he understood it nonetheless.

Sam shoved Nick hard. "Go!" His voice was urgent, but Nick didn't move. "Go!" Sam said again, shouting this time. "Run!"

Nick hesitated a moment longer, but when his brother began to skate, he at last dropped his sandwich and pushed his legs forward on the ice, digging his blades into the soft surface as forcefully as he could. Panic rose in his chest as Sam pulled ahead of him. He could hear the stranger's slippery footsteps right behind him, and the rasp of his ragged breath. The man was gaining on him.

"Wait, Sam," he cried. He was choking for air, barely able to make a sound. "Wait up, Sam!"

In seeming slow motion his skate got caught in a deep rut in the ice. His right foot was yanked away from him. His knee torqued, whipping him around and knocking him off balance. He tried his best to catch himself, but even as he struggled he knew that he was going to fall. His hands hit the ice first, then his knees and his elbows and his chin. The metallic scrape of his skates catching the ice and the cacophony of his tumble crashed around him as he skidded to a rough stop on the unforgiving surface of the frozen lake. His mouth was full of snow. "Sam!"

The ice turned red in front of him as he shouted, and his lips felt warm and tasted briny. A bloody stain leached across the ice. The man was just behind him, nearly on top of him. Nick writhed on the ice, preparing himself to resist, certain that the man would catch him and kidnap him and that he would never see his parents again.

"*Sam!*"

Nick's eyes were squeezed closed when Sam's hands grasped his shoulders. When he opened them again, the rusty blades of Sam's skates were glinting just next to his eyes. "Get up!" his brother was saying, yanking his arm. "Come on, Nick. Get up!" When their eyes connected, time stopped for a split second. Nick wasn't aware of Sam's hands hoisting him from the ice. *You're my brother.* The words passed unspoken through his mind. *Thank God you're my brother.* "Come on. Run, Nick. You're going to have to run."

Nick rose to his knees, then, scrambling, was back up on his skates. The left lace had come loose and the skate wobbled on his foot, but he pushed off anyway, propelling himself forward. He imagined that Sam was next to him. A few moments later, though, the sounds of flight resolved into nothing more than his own panicked breathing and slicing strokes. He realized that he was fleeing alone. He shifted his skates sharply to the left and, with a fizz of shaved ice, slid to a short, controlled stop. He was dizzy, so nauseous that he thought he would throw up. Sam was still standing in the same place where he had fallen, waiting for the man to catch up to him. He glanced over his shoulder at Nick. "Run, Nick," he shouted. "Run!"

"Come with me," Nick replied weakly. He couldn't understand what his brother was doing. He couldn't fathom the sacrifice. The man reached Sam before Nick could think what to do next. He felt himself burst into frightened tears, powerless to protect his brother from the approaching violence.

Just as the man reached Sam, the ice broke. The two of them plummeted into the water together. Sam had time to shout for help before his head went under the water. "Nick!"

His brother's voice ripped through Nick's body with the force of lightning, and Nick skated as fast as he could, back in the direction he had come, back toward Sam.

Nick didn't remember much after that. Sam told him, though, that he had skated right to the edge of the hole in the ice and, lying down, had pulled his older brother out of the water. The next thing that Nick remembered was stopping at the side of the lake to lace his boots back on.

Shaking uncontrollably, Sam was peeling off his wet jacket and shirt. Nick took in his brother's bluish skin, then quickly tore off his own jacket and sweater and gave them to his brother to wear. Nick noticed that Sam's face was twisted with fear. "We've got to go, Nick," he said. Nick had the impression that his brother was barely seeing him. He watched as a wad of mucus stretched from his nostrils, then slid down his face.

Collecting his things into his arms, Sam took a few halting steps away from the lake. Nick held his elbow, keeping his brother from losing his footing in the slippery snow as they climbed the embankment. Once they reached the road, the two brothers ran the rest of the way home, their skates digging into their ribs, their hockey sticks gripped in their frozen hands.

* * *

Nick woke Sam late that night, holding the lens of a flashlight against Sam's mattress, shaking him on his arm. Sam awoke in a cold sweat and yelped, then saw his brother's face in the eerie reddish glow emanating from the flashlight. "What?" he said. "What is it?"

"I'm scared."

"I know," Sam said. "But don't worry. No one's going to find out. No one knows where we were today."

"It's not that," Nick said.

"What?"

"What if that man followed us home?" Nick asked.

"What are you talking about?" Sam asked him. His face was a collage of shadows in the dimming light of the weak flashlight, gradually darkening as the batteries died. "He didn't follow us anywhere. Don't you remember what happened?"

Nick felt stunned. He wasn't sure what his brother was asking him.

"You really don't remember what we did?"

Nick shook his head.

"You can get in bed with me if you want." Sam lifted the covers to let his younger brother climb into the narrow bed next to him.

"I'm scared," Nick said. The batteries gave out before he switched the flashlight off, and Nick was still awake when the room went black.

chapter 9

A few nights after Sam's murder, Nick woke up in a panic, certain that Sam's mutilated body was lying in bed next to him. The room was pitch black. The dim green numerals on the old digital clock on his nightstand cast the only light in the thick, musty darkness. 4:02 A.M. The shades were pulled closed, but it would hardly have mattered had they been open. Outside the nighttime sky was heavy with storm clouds. Nick became aware of the windswept patter of rain being blown against the window glass. He reached a hand out, blindly searching beneath the covers for the corpse next to him. His heart leapt in his chest when he felt the smooth skin of Sara's slender shoulder instead. Nick thought that it felt like ivory.

"Are you awake?" Her voice shattered the night with the intensity of a china cup dropped onto a tile floor.

"I don't know."

Nick was aware of the perspiration on his face before he was able to comprehend the passage of time. A light had been switched on next to the bed, revealing the dinginess of his cramped one-room apartment. Sara was sitting on the edge of the mattress next to him, peering down at him with a glass of water in her hand, concern evident on her face. Nick glanced at the clock. 4:50. Forty-five minutes had somehow disappeared.

"I was dreaming," Nick said. "A terrible dream."

"Here." Nick realized that Sara was holding something toward him. A small orange tablet, barely the size of the head of a pin.

Nick shook his head. "I took one already."

"You need to sleep, darling." Sara set the glass down on the dresser, then placed the tranquillizer next to it. When she faced Nick again, her eyes had turned to glass. It took Nick a few beats to understand that she was crying. When she blinked, a tear tumbled down her cheek, then crystallized into a diamond on the cusp of her chin before freefalling toward the bed.

"I don't know what's real," Nick said.

"The doctor said you were going to have trouble accepting Sam's death, Nick." Sara didn't mean to touch his face. But she did. Her fingers were as cold as ice on his forehead, then gently gliding through his hair. "And I don't blame you, sweetheart. It's only been a few days. You've barely slept."

Nick shook his head. "No," he said. "I don't mean that. I know that Sam's dead."

Sara waited for her lover to continue.

"I meant about my dream. The last few weeks, I keep having the same dream. I'm back in Madison. In Wisconsin. Sam and I are kids."

"Shhh." Sara was settling back into bed next to him.

"Leave the light on," Nick said.

"I will." Again, Sara waited for Nick to continue.

"I'm just not sure I'm dreaming."

In his arms Nick felt Sara shiver. "What do you mean, Nick?"

"I feel like—I mean, maybe I've been awake. Maybe it's not a dream." Nick grasped the profundity of his own terror. "I can remember bits and pieces of the day. Waking up. Listening to the radio with Sam. Then walking to the lake with our skates. We played hockey for a while, and then I remember sitting on this wall to eat. I was cold. Really cold. After that, though, it's like there's nothing there. Except in my dream, a man approaches us. A homeless man, dressed in a long black coat. He chases us. He wants to hurt us, I think. I'm just not sure—I can't hang on to it all at once. But maybe it's something that really happened to me. You know, something I forgot somehow. Something I'm remembering."

Seated on a black fiberglass chair in a precinct hallway the next morning, opposite a utilitarian, fluorescent-lit office, Nick was still turning the nightmare over in his mind. His elbows were on his knees. Detective Adam Stolie had closed the door and partially covered the glass partition separating them with a miniblind, but Nick could see the figures of the two men inside. He was barely aware of the detective, though, or of his bleak surroundings or the policemen scattered through the busy station house. In the days since his brother was killed, his mind had continued to find its way back to the snow day in Wisconsin nearly two decades before, trying to get used to this new memory. He couldn't understand how he had been able to forget such a distinct moment in time.

Detective Stolie had brought Nick in for questioning

a couple of hours before. He hadn't arrested Nick. He had told Nick, though, that he didn't really have a choice except to come downtown. If Nick refused, he had orders to take him into custody. Five days had passed since Sam was found murdered in the parking lot. As yet the police didn't have leads on anyone. They had found no evidence supporting Nick's statement that the brothers had been attacked by a vagrant man.

Stolie was speaking to his lieutenant, a silver-haired man with piercing eyes whose name Nick had failed to get when they were introduced. The lieutenant had examined Nick as they shook hands. Nick read his skepticism. The middle-aged lieutenant wasn't buying his story. There was no vagrant. There was no group of college students getting into another car a block or two away who might vouch for Nick's story. Nick had killed his brother, simple as that. It didn't matter that he had been badly beaten himself. That only proved that Sam had put up a good fight. Nick had returned barefoot to the scene with blood on his hands, and the lieutenant was ready to close the investigation and bring the case to the district attorney. Every now and again, Stolie or the lieutenant would raise their voices, and Nick was able to hear bits and pieces of their conversation through the closed door.

"His fingerprints were on the knife," the lieutenant said for the third or fourth time.

"I'm not arguing with you," Stolie said. "I know it doesn't look good."

"It's not how it *looks*, Stolie," the lieutenant retorted, interrupting him. "His fingerprints were on the knife."

"I was there. You weren't. I saw his face. He didn't kill his brother."

"Since when did you become a shrink? It's not just

his brother we're talking about here, and you know it. A month ago, it was that prostitute—Claire Scott." Claire Scott had last been seen alive working the streets on First Avenue two days before her body had been found. "Our boy Nick was the first one there at the crime scene that day, too. Down on the Green River, right where Ridgway used to dump his victims, rocks shoved up their vaginas. Am I right? And then last week it was that bum behind the Safeway. You're the investigating officer. Still no leads, I take it."

"Dickenson, yeah," Stolie said. "The guy was homeless." He shook his head. "It's pretty hard to follow his tracks."

"Our boy Nicholas was right on top of that one, too. Wasn't he?"

Stolie straightened and looked the lieutenant in the eye. "He's a photographer. That's what he gets paid for, to get to crime scenes before we rope them off."

"All I'm saying is, keep your guard up. Think about it. He's been a thorn in our side for the last couple of years. Someone gets killed, and he's there with his camera ten minutes later. Like magic." Shifting on the edge of his desk, the lieutenant folded his arms across his chest and nodded toward Nick. "For all we know at this point, we've got the Street Butcher sitting out there in the hallway. Under our noses."

Stolie's voice remained patient. "All we've got right now are three unrelated homicides. A prostitute, a bum, and Nick's brother."

"What we have, my friend, are the makings of a serial murder spree. What we have is a city that's starting to get scared."

"You really see a connection between the crimes?"

"You don't? Three people stabbed multiple times.

Not murdered—butchered. Three ugly homicides with a link to street people." The lieutenant assessed his subordinate with a long look. "You've got a hunch this boy's telling the truth, okay. But why stick your neck out? Because it's your neck you're sticking out, Stolie, and mine with it."

Stolie stood up straight. "Listen, you take what we've got to the DA, and he's not going to be able to get the charge to stick. Nick got pretty badly banged up. We've got nothing at this point. About all we've got are his fingerprints."

"On the knife."

"He could have grabbed the knife." Stolie waved his hands in disgust. "Maybe he tried to pull it out of his brother's chest. The DA will throw an arrest right back into our faces. We don't even know what we've got here ourselves yet."

The lieutenant let the detective's objections hang in the air, listening with a cynical smile.

"All I'm saying is give it a few days." Stolie refused to accede to the lieutenant's rank. "Let's see what we can turn up first. There's Sam Wilder's partner—Blake Werner—for one thing. The guy seems to have dropped off the face of the earth. We can't even find him. Coincidence? I don't think so, and the DA's office is not going to think so, either. They're going to want to know we've questioned him. Our case isn't complete until we bring him in."

The lieutenant pushed away from his desk. "You've got two days, Detective. Two days, that's it. And then we arrest the brother."

Stolie walked briskly to the door and whipped it open. His eyes connected with Nick's as he stopped to pull the door closed behind him, and Nick wondered why this man believed him. It was clear that he didn't like the heat he was taking from the lieutenant.

"I don't have enough to book you," the detective said, his agitation rupturing his reserve. He eyed Nick as he stood up from the chair. "I'm going to let you go. You stay close, though, you hear?"

Nick nodded his agreement.

"I'm on a short leash with this, understand? That means you're on an even shorter one." The detective's nostrils flared. "I know how crazy this all must seem to you right now. Your brother hasn't even been buried yet, and here we are putting you through this. But you're in serious trouble, okay?" He took a breath, then went on more slowly. "You got anywhere you can go? Someone you can go to for help, I mean."

Nick thought about the question. He hadn't put it into words before: *He was by himself now.* "My parents died when I was seventeen. In a car accident." His father had driven their Chevy Impala head-on into a sixteen-wheel truck. His parents' remains had been unrecognizable. "Sam and I were alone. He was all I had left."

Stolie looked away from him, then turned back and placed a hand on Nick's shoulder. He took another deep breath, and when he next spoke, his voice had softened noticeably. "I'll do what I can," he said. "Now get yourself out of here. Go on home. There's nothing for you to do here, and I've got to get to work or we'll both be in trouble."

Nick was exiting the station house when a thought occurred to him, and he retraced his steps. He had to ask one of the officers where Stolie had gone. He found him at a desk, about to make a phone call. "What about my shoes?" he said.

Stolie hadn't seen him approach, and he looked up at Nick in surprise. "What's that?"

"My shoes," Nick said again. "I was wearing a pair of black and orange Nike running shoes. Did you ever find them?"

The detective didn't respond.

"Did you search for them?"

"Not specifically," the detective said. "But we combed the area pretty thoroughly, all the way to Elliott Bay Park—where you said you woke up. Next to the gravel dock." He looked pensively at Nick. "Why?"

"You don't think it's weird?"

Stolie shrugged. "Maybe this guy you say attacked you tossed them into the bay. Maybe they sank."

Nick considered the thought. "Yeah, maybe," he said. Then he headed back out into the corridor.

"Listen," Stolie called out after him. "You remember anything, you let me know. As fast as possible. Understand?"

chapter 10

Nick had forgotten all about his lunch appointment with Laura Daly. He wasn't hungry, and the last thing on his mind was the *Seattle Telegraph.* His cell phone vibrated in his pocket as he was stepping down the worn concrete staircase from the precinct house. He stopped to pull it from his pocket, taking refuge from a lightly falling rain beneath the branches of an old, gnarled maple tree, aware of the sound of raindrops tapping against its desiccated brown and orange leaves.

"Nick? It's Delilah. From Laura Daly's office."

"Delilah, yes," Nick said. A car sped past. A small whirlwind trailed in its wake, sending a blast of cool, wet air against his face. "Sorry. I'm in the street. It's a bit difficult to hear."

"That's okay," Delilah said. "I understand."

Nick cringed at the consideration in the woman's voice. More than anything else since Sam's death, that's what he had come to resent: everyone's goddamned superficial pity.

"Ms. Daly asked me to call. She wanted me to remind you that you have a lunch scheduled today at noon."

"Is that today?"

"Yes." Delilah paused. "Ms. Daly thought you might have forgotten."

"It's at Enrico's, isn't it?"

"At the Metropolitan Café. Laura is already there, waiting for you."

After hanging up the call, Nick stared at the phone for a few seconds, until a cascade of cold and heavy raindrops spilled off the leaves above his head, sinking through his hair and running icily down his cheeks.

Ten minutes later, Nick was seated across a table from the senior editor of the *Seattle Telegraph* in a crowded restaurant downtown, a couple of blocks from the newspaper office. Half the bistro's clientele worked for the paper, and the room had fallen silent when Nick pulled the glass door open and stepped inside. Everyone had stopped eating, seemingly in unison, to look up at him and then over at Daly.

"You got us some pretty good pictures of the Claire Scott murder a few weeks back," Laura Daly was saying. They were seated at a table next to the front window. The crowded restaurant was so old that its floors were uneven and the tabletops were out of plane. Nick glanced at the party next to them, wishing that Daly would lower her voice, aware that people were listening. "It's a shame how gory the murder was. You know, we ended up having to go with some stock photos—an old mug shot from last year when the police picked her up for soliciting. The stuff you brought back—" Daly stopped short and shook her head. “Christ. It was too grisly to print. Stabbed twenty-one times, right?”

“Twenty-three,” Nick said.

“And then the bite marks.” The editor’s disgust was visible in her expression. The police had determined that the killer had bitten her. Not hard enough to pierce her skin and leave evidence they could use to identify the killer. No teeth marks they could match with any certainty to a dental plate. Hard enough, though, to have disfigured her with bruising.

“It was pretty unsettling,” Nick admitted.

“And then last week it was the same thing. With that other murder. The hobo they found in the Safeway parking lot.”

“Dickenson,” Nick said.

“Yeah, Dickenson. He was stabbed more than twenty times, too, right?”

“Twenty-six,” Nick confirmed.

“And then sliced up with a broken beer bottle? And his left hand. Jesus.”

Nick closed his eyes, and his head was filled with the image of the bum’s hand, shredded into a hundred slivers of flesh.

Nick was standing over the remains of Dickenson’s body, shielding his camera from the rain, framing a shot. The corpse had been found in a Dumpster behind the Safeway on Fifth Street, just a few blocks from the *Telegraph* building. The police had opened the lid of the Dumpster in the morning after they arrived on the scene. Two hours later, the runoff from the roof of the supermarket had filled the bin, and the bloated body was floating in filth, pulled by a weak current to the edge where a few holes had rusted through the steel. The dead man's blood had turned the water seeping down the side of the Dumpster weakly red. Stepping back from the corpse, Nick snapped a quick picture of the pink water puddling at the feet of a uniformed cop.

When Nick looked back up at the Dumpster, he noticed the man's shredded hand for the first time. It had been submerged beneath the corpse, but with the water rising inside the bin, the body had twisted and the torn, gruesome arm floated in bits and pieces to the surface. Nick had opened his mouth to ask the cop how Dickenson had died. He shook his head instead, turning away from the body.

"You got what you need here?"

Nick looked up at Detective Stolie. He hadn't seen him approach. "Just one more," he said. "Give me a second."

As Nick was putting his camera back into his bag, he glanced up at the crowd gathered behind the police tape about ten yards back from the crime scene, and a familiar face caught his eye. By the time that he reached the small crowd, though, the boy was gone.

Nick tracked him down the next day.

"So you're Daniel Scott? Your mother was Claire Scott?"

"That's right."

"You're her birth son?"

"What do you mean?"

"She gave birth to you. She was your real mother."

"Yeah."

"Do you know your father?"

Daniel didn't answer.

"Do you mind if I tape this interview, Daniel?"

Daniel leaned his head into his hands. His hair was long, and he combed it back with his fingers. He seemed to make a concerted effort to regain control over himself. They hadn't been sitting inside the diner very long. Nick clasped a small tape recorder in his hand on the red Formica tabletop, waiting for the teenager to respond.

Nick had waited for him outside the grim concrete high school on Eighth Avenue, standing at the chain-link fence that bounded school property. At three o'clock, the bell had rung, signaling the end of the school day. There was no guarantee that Daniel would be at school, but Nick had no other way of locating him. The school's administration had an old address on file, and now that his mother was dead, he wasn't easy to find. No one had any idea where the boy might be sleeping.

"So what do you say? You mind if I tape this?"

"What are you going to ask me?"

"About your mother mainly."

"Are you looking for who killed her?"

Nick didn't want to lie. "I'm a reporter," he said. "Not a policeman. I'm not looking for your mother's killer. The truth is, I don't think anyone is. That's one of the things I'm going to write about."

"Because she was a whore."

Nick didn't argue. "Because she was a prostitute."

"You didn't know my mother, did you?"

"No. The first time I saw her, she was already dead. Out by the Green River, where she was found. That's where I saw you the first time, too. When the police brought you there to ID her body."

"Okay." Daniel dropped his gaze, once again combing his hair back with his fingers. "You can record this if you want to. It's up to you."

Nick had spotted Daniel as he pushed his way out the school doors and started down the steps. Daniel took off the moment he saw Nick. He shoved through the crowd on the stairs and tore down the street. Nick shouted for the boy to stop. Knocking into a few students, he sprinted after him.

Nick didn't see the car pulling away from the curb halfway down the block until it was too late, and as the car screeched to a stop, he glanced into it sideways before he was able to jump out of its way. He cradled his camera as he fell, ripping a small gash in his jeans when his knee hit the pavement. By the time he was back on his feet, Daniel had disappeared. Ignoring the angry shouts from inside the car, once again he sprinted down the street. His heart pulsed inside his ears, his breath burned his lungs. He didn't see the small alley on his left until he was on top of it. Even before he could hear him, though, he knew that this was where Daniel had hidden himself. Slowing to a stop, he took a few tentative steps into the alley. Struggling to quiet his breathing, he kept his ears peeled, peering closely into the shadows.

"So tell me why you ran, Daniel."

"What?"

"When you saw me." Nick looked down at the recorder on the Formica tabletop, making sure that the tape was still spinning on its reel. "You ran."

Daniel shook his head.

"Did you think I was someone else? Has someone been looking for you?"

Daniel took a deep breath before responding. "Not for me."

Nick understood that he had stumbled onto something. "Who did you think I was, Daniel?"

"I saw you yesterday, too."

"I know. I saw you, too."

"At the Safeway. Where they found that body."

"You ran from me then, too, didn't you?"

Daniel didn't respond.

"Why, Daniel? Who did you think I was?" Nick asked again.

"One of the doctors."

Nick took the information in. "One of which doctors, Daniel?"

Daniel shrugged. "You know, a social worker. One of the doctors."

"I'm not sure I understand why you'd run, then. If you thought I was a doctor."

Daniel hesitated. "People say they've been giving them bad drugs."

"Do you believe that?"

Daniel didn't answer.

"Doctors are there to help people, aren't they?"

The boy assessed the man opposite him. "You've never lived on the streets, have you?"

Nick ignored the temper the boy's question triggered, burning hot inside his chest. "Tell me what that means, why don't you? To live on the streets."

Again, the boy shrugged. "It means different things."

"So—what—you sleep on the sidewalk? Is that what it means?"

The boy considered the question. "It means I'm always moving. I have slept on the sidewalk, yeah. But I'm not sleeping there now."

"Where are you sleeping?"

The boy smiled.

"But you go to school."

"Yeah. That's what Mom wanted. I go to school."

Nick had waited for his eyes to adjust. Then he took a few more steps into the shadows. Three steps into the narrow alley, the light seemed to drain from the day. He glanced upward, at the brick and concrete buildings rising four stories above him on either side. As far as he could determine, the alley stretched the better part of the city block. The cobblestone corridor seemed to vanish into a black hole, though, so Nick figured it was a dead end. Daniel must be trapped. The scrape of a lone gravelly footstep echoed down the length of the alley. *Daniel?* Nick took another hesitant step forward. *I just want to talk to you.* The doorways in the buildings lining the narrow street were so dark they were black. Nick peered into the shadows, looking for movement.

He saw the blade glinting in Daniel's hand before he spotted the boy, hidden in a shallow doorway, waiting for him. The boy had tricked him. He had led him down the alley, now he was going to ambush him. Nick's heart pounded in his ears. He was blinded by fear. Yet Daniel wasn't preparing to attack him. The boy wasn't moving at all. He was standing still in the black doorway, the knife clasped in his hands. His eyes were closed, and tears were streaming down his face.

"So what are you going to do now, Daniel?"

"Now that my mother's dead?" the boy asked.

Nick looked at him across the booth. "Yeah, now that she's dead. Where are you going to go? How are you going to live?"

The boy took his time, and when he spoke, he didn't answer directly. "In a way it's going to be easier," he said at last. "When Claire was alive, I was worried all the time, you know? She was a whore, I know that. But she was my mom, too. It was my job to protect her."

Nick had turned the tape recorder off when he thought to ask Daniel one last question. He had already put his things back into his bag, and they were on their way out of the diner. Nick stopped Daniel as they stepped into the street. "Did you know Dickenson?" he asked him.

Daniel shrugged. "Not really."

"But you'd seen him before?"

Again, Daniel shrugged. "Sure. He was around."

"What do you make of what happened to him?"

"What do you mean?" Daniel was looking down the street, as though he was figuring which way to walk.

"His hand," Nick said. "Why do you think someone would do that to his left hand?"

"He was married."

"What?"

"Not anymore. His wife is dead. But he had this ring. This big gold ring with a diamond in it."

"His wedding ring," Nick said.

"Yeah. That's right. His wedding ring. It was probably worth something, but he never took it off. Everyone knows that. Dickenson was really proud of that ring."

"Your pictures didn't leave much to the imagination," Laura Daly was saying. "The irony is, your work was so thorough we couldn't use it."

It took Nick a moment to focus. He had lost himself in his memory. "You know," he said, glancing across the table at the senior editor, trying to hang onto the thread of the conversation, "I'm not exactly sure why you haven't printed some of those pictures." He looked at his hands on the white linen tablecloth in front of him, wondering why they weren't trembling. He felt sick, queasy.

Daly smiled, unaware, leaning forward onto her elbows. "You're too young to remember. You moved out here what—ten, eleven years ago?"

"When I was nineteen," Nick confirmed. "To go to the university."

"It's a beautiful city, Seattle," the editor said. "We're pretty proud people. We have a reputation, though, for being home to some fairly notorious murderers over the years."

"Ted Bundy," Nick said.

"And then the Green River Killer."

"Gary Ridgway."

"Yes," the editor said. "That's right—Gary Ridgway. Forty-eight acknowledged homicides. Probably the most prolific serial killer in U.S. history, a Seattle native. You can understand how people around here are gun shy. The Claire Scott murder by itself was probably enough to set people off. Another prostitute from downtown Seattle kidnapped and slaughtered and dumped in the woods. Left to rot on the banks of the Green River. People get scared it's going to start happening all over again."

"So you censor the news."

Once again the editor smiled. "Back when I started out, I was a lot like you. I thought it was my job to tell the truth."

"Isn't it?"

Daly shook her head. "It's my job to sell papers. Today, tomorrow, and the day after that. I don't trade in truth. I trade in credibility." The editor leaned toward her young reporter. "Can you believe that we've been criticized for the stories we've been running? You know what they're saying? They're saying we're trying to take advantage of the public's paranoia. They're calling us terrorists. *Terrorists.* If the people only knew. If they could see the pictures we *haven't* printed."

"You didn't invite me here to bitch about your critics," Nick heard himself say. He felt nervous, watched. He concentrated on his hands, trying to steady himself.

Settling back in her chair, Daly examined the young man in front of her.

Nick tried to hold her gaze but couldn't. "I'm just wondering where this is going," he said.

"No—you're absolutely right." The editor raised a hand to cut off Nick's apology. "You deserve my candor, Nick, so let me level with you."

Nick glanced at his boss, then back down at his hands, waiting.

"We've been pretty careful with the news so far. Claire Scott gets killed and dumped in one of Ridgway's graveyards, and we write columns telling people it's a one-off thing. Dickenson gets stabbed a couple of weeks later, and for the most part we reassure people the two murders aren't related. I'm not publishing lies. I'm writing what credibility demands me to write." The editor looked at the young man, trying to gauge him. "But now with your brother, we've got three murders in three weeks. All of them stabbings."

Nick waited for Daly to continue.

"Credibility. That's what it all boils down to. I've got my credibility to think about. I like you, Nick. You know that. And it's more than that. I know you. I believe in you. The time has come, though, where I have to run what I've got. From every angle. Understand?"

Nick turned the words over. He understood that the editor would have drawn the same conclusion as the police. Until he was able to remember what happened, he was a natural suspect.

"You're one of my reporters. One of my best photographers. Hell, tomorrow morning I'm going to be running that piece you wrote a couple weeks ago. The story about Claire Scott's son—what was his name? Daniel, right? But you're also part of the story now. You understand that, don't you?"

"So what does that mean, Laura? You're going to investigate me? Is that what you brought me here to tell me?"

The senior editor sat back in her chair, flustered. "Don't be ridiculous, Nick. We know each other better than that. I just wanted to make damn sure we had this conversation before you read about yourself in the paper." Daly herself seemed surprised by the harshness of her words, and she took a few seconds before continuing. "You can understand my taking you off the murders, though, can't you?" she said. "At least for the time being."

Nick didn't respond.

"If it was baseball season, I'd send you out to the park to cover a few games. Seriously."

Nick knew how closely the editor followed the Mariners, but he couldn't bring himself to return her smile.

"There's no reason you can't work on something else," Daly said into the awkward silence. "There's the Hamlin gala tonight, for example. I'm sure you've been invited, haven't you?"

"It's too soon," Nick heard himself say, cutting Daly off.

"I understand," Daly said, reminding Nick of the sympathy that Delilah had shown him a few minutes before, on the phone. "These things take time." When Daly lifted one of her hands, Nick noticed how slack the skin on her arm was. There were deep creases in the thin, waxy skin between her knuckles. The editor's hand was nearly on top of his own before Nick understood that the middle-aged woman intended to touch him. He jerked away from the contact.

"I appreciate your concern," Nick heard himself say. "But I'm okay. Really. It's not Sam I'm talking about. I was talking about Sara. It's too soon for you to ask me that."

The twenty years that separated them were suddenly visible in the senior editor's face. "I see." Daly shifted in her chair, recovering her composure.

"I've only known her for a few weeks," Nick explained.

Daly nodded, taking her time. "I thought that an assignment like this might be good for you. That you might *want* to work a little."

Nick made an effort to meet the woman's steady gaze. "I appreciate that," he said. "But like I told you, Laura, I've only known her for a few weeks."

"The gala's a big event," the editor said, ready to press the point. "The cream of Seattle society's going to be there. Jason and Jillian Hamlin are about the closest thing to a king and queen we've got here in the Pacific Northwest. When they throw a charitable ball like this, they put on a real show. They've booked the whole of Benaroya Hall, and I hear the symphony's going to be there tonight playing dinner music while the guests eat meals catered by a chef they've flown in from Paris." Nick was aware of Daly's censure. "One of Hamlin's companies—Hamlin Waste Management—just earned a twenty-million-dollar bonus for cleaning up that toxic spill in Elliott Bay a month ahead of schedule." Daly shook her head. "As if he didn't have enough money already. They're going to bring the house down, Nick. You can be sure of that."

"Aren't you going yourself?"

"Me?" Daly smiled. "I'm a newspaper editor. That's all I am. The press isn't invited." She leaned forward. "You get pictures, and it would be a scoop for us. Not just the red-carpet stuff. Pictures from inside."

Nick shrugged. "I can't do it."

"Think about it some more," the editor said, apparently oblivious to Nick's increasing distress. "The pictures would make the Sunday supplement."

"Sara invited me as her guest."

"Ask her, why don't you? See what she says if you tell her you're bringing your camera." The editor leaned back comfortably in her chair and looked up to signal the waiter, turning her attention to the meal.

"I've got to go," Nick said.

"What's that?"

"You're ready to order?" the waiter asked, standing over Nick's shoulder. Daly lifted a hand to stay the tall, thin man.

"This was a mistake," Nick said. "I'm not hungry. I can't do this."

"Sit and talk to me, then," the editor said, changing her tone. She waved the waiter away. "We don't have to eat. You know you're more than just a reporter to me, Nick—"

"You wouldn't ask me to do this if that were true." Nick raised his eyes, expecting to have stung the editor with his words. The expression on Daly's face, though, remained gentle. Unfazed. "Look—I've got to go. I'm sorry."

"I wanted to talk to you, Nick. Seriously. Not just about the gala. I'm not being coy."

Nick wouldn't be persuaded. "Another time."

Laura Daly examined him, then seemed to give up. “Another time,” she echoed.

Aware of the shadow of deep concern darkening the editor’s eyes, Nick pushed his chair away from the table and strode to the exit. Daly was still watching him as he shoved his way through the doors past a few customers, and Nick knew it. He couldn’t decide what her expression was concealing. Was it concern for him? Or was she allowing herself to wonder whether he had slid a knife into his brother’s chest? Nick took a deep breath of fresh air, grateful to be outside.

chapter 11

After leaving Daly at the Metropolitan Café, Nick found himself drawn to the parking lot beneath Pike Place Market. This was his first visit back to the scene since Sam's murder, and he had to steel himself against an upwelling of memories.

At three o'clock, the sun had broken through the clouds, and the waterfront was crowded. A flock of seagulls was circling and screeching overhead. He wasn't certain precisely what he was looking for. Standing on the edge of the lot in the light of day, among hundreds of tourists and residents happy for the interlude of warm sunshine, he was convinced that he was grasping at straws. He looped the camera's leather shoulder strap around his hand a few times, letting the camera dangle at his legs. The cast aluminum body of the telephoto lens tapped against his knee. There wasn't anything for him to see here. Nothing to find that the police wouldn't already have found.

He was ready to give up when two girls caught his attention. He hardly noticed the yellow tube top that the blonde was wearing, or the brunette's long, slender legs. It was the way the blond girl was laughing that grabbed him. The shrill sound resonated in Nick's head, and despite the sunlight, despite the crowd of people streaming past him on either side, his world went black. Nick was shivering, dressed once again in his jacket. A mist was swirling around him, a foghorn was sounding over the water. A few students were talking loudly, drunkenly, a couple of blocks down, their words indistinct. A girl was laughing. And Sam was next to him, in step at his side.

Nick was grasping something cold and metallic in his hand. He didn't have to see it to know that it was the knife that had killed his brother. The handle and half its blade protruded unnaturally from his brother's chest, wedged savagely into his body. The silvery steel blade was covered in gore, but Nick could see that its edge was rough and dinged. Sam's last breath was gurgling from his lungs through a hole in his ribs. Nick looked down at his brother's disfigured face, then stood up and, leaving the knife lodged in his brother's chest, began to run.

Nick shook off the enveloping memory. As he came to, he could feel his heart pounding in his chest. He concentrated on the feeling of the sunlight on his face, warming his skin. He searched the parking lot for the two girls, but they were gone, swallowed into the crowd. He pushed himself off the light pole he had been leaning against, shaken by the vision, his legs weak beneath him. He was about to start home when, across the lot, something caught his eye.

In the midst of the throng, a lone vagrant was shambling toward the ferry landing.

The man had his back to Nick. All Nick was able to see at first was his ragged, greasy hair and the long, tattered coat he was wearing. An image of the killer's face filled Nick's mind. His watery blue eyes. The pocked, ravaged skin. Nick blinked, suppressing the memory, trying to focus his mind onto the homeless man in front of him instead. The man's shoulders were hunched as he shuffled through the late afternoon crowd, cutting diagonally across Alaskan Way. When Nick banged into a passerby, a man turned and gestured at him. The man's hands fluttered in the air in slow motion, and his mouth opened and closed in a curse, but Nick heard nothing he said. Except for the homeless man's slow and deliberate footsteps, the day had gone completely silent. Nick raised his camera to his eye and snapped a picture of the man. Then, taking a deep breath, he followed him.

Nick was trying not to draw attention to himself. He had kept a good distance between the homeless man and himself. For over an hour the man had led him across town. The man had paused at any number of waste bins along the way, searching through them for scraps of food. In front of the Art Museum, he stopped to stuff some newspaper into his ragged shoes. When he stood back up, a pedestrian handed him a dollar, then hustled away, spooked by something the man said in return. The last three or four blocks, with daylight fading, Nick thought he might lose him.

Nick paused on the edge of the park on Occidental, downtown. Around him, homeless men and women were gathering with their grocery carts of possessions, shouting obscenities at one another, jockeying for places on the scattered benches. As yet, Nick hadn't been able to get a good look at the man. He had him in the center of his telephoto lens now, though—a 400mm zoom that gave him 500 percent magnification. The sky was melting from a deep, purplish blue into a hazy gray twilight, and there wasn't enough light for Nick to snap a good picture. He clicked the shutter down anyway, to give himself some identification to look at later. Perhaps, if it wasn't too blurry, he would be able to enhance the image on his computer.

The man was talking to another homeless man sitting on a bench. The sky was getting darker, and it was becoming more difficult to see. Nick surveyed the area. The parking lots next to the long, narrow park were emptying out, and a few stragglers leaving their offices late were still on the streets. As night fell, the park was becoming a tent city. On the far side, next to a derelict building, several men had started a fire inside a rusted oil drum and were holding something over it, perhaps cooking themselves dinner. Their faces were lit orange, and plumes of black smoke billowed above them, undulating as they dissipated into the twilight, describing invisible currents in the air. Nick stifled a chill. Taking a step into the boundaries of the park, he had the sense that he was stepping into a jungle.

Nick stopped ten yards from the homeless man. Sidling up to the trunk of a tree, he could hear the man's raspy voice. He had to listen carefully to the choppy, broken conversation to understand that the man was buying drugs from the bum seated on the bench. Once again, Nick raised his camera to his eye. There wasn't enough light, though, to get a picture.

"You say you got Vicodin tonight?" the homeless man said.

"I din' say that."

"But you do."

"I got six tabs. I got three Valium. I got a Xanax. I got me some generic hydrocodone. Some OxyContin, too."

"No generics. The Vicodin ain't generics, are they?"

"They're Abbots, man. 'N the OxyContin's Watsons."

"Don't want no generics. People are talking. There's some strange shit going down."

"Tell me about it."

"How much for the Vicodin?"

"Always the same, man."

"Six tabs you say?" The homeless man reached into the pocket of the long, ragged coat he was wearing and pulled out some crumpled bills. One of them, Nick reflected, must have belonged to the person who stopped to give him a dollar in front of the museum. "Gimme the Vicodin, and give me two of the Oxys."

"You two dollas short, man."

"Wait up, wait up." The man reached into the pocket of his pants and brought out a handful of change. He counted through it, then, taking a quick glance around him over both his shoulders—as though he could feel Nick's eyes on him—handed the coins to the other man. He took the pills in return, examining them in the dark light before shoving them into his shirt pocket.

"You got enough for a bed, man?"

The homeless man shook his head. "I'll go inside and get me somepin' to eat, but I'm outside tonight."

The other man shrugged his shoulders and settled back onto the bench. He mumbled something that gave his friend pause. Nick waited for the homeless man to disappear into the shadows, then followed. He was aware of the second man's eyes on him as he approached the bench where the exchange had taken place. As he walked past, the man let his breath out in a single shrill whistle. Nick hesitated in midstep, a chill crawling up his spine.

* * *

Nick paused in front of a tall brick building a few blocks east of the park. He had passed through Pioneer Square a thousand times, and while he had always known that homeless people gathered here, he had never once noticed this particular building. A large sign was taped in a ground-floor window, its words spelled out in marker on an aging piece of cardboard: SEATTLE EMERGENCY SHELTER. Nick looked up at the shabby building. From the number of ragged hobos lined up outside, he figured the building must house a shelter and a food program, as well as other services upstairs. It was dark now, and the street lamps in front didn't cast much light. Nick could barely make out the words etched into the stone lintel above the front doors: HUDSON HOTEL.

Nick crossed the square just in time to see the doors close behind the homeless man. He had cut the line and let himself inside. Nick took a deep breath to steady himself. A number of people noticed him as he approached the building, and he was aware of the way they were eyeing his camera. Still, he had no alternative. He hadn't yet gotten a good look at the man's face; he needed to follow. He walked up the stairs to the entrance.

"Hey, Professor! You got a dolla' fo' me?"

"You got yo'self a fine camera, man."

"You ken take my pitcher fo' a dolla', Professor."

The handle of the door felt grimy in Nick's hand. He yanked it open, then pushed his way through the crowd. The line stretched into the bowels of the building. He turned toward one of the men. "What are you waiting for?" Nick asked him.

"Clark Kent," the man mouthed. "Are you Clark Kent?"

Nick took in the rags the man was wearing. The spectacles propped on his nose were missing a lens. He turned to the man next to him. "What are you in line for?"

"Dinner," the man said, staring at Nick's camera.

Nick pushed his way down the dim hallway. The walls were veneered with greasy green tiles, and the ceiling was gray with years of accumulated grime. Nick felt claustrophobic. He craned his neck as he rounded the corner, able to see down to the end of the line, which terminated in front of a set of double doors leading into a steamy dining room. There was no sign of the homeless man. He had lost him somehow.

Nick scanned the line of ragged, hungry men. Their voices had dropped to whispers, and they shuffled out of his way as he moved down the corridor, gathering again at his back, cutting off his retreat.

The smell of the food cooking in the dining room grew stronger as he approached the double doors, until it became overpowering. The smell of cheap beef simmering in pungent vegetables, mixed with the steamy smell of spaghetti smothered in canned sauce. The air was becoming stuffy, stagnant, the walls close. The men in line reeked of the street, as though they were festering in their own urine and excrement. Nick was surrounded by hands wrapped in cloth, by toothless smiles and unshaven faces.

When he reached the double doors, he turned to a tall, gaunt man with short brown hair and a rat's face. The man took a step back, as if Nick were going to ask him to move aside. "I'm looking for someone," Nick said.

The man didn't respond.

"He was just a few steps in front of me. Did you see him?"

The man's eyes darted toward a door on the other side of the hallway that Nick hadn't noticed before.

"He went in there," someone else said.

"Like he was runnin' from you."

Nick took an awkward step to the large metal door and pushed on its handle. The door swept open in front of him, revealing a filthy, fluorescent-lit men's room paneled in the same grungy tile as the hallway. Its floor was covered with a slick layer of oily mop water. The stench of human waste and ammonia revolted him, burning the insides of his nostrils. He steeled himself and stepped inside. The door swung closed behind him.

A man was standing next to a urinal, peeing. Another man was in one of the four stalls, sitting on a toilet. A fan was blowing overhead, its blades rattling and clanging metallically as it turned in its old tin housing. The fluorescent light overhead flickered. Nick noticed none of these things. The homeless man he had been following was standing in front of a sink to his left, the water running from a broken tap. His hands were resting on the basin. He was staring back at Nick in the mirror, waiting for him.

Their reflections were side by side in the glass—Nick's face, tense with stress, still healing from the battering he had received the night of Sam's murder, counterpoised with the homeless man's street-ravaged countenance. Nick looked into the vagrant's light brown eyes and realized that he had been chasing a ghost. This sinewy, tired man was not the blue-eyed man who had attacked and killed Sam.

Nick had come too far, though, to turn around. The door was clicking shut behind him, there was no retreat. He was inside the bathroom, two steps from the man he had followed across town from Pike Place Market.

The man at the urinal zipped up and turned to leave,

pushing past Nick to get to the door. Too late, Nick caught sight of the homeless man's eyes narrowing in the mirror. He leapt at Nick, grabbing him by his shirt and slamming him up against the hard tiles. In the mirror, Nick saw his camera swing backward from the force of the man's attack and bang against the wall. The man's dirty, scaly hands sank into his clothing. The man's knee pinned his thigh. His breath was hot and sour in Nick's nose. His eyes had become unfocused and wild.

"What you want, boy? You want somethin' I got?"

Nick shook his head.

"You been followin' me. You think I ken't see?"

"I made a mistake," Nick said. He wanted to resist, but the man clamped his fingers around Nick's throat.

"You want my pills, that it?"

"No." The pressure from the man's hand was choking him. He couldn't breathe, and the room became dim and blurry in front of him.

"You make yer mistake with someone else, got it, boy?" The man's leg gouged into his thigh. His dry, crusty fingers cut into his throat. He was closing his hand around Nick's windpipe.

Nick tried again to struggle free. An image of Sam attacking him on the snow-covered lawn in front of their house in Madison blinded him as his head slammed back into the hard wall. The whiteness had drained from the day as Sam had strangled him, until Nick had been engulfed in blackness. Then at last the man released him from his grip. He elbowed Nick in the ribs, took a quick step around him, and pulled the door open, letting himself back out into the hall. Nick was aware of the swell of voices in the hallway as the door opened and closed.

Gasping, Nick slid into a heap on the floor.

* * *

Nick wrapped his arms around his knees. His camera was on the floor next to him. As far as he could tell it hadn't been damaged. Imagining that he was alone in the bathroom, he was breathing easier now, recovering. He was contemplating his retreat through the crowd of homeless men, about to push himself to his feet, when he heard a noise from the stall: the sharp echo of a hardened plastic toilet seat banging against the porcelain bowl, followed by the loud rustling of clothes. He looked up.

His blood froze in his veins.

Beneath the gray Formica partition of the stall, Nick caught sight of the shoes the man inside was wearing. *His* shoes. The pair of black and orange Nike running shoes that he had lost the night that Sam was killed.

The man hiked his pants and closed his belt, then shuffled around, moving to exit the stall.

Part 3

chapter 12

After Sam dropped Nick and Sara off at the ferry landing on the day of their first date, Nick didn't see Sam again until they met for dinner several days later at an Italian restaurant off the steps below Pike Place Market. Nick hadn't called Sam since that afternoon, and he knew that his brother would be worrying about him. Nick didn't bother to dress for the occasion. He showed up twenty-five minutes late in jeans and a T-shirt: no sweater, no jacket, despite the fact that it was so cold that parked cars were covered in frost and puddles in the street were glazed with thin, glassy sheets of ice.

Sam stood up from the linen-topped table when Nick arrived, pulling it to one side to make room for his brother to sit down in the cramped restaurant. The silverware clinked on the table, and the red wine he had been drinking sloshed back and forth in his glass. Sam couldn't disguise his concern. Nick didn't give him a hug or even a touch on the shoulder. As Nick squeezed into his chair, he realized how disheveled he must have looked.

His hair was uncombed, and his eyes were puffy and tired. Perhaps it hadn't been a good idea to come.

"What's up, Nick?" Sam asked his brother. "You're looking worse and worse."

Sam's wine spilled as he sat back down, and Nick watched it seep into the white tablecloth. "Am I? I'm feeling pretty good," he said. He realized after the words were out of his mouth that he was lying. He was happy, but he wasn't feeling *good.* Physically, he was feeling poorly. He wasn't sleeping much, and he was waking up dizzy and disoriented. "I'm having fun—with Sara, you know?"

Sam's smile spiked the corners of his mouth. His eyes, though, remained critical. "You're seeing a lot of that girl, aren't you, bro'?"

Nick nodded. He was thinking about the expression in his brother's eyes, trying to understand what it meant. Sam wasn't pleased.

"She's spending nights with you, at your apartment?"

"Every night but one since we met," Nick said. *That's it,* he told himself. *He's not just jealous. He's angry.*

"Every night? That sounds pretty serious."

"Yeah, well, keep in mind we only met a few days ago." *Angry with me for spending so much time with her.*

"Still," Sam said. "Even if it's just a few days, the two of you are practically living together."

"I don't know."

"What do you mean, you don't know? Look at you—*I* can see how serious this thing is. Anyone can."

"It's sexual," Nick said.

Sam sat back in his chair. His hands were on the table, and Nick noticed that he was crumpling the white tablecloth in his fingers. Following Nick's stare, Sam relaxed his grip, then reached forward and picked up his wine.

"Let's not talk about it," Nick said.

"Why not? I think you should talk about it."

Nick refused. "It's making you uncomfortable."

"Me?" Sam forced a laugh. "Why should it make me uncomfortable, Nick? It has nothing to do with me. I'm just worried about you, that's all."

"There's nothing to be worried about."

The waiter approached their table, interrupting them to inquire if Nick wanted something to drink. When Nick asked for a glass of water, his brother spoke over him. "Bring him a glass of the same wine," he said, and then to Nick: "It's a Merlot, and it's a pretty good one."

"I've been drinking too much," Nick said when the waiter was gone.

"Yeah, well. One more glass of wine won't hurt you then." He lifted his glass and took a sip. "So tell me, little bro'. If everything's so goddamned great, why the hell do you look like shit?"

Nick had already been awake at five that same morning when Sara crept out of bed. She moved so stealthily that the covers barely rustled. Nick opened his eyes in slits, spying on her. She didn't look back at him. She lifted herself off the uncomfortable mattress and walked naked across the room to the bathroom door. Nick was aroused by her slender silhouette, by the way her breasts lifted proudly from her chest and how muscled her long legs seemed as they disappeared into the cleavage of her small ass. He stilled himself, puzzled that she was up so early.

She didn't go into the bathroom, and she didn't switch

on a light. Quietly she pulled on her clothes, lifting her string panties up over her legs, then snapping her lace bra behind her back. It occurred to Nick that she must have gathered her clothes by the bathroom door before they fell asleep. The room was too much of a mess for her to find her things so easily otherwise. Nick measured his breathing. He waited for her to latch the door carefully behind her, then pulled himself up out of bed and, fighting off a nearly crippling dizzy spell, followed her from the apartment. The engine of her large Mercedes was turning over in the parking lot as Nick slipped down the concrete stairwell. He took the rest of the stairs more quickly, crossing through the shadows in the lot to his car as the red glow of her powerful taillights vanished from the misty, early morning air. The Toyota's engine rattled then turned over, and Nick gave chase.

The streets were practically empty. Nick had to hang back to avoid being spotted. He allowed two to three blocks between them. Her car was easy enough to follow, even from a distance. Its headlights shone so brightly that the slick black body of the car seemed to be shadowing its own halo. Nick's headlamps barely poked two weak shafts of candle-colored light into the darkness.

The wind, whistling through the failing seals around the Toyota's windows, tossed the light car from side to side. Down Roosevelt Way, the cedar and elm trees lining the street churned overhead. When a branch broke loose and hit the pavement in front of the Corolla, Nick slammed on the brakes and nearly skidded off the road. He had seen the movement out of the corner of his eye, and for a split second he thought a person was running in front of the car. He even imagined a flash of the person's face, twisted in fear, prepared for the fatal impact.

Shaken by the vision, Nick huddled over the steering wheel, taking deep breaths.

He caught up with Sara's Mercedes again crossing the bridge over Portage Bay, and from there he followed her all the way to Bellevue. Easing off the gas, he was a quarter mile behind her when she dropped onto Shoreland Drive and meandered down the tree-lined lane toward Chism Park.

For as many years as he had lived in Seattle, Nick had never ventured into this part of Bellevue. He gawked at the huge houses hidden by trees, set back hundreds of feet from the road. He didn't notice when the Mercedes slowed in front of him, and he was almost on top of her when Sara turned into a driveway and pulled to a stop in front of a gigantic electric gate. Nick continued past her without slowing down, catching sight of the looming house at the end of the long white gravel driveway out of the corner of his eye. He turned the car around and came to a stop a few hundred feet before the gates. Above him, with the engine off, the wind storming through the gigantic old growth trees became a roar.

The sky was lightening into a soft gray as Nick got out of the car. Hunching against the cold, he walked to the gates in front of the Hamlin house. He could barely comprehend the imposing scale of the mansion at the end of the long driveway, beyond a field of freshly mown grass and plantings of flowers and hedges and trees. The only houses that Nick had seen larger than the one in front of him were the aristocratic palaces in England after which the Hamlin house had been designed. Its sandstone walls gleamed in the approaching light of dawn, and its hundreds of windows sparkled like so many diamonds. As Nick stood staring in at the house, a light flickered in a large window on the second floor. The house was much too far away for Nick to be able to see anything inside, and at last, feeling cold and insignificant, he thought about returning home. He was walking back to his car when, unexpectedly, he heard the sound of an engine turning over. He glanced over his shoulder, then took his hands out of his pockets and jogged the rest of the way to the Toyota.

In another minute, Nick was tailing the black Mercedes again. The narrow roads fronting Lake Washington were deserted at this time of the morning, and he didn't want to risk being spotted. Once on the expressway, it became much easier to keep Sara comfortably in sight. A number of other cars were beginning their morning commute, and he blended into the traffic as he followed her over the bridges across Mercer Island into downtown Seattle. Where was she heading?

Nick got caught at a traffic light about half a block behind her when Sara pulled to a stop in front of the Four Seasons Hotel and switched off her engine. He leaned forward against the steering wheel, trying to get a good view of her through the misty windshield as she stepped from her car. A tall doorman dressed in a long black coat and top hat held her door open, then led her to the curb.

The traffic was moving again when another man came out of the hotel toward Sara. Nick wasn't able to get a good look at him, but Sara leaned into him and gave him a kiss on the cheek, her hand intimately finding his chest.

The cars lined up behind Nick honked their horns. A sudden wave of fatigue washed over him, and he gripped the hard plastic steering wheel. Easing his foot off the brake, he passed through the intersection, just in time to catch a glimpse of Sara disappearing inside through the hotel's plate glass doors, arm in arm with the man whose face he had not been able to see.

"I think she's seeing someone else," Nick said to his brother.

"What?" Sam sat back in his chair, surprised.

"You asked me why I'm not sleeping. I look like shit, you said."

Sam held onto the edge of the table, visibly stunned. "How do you know?" he asked. "What makes you think she's seeing someone else? And even if she is, you're just at the beginning of the affair, right? What makes you think this is supposed to be exclusive?"

Now it was Nick's turn to pause. "I never said I thought it was exclusive."

"You're acting like she's the love of your life."

"Maybe she is. But I told you already, it's sexual right now. And that's all it is. Haven't you ever had a purely sexual relationship?"

Sam nodded but didn't respond.

"I followed her," Nick admitted.

"What?"

"This morning. I was awake all night. I couldn't sleep."

"You really do look tired." Sam examined his brother. "I mean it."

"She got out of bed at five, and I followed her."

Once again, Sam leaned back in his chair. The veins in his neck turned red, bulging beneath the collar of his white dress shirt. "Where?" he asked.

Nick shook his head. "I saw her with someone else."

"Where?" Sam asked again. This time, the word came out with the force of a demand, and he shifted in his chair, then softened his voice. "Where did she go when she left your apartment, Nick?"

Nick leaned back to let the waiter set the glass of Merlot down on the table in front of him. Then he rested his elbows on the table, narrowing his eyes at his taller, broader brother. "What does it matter? Like I said, it's only sexual between Sara and me." He drew his lips against his teeth, fastening his hands under his chin. "I know I should put a stop to it," he said, "but I can't. You know what I mean? I *can't.*"

chapter 13

The phone woke Nick at twelve-thirty the next afternoon. He reached for it, then propped himself onto his elbow on the hard, uncomfortable mattress, staring blankly at its display. His throat ached from the night before.

After leaving Sam at the restaurant, he had met Sara at a nightclub. For the first time in years, he had smoked a cigarette and sniffed a couple of lines of coke. Nick closed his eyes, trying to piece the night together. He could barely remember anything after the coke. Just looking into Sara's eyes and laughing, dancing with her in the crowded room, jostled by sweaty bodies, hypnotized by the loud music and the pulsing shafts of green and purple laser light caught in the club's smoky air like the threads of a jagged spiderweb.

He let the phone ring six times, aware that his croaking voice would betray him. He swallowed to try to moisten his mouth, then, sitting up on the side of the bed, away from Sara, pressed the button to accept the call from Laura Daly.

"Hello?" Nick's greeting was a rasp.

"Nick? Is that you?" Nick understood from Daly's tone that she hadn't recognized him.

"Yes." Nick cleared his throat. "Sorry." Sara moved under the blankets, and Nick stood from the bed to walk to the bathroom. He winced, remembering that he had forgotten to turn in the photographs of the toxic spill on Elliott Bay. From the bathroom doorway, he glanced over his shoulder at the reason for his screwup.

Sara's face was resting like an angel's on the lumpy pillow he had owned since college. He had a sudden image of this same face, twisted with passion, his fingers in her mouth, almost brutally, stretching her lips, as he pinned her writhing body beneath his. She had screamed when he finally allowed her to move, then had choked on his fingers, and he had dropped his hand to her neck. He hadn't known that he would slap her until he felt the smack of her cheek on his fingers. He watched her skin redden, then squeezed her throat and slowly but rhythmically slammed himself into her, again and again until her body knotted up into a tight ball underneath him.

"You're calling about the assignment," Nick said into the phone, turning away from Sara. He wanted to collect himself for the call, but the mess in the room distracted him. The floor was covered with their clothes, and his camera bag was open and his equipment scattered throughout the apartment.

"You didn't even speak to Rogers," Daly said evenly.

"I missed the deadline, I know. I can bring the pictures downtown today."

"Rogers had some fairly specific requirements for the pictures. Things he wanted to see accompany the text. You know how it works."

Nick closed his eyes, unable to offer any excuse.

"I doubt your pics are going to fit, and you know as well as I do that it's too late anyway. They say the EPA is going to award the contract for the cleanup within the week. This story's got to run now. Why didn't you call me?"

Nick brushed his hair back, away from his face. His skin felt sweaty to the touch, as if he had been hot in his sleep. "I'm sorry."

"Sorry doesn't really do much for me, Nick."

"I know." Even as Nick acknowledged Daly's point, though, he felt a wave of resentment rise in his chest. He tried his best to battle the irrational emotion. "Listen," he said, a bitter edge creeping into his voice, "you don't have to lecture me, Laura. I know that I messed this one up."

"I'm not lecturing you." His boss sounded surprised. "I was depending on you, that's all. You had plenty of time to talk to Rogers, and you didn't. I didn't step in. I let you try to do it on your own."

"You gave me the rope and let me hang myself with it," Nick said.

The phone went silent for a couple of seconds. When she next spoke, there was confusion in Daly's voice. "I *relied* on you."

"So what are you saying?"

Daly sighed. "Maybe you should come on down here. Maybe we should talk about this in person."

"Are you planning to fire me, Laura?"

"You know, Nick, I don't like your tone of voice. I don't know what's going on with you right now. I'm asking you to come on in so we can sit down and discuss it."

Nick's body was stiff with tension. He was filled with regret. Daly was a good boss. He didn't know where his anger was coming from. Sara's hand was suddenly on his stomach. She had come up behind him naked, her fingers smooth and cool on his skin. "Okay," he said. "Listen, I'm sorry." Her nails were digging into his skin. "I'll come in. We'll talk."

"Without delay," Daly said firmly.

Before Nick had the chance to say more, Sara took the phone out of his hand and flipped it closed and tossed it onto the floor, where it got lost in the clutter. She wrapped herself tenderly around him and brought him back to the bed. Nick forgot everything but the sensation of her hands pulling him into her.

"Hurt me," he heard her say.

"What?"

Hurt me. Nick was certain she had spoken the words, but they seemed to have lost all meaning.

"Make love to me," she said, as though she were repeating herself.

"Wait a minute." Nick hadn't thought to speak. He hadn't thought to push Sara away from him. But he did. His arms were stiff in front of him. His hands were on her shoulders.

"Make love to me," she said again. "Please, Nick. *Hurt me.*"

"No." He shoved her away from him, not roughly but not gently, either. She looked at him in surprise.

"What is it, Nick?"

The anger in her voice didn't escape him. Neither did the note of pain. He kept her away from him for a few moments longer, then all at once wanted only to hold her. "Just hold me," he said.

"Nick?"

"I just want you to lie down with me and hold me."

Sara took his shoulders gently in her hands and pulled

him down onto the bed next to her. She let him twist onto his side, away from her, then drew herself into him, crushing her breasts against his back.

"I didn't know I was going to feel like this," she heard him say.

I didn't know I was going to feel like this, either. The words were on her tongue, but Sara couldn't speak them.

"I don't want you to go away."

"I'm right here," she said.

"I thought I could do it."

Sara waited.

"I thought I could accept anything, just to be with you. But I can't."

"You'll only know when you fall."

Nick let the words sink in, turning them over in his mind.

"When you fall, I'll be there to carry you, Nick. We'll carry each other. Then you'll see. Then you'll know."

Downstairs in the apartment building's small lobby, Laura Daly's face was red with anger. After making love to Sara, Nick hadn't gone in to the paper. He had drifted back to sleep. It was four o'clock when the buzzer woke him up. Standing disheveled in front of the older woman, he could taste the editor's profound disappointment. Nick hadn't just tripped, he had tumbled in this woman's esteem.

"I appreciate your coming all the way here," Nick said. "But I'm fine."

"Don't flatter yourself, Nick. I had some business to take care of at the university. I only stopped by because I need to vent. I put my faith in you. You're letting me down."

"I don't know what to say."

"You can begin by explaining yourself."

Nick dropped his eyes. "I'm going to resign," he said.

"What?" Daly was clearly taken aback.

"I'm going to quit," Nick said again. The building's heat was switched on too high, and Nick could feel sweat gathering on his scalp, soaking his shirt beneath his arms. He felt dizzy. The lobby walls were closing in on him. "Let's go outside," he blurted out.

Daly examined him in puzzlement. "Are you all right?"

"I need some fresh air, that's all. Do you mind?"

Nick pushed the door open and stepped outside into the small parking lot, trying to recover himself. Daly's cab was parked at the curb, its motor still running, a jet of exhaust rising in the air behind it. Nick felt nauseous.

"What's this all about?" Daly asked. The anger in her voice had been replaced with worry. "I have to admit, I'm concerned about you."

"It's not about anything," Nick said. "I'm quitting, that's all."

"Do you have a history of—I mean, is this the first time that you've done something like this, or do you have a history of—"

"Of what, Laura?"

"Well, of behavior like this."

"*Strange* behavior, you mean." Nick took a deep breath. "No, I don't. Look, I'm not sure what's going on. I'm with this girl. And I don't know—maybe I'm in love with her, or maybe it's something else. But I haven't been sleeping. And I haven't been able to do my work. I keep getting these images, you know—these flashbacks—back to when I was a kid. Things I haven't thought about for years. Until now, things I haven't even been able to remember."

Daly assessed the young man in front of her. "Have you thought about seeing someone?"

"A psychiatrist?"

"I don't know. Anyone. A counselor. Someone who can help you through this."

Nick shook his head. "I'll work it out. I don't need help. I just need a bit of time with it."

"You can take a leave of absence," the senior editor suggested.

"I don't want a leave of absence. I'm quitting."

"Okay, then."

"You were going to fire me anyway, weren't you?"

Daly waved a hand at him. "It's not black-and-white like that. I was going to give you a warning. As it is, maybe this is for the best. Take some time. Do what you have to do." She looked Nick in the eye to stress her sincerity. "I'm not going to let you quit, though. I'll take you off staff, but I want you to work freelance. Whenever you're able. Okay? You've worked too hard to throw it all away."

"I appreciate that."

"Your work is too good, Nick. You're one of my most talented photographers."

Nick took a shallow breath and held it. The trees surrounding the lot loomed like dark effigies above him, and the ground spun beneath him like a gigantic carousel, picking up speed. The taxi's engine was getting louder. Its exhaust was choking him. He focused on Daly's face, trying to regain his equilibrium. "I know that's really how you feel."

"Tell me something, Nick." Daly's voice came from a distance. "Before I go. This girl you say you're with. Are you still seeing Sara Garland?"

Nick's skin was crawling. This had never happened before—never. There was a voice in his head. A voice he didn't recognize. Someone telling him to turn around and to look behind him. *Turn around, Nick. Turn around now.* He squeezed his hands into fists, fighting the urge to twist around.

"Nick? Are you dating Sara Garland?"

Nick nodded. He was biting his lower lip. He tasted blood. He told himself to relax his jaw. In front of him, Daly didn't seem to notice.

"Because I did some checking up on her, and I found out a few things that maybe you might want to know."

Turn around, Nick. Look behind you.

Nick closed and then opened his eyes, trying to relax, waiting for Daly to continue.

"She's had kind of a checkered past."

"What's that supposed to mean, Laura?"

"She's been in and out of rehab. She's spent a lot of time in Hollywood. Running around with the people we like to read about in the tabloids. Taking a lot of drugs, having a good time."

"She's only twenty-six."

Nick didn't notice Daly's pause. "I just thought you'd like to know," she said. "You're swimming in pretty deep water."

Turn around, Nick.

"I know that already, Laura."

"She came into the Hamlin family when Jason married Jillian seven years ago. You should see her picture back then, when she was nineteen."

"She's beautiful now."

That's not what Daly meant. "There was some talk. Some nasty rumors."

"What kind of talk?"

"She would have been difficult for any man to resist."

Turn around.

"Am I supposed to thank you for this?"

The older woman shook her head, becoming aware of Nick's increasing distress. "Just keep your eyes open, okay? You're not a kid anymore. You know what you're doing. But watch yourself."

Now!

Nick's fingernails were digging into his palms. He could barely restrain himself any longer. When Laura Daly at last got back into the cab, he swiveled around, his eyes climbing the building to the window of his apartment. For a split second, he was certain that Sara was standing there naked, looking down at him. An instant later, though, the window was empty, and Nick was standing alone in the parking lot.

chapter 14

Some evenings later, the two brothers arranged to meet for drinks at the Blue Note, a jazz club on the waterfront beneath Pike Place Market. At just after midnight that night, Sam would be murdered.

Sara was waiting with Nick in the small lot behind his apartment building at eight o'clock when Sam arrived to pick his brother up. As Sam pulled the BMW to a stop, they were standing close together, touching one another with their hands. "I'm not sure why I'm even going," Nick whispered into her ear.

"Why don't you come with us?" Sam asked Sara, leaning his head out of the driver's-side window.

Sara shook her head solemnly, and Nick was grateful for her reluctance.

"Come on," Sam cajoled. "It's going to be fun. There's a new band playing, up from New Orleans."

"I'll see you later tonight," Sara said to Nick, ignoring his brother.

"I'll try not to be too late."

"Just give me a call when you're on your way home," Sara said. "I'll meet you back here."

Inside the club, the music played quietly. The band was led by a young guitarist who called himself Ricky Rainbow. Watching him, Nick had the impression that he was reaching down into the guitar to pluck notes from inside it, one after the next. He had to remind himself that the man's fingers were strumming its strings. He sipped his vodka tonic, keeping his eye on the small band at the front of the small, dark club.

"He's pretty good, isn't he?" Sam said. "He can't be more than twenty. He's a real talent."

"I don't know what's happening to me," Nick said.

"Imagine being twenty years old and being able to play like that."

"Did you hear me, Sam?"

Sam turned toward him. There was a look on his face that Nick couldn't read.

"I said, I don't know what's happening to me."

"I heard you, Nick. I just don't know what you'd have me say. I'm not sure I even understand what you're trying to tell me."

Nick was overcome by a wave of dizziness. He couldn't make sense of his brother's apparent hostility.

"I need your help, Sam."

"You need *my* help? Come on, bro'. You've been ignoring me for the past couple of weeks."

"I've been feeling strange," Nick said. The music was getting louder, and Nick wasn't certain his brother could hear him. "I thought it was going to get better, but it's only been getting worse."

"You and Sara are getting pretty damned serious." Nick was confused by the bitterness in his brother's tone. "That's all I see happening. You should be on top of the world. But

I don't know, maybe it's not the relationship you thought it was going to be." Sam let his words trail off, as though he was himself perplexed by the tone of his voice.

"I'm seeing things."

"What the hell are you talking about, Nick?"

"Things. I don't know. Images."

Sam shook his head. "Come on, wake up. What the hell do you mean? Hallucinations?"

Nick nodded his head. "Yes. Hallucinations. I'm looking at something right in front of me, and it becomes something else."

"You're still not sleeping, are you?"

"Or I'm hearing something. Like right now. The guitar. I know it's a guitar, but I'm hearing it as a voice."

"What do you mean, Nick?" Sam could barely contain his disbelief. He leaned toward his brother, challenging him to explain.

"He's holding a woman in his hands, and he's making her sing."

Sam smiled, unease creasing his brow. "He's playing a guitar. Come on. You know that."

"It's like I'm dreaming when I'm awake."

"Maybe you should see someone."

Nick's lips formed a grim line. He raised his eyes.

"It sounds to me like you're worn out, but this is too big for me. I'm your brother. I love you, Nick. But I'm out of my depth here." Sam reached across the small table and grabbed his brother's shirtsleeve. "There's a doctor I know. A psychiatrist. I'm doing some work with him at the company. He's a real good guy. Alan Barnes. I'll give you his number."

"I couldn't even if I wanted to," Nick said, embarrassed. "These guys charge a fortune."

"I'll pay." Sam gave Nick's shirt a tug. "You know that.

Don't think about the money. You go see Barnes, and have him send the bills to me."

Nick's gratitude was heartfelt. "I keep remembering things," he said at last.

"Tell it to the doctor, bro'."

"Things about you, Sam."

His brother remained silent.

"Things that happened to us. Only I'm not so sure whether they happened or not."

The music was getting louder, drowning out Nick's words.

"Tell me what happened that day," Nick said. "Tell me what happened on the lake. After that man fell through the ice."

"You saved my life," Sam said. "You want to know what happened that day on the ice? You saved my life, Nick."

Nick shook his head. "What did I do to him, Sam?"

Sam was looking at him. The music had gotten too loud to continue this conversation.

"Tell me what happened," Nick said. "Tell me what I did."

Sam lay his hand onto Nick's forearm. Nick registered his brother's alarm, and he became aware of how rapid his own pulse was through the thin fabric of his shirt, beating against Sam's fingers. His face was unshaven, his hair unwashed. He understood how disoriented he must have appeared to his older brother. "You really do need to see this guy, Barnes," Sam said. "I mean it."

"Why won't you just tell me? Damn it, Sam. Damn it! Can't you see how broken up I am?" Nick yanked his arm from Sam's gentle grip.

"He was going to rape us," Sam said. "The bastard was going to kidnap us, Nick. Molest us, I don't know."

"Maybe he just wanted to steal our food or our jackets. Or maybe he just wanted to talk to us." Nick leaned forward, dropping his head in his hands, then slid his palms up over his ears. "I gotta get out of here," he said, twisting his head from side to side. The music was pounding inside his skull. The beat of the drum had become footsteps, the guitar a woman's scream. "Jesus. I've really got to get out of here."

Sam was getting to his feet. "Sure," he said, reaching to place a hand onto Nick's shoulders. "Sure, Nick. It's getting pretty late anyway. You need to get yourself some sleep."

Nick walked two steps in front of his brother, pushing his way past the crowd of tables and the people standing in a crush along the bar. He threw the door open, let the cool, moist air splash against his face, grateful for the salt breeze blowing in off the water. The sound of the music inside the club faded as the door closed behind them. Their footsteps echoed as they walked down the deserted waterfront in silence, toward the parking lot beneath Pike Place Market where Sam had parked his car. The blackness of the night surrounded them, hiding the stricken expression on Nick's face, the blank expression on his brother's.

"Maybe Sara has something to do with all this," Sam said as they approached the lot. A few steps back, he had slipped $600 in twenties into the pocket of Nick's jacket, and he was rubbing his hands together, as though the bills had left a grimy residue on his fingers. His breath steamed in the cold, foggy air. "I don't know. Your obsession with her, it kind of reminds me of the way you were back in Madison. With Elizabeth, I mean. You remember Elizabeth Munroe, don't you, bro'?"

These were the last words that Sam spoke to his brother.

Part 4

chapter 15

Inside the men's room at the Hudson Hotel, Nick focused on the orange and black Nikes visible beneath the bottom edge of the gray toilet partition. He raised himself on one knee. His head was spinning from his confrontation with the homeless man. The bum had been strong, and his sudden violence had caught Nick off guard. The back of his skull was aching where it had connected with the tile.

Pushing himself up onto his feet, he watched the man inside move to exit the stall. He poised himself to intercept him. Just as the stall door began to swing, though, the bathroom door burst open, and three homeless men trundled in, shoving one another, pushing toward the sink and the urinals. The man wearing Nick's shoes got lost in the commotion, blocked from Nick's view. His hand, bound in dirty rags, darted out and grabbed hold of the door before it shut behind the three men. He pushed his way into the hallway before Nick was able to see his face.

Nick had to see the man's eyes. He had to identify him as Sam's killer.

Nick took a quick, impulsive step toward the door, but one of the men raised his hands to Nick's chest, stopping him. He was looking Nick up and down, measuring him, realizing that he was out of place, lost. This photographer didn't belong here inside the shelter.

"Where you going in such a hurry, chum?"

Nick tried to push the man's hands away from him. The violence attracted the attention of one of the other men. "What's a camera like that cost you, friend?"

"You cut yerself?" the first man asked, peering at Nick's face.

"Let me pass," Nick said.

"How you cut yerself like that?" The man raised one of his dirty hands to touch Nick's cheek.

Nick felt his blood boil. The man wearing his shoes was getting away, and these men were slowing him down, antagonizing him for no reason except that he wasn't one of them. He pushed the man away from him. His fury surprised the man, and he stumbled backward against the wall, then fell to the floor, dazed and confused. The other two men took a step back, assessing Nick through fresh eyes. The blade of a homemade shank flashed in the fluorescent light, and the man holding it laughed, opening his mouth wide and baring his teeth. When Nick looked into his eyes, he felt a cold sweat break out on his face. The man was insane, like an animal excited by violence.

The shiv swished in front of Nick in a dazzle of light, and the crazy man howled. The anger that had welled up inside Nick's chest melted into panic. When he took a step backward, retreating from the shiny blade, the man on the floor grabbed one of his legs, nearly tripping him. Nick tried to pull himself free, but the man yanked back, and Nick lost his balance. His eyes darted toward the door.

"Get off me," he said, turning on the man at his feet. He planted his trapped leg on the ground as solidly as he could, then twisted and kicked the man, aiming at his head. The man reacted quickly enough to protect himself. Nick's foot landed ineffectually against his hands, but at least he had freed himself. He faced the other two men. "Get that knife out of my face," he said, surprised by the strength in his voice.

Once again the crazy man howled with high-pitched, demented laughter, slicing the blade in front of Nick's face.

"Grab 'im, Willy," the man on the floor said.

Nick turned to face the third man. He hadn't yet appreciated how big the man was—easily half again his own weight and three or four inches taller. Nick tried to read him, aware of the resentment welling in his eyes. The man took a step forward, raising his huge hands from his sides. The crazy man screamed feverishly, and the sound reverberated through the small tiled room, piercing Nick's eardrums. The blade glinted in the light.

Then the door burst open. A man dressed in an elegant gray suit and red silk tie stepped into the bathroom, letting the door close behind him.

"Dr. Barnes," the large man said, taking a step backward. Not, Nick thought, as if he respected the doctor, but as if he feared him. The man at Nick's feet pulled himself up from the floor. The shiv disappeared back into the crazy man's pocket. The room fell so quiet that it felt to Nick as if his ears were ringing. Nick stared at the doctor, trying to remember where he had heard the doctor's name before. It wouldn't hit him until sometime later that Sam had mentioned Dr. Barnes to him at the jazz club on the night of the murder.

Barnes glanced at Nick, and Nick understood that the doctor wanted him to leave. Nick would have liked to thank him, but he knew that the peace that Barnes's presence had restored was fragile.

"He brought his camera in here," the man with the knife said.

"He pushed me down fer no reason," the other man said.

"I din' mean nothin', Dr. Barnes," the large man said. "I din' mean ta hurt him."

"It's okay, Willy," Barnes replied. "You, too, Clarence," he said to the man with the knife. "Nothing happened. Right?"

"Nothin'," the large man said.

"You okay?" Barnes asked Nick.

Nick assessed the doctor. He looked about forty, tall and athletic. He was looking at Nick not with concern but curiosity, taking in his dangling camera, trying to figure him out. "I'm fine," Nick said at last. "Thanks."

The crazy man chirped softly. The sound a dove makes, Nick thought, only it sounded threatening somehow. Nick resisted the impulse to look at him.

"You got stars in your eyes, Jerome?" Barnes said.

This made the crazy man laugh, only lightly this time.

"Why don't you get yourself on out of here?" Barnes said to Nick.

Nick hesitated, then, gathering himself, took the doctor's advice. He found himself wondering what would transpire behind the door after it closed behind him.

Back out in the hallway, the noise of the disorderly

line of men died the moment Nick left the bathroom. A path cleared in front of him, all the way to the front of the building. Nick stepped from the dimly lit, steamy hallway into the dark, cool night, aware of the fresh air filling his lungs, glad for his freedom.

The man wearing his shoes would be long gone by now, he figured. But Nick had something to go on at least. A concrete lead he could take to Stolie.

chapter 16

Nick stood on the sidewalk in the shadow of the Hudson Hotel, peering across the street into Pioneer Square. It was getting late, and he had to hurry to meet Sara for the gala. Cutting back through the square would save him a good ten minutes. Still, he was hesitating. The park was lit with only a smattering of working street lamps, and the light from the street barely penetrated the darkness. The vagrants Nick had seen earlier had vanished into nooks and crannies, but Nick could hear a few muffled voices from somewhere inside, without being able to place them. Nick shivered, uncertain whether to continue. The wind picked up, and the trees rustled, drowning out the voices and throwing geometric shadows across the pavement at his feet, giving depth to the night.

Nick became aware of a man staring back at him. Nick's breath caught in his throat. He maintained his composure, determined not to give himself away.

At first, the man was barely discernible from the shadows some twenty or thirty feet into the park. Nick kept still, concentrating on the dark figure out of the corner of his eye. Gradually, he brought the man into focus. The silhouette of the man's long black coat. The greasy clumps of his long hair. The rags on his hands. And then at last, emerging from the darkness, his own orange and black running shoes on the man's feet, their silvery reflective strips glimmering in weak light. Nick's heart pounded against the walls of his chest. Nick glanced up at the street lamp next to him. Its dull yellow glow briefly defined his face, revealing him to the killer across the street.

The man's eyes narrowed. Then he turned and ran. Until that moment, Nick wasn't certain that he was going to give chase.

Impulsively, Nick sprinted after him. The light from the street lamp faded behind him. He was aware of the terrain changing through the soles of his shoes as he crossed from pavement onto a patch of lawn. He followed the man's footsteps, sometimes closer, sometimes becoming more distant. Still, he lost him in the shadows. The broad trunk of a tree loomed out of the darkness, and he swerved to avoid it. In another instant, he raised his hands to protect his face from some overgrown brush.

Nick didn't see the body until it was too late. It emerged in front of him like a black bundle of rags. His foot sank into something soft, something fleshy. He tripped head over heels, landing a few feet beyond the corpse, the palms of his hands scraping against the gravelly soil.

Holding his breath, squinting at the vague outline of the lifeless body behind him, Nick sat still, listening for the man he had been chasing. Nothing. Except for the wind rushing through the trees, the night was silent.

Picking himself off the ground, he approached the

dark, shapeless corpse. He took his cell phone out of his pocket. It hadn't entered his mind yet to call for help. What he needed was light. He flipped the phone open, illuminating its LCD screen, and directed its dim bluish glow toward the body like a flashlight. The body was lying facedown, hidden in shadow, but it passed through Nick's mind that there was something familiar about it.

He reached his hand toward the corpse. His fingers were on its shoulder when he realized that this wasn't the body of a man, but rather only of a boy. *He's still warm.* Nick lifted the dead boy's shoulder and turned him over.

For a split second, before the phone's LCD panel abruptly went dark, Nick stared into the face of Daniel Scott. His eyes were wide open but entirely blank, like a blind man's eyes. His mouth mimed a hideous, silent scream.

Nick dropped the boy's limp shoulder, jerking away from the contact. He was up on his feet, running, before he knew what he was doing. He didn't see the park bench in front of him. It hit him like a missile. His shin cracked as it struck its unforgiving wood slats, and, crying out in pain, Nick spun to the ground. He was up seconds later, running again, trying to escape the rasp of his own breathing, fighting to make sense of the shadows in front of him, chasing the distant sounds of the city. The rush of his scrambling, frenzied flight through the park crescendoed into a roar. And then, with the intensity of an explosion, there was only silence.

When Nick opened his eyes, the spiny treetops above him were lit white against the black sky. He stared at the rustling branches, dazzled by the crisp halogen halos clinging to the trees' remaining leaves.

An aura of bright light was emanating from the center of the park. Gradually, Nick became aware of the distant babble of voices, then the squawk of a police radio and the hum of a few idling engines. His shin was throbbing where he had collided with the bench. Sharp needles of pain shot through his body when he raised himself onto his elbows, then picked himself up onto his feet.

"You fan out over there. If there were any witnesses, we're gonna want to talk to them."

The policeman's voice was close, no more than twenty feet away. Nick looked down at his clothes, trying in the dim, shadowed light to assess his appearance. Wondering how long he had been out, he ran his fingers through his hair and wiped off his face in the crook of his elbow. He searched his pockets for his phone. Unable to find it, he scanned the area around him, trying to recall if he let go of it after he had used it to light Daniel's body.

The footsteps and voices came closer. "Hey. You there!"

Nick bent down to pick up his camera, then raised his eyes to the policeman. He squinted in the beam of his high-intensity flashlight.

"Step out where I can see you."

Nick realized that he was standing half tangled in the branches of a large bush, and he took a careful step away from it, into the beam of light. "It's okay," he said at last, finding his voice. "I'm a photographer. With the *Seattle Telegraph.* I heard there's a body out here somewhere. Another killing."

"Stay where you are," the uniformed officer said.

"You mind lowering that flashlight?"

"Put your hands in the air, sir."

"My name is Nick Wilder. I told you, I'm a photographer with the *Telegraph.*"

The officer placed his hand on Nick's chest, frisking him. "You got any ID?"

Nick reached carefully for his wallet. "That's my press card," he said, holding his wallet into the light. "And my driver's license."

The officer peered at Nick's face, then at last lowered the flashlight. "The crime scene's over there," he said, pointing its beam into the darkness. "Why don't you come with me? I'm not sure what the CO wants us to do about the media."

"Am I the first one on the scene?"

"We've only been here ten minutes ourselves," the officer said.

Detective Stolie was kneeling beside the corpse when the cop led Nick into the clearing where Daniel Scott had been killed. A small generator was running nearby, and several portable halogen lamps had been plugged into it. Directed in a circle around the crime scene, they gave the park floor the atmosphere of a lit field at night, as though a bubble of daylight had been trapped beneath the canopy of branches overhead.

Stolie had flipped the body over, and Nick could see Daniel's face clearly. The soil beneath him was soaked with blood, and his thin clothes had been shredded and punctured with stab wounds. Nick winced at the violence inflicted on the boy. He was raising his hands to shield himself from the horrifying vision when Stolie glanced at him over his shoulder.

"Do me a favor," he said to Nick, "and keep back, would you? The scene's still fresh." He turned toward the cop who had led Nick into the clearing. "Stand him over there by that bench, would you? Then get back out there. Search the park. We need witnesses." He watched Nick step toward the bench where he had banged his shin. "No pictures yet," he said.

Nick didn't notice his cell phone, lying on the ground just beside the bench, until Stolie stood up. Peeling the latex gloves from his hands, the policeman waved a crime-scene photographer over. Nick took a step toward his phone. The detective turned to face him, though, before he could lean down to pick it up.

"It looks like we got ourselves another one," Stolie said. "Would you believe it—no one other than the prostitute's kid."

"Claire Scott's boy?" Nick barely recognized his own voice. "Daniel?"

Stolie was looking down at his watch. His mind was elsewhere, and he didn't seem to notice how quickly Nick had remembered the boy's name. "Body's still warm. I doubt he's been dead more than half an hour. How'd you get here so fast?"

"I was in the neighborhood." Watching the taller man approach, Nick tried to sound unconcerned. He resisted the impulse to drop his eyes to the steel gray cell phone in the dirt at his feet. "What about you?"

"Hmmm? We got a 911 call. Anonymous."

"You mind if I take a couple of pictures now?"

The detective glanced behind him. The police photographer was positioning himself above the body, adjusting his camera to the light. "Why don't you give us a few minutes first, huh?" Approaching, he looked Nick in the eye. "Maybe you and I should have a little talk." Remembering something, the detective stopped and signaled to a group of cops standing at the edge of the light. "Yo,

Harris," he called, raising his voice to get another policeman's attention.

Nick used the interruption to take a small step closer to his cell phone.

Stolie dangled the stained latex gloves he had been wearing in the air. "Bring me a baggie, would you? I've got to catalog these."

A cop gathered a few things from the evidence staging area and headed toward them, making a large detour around the corpse to avoid disturbing the crime scene.

"I have to admit, Nick," Stolie said, turning to face him again. "I'm surprised to see you here. You really sure this is what you want to be doing? So soon after your brother's murder, I mean."

The cop approached Stolie, and Stolie slid the latex gloves into a large Ziploc bag.

Again, Nick used the pause to inch toward his phone.

"Mark it with the others," Stolie said to the cop, still working the gloves into the bag. "You know what you're doing with this, right?"

"Sure," the cop reassured him. "I've been doing it all night."

Stolie watched the uniformed officer walk back around the body, then turned once again to confront Nick. "The truth is," he said, "you showing up here saved me a trip."

Straightening, Nick returned his gaze, confused.

"I was on my way over to your place when I got this call." The detective was scrutinizing him. "Listen," he said, "it wasn't going to be a friendly visit. I don't have good news. I've got orders to place you under arrest."

The words sank in. "I don't understand."

"For the murder of your brother."

"You really believe I murdered Sam?"

"It's not what *I* believe. It's what the lieutenant wants. You're our only suspect. I told you before. You're the only one with a motive, and you were there. You don't have an alibi."

Nick was shocked. "What motive could I possibly have to kill my brother?"

"That's the thing—"

"You told me just this morning," Nick continued to protest, "that I had two days. You told me you were going to try to find the killer."

The detective checked behind him, glancing at the few police officers gathered around the corpse. He lowered his voice. "That's the thing," he said again. "There's been a new development since this morning."

"What new development?"

"We know about the life insurance policy, Nick."

"What insurance?" Nick asked.

"Your brother had a one hundred thousand dollar life insurance policy. You were the sole beneficiary."

Nick was stunned. "You think I killed Sam for one hundred thousand dollars?"

"Are you saying you didn't know about the policy?" Stolie countered.

Nick shook his head. "No," he said. "I didn't know it existed."

"The thing is," the detective said, "the policy was taken out just this summer. June tenth, to be exact. And it was taken out online. It's one of those no-doctor-visit policies. No one had to see anyone else. No one even had to pick up the phone. A couple of clicks, and the policy was issued."

Nick's mind was whirling. "What are you saying?"

"Did you know," the detective asked him, "that we can

trace the computer now when you go online onto a Web site and order something? Whatever—a pair of jeans, a bottle of shampoo, books. An insurance policy."

Nick took a deep breath, waiting for the detective to complete his accusation.

"The policy on Sam's life, Nick. It was ordered from your computer."

Nick felt the air escape from his lungs. It felt as if he had been hit in the solar plexus. He was aware of the warmth of the detective's hand on his shoulder, keeping him from falling.

"You have to understand," the detective said, "it looks pretty bad. Lieutenant Dombrowski thinks we've got enough now. To make the charges stick, I mean."

"Wait," Nick pleaded, sensing that the detective himself did not want to make the arrest. "Wait a second. When did you say the policy was taken out?"

"In June."

"Sam borrowed my computer this summer." An image of his brother standing at his door, holding a small black case, thanking him, flashed through Nick's mind. "This was months ago—I practically forgot."

"He had his own computer at home," Stolie said, skeptical, "and he had another computer at his office."

"His computer froze up, and he borrowed my laptop for a week." Nick understood how convenient his explanation sounded. "Sam worked from home a lot. I'm telling you, I let him borrow my laptop."

The detective was shaking his head. "I don't know how you could prove it."

"You could look at any e-mails he sent. Maybe you could trace those to my computer, too. Or anything else he bought online in June. I don't know—you could find out where he took his computer to be repaired."

The detective nodded uncertainly. "I suppose we could do that."

Nick seized the opportunity to try to exonerate himself. "There's something more. I told you, I was down here already—that's why I was able to get here so quickly."

The detective's eyes didn't leave Nick's face.

"You didn't ask me what I was doing down here."

"Why don't you tell me?"

"I found the man who took my shoes."

"What?" Stolie couldn't mask his incredulity. "Where?"

"At the homeless shelter. Right there, on the other side of the square." Nick remembered the large cardboard sign in the window of the tall brick building. "The Seattle Emergency Shelter."

"The Hudson Hotel?" the detective said.

An image of the building's name, scored into the sandstone block above the front doors, came to Nick. "Yes," he said. "At the Hudson Hotel."

"The man who took your shoes— How did that work? You remember losing them now?"

"No." Nick quelled his frustration. "And I didn't get a good look at him. I only saw the shoes under the partition of a men's room stall." Nick brought the killer's watery, light blue eyes into his mind. "I didn't get a look at his face. I saw the back of his head—his hair. I saw his hands. The rags on his hands. But I couldn't tell you for sure if it was the same man who attacked us."

"This doesn't give me much," the detective said.

Nick had to stifle his impulse to tell Stolie that he had chased the man into the park—right before he had tripped over Daniel Scott's dead body. He had blacked out, and he couldn't account for the time. He tried to think instead of some way to prove what he was saying.

"There was a doctor there," he said. "I think his name was Barnes."

The detective made a quick note on a pad, then slipped it back into his pocket.

"He was in the men's room at the same time I was. Maybe he saw the man, too. Maybe he can identify him. He seemed to know the people there."

The detective's breath steamed from his mouth as he exhaled.

"So, are you going to arrest me?" Nick asked, breaking the silence.

The detective pondered the facts. Then he cracked a small smile. "I can't arrest you if I can't find you."

Nick couldn't mask his relief. "You believe me, then."

Stolie touched him on the shoulder. The light caught the detective on the side of his face, and Nick saw the sincerity in his eyes. Once again, despite his gratitude, Nick found himself puzzled by the man's sympathy. "Listen," the detective said. "Lieutenant Dombrowski will have my head if he finds out, you got that?"

"I understand."

"Don't queer this up for me."

"I won't," Nick said. "Thank you."

Stolie looked away. Nick's appreciation seemed to hang in the air between them. "Don't thank me," the detective said. "I'll head over to the Hudson Hotel after I close up shop here." His voice hardened. "Just pray I find your man. If this goes on much longer, there won't be anything more I'll be able to do for you."

Nick held his camera up. "So what—you think I can get a couple of pictures now?"

Stolie assessed the scene for a few seconds. "Sure," he said. Nick was aware of the moment when the detective's eyes caught sight of the phone at his feet. He tried to keep his own eyes leveled at the detective's face. "That yours?"

"What's that?"

Stolie pointed at the phone, and at last Nick allowed himself to lower his eyes. He bent down and picked it up, flipping it open to light its screen.

"Yeah, thanks." Nick glanced nonchalantly back up at the detective. "I must have dropped it."

"Come on," Stolie said. He led Nick toward Daniel Scott's body. "Let's get this wrapped up. I'm sure you've got places you'd rather be."

chapter 17

Sara Garland's huge, sleek Mercedes was parked in the small gravel lot behind Nick's apartment building when he pulled up in his rusting white Corolla. When she stepped from her car, concern was etched onto her face. Nick was more than an hour late for the gala.

Nick glanced above Sara's shoulder as she closed the distance between them. His neighbor, Reggie—a perennially stoned student in his last year at the university—was looking down at him from the third floor, his curly brown hair a tangle on his head. Reggie's girlfriend joined him at the window. She wasn't wearing a shirt, and Nick could see her breasts squeezed beneath one of her arms. Their eyes met, but neither Reggie nor his girlfriend looked away. Nick had become used to their morbid curiosity in the days since Sam's murder.

When Nick embraced Sara, the relief he felt upon seeing his lover was eclipsed by a sense of panic. The last thing he wanted was to lose her. Her beautiful face was half hidden in shadow. Her golden and platinum blond hair was radiant, almost glowing. Leaving her hands on his shoulders, she drew away from their kiss, peering into his eyes. "Where have you been?" she asked him. "I've been so worried."

Aware of her anxiety, Nick was nevertheless unable to respond. He found himself hypnotized by the refracted light emanating from the large diamond earrings she was wearing. *The police think that I killed my own brother. They think I stabbed him to death. They think I slashed my brother's face and kicked his teeth into his throat.* "I've been thinking about Sam," he said at last, unwilling to admit to Sara that he had blacked out. As much as he needed a friend, he was scared of what she would conclude if he told her about Daniel Scott. He was going to have to shoulder these secrets alone. "I haven't been myself. I'm sorry."

"Haven't you been able to remember anything more?" she asked him.

Nick shook his head. A sense of helplessness welled up inside him. He wished that he could give Sara the reassurance she must need. "I don't know why you stay with me," he heard himself say. He hadn't meant to voice his doubts. The headlong rush of events had shaken him.

"You're grieving, darling." She gave his hands a gentle squeeze. "I understand that. I'm here for you, and I'm not going to let you go. I promise."

Nick had to fight a sudden urge to break down.

Sara's face lit with a genuine smile. "Let's go upstairs. It's late. You have to change if we want to get to the gala in time for the dinner."

"The gala," Nick echoed. He would be meeting Sara's parents for the first time, thrust into the spotlight with this impossibly beautiful woman. After the day he had had, Nick wasn't certain whether he had the resolve to attend the lavish celebration. He had been thrown to the filthy, urine-stained restroom floor in the bowels of the homeless shelter. He had stumbled over Daniel Scott's corpse and then been grilled by Stolie. *He had come face-to-face a second time with his brother's killer.* His shin was still throbbing where he had collided with the bench, and he could still feel the grime of the men's room on his hands and the tickle of his own dried sweat under his clothes.

"My parents are expecting us," Sara said, reading his hesitation. "It will mean so much to me."

"I'll try, Sara."

She leaned into him and gave him a hard kiss. "You can do it," she whispered into his ear. "I need you to be strong."

"I don't deserve you."

"Do you think I'm with you just to have a little fun, Nick?" She waited for him to understand. "Is that what you think?"

"We've only known each other a few weeks," Nick said. "What do you really know about me?"

Jason Hamlin was aware of the instant when his step-daughter entered the room. Hamlin had positioned himself midway up the broad red-carpeted staircase that swept down from the mezzanine of the concert hall. He was engaged in idle conversation with William Gutterson, Seattle's chief of police. His muscular arms were folded across his chest, stretching the fabric of his crisp black tuxedo. The party spread out beneath him through the lobby and into the banquet rooms. The entire space had been elaborately decorated in broad swaths of silk patterned in a jungle motif. Huge cutouts of endangered animals were suspended from the ceiling on invisible wires, twisting in beams of carefully directed light. Hamlin's posture stiffened, and he let his arms drop to his sides. Unconsciously, he closed his hands into dry fists.

The chief of police noticed the change in the man's demeanor. He paused in midsentence, realizing that Hamlin was no longer listening to him. Following his host's gaze over the coiffed heads of the elegantly dressed guests, he spotted the object of Hamlin's attention. "Your daughter is a beautiful woman," he observed. The chief of police was aware of the muscles working beneath the taut skin of the other man's cheeks.

"Hmmm?" Hamlin mumbled, distracted. "What's that?"

Hamlin's eyes had been fastened on the young man who had walked into the hall next to his stepdaughter. A thin young man with long hair, dressed incongruously in a regular sports jacket and tie in an ocean of tailored dinner jackets and gowns. Yet the man moved gracefully, Hamlin thought, with an air of self-possession. Nick's unease only became apparent gradually, after Hamlin watched him enter the party. Sara's hand was resting lightly on his shoulder, but Hamlin had the impression somehow that the young man was hanging on to her instead.

Gutterson nodded in Sara's direction. "I've never seen a more beautiful woman," he said, repeating himself.

Like Gutterson, Hamlin was struck by Sara's beauty. She had dressed for the evening in a simple black dress, but no one in the room looked more elegant. He watched a small circle form around her. "Yes," he said, finding his voice, "she is beautiful." He glanced toward his wife Jillian a few steps below him, conversing with a few women. "She takes after her mother."

"Who is that with her?" Gutterson asked. "I'm sure I've seen him before. Recently."

"I don't know his name," Hamlin said, irritated that he didn't. "Sara told her mother and me that she was bringing someone special tonight. I wasn't paying much attention, though, I have to admit."

Gutterson didn't miss the icy stare in his host's eyes. *You're paying attention now*, he thought to say. He knew Jason Hamlin well enough, though, to keep his mouth shut.

"Are you going to find him?"

Neither Hamlin nor Gutterson had noticed the woman approach, and the two men turned reluctantly from Sara. A tall, elegantly dressed woman was standing on the stair next to the chief of police, looking at him expectantly. Her hair was dyed a tasteful shade of chestnut, and she had seen the best surgeon in Seattle about the wrinkles around her eyes. Her age, Hamlin thought, was apparent only in the loose, wrinkled skin on her arms. "Natalie," he said to her in brusque greeting.

She smiled in return. "It's a wonderful gathering, Jason," she said to him. "You outdid yourself."

"It's my pleasure. Have you tried the champagne yet?"

She held up a crystal flute half full with sparkling wine. "So what of it, Bill?" she said, turning once again to the chief of police. "The Street Butcher. Are you going to find him? Charles works downtown. So does my eldest son. I'm worried for both of them."

"You're correct to be vigilant, Natalie," Gutterson said, straightening up. "But I wouldn't spend too much time worrying if I were you. So far the violence seems to be confined to a pretty small community."

"Another serial killer stalking the streets of Seattle, nothing to worry about?" The woman glanced at Hamlin for support, appalled. "The city is crawling with homeless people. It's downright scary. And what about that man—the biologist? He wasn't homeless. He was one of us, Bill. The whole room is buzzing about it. You really must catch this maniac."

Across the soaring room, Nick felt totally at sea. Sara's hand was resting lightly on his shoulder, but he had the impression that she was carrying him into the party, holding him up onto his feet. As he followed her into the crowded hall, the guests parted in front of them, then closed behind them, cinching them in more and more tightly as they moved toward the center of the lobby. Everyone seemed to know Sara, greeting her by name as she passed. Nick was aware of their eyes scrutinizing him, their surprise at his inappropriate clothes. He glanced down, following an elderly woman's eyes to his feet. His old dress shoes appeared humble and clumsy against the plush red carpet, dross in a surfeit of glistening patent leather.

When Sara stopped to talk to a couple she knew, a wave of panic washed over him. *What if Sara left him alone there to fend for himself?* But she didn't. She pulled Nick close as she engaged in easy conversation with the young woman. When the woman's partner started talking to him, Nick nodded at him, smiling when the man smiled, listening to the rhythm of Sara's voice as she responded for him. The woman in front of Sara, Nick noticed, was adorned in so many diamonds that she seemed to be surrounded in a prismatic aura of light. And then they were moving forward again, finding their way toward the red velvet bar.

"You're doing beautifully," Sara said.

"Maybe some water will help," Nick said.

"We're almost there, darling. I'll get us a couple of

glasses, and then in a few minutes we can go sit down at our table."

"You don't have any idea how wonderful you are," Nick said.

"I told you, darling." Nick felt her hand find the small of his back. "I'm not going to let you go."

"It's a party, my dear. You're supposed to be enjoying yourself." Nick became aware of the woman's voice before he saw her. His eyes tracked the words, and he found himself looking at Sara twenty years older. Only the woman addressing him was decidedly more formal than Sara, much more reserved—wooden even.

"You must be Jillian," he heard himself say. "Sara's mother."

"How good of you to notice."

Sara's fingers clenched his shoulder. Nick remarked that she didn't move to give her mother an embrace. "Mother," she said, "this is—"

"You must be Nick," Jillian Hamlin said at the same time.

"Yes," Sara confirmed. "Nick Wilder. The man I told you about."

Jillian studied Nick's face. "You don't like big gatherings like this," she observed. "Well, I don't blame you, dear. It was an acquired taste for me as well."

"It's nice to be here with Sara," Nick contradicted pleasantly. "And it's nice to meet you."

Jillian acknowledged the hollow compliment with a tight smile.

"Nick works for the *Telegraph*, Mother."

"You do? How fascinating. And what is it you do there, Nick? Are you a reporter?"

"He's a photographer, Mother. And a good one."

"I'm sure he is."

"I do some reporting, too." Nick made an effort to find his voice. "But I'm not really working for the *Telegraph.* Not anymore."

"No?"

"I work freelance now. Assignment by assignment."

"Jason will be impressed," Jillian said.

"I'm not so sure," Nick said.

"Don't be so modest." Sara gave his shoulder a squeeze. "Of course Jason will be impressed. He'll have every reason to be."

"Why don't you let me speak for myself?" Once again, Nick was aware that he was being addressed before he saw the speaker. His eyes alighting on Sara's stepfather, he found that the voice matched Jason Hamlin's angular, symmetrical face. He felt Sara's fingers slip at last from his shoulder. "Jason Hamlin," the powerful, charismatic man in front of him said, introducing himself. "And you are?"

Nick hesitated. He glanced at Sara, waiting for her to speak for him, but her eyes were veiled, dropped to her feet.

"Mr. Wilder, isn't it?" Jillian offered.

"Yes." Nick tried to smile. His hand felt damp and weak inside Hamlin's dry grip. "Nick Wilder. I'm pleased to meet you."

Hamlin let go of Nick's hand and touched him on his shoulder. "I have a little emceeing to do, Nick," he said. "But I'll make a point to catch up with you later."

Nick watched the possessive way the financier wrapped an arm around Sara's shoulders in greeting. She was a tall woman. From the moment he had met her, Nick had been conscious of her strength. Caught in Hamlin's grip, though, she looked small and helpless. He was glad when Sara's stepfather let her go, and he was relieved once the man was gone.

After finishing dinner, Nick stood from the table where he and Sara had been seated and excused himself to go to the men's room. He had barely touched his food, but he had drunk a glass of wine, and he felt flushed. He stood in front of the mirror, his hands pressed against the edge of the washbasin. "This is a party," he said out loud to himself, repeating the words Jillian Hamlin had first spoken to him. "You're supposed to be enjoying yourself." He twisted the taps, plunged his hands under the stream of cold water, and splashed his face, then yanked a few paper towels from the dispenser. "Only another hour to go," he said to his reflection. "You go out there and enjoy yourself."

Nick searched the large room for Sara as the door to the men's room swung closed behind him. A small prickle of fear rose in his chest when he didn't locate her at their table, and he made a conscious effort to calm himself. His gaze traveled from face to face across the expansive party, as if he were watching a slide show. Voices welled up against the walls, coalescing into a mechanical sound, Nick thought, like the rumble of a gigantic engine. All at once, from out of the cacophony, a single voice distinguished itself. *No, I've never seen him before, either. I have no idea where he's from.* His eyes followed the voice to a woman, watching him from about thirty feet away. He tried to block out the woman's voice, concentrating instead on the classical music drifting into the room from the orchestra, searching one more time for Sara.

All the way at the other side of the party, engaged in a close conversation with another man, Jason Hamlin was also watching him. When Nick caught sight of him, he realized that he recognized the heavy, dark-haired man Hamlin was speaking to. He couldn't immediately place him, but he had seen the man before, Nick was certain of it.

Nick waited for Hamlin to drop his eyes, then reached into his jacket pocket and pulled out the small, high-resolution digital camera he carried when it wasn't convenient to lug around one of his SLRs. His first picture was a broad canvas of the room, which he would be able to enhance later on his computer. Then he zoomed in on the two men and took a close-up of their faces. He checked the screen to make sure he had captured a good picture, then slipped the camera back into his jacket and cut through the guests, heading toward them. Nick had meant it when he told Laura Daly that he didn't feel comfortable taking pictures here for the paper. He didn't want to betray Sara's trust. Seeing Hamlin with this other man, though, had piqued Nick's interest, and, despite his reluctance, he wanted to figure out who the man was.

Hamlin was a good three or four inches taller than the other, mustached man, and he was leaning into him, crowding him. As Nick closed the distance between them, he could see the man's unease. Sweat had gathered on the man's forehead, above his bushy eyebrows. *Where had he seen him before?* This was a man with authority, a man used to getting his way, but Hamlin was making him nervous. Before Nick was able to get closer, Hamlin led the man away from the party, directing him through one of the open doorways into the concert hall.

"Have you seen Sara?"

A tall, thin man was standing in front of Nick, waiting for a response. "Sara?"

"You're Sara's date, aren't you?"

"Yes."

The man held out his hand. "Grant Jones," he said. "I'm an old friend of Sara's. Can't seem to find her anywhere."

"Nick Wilder," Nick said distractedly.

"I saw her going upstairs with her mother," another man said. "About five minutes ago. I was looking for her, too."

"If you'll excuse me," Nick said. He pushed past the two men in front of him, making his way to the doorway where Hamlin had disappeared, ignoring the voices behind him. *Where did Sara meet him? You know, I have no idea. Just like Sara—she's always been headstrong.*

The hubbub of the party fell away as Nick stepped through the doors into the empty auditorium, replaced by the crisp notes of the Seattle symphony performing without an audience on the stage far beneath him. He scanned the rows of plush seats until he spied the diminutive figures of Hamlin and his guest seated in the middle of the auditorium. The man's sweaty face glowed red with the reflection of the velvet covering the seats. Nick reached for his small camera to get another picture of the two men.

"Excuse me, sir. There's no photography allowed in here."

Nick hadn't heard the guard approach, and his command gave him a jolt. He swiveled toward him, surprised by how large the man was. The guard's voice had traveled through the empty auditorium. Jason Hamlin turned to face him as well.

"I've never seen the concert hall empty like this before," Nick said.

The imposing guard took a small step toward him until he was uncomfortably close. Before Sara slid next to him, Nick thought the man was going to wrench the camera out of his hand.

"It's okay," Sara said. "He's with me." She nodded a discreet greeting to her father, then took Nick's elbow and led him back to the gala.

chapter 18

Unable to sleep, Nick was behind the wheel of his old Corolla before eight the next morning, on his way in to the *Telegraph.* He twisted the key in the ignition, then released the parking brake. The car was rolling across the lot when a black stretch limousine glided to the curb, blocking his exit. He waited behind the wheel, contemplating the limousine. It took him a few seconds to understand that its driver was intentionally penning him into the lot. Nick tried to peer through its obscured windows, then, flustered, stepped out of his car.

The limousine's side window slid down with a high-pitched mechanical hum as Nick approached, and he found himself looking down into the eyes of the large bodyguard who had accosted him inside the auditorium.

"Nick Wilder?"

Nick nodded, taken aback.

"I've been instructed to pick you up, sir."

Nick glanced over his shoulder at his car. He had left the motor running when he got out. "What's this about?"

"Mr. Hamlin sent me. He would like you to come downtown to meet him."

"For what reason?"

"That's not my business, sir."

"I'll follow you, then."

The large man didn't smile. "No, sir. Those aren't my orders."

"I see." Nick tried to peer into the back of the car, to see whether it was empty, but the windows were too dark. "Give me a minute," he said, making up his mind. "I have to park my car."

"As you wish, sir."

Fifteen minutes later, the limousine pulled into the basement of one of the tallest buildings in downtown Seattle. As the car started down the ramp into the garage, Nick glanced up through the moon roof at the building's glossy green glass façade. It was a cold, dark morning, and the skyscraper seemed to disappear into a cloud of drizzly mist. After pulling to a stop on the first level, the bodyguard accompanied Nick into the elevator and pressed the button for the top floor. The ultra-sleek elevator whined as it accelerated powerfully upward. Seconds later, its doors slid open to reveal a suite of private offices drenched in natural light.

Despite how dreary it had been at the base of the building, it was so bright atop the tower that Nick had to shield his eyes. He squinted toward a wall of windows, surprised to find that the elevator had carried them above the fog. Tips of the taller buildings poked through the blanket of mist. Taking in the expansive view, Nick had the sensation that he was riding over the clouds in a plane.

"This way, sir," the bodyguard said. At eight o'clock, the offices were empty. Nick followed the bodyguard down a long, teak-paneled corridor to a door at its end.

Jason Hamlin, cleanly shaven and dressed casually in jeans and a charcoal sweater, was seated behind a massive desk in a room that spanned the length of the penthouse suite. Framed by a wall of glass, the view behind him stretched all the way to the Olympic Mountains. He didn't stand to greet Nick when the guard rapped on the solid door. Dismissing the guard, he let Nick traverse the spacious office to the edge of the huge desk, then, leaning back comfortably, waved a hand at a couple of guest chairs. "Take a seat," he instructed, making no pretense at civility.

Nick stood in front of him, surveying the room. Three flat-panel plasma displays lined the far wall, each of them tuned mutely to a different program. An Oriental carpet covered the floor. In Hamlin's presence, he felt ragged and poorly dressed. He hadn't slept well, and he had gone straight from bed to the car. He ran a hand over his unshaven face, then through his unkempt hair. At last, realizing that Hamlin was waiting for him, he sat down. "I've never seen such an extraordinary view," he said.

"Let's dispense with the bullshit, Wilder. Okay?"

Nick knew that this wasn't a social call, but Hamlin's ugly candor surprised him. "What's this about?" Nick asked. "Exactly."

"No great mystery there, Wilder. I'm surprised you even have to ask." Hamlin leaned forward in his chair and set his forearms down on the edge of the massive desk. "You're going out with my daughter. I thought it was time we get acquainted."

"You do this with all her friends?" The words were out of Nick's mouth before he had the opportunity to reflect whether it was a good idea to provoke the powerful man.

"Only the ones she's sleeping with," Hamlin said with an unexpected smile. "I'm a pretty protective father. Some people might say overprotective." He shrugged and loosened his neck, a fighter stepping into a ring. "Sara's a beautiful girl."

"Does she know about this?"

"This meeting?" Hamlin laughed. "Hell no. And she's not going to know about it, either. Is she, Wilder? I think this is something best kept between men." He settled back in his chair, keeping Nick in his sights.

Nick was distracted by the artwork hanging on the wall. Hamlin appeared to own an original Warhol and a small Picasso oil-on-canvas. Nick didn't know whether the art held any significance for Hamlin. But he recognized that the paintings served their purpose. The wealth they represented was staggering. He returned his attention to the older man, awed despite himself. "So what is this, then," he said, trying to regain some of his righteousness at Hamlin's presumption. "Some kind of inquisition? You want me to convince you I'm worthy of your daughter?"

"Something like that," Hamlin said. "Only don't kid yourself. I already know who you are, and you'll never be worthy of Sara." He reached across the glistening desktop to a thin manila folder lying in its center and flipped it open, revealing an eight-by-ten black-and-white photograph. After looking at it himself, he slid it across the desk toward Nick. Nick recognized the photograph. He didn't move to touch it. "You've been seeing Sara for about a month now. You didn't think that I might do a little background check on you in the meantime?"

Nick shook his head. As obvious as it was, the thought had never crossed his mind.

"That's the photograph that landed you the job at the *Seattle Telegraph.* Am I right?"

"I had the job already," Nick said, "when I took that picture."

"You were on probation. After that picture, you were a photographer."

"I guess that's right."

"A group of tree huggers protesting the construction of the new science lab at the university. Huh?"

Nick was conscious that Hamlin was trying to intimidate him. "The university's private security company decided forcibly to remove the protestors one night," he said, "despite the court's stay of the proceeding against them. I just happened to be there that night. So I snapped a few pictures."

"You have any idea how much those pictures cost me?"

Nick was confused. "How could this picture hurt you? It didn't have anything to do with you."

"Because of this one little picture, the court placed a permanent injunction on the project. Take a guess whose company had been awarded the contract to build that hundred-million-dollar science lab."

Nick didn't know what to say. He glanced down at the photograph. A university security guard had reached up into a tree and grabbed hold of a protestor by the ankle. Nick had focused the shot on a student calmly looking back at him from the middle of the melee, but the photograph had caught the protestor frozen in his rough flight to the ground. The guard's face was a reflection of his exertion, the protestor's a shocked question mark of surprise.

"It was a good photograph," Nick said. "I'm sorry if it inadvertently cost you some money."

The older man harrumphed. "A one hundred million dollar contract. Not just *some money*." He furrowed his brow, determined to maintain control of the conversation. "I knew your brother," he said. "Sam. Did you know that?"

The words gave Nick a small jolt. He knew already that Hamlin had been fronting Sam's company start-up funding. There was enormous money chasing biotech projects in Seattle, and Sam and his partner, Blake Werner, had been on to something big. Nick hadn't realized, though, that Hamlin had known Sam personally, by name. Nick made an effort not to reveal his surprise. "Sure," he said. "I guess I'd heard."

"He was an ambitious man, your brother. A real determined man. He had his eyes on the prize, and he wasn't going to let anything or anyone stand in his way. It's unfortunate he was murdered, and I feel for you. Believe it or not, I really do."

Nick felt himself bristle. Sam had only been dead a week. His mutilated body still lay in a mortuary, released by the police the day before.

"The question in my mind, though," Hamlin continued, oblivious to Nick's increasing indignation, "isn't how much compassion I'm supposed to be showing you. It's whether my daughter should be sleeping with some stranger whose brother just got himself stabbed to death on the street. Sara deserves the best this world's got to offer. I'm sure you'd agree, wouldn't you?" He closed the manila folder over the photograph. "You're damaged goods, Wilder. A wounded stray."

Nick liked Hamlin less with every passing moment. His hands were sweaty and his chest was tight, but he couldn't find his voice. Against his resolve, he had allowed the older man to bully him.

"Here's the way I see it." Hamlin leaned forward, engulfed in the glare of the bright light streaming through the huge plate of glass behind him. "Picture yourself at a crossroads. Looking one way, you've got a good job, a promising future. You're a talented photographer. I'll give you that. You make the right decision now, and there's no telling how far you'll go. Walk down the other road, though, and what do you see?" Hamlin's icy blue eyes bored holes into Nick's face. "Sara?" Hamlin's lips formed an empty smile. "Do you honestly believe that you've got any sort of a future with Sara? Just how long do you think she'll stay with you?"

Nick broke his silence. "If that's true," he heard himself say, "if she's just playing with me, then why are we having this conversation?" His voice cracked, his heart pounded in his chest. All at once he could barely contain his rage. "Why did you feel the need to drag me down here to your office to threaten me?"

Hamlin continued looking at Nick, trying to stare him down. Nick returned his gaze, practically choking on his breath. At last, lacing his hands behind his head, the older man leaned back in his chair and raised his eyes to the ceiling. "Get out of my office, Wilder," he said. "From now on, I'm going to be watching you. Understand?" The chair groaned beneath him. "Consider yourself warned."

* * *

Nick was turning the confrontation with Jason Hamlin over in his mind later that morning. He was determined not to let the powerful man's threats deter him. With the rush of everything happening around him, the single stable element in his life was Sara. Not just emotionally, but practically as well. In the days since Sam's murder, when decisions had to be made, Sara had helped Nick make them. She had even been the one to organize the disposal of Sam's body. After the police released Sam's remains to a mortuary, Sara had taken it upon herself to visit the director, and without telling Nick she had paid for the cremation. Sara had become part of his life. Nick needed her, no matter what the consequence.

Nick stopped walking in front of a small antique jewelry store downtown. A long, thin silver chain with delicate, flattened links, scintillating in a halogen beam, had caught his eye. He glanced up at the lettering on the awning above the storefront, then approached the window. He hesitated, aware that his finances were pretty well tapped out until the payout on Sam's insurance policy came through. Then he made up his mind and opened the door. He needed something tangible to demonstrate the depth of his feelings to Sara. Perhaps this chain wasn't much, especially to a person used to real jewelry. Nevertheless, Nick wanted to see it around Sara's neck.

chapter 19

At five that afternoon, Nick was standing on First Avenue, across the street from a rundown transient hotel Night had begun to engulf the city. A group of women dressed in miniskirts and tight jackets had gathered at the entrance to the hotel, huddling together under its small rusting canopy to escape the drizzle. Trails of cigarette smoke wafted into the dark, misty air above their heads. Nick raised his camera to his eye and took a couple quick snaps of them, wondering if they had known Claire Scott. There weren't that many streetwalkers left in Seattle. Prostitution had moved to the Internet and into the strip clubs. Nick listened to their hard voices. *That's right, girl. Keep it covered in plastic. Swallow at your own risk, baby.* The string of nonsensical words dissolved into cackling laughter.

One of the women clicked open an umbrella and, craning her head toward the heavy sky, ventured onto the sidewalk. The others followed her in a pack. Nick waited until they had disappeared, then, glancing up at the five-story hotel's grim brick façade, crossed the street to its entrance.

Nick entered the fluorescent-lit lobby, aware of the floor's worn linoleum through the soles of his shoes, taking in the dark water stains on the walls. The clerk at the front desk eyed him from behind a greasy partition of bulletproof glass. "I got no rooms," the old man said. "I'm full up."

Nick rested his hands on the stainless-steel counter in front of the window. "I'm not looking for a room."

"We don't got any," the man said again.

"I'm looking for someone. A man named Blake Werner."

"He expecting you?"

"No." Nick noticed the tiny pieces of crust around the man's eyelids and the black gap in his mouth where a front tooth was missing. "Is he here?"

"He's here, okay. I don't figure he could be anywhere else."

Nick pulled a twenty-dollar bill from his pocket and laid it on the small, grimy steel tray at the base of the window. "What room is he in?"

"Take the elevator." The green bill disappeared from the tray, and a raspy buzzer sounded behind the doors leading from the lobby into the hotel. "Fifth floor. Down to the left. Room four."

The elevator opened onto a narrow, unlit hallway. Nick could hear voices through the hotel's flimsy walls as he made his way down to Werner's room. The number 4 was tacked to an old painted wooden door, dangling askew. He stood for few beats, listening. When he knocked, the number rattled, then dropped back into place. Nick could hear someone sitting up on a bed inside the room, followed by the hack of a man coughing.

"Blake?"

Farther down the hallway, another door opened. Nick glanced down the close corridor, aware of the eyes looking at him from a tight crack in a doorway. He knocked again.

"Who's it?"

The words were slurred and forced. Nick hesitated, then placed a hand on the knob and tried the door.

"Who's there?" the man inside repeated, panicked, when the locked door rattled in its frame.

"We met a couple of years ago," Nick said. "You worked with my brother."

Werner paused, absorbing the information. "What d'you want?"

"Nothing. Just to talk to you for a few minutes."

"Go away." Nevertheless, the bed groaned beneath the man as he stood up, and the floorboards creaked as he moved across the small room.

Nick waited. The smell of alcohol nearly overwhelmed him when the man pulled the door open. Dressed in jeans and a grubby shirt, unshaven, his hair in a greasy heap on top of his head, Werner was barely the shadow of the man Nick remembered.

"Not quite what you were expecting," the man said with a knowing, bleary-eyed smile. He reached a hand toward Nick. "Blake Werner," he said unnecessarily when Nick clasped his hand. "But I guess you know that already. *Dr.* Blake Werner."

"Yeah," Nick said. "I remember. We met."

Werner shrugged. Even as pathetic as he was, he was a beguiling man. Nick understood from his eyes that he was painfully aware of his own failure. He took a few halting steps back toward his bed, so incapacitated that he nearly fell before reaching it. "Help yourself to a drink," he said, pointing at an open bottle of whisky on top of a beaten-up bureau. "Sit down. My home is your home. So you're Sam's brother—right?"

Ignoring the alcohol, Nick pulled a chair over from the desk. "Yeah. Sam's brother."

"How is it the old saying goes? Any brother of Sam's is an enemy of mine, or something like that."

Nick smiled uncomfortably. "I haven't heard that one," he said.

"I don't sleep anymore," Werner said, as though he were answering a question Nick had posed. "I dream all the time. I can't seem to stop dreaming. Goddamn it. But I can't sleep."

The lanky man had huge dark circles underneath his eyes. His hands were trembling uncontrollably.

"Yeah," Werner said, following Nick's gaze, "it's like I've got Parkinson's disease, isn't it? I used to run marathons. Honolulu. New York." His eyes lit. "You remember the Seattle marathon, right? What was that, just two years ago? Seven forty-five a mile. I finished with your brother, and you know what a good runner Sam was. Today"—Werner shrugged—"I couldn't even find the starting line."

Nick took a quick look around the room. A small TV in the corner was switched off, its screen blank. The cramped space was littered with fifteen or twenty books, scattered around the floor as if they had been thrown there, their spines broken, their covers torn, some half-buried in heaps of soiled clothes. Above the bureau, Werner had tacked his Harvard diploma to the dirty wall. "You've been here a long time," Nick said.

"Too long."

"How long?"

Werner shook his head. "I really don't remember." He

tracked Nick's eyes to the bureau. "Say, friend," he said, alert. "Do me the favor of handing me that bottle, would you?"

Nick reached for the whisky.

"I don't need a glass," Werner said. "There's no one here to impress. Just Sam's brother. One of my sworn enemies." He took a large swig, then handed the bottle back to Nick. "Put that back where you got it, would you? Or I'll finish the whole thing. Then what'll I do, huh?"

"Listen, Blake," Nick said. "There're a few questions I want to ask you, okay?"

Blake shrugged his acquiescence.

"About Matrix Zarcon."

"You were a reporter, right?"

"Yeah, that's right."

"So why not ask your brother, then? If you've got so many questions. I don't want to revisit that sorry piece of history."

It took Nick a moment to understand what Werner was saying. "You haven't heard yet, have you?"

"Heard what?"

"Sam's dead," Nick said.

Werner looked confused, then broke into an odd smile. "You're kidding me, right?"

Nick shook his head.

"What, someone finally kill him?"

"Why do you say that?" Nick asked, stung by the off-hand remark.

"You mean, how do I know?" Werner laughed, then began to cough. He held his crooked elbow up to his mouth, and when he brought it away Nick was aware that his forearm was freckled with blood. "Chalk it up to wishful thinking."

"You really didn't like my brother."

Werner seemed not to hear. He took a crumpled cigarette from his shirt pocket and stuck it between his lips. "You're a smoker, right?"

Nick shook his head. "I quit."

"Once a smoker, always a smoker. It's like riding a bike. You never forget how." Werner harrumphed, half to himself. "You got a match?"

Nick ignored the interruption. "You didn't like Sam," he repeated, mastering his annoyance.

"Sam? Nobody liked Sam."

"Why?"

Werner squinted at Nick, a slightly amused expression lighting his otherwise dark eyes. "Let me ask you something, friend." He stuffed the unlit cigarette back into his pocket.

"Sure."

"How well did you know him?"

"What?"

"I really mean it, friend. How well did you know your brother?"

Nick had taken shelter beneath the metal bleachers set up inside Memorial Stadium. He had arrived at the park next to the Space Needle early, two hours after the start of the race, in time to catch the first elite runners crossing the finish line. It had been raining earlier, and the marathoners were drenched and miserable as they entered the stadium. Their determination was audible in their footsteps over the excited cheers of the onlookers.

An hour later, the runners' footsteps weren't so emphatic anymore, and the crowd had become subdued. The sun peeked through the clouds, even as a few sprinkles chased the slower, spent runners into the stadium. Nick leaned under the edge of the bleachers to light a cigarette, then, squinting, taking a deep drag, stepped out into the momentary burst of sunlight. He didn't want to miss Sam crossing the finish line. Sam must have repeated his instructions ten times. *Be there with your camera, bro'. Don't be late.* He had made Nick promise.

Nick was aware of the girl's giggles. She was sitting on the bleacher above him, just out of his sight. His attention, though, was drawn to the man in the cowboy hat in front of him, who had turned around to berate him. "Look where you are," the man said to Nick. "You're at a marathon, for Christ's sake. And you want to light a cigarette?"

Nick took another deep drag before dropping the cigarette to the ground. The lit ember tumbled through the air, then drowned in a puddle at his feet.

"Yeah, you're at a marathon, for Christ's sake," he heard the girl say.

Nick took another step out from beneath the bleachers, craning his neck to see who was teasing him. "Do I know you?" he asked the girl.

"Yeah." Her face flushed. "Media and Politics? Professor Rigby's seminar?"

"Oh." Nick felt silly. He placed her now from his class Tuesday and Thursday afternoons. "I'm sorry. I didn't recognize you."

"You're not running in the race?"

"My brother's the athlete." Nick held his camera up for the girl to see. "I'm just here to take a few pictures."

"Assuming he makes it."

"He'll make it," Nick said. "If I know Sam, he'll cross

the finish line one way or another." Nick realized that the girl was wearing running shorts. "You finished already?"

"Yeah. I beat your brother, I guess."

Nick squinted toward the finish line, searching for Sam's face among the runners coming into the stadium for the final lap of the long race. "He's not going to like that," he said.

"You're Nick, right?"

"Yeah. Nick Wilder."

"I like the things you say. Your comments, I mean, in class. Like what you said last week, about the way networks turn news into entertainment."

Nick took a small step back to get a better view of the girl, doubly embarrassed now that he hadn't recognized her. "Thanks," he said.

"You have another of those cigarettes?" she asked him.

Nick gauged her. "You're not kidding, are you?"

She smiled. "After twenty-six miles, I deserve a little vice, right?"

Nick noticed Sam enter the stadium as he lit their cigarettes. Even from this distance, Nick recognized Sam's aggravation. His brother was scanning the bleachers, looking for him, worried that he hadn't shown with his camera. "There," Nick said. He pointed across the field. "That's my brother now."

The girl followed Nick's direction. "He looks like you, doesn't he?"

"He's better looking than I am," Nick said.

"I wouldn't say so," the girl said.

"You haven't seen him up close yet." Nick raised the camera to his eye. He brought Sam's sweaty face into focus through the powerful telephoto lens and snapped a picture, then held the digital camera up for the girl to see.

"Yeah, you're right," she said glibly. "He's much better looking."

"That's what all the girls end up saying," Nick said.

Nick raised the camera back to his eye, this time bringing Blake Werner into the picture, too, next to Sam. Sam had thrown an arm over Werner's shoulders, and the two men were running in step. Nick saw the tension on Sam's face. He waited for him to smile, then snapped a picture of the two friends. Werner had come in from Boston the day before, just for the race.

"You're a good brother," the girl said. "My brother wouldn't brave the cold to take my picture."

"I owe Sam a lot," Nick said. "He's not just better looking, he's putting me through graduate school."

Nick was still smoking the same cigarette when he jostled his way through the crowd at the track to get a picture of Sam crossing the finish line.

"Jesus, bro'," Sam said, arm in arm with Werner, stumbling toward his younger brother, "those things'll kill you. Don't you know that?"

Nick let the cigarette drop to his feet. He tucked his equipment back into his camera bag.

"You get the pictures?"

Nick snapped the camera bag shut. "What do you think?"

Relaxing, Sam gave his brother's shoulder a squeeze. "Come on," he said. "Let's go get a beer. Blake's buying."

"You play with fire, you get burned. That's what they say, isn't it?"

Werner was rocking on the bed, too drunk, Nick realized, to remain sitting up much longer.

"Tell me what you mean, Blake," Nick said.

"Sam knew how dangerous Zarconia was."

"What do you mean, dangerous?"

"It's unstable. It's a new drug. Genetic. You know how small a dose is? You just take a grain of the stuff. You can hardly measure it. It works on a molecular level. In your brain. It acts on certain receptors—basically, it supercharges your dopamine. You ever take Ecstasy, friend?"

"Sure."

Werner raised his hands, then let them drop into his lap. "It was mine. All mine."

"What are you saying?"

"I was the one, not your brother. I was the one who made it. It was my research. My baby."

Werner was starting to ramble. Nick wanted to back him up to the beginning. "I never heard how you ended up working with Sam," he said.

"Hmmm? We met at the university, the year before I went back to Boston to get my master's. He was a lousy student, did you know that? A damn lousy excuse for a scientist. But he was good with money, you know? And I wasn't."

"So you went into business together?"

Werner shook his head. "I invented Zarconia, I told you. When I was at Harvard. That's what I did. It was Sam's idea to start the company, Matrix Zarcon. Give him credit for that. Your brother was one smart son of a bitch, friend. He convinced me to put the patent in the company's name. What I didn't quite understand was that the company belonged to him. Once he had what he needed, I was history. He kept the prize for himself."

Appalled by what he was hearing about his brother, Nick nevertheless didn't doubt that Werner was speaking the truth. "Wasn't there anything you could do?"

Werner smiled. "He fired me, friend. Kicked me to the curb."

"There wasn't any way you could protect your interests? Legally, I mean. Couldn't you have sued him for fraud?"

"What would have been the point? You're not listening to me, friend. Zarconia was more dangerous than good. Like brushing your teeth with nitroglycerin. As far as I was concerned, there was zero chance of ever getting it tested." Werner again raised the crook of his elbow to his mouth and coughed. "And then anyway, there were the pictures."

"The pictures?"

"The photographs, friend."

Nick was lost. "I'm not sure I understand."

"You should remember. You took them. The day we first met. At the marathon."

"I remember," Nick said. "I took photographs of Sam and you, crossing the finish line. But I can't see—"

Werner waved a hand vaguely in the direction of the diploma he had tacked to the wall above the bureau. "The day I was running the marathon in Seattle, I was also in Boston, taking my final exams for my master's. Or a friend of mine was. All Sam had to do was bring the pictures to the university. I would have lost my degree."

The information stunned Nick. "The pictures were proof you cheated on your exams," he said, remembering how vehement Sam had been. "That's why he wanted me there."

"Like I said, friend, how well did you know your brother?"

"I'm sorry."

"It's not your fault. Sam had us both fooled." Werner's smile could have been a wince. "As far as I could see, my degree at Harvard was worth a hell of a lot more than a share of Matrix Zarconia. I never imagined that Sam would pull off the financing he did. How could I? Jason Hamlin's a pretty big fish to reel in your first time out."

"So he forced you out of the company."

"Check. But hell, I've still got my diploma, right? And as for your brother—" Werner laughed, fastening Nick with a blurry stare. "All that stuff he was doing with Hamlin? Raising funds. *Capital*, he called it. Testing the drug. The FDA in one hand. Hamlin's venture capital in the other. You know what it was, friend?"

Nick looked at the broken man in front of him, waiting. Sorry for him, sorry for himself. But somehow most sorry for his brother.

"A house of cards. That's what it was. A goddamned house of cards. He knew how dangerous Zarconia was. He knew the potential, but he knew the risks, too, friend. He knew. He was playing with fire. Looks like he got burned."

Nick handed the bottle of whisky back to Werner on his way out of the small, filthy room. As he pulled the door closed, Werner was sitting unsteadily on the edge of the bed, holding the half-empty bottle to his lips and taking a greedy swig. The vision remained with Nick in the elevator as he descended to the lobby, serenaded by the whining groans of the ancient cables overhead.

chapter 20

Nick woke in a sweat at dawn the next morning, gasping for breath, in the throes of a nightmare. He placed where he was. He recognized the door in front of him, the doorknob as he reached his hand to turn it. He had stood in this short hallway a thousand times before. The door swung slowly open in front of him. And he took a cautious step into his parents' study in Madison.

Seated behind his desk, examining some papers, his father looked up at him, surprised. Nick's first reaction was to approach his father and to embrace him. Nick realized only slowly that his father was dead. His face was bloodied, disfigured from the accident with the truck that had killed both his parents. His lips were swollen, purple. Like Sam's, his teeth had been broken, forced backward into his mouth.

Lying in bed, Nick's eyes were open already, but he struggled to open them wider, trying to see, writhing to untangle himself from his heavy blankets. At last the dark bedroom in Seattle came fuzzily into focus, replacing the vision from his nightmare. Nick settled back into bed, his heart racing in his chest, his breath caught in his throat. He dragged his hand across his sweaty face, through his hair. It felt as if he hadn't slept a single minute since the cops had unzipped the body bag and he had looked into his brother's lifeless eyes. Trying not to wake Sara, he crept out of bed. It wasn't yet six A.M., but he didn't want to close his eyes again. He looked around the grungy room, then decided to head in to his office.

The rain was coming down hard, and Nick got drenched running from the parking lot to the doors of the *Telegraph* building. He slid his cameras and his phone across the table to the security guard.

"I haven't seen you in this early in six months," she said, leaning back in her chair to look up at him.

"It's been awhile," he acknowledged, grateful for the small, everyday banter.

"I thought they fired you, didn't they? Hey, you got your security pass or an ID card or something?"

Nick reached into his back pocket for his wallet. "They didn't fire me." He held his ID out for her to see. "I quit. But I still work freelance."

"Were you right there when it happened? Did they catch him yet?"

"What?" Nick wasn't certain what the guard was asking him.

"If it was me, I'd a killed the man."

Incensed, Nick gathered his things into his hands. "You can give Laura Daly a call," he said, "if you have an issue with my clearance."

* * *

At six-fifteen, Daly stopped in front of the desk Nick was using. Nick looked up at her as the editor lowered herself into a red vinyl chair. She flinched a little as she sat down, like she was feeling some pain in her knees. Nick assessed her dispassionately, waiting for her to speak. Dressed casually against the morning cold in a thick navy Mariners sweatshirt over her usual white cotton shirt and dark gray trousers, there was little soft about the senior editor's appearance. Nick had always thought that she went to pains to remove any hint of the feminine from her bearing.

This early in the morning, the office was almost empty. Several reporters were sitting in front of computer terminals, working on stories with imminent deadlines, and a few stragglers from the night shift were gathered at the coffee machine. Their voices rose and fell indistinctly across the huge newsroom, but the voluminous space was otherwise silent.

"I think I owe you an apology," Daly began. Her tone was deliberately casual. Nick, though, was aware of the depth of her sincerity. He understood that she was worried that she had offended him, that she didn't want to lose his regard. "About the gala, I mean. You left the restaurant pretty upset."

"Forget it, Laura. It's not your fault. I shouldn't have reacted like that. I've been pretty stressed."

"I didn't mean to push you," she continued. "This is all new to me as well, you know what I mean? I don't know what to expect. I thought maybe it might help to have something concrete to work on."

"You don't have to worry about me. I'm figuring things out."

Daly shifted a little in her seat, settling in. "When Harold disappeared, I forgot how to sleep for a while."

Waiting for her to continue, Nick watched her brush a few strands of gray hair behind her ears. He knew the stories. In her thirties, when Daly had gotten pregnant accidentally, outside any serious relationship, she had decided to have the baby herself. She had raised her son alone, all the way through high school, only to lose him in a tragic twist of fate when he was eighteen. As long as Nick had known the editor, however, this was the first time she had ever herself mentioned her son to him.

"It got so bad I went to see a shrink—though that's not something I tell too many people. You know what the therapist told me?" Daly raised her eyes toward the ceiling, remembering. "She said, as hard as it is to accept, Harold made his own choices. Not me." Daly paused, as though she was once again listening to the therapist's counsel. "I can't blame myself."

Nick remembered that Daly's son had traveled with the high school baseball team to a state tournament a few hours away in Spokane, just a few months shy of his graduation. Harold didn't want to go. He hadn't wanted to try out for the team in the first place. Daly had pushed her son to make the overnight trip. Then Harold disappeared when the team stopped for dinner at a fast food restaurant. He had gotten up to use the restroom and had never come back. No one saw him leave the building, and no body had ever been found. Laura used the paper to organize a statewide search. Harold, though, had vanished.

Daly blinked back the memory. "I think I was *afraid* to sleep, because every time I did I would dream that Harold was in the room, reaching out for me. And every time I woke up, I lost him again." When she glanced at Nick, her gentle smile caught him off guard.

"I'm sorry," Nick said. He wasn't certain what else to say.

"Don't be." Daly reached out to touch Nick on his arm. "I don't think about it so much anymore. You should know that. I'm only telling you because I want you to know I understand. I was pretty upset with my shrink when she told me that Harold was the one who was responsible. That he was gone and that I should stop waiting for him. Looking back, though, I think I understand what she was trying to tell me. Not to internalize the loss. Not to spend too much time looking for answers inside myself. There's a lot in your life that is simply outside your control."

Nick didn't know how to respond. "Yeah," he said at last, trying to return the editor's smile. "You're probably right. I'm doing the same thing."

"Well, it's natural, I guess. But heaping guilt onto yourself isn't going to bring anyone back." Daly straightened in the chair. "Anyway, I couldn't sleep, either. So I worked instead. I spent so much time here, Hamlin ordered a wardrobe into my office for me and told me I might as well bring in a change of clothes. It's still there—the cedar wardrobe in my office." Daly nodded and pointed toward her office. Nick could see the large, misplaced piece of furniture through the glass partition that separated the senior editor's office from the rest of the newsroom. "You don't think of Hamlin like that, do you? This was seven years ago now, back when Jason first bought the paper. Back then he was the first man in every morning. When he bought the paper, we were losing ten thousand dollars a day. He came down here and ran the place himself, turned the paper around." Daly stopped speaking when she realized that Nick wasn't following the story, and Nick became aware of the woman's careful scrutiny.

"You really don't need to worry about me," Nick repeated.

The senior editor continued to examine him. "It's only been a few days," she said. "I'm just making sure."

A thought occurred to Nick. "Listen, Laura," he said, determined to change the subject, "what can you tell me about Adam Stolie?"

"Stolie?" Daly narrowed her eyes. Nick could see from her expression that she, too, was grateful for the change of focus. "The detective?"

Nick waited.

Daly pursed her lips. "I haven't had much to do with him. He worked the Henderson case, I think. He was the one who made the arrest. Three, four years ago—a bit before your time—when they arrested the wrong man. He's on homicide. One of Lieutenant Dombrowski's boys." Daly seemed lost in the train of her thoughts, then put two and two together. "He's the one they got assigned to your brother's case?"

"Yeah." Nick hesitated, uncertain how much to share. "You know, I've butted heads with this guy before at crime scenes. As far as I've been able to tell, he doesn't like me. Now he's the only one standing between me and a jail cell. I'm not sure what's motivating him."

Daly considered the point. "Maybe it's the Henderson thing," she said. "Maybe he doesn't want to make another mistake like that." She searched her memory. "If I remember correctly, Stolie experienced a family tragedy, too—about the same time as the Henderson arrest was going bad on him. I'm not sure I've got this right, but I think his brother died about that time.

Leukemia maybe. Something prolonged. I can look it up."

Nick remembered how much genuine concern the detective had shown him. "That would make sense." He squinted, shaking his head. "You don't have to look it up."

"Lieutenant Dombrowski, on the other hand, that's a man to watch out for. I've crossed swords with him a number of times." Daly scowled. "He's a political beast, that man—and heading straight for the top. He'll be our police chief when Gutterson steps down, mark my words. If he's the one who's got you in his sights, I'd—" Daly stopped herself. "You sure you're up to this?"

Nick forced a thin smile. "I'm fine," he said. "Really. It's good to know what I'm up against. If this is actually going to happen, I'm not going to be able to avoid it anyway."

"You might as well be prepared," Daly agreed.

Nick looked away. One of the men on the other side of the newsroom was laughing, and Nick followed the sound to its source. The man leaned forward and looped an arm over another man's shoulders. *You're killing me, Tom,* Nick heard him say. *You're absolutely killing me.*

"Listen," Daly said, shifting forward in the chair, "something occurred to me when I was thinking about the crime. Something that might be of interest to you. A story came across my desk about a month or two ago, out of Milwaukee. You hail from Wisconsin, don't you?"

"From Madison," Nick confirmed.

"I doubt you'll remember the story, because it didn't get much play. A suburban couple, well-to-do, were murdered a couple of months ago—pretty brutally, in their sleep. Their teenage kids were at home at the time.

Apparently they didn't hear a thing. The police thought it was odd the boys could sleep through the noise, and they were considered suspects for a couple of days—that's what made the story interesting. Long story short, the murder turns out to have been committed by a homeless man with no connection to the family at all. He just wanders in off the street one night and kills these people in their bed. Stabs them each twenty or thirty times."

Nick felt himself shiver. An image from his nightmare flooded his mind. His father's eyes were hollow sockets. Opening his mouth to speak, blood spilled down his chin. Sam appeared in the study with them, and Nick cried out to him: *He's dead, Sam. Dad's dead.* Sam's face twisted into a smile, and Nick realized that his brother was holding a bloody knife in his hand.

Nick fought off the vision, focusing on Daly instead. "How did they end up catching him?" he heard himself ask the editor.

"The police found the homeless man dressed in a pair of the victim's trousers, selling some of the wife's jewelry."

"In Milwaukee, you said."

Daly nodded, then pushed herself up from the chair, once again wincing as she straightened her knees. "I'll send you a link from my office. I thought maybe it was something you'd want to check out. Another homeless killer." She stretched and looked around the newsroom. "Yeah, it helps to keep yourself busy. Especially if there's no baseball to watch." She rapped her knuckles a few times absently on Nick's desk, then wandered off toward her office.

* * *

When the rain cleared later that morning, Nick ducked out of the newsroom to visit the mortuary. The director had called to let Nick know as a matter of procedure that the cremation would be carried out in the afternoon. There was nothing for Nick to see. Sam's remains weren't resting in a casket. No funeral would be held. Sam wasn't religious, and the body itself was too mutilated to view. Nevertheless, Nick understood that this would be his last chance to say good-bye to his brother.

Nick sat in the small chamber where the mortuary held its memorial services. Sam's body was lying somewhere else inside the building, Nick didn't know where. In a refrigerated drawer in the basement, perhaps. Nick was holding a large yellow envelope in his hands—Sam's personal effects, which the director had turned over to him a few minutes before. Nick hadn't been expecting the rush of emotions.

An image of his brother's face hovered in front of his eyes. Not a memory of Sam himself, but of a photograph taken when they were kids. In the snapshot, Sam was standing next to him in front of their house in Madison, holding his lunch box, on their way to Nick's first day of school. Nick was remembering how brave Sam had always looked to him in that picture. Nick had been smiling, too, but he understood that his ease belonged to his brother. Sam had always made everything so effortless for him. He had blazed the trail, Nick only had to follow.

Something kept tugging at Nick. An impulse that wouldn't go away. *He wanted to see Sam.* Until he saw him again, he couldn't accept that Sam was dead. This thought brought him back to Laura Daly and to the loss of her son. Harold Daly had simply disappeared. Laura never had the chance to close the door. The days she had spent expecting her son to reappear in her life had melted into a tragedy too slippery to grasp. Nick glanced at the raised platform at the front of the room, where an empty coffin was staged, surrounded by a profusion of flowers. *What would Sam have done? Would he have demanded to see Nick's body?* Nick knew that Sam wouldn't have accepted *no* for an answer.

At last, Nick split the yellow envelope open, then tilted it upside down to empty its contents. There was only one thing inside. The police had confiscated the rest of Sam's personal effects—his cell phone and whatever else he had in his pockets. The heavy steel wristwatch their parents had given to Sam as a graduation gift slid into his hands.

Nick sat staring at it. It had never occurred to him before how out of character it was for Sam to wear it. Everything else Sam wore reflected his success. This clumsy watch provided the only hint that Sam, too, missed their parents. That their childhood back in Wisconsin meant something to him.

Nick dropped the heavy timepiece into the envelope, then stood up and found his way back outside.

chapter 21

Back at the *Telegraph*, Nick was staring at the screen of his computer. His eyes appeared to be focused, but he wasn't seeing anything on the plasma display. Instead, he was lost inside a vivid recollection from a decade before, sparked by images from the nightmare that had woken him early that morning.

Sam was standing beside their father's desk in their parents' study, alone in the room, looking at Nick over his shoulder, startled. Next to him, the drawer to a black metal filing cabinet was pulled open. The second that Nick had pushed open the door and wandered into the room, he understood that his brother was doing something wrong. The cabinet was kept locked, and as far as Nick knew his father held the only key. Nick saw that Sam had taken a file from the drawer and had spread it out on their father's desk.

"They've got twenty-three thousand dollars in their checking account," Sam said with a strange smile.

Despite his unease, Nick was surprised by the information. "Is that all?" he asked.

"That's just their checking account," Sam said. "I haven't been able to figure out their savings yet. But they've got at least twice that. Some of it's in stocks, and it's in a couple different banks."

"What are you looking at?"

"Come here. Take a look." Sam waited for his younger brother to approach the desk. "These are their statements. See? Here's the check they wrote for me last week to the admissions office at the University of Washington. Seventy-five dollars. And here's one they wrote to your school. For soccer fees, I guess."

"Why are you doing this?"

"Why?"

"Yeah, why?"

"Aren't you curious?"

Nick realized that he wasn't. "I don't care."

"It's only right that we know," Sam said. "It's important. Maybe not for you yet. But me, I'm going to college next year. Maybe I'll want a car. Who knows? I want to know what they've got."

Nick shrugged. "Nothing's going to change if you know," he said. "Not for me, and not for you, either."

Sam frowned at his little brother. "That's what you think."

"Aren't you afraid Dad's going to find out?"

Sam was examining the papers on the desk again. "No," he said, dismissing Nick's concern. "They won't be home for another hour. I know where everything goes."

When the phone on their father's desk rang, both boys jumped. It was a mechanical ring. The loud, jarring sound of a small steel bell being struck by a tiny hammer. "Jesus," Sam said, recovering himself.

"See?" Nick exclaimed, as though the phone's ring had snuck up on them and proved his point. "You're going to get caught." He reached for the phone.

"Don't answer it!"

"What?" Nick put his hand down onto the beaten-up, heavy receiver anyway.

"Don't pick it up, Nick!"

"Why not?"

"Wait a second. Let it ring a few times first. What if it's Dad? You don't want him to know you're in the study."

Nick waited through the course of another rattling ring, then picked up the phone. The man from the power plant didn't want to speak to him, though. Michael Simmons was their father's boss and, after fifteen years at the plant, a family friend. "Put Sam on the phone," he said to Nick, and Nick understood that something had happened.

Sam's face went blank when Nick handed him the phone, and his expression didn't change during the short conversation. He hardly spoke. He listened to whatever Simmons had called to report, then told the man that he would talk to his brother about it. Then he handed the receiver back to Nick.

After Nick hung up the phone, the two brothers looked at one another. Sam didn't have to speak the words. Nick understood that his parents were dead.

"Dad was driving," Sam said. "You know how much ice there is on the road."

Nick felt his legs begin to shake. He collapsed into the chair in front of his father's desk. The room was going black all around him.

Their father had lost control of the car and driven head-on into a speeding truck. He had died on impact.

Their mother had survived until the ambulance arrived fifteen minutes later, slowly bleeding to death, trapped inside the twisted metal wreckage of the totaled car. Her weakening cries were audible to the small group of people who gathered around the crash, gawking at the scattered mess the truck had left in its wake.

"I want Mom," Nick said. "I want Dad. Let's go. Let's get them."

"They're dead, Nick," Sam said. "It's too late. They're already gone."

"Yo, Nick. Nicholas Wilder."

Lost in his reverie, Nick didn't hear the voice at all. A man appeared at his desk, waving a sheet of paper in his field of vision. Nick took his eyes from the computer screen.

The man's name was Johnnie. One of the newspaper's best researchers, he was three or four years older than Nick, prematurely gray. He tossed the sheet of copy on Nick's desk. The headline screamed out at him: *Homeless Man Robs Store, Two Dead.* "This came in from New York a few hours ago. I was just setting it. Laura thought you might want to see it."

Nick regarded the news story. "Sure, thanks."

"You look like you could use some sleep, buddy."

Nick glanced up at him, then shrugged. "Couldn't everybody around this place?" He twisted the sheet of paper around and began to read.

Fifteen minutes later, he walked into Daly's office, a manila folder tucked under one of his arms. Daly didn't lift her eyes from the proof she was redlining by hand. "A pretty interesting series of coincidences," the editor said, carefully X-ing out a few sentences from the body of the story. "Wouldn't you say? A string of unprovoked, brutal murders in three different cities. Seattle. Milwaukee. New York. All of them stabbings, all of them committed by homeless men." She raised her pen from the galley, at last looking up at Nick. "Sounds like a story, doesn't it?" Self-consciously, she took the half-glasses from her nose and pinched them closed, then tossed them into an open drawer.

"Will you pick up my costs, Laura? I'd like to see if I can get a couple of interviews."

Daly didn't seem surprised by the request. "You give me a story, Nick, and I'll pick up your flight and a rental car. If you're flying out there just to satisfy your own personal curiosity, though, you're on your own time."

"I understand."

Daly gave him an assessing look. "You've already booked your flights, haven't you?"

Nick didn't have to respond.

"So what are you waiting for?" The senior editor looked back down at the proof, finding her grip again on the red pencil she had been using to scribble her corrections.

Nick remained standing where he was. "I know I've been messing up pretty badly," he said.

The gray-haired woman glanced back up.

"I wanted you to know, though. I took your advice. At the gala, I took some pictures."

Daly set her pencil all the way down, a small smile turning up the edges of her mouth. "Is that right? You get anything good?"

Nick shook his head. "Not exactly what you had in mind."

"No?" Daly pursed her lips, waiting for Nick to explain.

"I didn't get the spread you imagined for the Sunday magazine. I did get these, though." Nick set the manila folder down on the senior editor's desk.

The first photograph was a digitally enhanced picture of Hamlin talking to the stout, mustached man as Nick had first seen them. The resolution was so good that Daly could see the beads of sweat on the heavier man's forehead. Daly examined the picture, then slid the photograph over to one side in order to look at the one underneath: a picture of the two men seated in the middle of the empty auditorium, the heavy man's face glowing red with the reflection of the velvet, his distress etched across his brow.

"Who is he?"

"You don't recognize him?"

Daly shook her head. "He looks familiar. But no, I don't."

"I asked around here this morning. Something about the way Hamlin was talking to him bothered me."

"The way he was pressing him," Daly suggested.

Nick shrugged. "I guess. He was really going at him."

"So who is he?" Daly asked again.

"Ralph Van Gundy."

"That's Ralph Van Gundy?" Daly leaned back in her chair, surprised. "The head of the Washington state EPA?"

Nick nodded. "I guess there's nothing wrong with Hamlin inviting a commissioner from the Environmental Protection Agency to the gala—"

Daly harrumphed. "He's not just a commissioner. He's the man responsible for awarding the Elliott Bay contract to Hamlin's waste-management company last month. That contract netted Hamlin twenty-five million dollars, what, just two, three days ago?"

"All the more reason Hamlin might want to invite him to the celebration. There's nothing wrong in saying thank you."

Daly gave Nick a measuring look. "You know there's something wrong here yourself. That's why you took these, huh? You knew there was something wrong even before you knew who this man was."

Again, Nick shrugged. "Well, the pictures are yours anyway."

Daly slid them back into the manila folder, then held it up toward Nick. "No," she said.

"You don't think it's worth checking out?"

"I didn't say that. You know there's nothing I'd like more than to get my hands around Jason Hamlin's neck." The words had come out more bitterly than the editor intended.

Nick took the folder from Daly. "Why don't you keep these, then?"

Daly shook her head. "I can't."

"Because he owns the paper."

"It's more complicated than that." Daly leaned her elbows onto her desk, then rested her face in her hands, grinding her palms into her eyes. "Like I told you, Hamlin and I go back a number of years now."

"You're afraid of him."

"He knows where a number of bodies are buried," Daly said. "Let's put it that way. You do a man like Hamlin a few favors, you end up in his debt. You understand what I'm saying?"

Nick nodded. "Sure."

"It can wait until you get back. And like you say,

there's probably nothing there anyway. No smoking gun. But keep those pictures. Even if I can't, there's no reason why a freelance photographer who doesn't officially work for the paper can't take a run at him." Daly looked down at her watch. "What time did you say your flight was?"

"Yeah," Nick said. "I know. I better get going."

chapter 22

Henry Dean had entered a boutique on Fifth Avenue in Manhattan, armed with a broken bottle. Without warning he had attacked the first person who crossed his path. Witnesses reported that he literally cut the woman to death. He attacked her so violently that his arm had become a blur. When he was finished with her, he left her on the floor in shreds, blood pumping from her throat, her intestines oozing from a gash in her torso. After that, he turned on the store's clerk and swung the broken bottle at him so savagely that he nearly severed the man's head from his neck. Three other people in the store had no escape. The attack happened so fast, they fell to their knees and cowered against the wall, expecting to be killed, too. The carnage stopped, though, as abruptly as it began. Dean dropped the broken bottle and walked to the counter and grabbed a pair of Ray-Bans. He ignored the cash in the register and left the store with the sunglasses. Fifteen minutes later, the police subdued him only a block away, standing on a corner panhandling, covered from head to toe in the drying filth of his victims' blood.

Nick had expected a monster. Instead, he found a small, wiry man with a thin face and well-groomed short brown hair. His street clothes were visible beneath the oversize orange coverall issued by the jail. His wrists and ankles had been shackled to a steel chair, and he didn't move when Nick entered the holding cell at Rikers Island, New York. He didn't even raise his eyes. Nick had the impression that the man was catatonic. "Henry. Henry Dean," Nick said. The man didn't respond, and after a few minutes, the officer who had ushered Nick in terminated the interview.

"Has he been seen by a doctor?" Nick asked the officer on his way back out through the jail.

The officer shrugged his shoulders. "I don't know anything about that, sir."

"Has he been like this for long?"

The officer didn't acknowledge Nick's question.

A few hours later, Nick was on Highway 18 in Wisconsin, skirting the edge of Madison, keeping the white Ford Taurus he had rented at the airport in Milwaukee at a steady seventy-five, heading for the prison at Boscobel.

It was a bright autumn morning, and the trees along the highway were laced with gold. This was the first time Nick had been back to Wisconsin since he had followed Sam to Seattle over a decade before, after his parents had died. Nick's thoughts, though, were elsewhere. As he made the turn from Highway 12 onto Highway 18 through Madison, something in the back of his mind was troubling him. Something particular about Henry Dean in his cell in New York. Something Nick had seen but couldn't quite define.

Nick pulled the Taurus to a stop in front of the huge concrete prison at Boscobel just before noon. He glanced down at the green digits of the clock before switching off the engine. He had made good time. He sat for a moment in the driver's seat, staring up at the looming maximum-security facility. The atmosphere was deceptively peaceful, almost sterile. At last, Nick opened the door onto the newly paved parking lot and stepped from the rental car. A cool breeze touched his face, carrying with it the indistinct sound of a voice issuing commands over the static of an industrial intercom from somewhere behind the prison walls. Nick gathered his jacket around his shoulders and headed for the entrance.

The prison guard who led Nick from the carpeted front offices to the interview rooms was solicitously helpful. "I haven't had much contact with him myself," he was saying to Nick. "But from what I hear, he's been no problem at all inside. Keeps to himself. Doesn't make no noise. Stays outta trouble."

"Tell me about the trial," Nick said.

"What trial?"

"You must have heard about it on the news."

"There weren't no trial. Warren pled guilty."

"I see." Nick tried to remember what he had read. "I thought the two Gilbert boys were arrested for the murder."

"That's almost right," the guard confirmed, continuing down the wide corridor. “The police thought they killed their parents in their sleep. Like them boys out in California who killed their parents for the inheritance.”

“The Menendez brothers.”

“That’s it, the Menendez brothers. The police didn’t arrest them, though. It didn’t go nearly that far. They found Warren after a day or two, on the street. Wearing some of their clothes.”

“He confessed?”

The guard shook his head. “He didn’t have to. They found his blood in the Gilberts’ house.” They had reached the interview room, a stark, white-walled room furnished with a single table and two metal chairs. “Warren’ll be cabled and locked to this here chair.” The guard pointed at one of the painted gray chairs, and Nick noticed that it was bolted to the floor and a heavy link had been welded onto its sides to accommodate the prisoners’ cables. “Sometimes when they’re with their lawyers, we let their hands free, you know? So they can use a pen or whatever. With the press, it’s different. We leave you alone in the room with them so you can talk, but we keep them cabled.”

A few minutes later, James Warren was led hobbled into the austere room by another guard. His hair had been cropped short, but Nick recognized him from the articles he had read online. He moved as though his limbs were heavy as lead, like he had to control each movement independently. The guard shackled him into the chair opposite Nick.

“I’ll be just outside the door if you need me,” the guard said, straightening back up. “You won’t be able to see me, and I won’t be able to hear you. But I’ll be watching everything that goes on in here.”

When the guard closed the door behind him, its

glass panel became a bright mirror, and, catching sight of himself, Nick was surprised by how disheveled he appeared. He had boarded the plane to New York without a change of clothes, and he was dressed in the same jeans he had been wearing for a couple of days now, the same wrinkled shirt. James Warren and he could easily have exchanged chairs.

"Thank you for agreeing to give me this interview," he began. "My name is Nick Wilder. I'm with the *Seattle Telegraph*."

Warren raised his eyes. Nick understood from his expression that the man was perplexed by the distance he had traveled for the story.

"There've been a few crimes committed recently," he explained, "in New York and Seattle, that are pretty similar. Like the one you're in here for. I'm just following up leads."

"I don't remember doing it," the prisoner said. His voice was sluggish, so deep it sounded like it was being played back too slowly on an old vinyl record.

"You don't remember committing the murder?"

"I can see the bodies," Warren said. "But it's like I'm looking at a photograph. I don't know. Maybe it was a photograph."

"Do you think you're innocent?"

Warren shook his head. He didn't know how to answer.

"Why didn't you ask for a trial? Why would you enter a plea if you don't know that you're guilty?"

"They don't try people like me."

"It's your right."

"Do you really believe that?"

Nick looked at the man, struck by his apparent intelligence. "Did you know the Gilberts? Before, I mean."

"I never saw them once."

"What were you doing in their neighborhood? Mequon is a pretty wealthy suburb."

"I don't know. I don't remember how I got there."

"Does this happen to you often? Do you black out like this sometimes?" Nick realized that he was holding his breath. After the blackouts he had himself experienced recently, he wanted to hear Warren's answer.

Warren didn't respond. His face had gone unnaturally still. He closed and then opened his eyes. *A slow-motion blink,* Nick thought.

"Are you mentally ill, James?" Nick asked him.

"You always call me Jimmy," the prisoner said.

"What?" It felt to Nick as if he had been slapped in the face. "What did you say?"

"You know all this already."

"Do I know you somehow?"

Warren tipped his head back. "Come here, Doc."

Nick didn't move.

"Come closer, Doc," the prisoner said again, lowering his voice nearly to a whisper. "I don't want them to hear."

Nick waited, then rose from his chair and leaned closer to the prisoner. Warren pulled away, drawing him backward like a magnet. "How'd you get those cuts and bruises on your face, Doc?"

"What?"

"Come closer so you can hear."

Nick moved close enough to smell the man's sour breath.

"You're the one who told me to do it." Warren spoke the words like he was imparting a secret.

"What?"

"Aren't you, Doc?"

"I don't know what you're—"

"Come closer. Let me tell you something."

There was a loud rap on the door's glass panel: the guard warning Nick to keep his distance from the cabled prisoner. Nick looked toward the mirrored door just in time to catch sight of Warren's head rushing toward him. He shrank from the man's teeth, his gaping mouth, but Warren's head still grazed his own, hammering him in the forehead where he was already bruised. The room was filled with Warren's unrestrained laughter.

The door swung open and the guard rushed in. "That'll be enough, Warren," the guard said, shoving him backward in the chair. "You okay?" he asked Nick.

Nick took a deep, measured breath, shaken. "Yeah," he said. "Fine."

"I gotcha, Doc," Warren said.

"That'll be enough, Warren," the guard repeated. "The interview's over."

"Sorry, Doc. You heard the man. The interview's over."

"I'm going to take Warren out of here," the guard said to Nick. "I'll be back for you in a few minutes."

"Listen, Doc," Warren said as the guard unshackled his cables from the chair's arms and legs. "How is it back in Seattle? It starting to rain yet?"

A flash of recognition went off in Nick's head, blinding him—an image of Henry Dean, sitting like a statue, cabled to the chair inside the holding cell at Riker's Island. The collar of a dark blue T-shirt had been visible at the top of his orange jail-issue coverall. Nick hadn't paid attention to it at the time. It struck him now what had been bothering him since seeing Henry Dean. *The T-shirt.*

"That rain gets to you, doesn't it, Doc?" Warren's face rearranged itself into a broad smile. "After a while, it really starts to get inside your head."

Nick recognized the T-shirt. He had only been able to make out part of some green and white lettering on the shirt, but he knew the typeface. Henry Dean, arrested for murder in New York, had been wearing a Seattle Mariners T-shirt.

"It gets to where a man can't see, it rains so much. It gets to where a man has stars in his eyes all the time."

You got stars in your eyes, Jerome?

Nick felt his blood turn to ice. "Wait," he said.

The guard had unfastened the locks from Warren's chair. He was helping the prisoner to his feet, beginning to lead him from the room.

"Just one more question."

The guard stopped, holding Warren still next to him. The prisoner sagged on his feet.

"You're from Seattle. Aren't you?"

Warren didn't respond. Another smile spread across his face. He tugged on his cables and lifted his feet, step by lethargic step, leading the guard out of the room.

chapter 23

Nick was sitting in the shade of the birch trees in front of the house where he and Sam had grown up just outside Madison, on the short set of stairs where he had waited past midnight for Elizabeth to come home from the dance. He hadn't thought about exiting the highway at the interchange. His flight to Seattle was leaving from Milwaukee in another few hours, and he should have been on his way to the airport. He had pulled the Taurus off the freeway without thinking, wending his way down rural streets crowded with memories, following the familiar path back to his childhood home. Passing in front of Lake Issewa, he had slowed the car nearly to a stop, peering through the trees down the hill to the still pool of water. A vision of the lake frozen in winter flashed in front of his eyes. He could hear Sam shouting at him and laughing, the scrape of their skates on the ice.

Behind him, his family's old, three-story brick house was empty at midday. Nick had knocked on the Munroes' door, too, but no one had been home there, either. The fall landscape was vivid with color. A light northern breeze was blowing, rustling the leaves of the birch trees high above his head. Nick, though, was unaware of the breeze and the sounds. Caught up all at once in the currents of a memory, staring down the gently sloping green lawn toward the street, he was blind to the tableau in front of him.

You boys don't have to be skerred.

"Go!" Sam shouted to Nick. His voice sounded weak across the flat plane of the snowy, frozen lake. Nick was too afraid to move. "Go!" Sam shouted again. "Run!" Nick remained transfixed, looking back at Sam. He opened his mouth to speak, but his voice had deserted him. He leaned down, resting his hands on his knees and panting, trying to keep from vomiting. He couldn't figure out what his brother was doing. Why had Sam stayed behind? Sam glanced over his shoulder at him. "Run, Nick," he shouted. "Run!"

"Come with me!"

Nick watched as the man caught up to Sam. Nick's face was squeezed into a small red ball, and he couldn't think. His cheeks were wet with hot tears, and he realized he was crying. "Come on, Sam," he said under his breath. "Come on. What are you doing? Come on!"

Then the ice broke. It happened so quickly Nick couldn't figure out what he was seeing. The man had just reached Sam. He was grabbing him, about to wrestle him to the ground. The two of them went down into the water together. Nick remained where he was, motionless, unable to move.

Sam shouted for help as he plunged into the freezing water, before his head was submerged, and the sound of Sam's voice woke Nick. He skated as fast as he could back in the direction he had come, toward his brother. Closing the twenty yards between them in a matter of seconds, he didn't come to a stop until he was nearly in the water himself.

The ice began to crack underneath him, groaning beneath his weight, but Nick ignored the danger. He dropped to his knees, lay down on his stomach. Cold water seeped up onto the lip of the ice, soaking through his clothes, scalding him with its frozen heat. The hole was about five feet in diameter, and its surface had grown still. The lake was murky, opaque. "Sam!" Nick shouted. There was no sign of his brother or the man. He pulled himself forward, all the way to the very edge of the hole. "Sam!" He looked down into the water, but he couldn't see anything at all.

Moments later, when the man broke back through the surface, the sudden torrent of movement and sounds made Nick yelp. It took him a few seconds to realize that the man was more scared and disoriented than he was. The man was gasping for air. His face had turned blue and his lips had turned purple and his eyes were wide with terror. Ignoring him, Nick pulled himself back to the edge of the hole, realizing with growing horror that his brother had gotten trapped under the ice.

Becoming aware of a thumping noise and a slight vibration underneath him, Nick twisted around, then was able to make out the shape of a hand where the ice was nearly translucent, about two feet back from the hole.

Nick didn't consider his next move, he merely reacted. He crawled forward, thrust a hand into the water and, reaching back, caught hold of the sleeve of Sam's jacket. The ice bent dangerously beneath him, but he strained with all his might anyway, dragging his brother's limp body through the freezing water.

At first, there was no reaction from Sam. His body could have been a bundle of rags. All at once, though, Sam clasped Nick's arm, sending a wave of shock coursing through Nick like a bolt of electricity. This burst of adrenaline was quickly followed by another when Sam also began to pull. The wet surface of the ice was slippery, and, suddenly terrified—fighting frantically to find some traction—Nick felt himself being drawn into the water. He gritted his teeth and planted his free hand into the ice and spread his legs out behind him. Finally, he was able to hold his position.

Despite the lethal cold, Sam did the rest. Taking hold of Nick's hands and then hoisting himself on his brother's arms, he climbed up out of the water.

Nick had never seen his brother cry before. He had never seen Sam show a single sign of any weakness. He was crying now. He crumpled onto the ice next to Nick, coughing and shaking, sobbing, a huge, slick trail of snot seeping out of his nose and bubbling over his mouth. Nick, too, lay back on the ice, exhausted by the near disaster.

The man was still thrashing in the water in front of them, trying to pull himself up the way that Sam had. Without the benefit of anything to hold on to, though, he was being held back by the weight of his heavy coat and sweater and boots. In the freezing water, his muscles were stiffening, locking as he went into shock.

Sam was first to recover himself. "Come on, Nick," he said. "Let's go." Wiping his face clean, he clambered to his knees, then, shaking, stood up onto his skates. "Let's get out of here."

Time had slowed down for Nick. From his prone position, he watched his brother getting up, then pushed himself onto his knees and stood up as well. Next to him, Sam was moving in a panic. Nick recognized that he should have shared his brother's alarm. The day had taken on an unreal quality, however. Like he was standing back somewhere safe, watching all this from a distance.

"Now, Nick," Sam said, tugging Nick's sleeve. "We've got to run." When Sam skated off, however, rather than follow him, Nick turned back toward the man. *They couldn't simply leave him there, could they?* He picked up his hockey stick where he had dropped it, then, once again ignoring the ice threatening to break underneath him, reached toward the man with the taped blade of the stick as if he was trying to fish a piece of trash out of the icy water.

"Hey, mister," Nick said. "Hey!" The man struggled to face him, and their eyes met. Without articulating the thought, Nick understood that the man was too crazed to see him. The man's lips were so dark they were black. His eyes were so red that Nick thought maybe they were bleeding. Nick had the impression that the man's skin had shrunk. That it had been stretched taut over the skeletal frame of his face. The man's jaw was quivering with a mechanical intensity, like a machine plugged into a socket, syrupy spittle drooling out of his mouth.

Maybe it was because the man had wanted to rape them. He was getting what he deserved. Or maybe it was simply that, at ten years old, Nick couldn't envision what might happen next. But Nick made no effort to rescue the man. He didn't try to hook him with the blade. Despite the man's distress, Nick simply stretched the stick out toward the man as though he had all the time in the world, waiting for him to react. He didn't reflect that the man was practically comatose from the subzero cold.

When the man did reach for Nick's hockey stick, he moved spasmodically. His body twisted ineffectually in the water, and he overshot the blade. The agitation destroyed his equilibrium with the water, and he sank. Nick leaned forward on his skates to watch him disappear, stunned by the abrupt silence, tracking the man's movement beneath the turbulent green-black surface. When the man broke back through, gasping, screeching for air, the explosion made Nick jump. He wasn't ready for it when the man grabbed hold of the stick. Suffocating, unable to control his muscles anymore, the man yanked so hard that Nick lost his balance.

Beneath his skates, Nick felt the ice bend. For a split second, he thought he would be pulled into the lake. He heard the ice crack and groan and start to give. Unthinkingly, saving himself, he let go of the hockey stick. He jerked backward as the stick landed with a splash in the icy water.

The man fought to remain afloat. Regaining his balance, Nick watched helplessly as he slowly lost his buoyancy. When the man once again dipped beneath the surface of the water, this time Nick lost sight of him completely. As before, the abrupt silence stunned him, bookending the intervening rush of sounds. The water became eerily still. Nick squinted, listening to the raspy hiss of his own breathing, leaning forward over the broken edge of the ice, trying to peer into the murky lake. He must have stared at its glassy surface for ten full seconds before he realized that the man wasn't moving anymore. At last, comprehending, he dropped to his knees.

Nick wasn't aware that Sam was standing next to him.

He twisted in surprise at the sound of Sam's voice. "Stop it, Nick," Sam was ordering his younger brother. His voice was raised nearly into a shout. "Stop it! You'll fall in." Nick hadn't realized that he had been straining to reach into the icy lake. Not until he became aware of Sam's fingers digging into his shoulders, restraining him.

"Please, Sam," he said. "We've got to get him out of there."

Sam dragged his smaller brother roughly back from the edge of the hole, forcing him down onto the ice a few feet back. Then he took his own hockey stick and used it to lift Nick's from the water. After that, stepping as close to the edge as he dared, he reached his stick into the water and searched for the man with the end of its blade.

"What are you doing?" Nick asked his brother. *He wasn't trying to fish him out.*

Sam continued to prod the hole with his hockey stick. He didn't bother trying to explain. Nick was too young to understand that the longer the man went undiscovered, the less likely anyone would be able to piece together the series of events that had led to his untimely death. Too young to understand that they couldn't leave behind any evidence that they had been there. "He's dead," Sam said matter of factly. He didn't try to say more.

Once he found the corpse, Sam balanced himself on his skates and took the blade of his hockey stick and gave the dead man a firm shove backward, wedging him under the thick, frozen shelf. Nick turned away from the blurry image of the man beneath the frosty layer of ice. He lay backward. He was still breathing hard, but his tears had gone dry. He looked up at the sky. The clouds had thickened again, and it was beginning to snow. The lake would freeze over tonight, the hole would close. It would be months, he knew, before the man was found.

Sitting on the stairs in front of his family's house in Madison, Nick shuddered. The recollection felt unreal. Like a dream.

As far as Nick knew, if the body was ever discovered, the police hadn't conducted an investigation. The boys had never seen or heard anything about the man. Over time, Nick had suppressed the memory.

Fifteen minutes passed, and then, rousing himself, Nick walked down the lawn to the Taurus. He was cutting it short if he wanted to catch his scheduled flight back to Seattle. Shaken by his flashback, he was pulling the rental car's heavy door open when he heard an engine approaching. He turned and waited for the car to pass, his eyes connecting with Elizabeth Munroe's as she slowed to a stop in front of her parents' house.

Elizabeth's daughter looked just like her mother. She had long, dirty blond hair and light blue eyes, paper-white skin and freckles on her nose. She stood between her mother's legs, considering the strange man. She felt safe with the comforting weight of her mother's hands on her shoulders, her mother's fingers tangled in her wispy hair. She had yanked her mother's sweater hard enough to pull her off balance when she leaned forward to give Nick a quick kiss on the cheek.

"I'm sorry you can't stay longer," Elizabeth said.

Nick shrugged. "That's okay," he said. "I wasn't expecting to see you anyway."

"So what brought you back?"

Elizabeth's daughter was listening to every word. "I was passing through," he said innocuously. "I just wanted to see the neighborhood again."

Elizabeth smiled. "I can't believe how much older you are."

"Have I changed that much?"

She smiled, nodding her head. "Yeah. I'd like to tell you no. But yes, you have."

"You, too," he said. He looked down at her daughter. "How old is she?"

"How old are you, Emily?" Elizabeth gave her daughter's shoulders a soft squeeze. When Emily didn't answer, she tousled her hair a little. "She's four," she said to Nick.

"She's beautiful," Nick said.

"She's shy."

"That's how I remember you. Not like this."

Elizabeth's smile turned into an awkward laugh.

"I never would have imagined you with a daughter. So you're married now?"

"I'm Catholic. What do you think? Yes, I'm married."

"So it all turned out okay, then. In the end, I mean."

Elizabeth's eyes darkened. A gust of wind tossed a few strands of hair across her face. "How is Sam?" she asked.

Once again, Nick glanced at Emily. He didn't want to answer. When Elizabeth covered her daughter's ears with her hands, the girl struggled indignantly, craning her head to look up at her mother.

"Did something happen to him?"

Nick didn't respond.

"Did something happen to Sam?" Elizabeth asked again.

Nick shook his head, unable to find words to tell her

that his brother had been murdered. In the end, he didn't have to. Elizabeth was able to read it in his face.

"I can't say I'm sorry," Elizabeth said.

"What?" Nick was surprised by the callous remark.

"I guess I don't mean it," Elizabeth said. "But he deserved whatever he got."

Nick examined her, puzzled by the depth of her emotion.

"He beat you up. Don't you remember?"

"We were kids," Nick said. "That's what kids do."

"Not like that. He was so cruel to you. I could never understand why you didn't fight back. I always wished that you'd stand up to him."

Nick understood that she meant for her sake as well. "I couldn't," he said.

"I was your girlfriend. How could you let him take me from you?"

"I didn't want to. I didn't know what to do."

"You were like a powder keg, Nick. I never understood what kept you from exploding."

Nick dropped his eyes, rocked by the image of Sam's fingers wrapped around the rectangular, taped handle of his hockey stick as he went up onto his toes and wedged the man's corpse as far as he could beneath the ice. Emily was twisting back and forth in front of him, freeing herself dramatically from her mother's protective embrace. "Do you ever wonder," he asked, pulling himself back into the moment, "how things would have turned out differently? If you hadn't gone to that dance that night, I mean. If you and I had—well—" He didn't finish the sentence.

"No." Elizabeth shook her head.

"I wanna go see Grandma," Emily said.

Elizabeth acknowledged her daughter by combing

her fingers through the tangles of her hair. "I don't like to look backward anymore. Like you said, I'm just glad everything turned out okay in the end."

Nick smiled. He squatted down in front of Emily, eyeing her thoughtfully, then reached forward and tugged a few strands of her hair. "She really is beautiful," he said to Elizabeth. "I look at her, and I can only see you."

PART 5

chapter 24

"Where the hell have you been, Nick?"

Nick had switched his phone back on and called Stolie the moment the plane touched the ground. He had only been gone from Seattle for a day and a half, but he anticipated the detective's outburst. "I'm back in Seattle now," he said. "I'm sorry if I put you in a bind, but I wasn't running away."

"You didn't come back home to your apartment last night. I was worried about you."

"You don't have to worry. I can come to the station now, if you want."

The pilot's voice blared over the loudspeaker, announcing that the plane's gate was temporarily occupied.

"You're on a plane," the detective observed.

"I'm arriving at SeaTac."

"Where did you go?"

"It's a long story. I want to tell you, but later."

"Listen, Nick. I have some good news for you."

Nick knew what this must mean. "You caught him?" He held his breath.

"His name is Jackson Ferry."

Nick closed his eyes in relief. He had been expecting the police to take him into custody.

"We need you to come down here now," the detective was saying. "We've been looking for you since yesterday. I could arrange an escort for you, but it will probably be just as quick if you catch a cab. We need you to make an ID."

Nick was standing next to Stolie in front of an inch-thick piece of one-way glass. The police had gathered five other men from the street for the lineup. All of them were dressed in grimy, street-worn clothes. None was wearing shoes. Several of them had long, greasy hair. Nick, though, was only considering one of them. From the moment he had stepped up to the glass, his attention had been drawn to Jackson Ferry's ravaged face. His eyes were fastened on Ferry's. The detective had told him that the glass was mirrored on the other side, but Nick couldn't shake the feeling that the man was staring back at him, too.

An image from the night of Sam's murder filled Nick's head. Ferry was charging at the two brothers out of the blackness of the shadows. The rustling of Ferry's clothes echoed in Nick's ears. Closing his eyes, for a split second Nick was able to recapture a photographic image of Ferry's pocked and sallow face, his watery light blue eyes open wide with terror, as though he were being hunted.

"That's him," he said.

"Which one?"

"The third man from the left. The man with the blue eyes and long hair, wearing the black coat."

"You're sure?"

"Yes."

"That's Ferry," Stolie confirmed.

Nick continued to look at him. He was large, significantly taller and more muscular-looking than the other men the police had lined up. The skin on his face was reddish and leathery, deeply creased, his hair thick and scraggly and greasy. His lips were dark red, one corner of his mouth festered with sores. His hands were scabbed and filthy, badly scraped, powerful. *This was the Street Butcher, just inches away behind a plate of glass, the dangerous beast who had killed Sam.*

Stolie leaned forward and pressed a button on an intercom. "You can take the men back out," he said, his voice rumbling over a loudspeaker on the other side of the glass. Nick watched the two officers inside the room usher the men through a doorway. Ferry lowered his eyes, and Nick followed his gaze down to the dark brown, cross-hatched butt of one of the officer's guns as Ferry shuffled forward. When Ferry was just behind him, the cop seemed to feel his eyes on his weapon. He turned and, resting his hand on his holster, directed Ferry through the doorway.

Nick hadn't heard the other man approach, and he jumped at the touch of a couple of fingers on his shoulder. He turned to face the short and wiry gray-haired lieutenant he had met a few days before. Lieutenant Dombrowski nodded at him, his lips tightly compressed.

"Detective Stolie's filled you in already, Mr. Wilder?"

Nick took note of the lieutenant's nearly imperceptible Eastern European accent. "No," Nick responded, shaking his head. "I just got here."

"I brought him here to the window as soon as he arrived," the detective explained to his commanding officer. "We haven't had the chance to speak yet."

"You're a fortunate man, Mr. Wilder," the lieutenant said.

"I'm not so sure I would consider myself fortunate right now," Nick replied.

"No? Maybe not." He allowed himself a thin, slightly apologetic smile before explaining the remark. "Detective Stolie managed to track your man down. He had been sleeping the last few weeks at the Hudson Hotel, downtown. Detective Stolie tells me you know the place?"

Nick nodded.

"He was moving on apparently, going south for the winter, on his way to Frisco. Detective Stolie found a friend of his at the shelter, though—told him to look for Ferry down at the rail yard. We nabbed him at midnight, about to hop onto a train. Another five minutes, and he'd have been gone. You don't consider that fortunate?"

"My brother's still dead," Nick said.

Again, the lieutenant showed Nick his thin smile.

"We found him wearing your shoes," Stolie offered. "The black and orange Nikes. Just like you said."

"And a few things that belonged to your brother," Dombrowski added.

"His wallet," Stolie said. "His driver's license—a couple of credit cards."

"Ferry's clothes were covered in dried blood," the lieutenant continued. "We're having DNA tests run now. Initial testing confirms that it's your brother's. We'll probably find some of yours, too."

"The evidence supports everything you've told us," Stolie said.

"I wouldn't want you to leave Seattle again, though," Dombrowski said.

Nick looked warily at the lieutenant. "What about the other crimes? Dickenson. Claire and Daniel Scott. Have you questioned him? Has Ferry confessed?"

Stolie shook his head. "We've questioned him, but he hasn't told us much."

"He hasn't *said* much," Dombrowski corrected him. "About the only coherent response we've gotten from him is that he has absolutely no recollection of any of the murders. We've got the blood evidence, though. And Detective Stolie says you can place him near Pioneer Square the night of the kid's murder."

Nick remembered his conversation with Daniel Scott. "What about a ring?" he asked. "A gold ring with a diamond set into it—a man's ring."

Nick was aware of Stolie and Dombrowski exchanging a quick glance. "What about it?" the lieutenant asked.

"Did you find it on him?"

"In one of his pockets," Stolie confirmed. "Did it belong to your brother?"

Nick shook his head. "To Dickenson."

"I'll look into it," Stolie said. "Maybe someone who knew Dickenson can identify it."

Dombrowski was looking at Stolie through narrowed eyes. "You got anything else for us?" he asked, turning to face Nick.

Nick returned his stare, then looked away. "Is he legally sane?" he asked.

"He's sane enough to know what he did," Dombrowski responded. "Just like you or I would know it if we killed someone."

Stolie disagreed. He shot a glance at the lieutenant.

"He could barely speak his own name when we first found him," he retorted. "He seems a little more focused now. But he's mentally ill. There's no question. The memory loss is real. This guy is blacking out. He's not acting."

"So what will happen now?"

"We take the case to the DA," Dombrowski said, "and we nail him."

"Don't let the lieutenant upset you, Nick," Stolie said to him after Dombrowski had excused himself. They were walking together from the back of the precinct house, down a long, wide corridor that led past the holding cells to the street.

Nick considered his response. "I'm not upset," he said at last. "I'm just not certain this thing is over yet."

"No?" Stolie looked surprised. "What do you mean?"

"I came across two recent cases. Not here—one in New York, the other in Milwaukee. Random murders where the killer was a homeless man. The *Telegraph* arranged it so I could go interview them. That's where I was yesterday."

The detective was not impressed. "Someone murders someone else every half hour in this country—you know that."

"Usually there's a motive. These homicides were practically spontaneous. Both crimes were extremely violent, perpetrated by apparently mentally ill homeless men who have no subsequent recollection of the crime. Just like this one."

"When did these other murders occur?"

"One was just a few days ago, in Manhattan. The one in Wisconsin happened a few months ago."

"So what did you find out—anything interesting?"

"Yeah, maybe. I haven't been able to prove anything yet, but I think both the killers have a past history in Seattle."

Stolie considered the idea, then shook his head. "It's true these hobos can really move around the country. Look at Ferry. He was on his way down to San Francisco. If I hadn't caught him, he would probably have been there by now." He pursed his lips. "By the same token, that only makes it that less unusual that these other men could have a connection here."

"I suppose," Nick admitted.

"Listen, Nick." Stolie stopped walking. He turned upon Nick to make his point. "You've got my e-mail address. You can forward me the names of these two guys and I can dig around a little for you if you want. If I were you, though, I'd give it a rest." He pointed a finger at Nick's ravaged face. "As far as I can see, you're running on empty. I'm not a psychologist, but if I were in your shoes, I'd be in shock. You still haven't been able to remember everything that happened the night your brother was killed, have you?"

Nick shook his head, discouraged.

"Take some time off, Nick. Get some rest. Try to come to terms with your loss. It's going to take you some time to figure out how you feel." Stolie nodded toward the double doors directly in front of them, then once again continued in that direction. "This one's in the bag already. We've got our man. This bastard killed your brother. Just leave it with us. We'll take it to the DA, and like the lieutenant says, we've got Ferry nailed. He'll be behind bars the rest of his life."

Nick noticed the smell first. The antiseptic odor of the jail, laden with the heavy, industrial scent of oiled steel and the lingering stench of human excrement and filth. His eyes were focused on the double doors in front of them. The thick iron bars to his left were nothing more than a passing blur in the corner of his eye.

When Jackson Ferry leapt out at him, the sudden movement left Nick frozen in place.

Nick's mind burst with the image of Ferry emerging from the black shadows beneath Pike Place Market. Nick saw the knife in his hand, glinting in the dim light of the street lamp overhead. This image was rapidly replaced with another: Nick wrenching the knife from Sam's chest, staring at the blood-covered blade before dropping it onto the asphalt.

Ferry's trajectory toward Nick was broken by the steel that separated the two men. He crashed loudly against the bars, as if he hadn't seen them. Sliding his arms through the gaps, he swiped the air just in front of Nick's face. He grunted as he missed, straining to reach a little farther, his cheek pressed against the steel barrier.

Stolie was quick to react. Even as Ferry was first colliding with the bars, he grabbed Nick and yanked him back from the holding cell. The nightstick fastened to his black leather belt was in his hand, and he brought it down sharply against Ferry's outstretched arms. With a shriek of pain, Ferry fell to his knees, holding his bruised forearms with his hands.

"Guard!" Stolie shouted. The jail guard rushed down the wide corridor.

Ferry's eyes met Nick's. "I can hear what you're thinking, brother," he said in an intense whisper.

"Cuff him!" Stolie commanded the guard. "See that he's properly restrained." He turned toward Nick. "You all right?"

"Yeah," Nick said. "Don't worry, I'll be fine." His eyes were still locked with Ferry's. The man remained on his knees, allowing the guard to draw his hands behind his back. A smile spread across his face.

"The exit's straight down the hall, through those doors," Stolie said.

"Sure, yeah." Nick took a deep breath, then turned away from the powerful homeless man at his feet.

Walking down the steps in front of the station house, Nick wasn't aware of the man standing in the window two stories above, watching him. William Gutterson let go of the curtain, and it dropped back down in front of the glass. He was a tall man with strong shoulders, now becoming slightly stooped. He had begun to age, and he knew it. His hair was thinning. In the last few years he had put on twenty pounds.

He took a look across the office at Lieutenant Dombrowski, seated behind his desk. He was aware of the man's ambition. Dombrowski wasn't waiting for him to stumble. Any sign of weakness, and the lieutenant would give him a push. "You keep your eye on that kid," the chief of police said.

Dombrowski assessed the older man with a critical look. "You're going in front of the cameras in half an hour, Bill. Telling Seattle we've caught the Street Butcher—that it's safe to go back outside again. This is going to be primetime news. The headline story. You sure that's a good idea? It doesn't sound to me like you're convinced we've got our man."

"I've been around a few years."

"Sure you have, Bill. And you'll be around a few years more, too."

The chief of police looked his lieutenant in the eye, measuring his sincerity. "I know what I've got to do," he said. "The city wants reassurance, so that's what I'm going to give them. This guy Wilder, though—there's something about him that doesn't add up. He works for the paper, he seems like an ordinary man—but so did Ted Bundy. Bundy charmed the pants right off his victims, literally. Put a tail on this guy. I'm telling you, watch him. It was good work nabbing Ferry, but the last thing we can afford is to be wrong here. Not on my watch, Dom."

The lieutenant let the chief of police finish his rant. "Sure, Chief," he said to his superior, "you know me. I've got your back, just like I always have." To himself he remarked how tired the old man was going to appear on the ten o'clock news, even in the hour of his small victory.

chapter 25

At noon the next day, Nick was standing on the edge of Pioneer Square, staring across the street at the entrance to the Hudson Hotel. The sky had just burst, and all around him people were running for cover from the rain. Nick alone remained still, unfazed by the downpour. A woman wearing a translucent plastic slicker bumped into him, the spikes of her tattered black umbrella nearly skewering him in the eye as she passed, but Nick hardly noticed.

The rain soaked through his hair, and a few thick strands washed down into his eyes. At last he realized how wet his clothes were. He wasn't wearing a parka or carrying an umbrella. His gray sweatshirt had turned black, and water was streaming down his chest and legs. Tucking his hair behind his ears, he joined a crowd of pedestrians rushing across the street, making his way toward the Seattle Emergency Shelter, where he had first stumbled upon Jackson Ferry.

As before, a throng of homeless men were huddled in

the hallway leading to the dining room. Because of the rain, the line had degenerated into chaos. The doors to the dining room hadn't opened yet, and the air in the corridor was steamy and close. The men were milling around impatiently, hungry for their meal. A short man with a red face and bloodshot eyes, dressed in an army jacket and ripped trousers, was waving his hands violently, as though he had to fend the rest of the men off him. *Get the hell back, you bastard. Touch me again. Just touch me again, and I'll shove your fingers down your throat.* He was raging, but his eyes seemed focused on no one in particular. When Nick raised his camera to take a picture of him, one of the men hit the camera hard enough to jerk it away from Nick's eye. *You don't want to be doing that, buddy,* the man said to him. *It ain't nice to take no one's picture without permission.* Nick nodded a small apology.

Nick stepped in between a few men to reach the glass partition that separated the reception area from the public lobby. An overweight woman with thinning hair was sitting at the front desk, a carpal tunnel brace on her wrist. "I'm looking to talk to someone," Nick said to her. "An administrator."

"Are you a resident here?" she asked him.

"No."

She gave him a closer look. "Are you a social worker?"

"No. I'm a journalist." Nick glanced down at his camera. "I'd like to talk to whoever's in charge. Your director. Whoever can tell me something about a couple of your residents."

"Are you writing some kind of story?"

"I'm with the *Telegraph,*" Nick answered.

The woman picked up her phone and spoke a few inaudible words into the receiver, then buzzed Nick through a beaten-up door. "Take a seat," she said, pointing toward a few vinyl chairs. "Carla Lewis—that's our ED—she'll see you in a few minutes when she's got time."

Carla Lewis was a short and squat woman with a chubby face and a shrill voice. She regarded Nick skeptically from behind her square glasses. Her office was stuffy with the smell of cigarette smoke, though she had opened a window to air it out. Rain was splattering against the windowsill, and Nick found himself shivering, his skin clammy and uncomfortable beneath his drenched clothes. "So you're with the *Seattle Telegraph*?" she asked him.

Nick showed her his press card. "I'm wondering if you keep files on the people you serve here."

"Is the *Telegraph* doing a piece on the shelter?"

Nick put his wallet back into his pocket. "I do work for the *Telegraph*," he said carefully, "but I'm not here in connection with any story. My name is Nick Wilder. You can give my editor a call if you want to. Laura Daly. But she'll just tell you the same thing. The paper's not doing any reporting on the shelter right now—at least, not that I'm aware of."

"So why are you here, Mr. Wilder?"

"Do you know a man named Jackson Ferry?"

The director's eyes narrowed. "Do you mind if I smoke a cigarette?"

Nick shrugged.

"I know who Ferry is." She pinched a cigarette between her lips and lit it. "But I don't know that I ever met him." The putrid smell of her cigarette quickly permeated the room. "He's been arrested, accused of murdering a man a couple of days ago."

"My brother," Nick said.

"What?"

"The man he killed was my brother. Sam Wilder."

The director let a stream of smoke out through her nose.

"I was wondering what you can tell me about him. About Ferry."

"Like I said, Mr. Wilder, I didn't know Ferry myself. He had a room here for the past few months, upstairs. So I saw him coming and going a few times. I know his face. He's a diagnosed paranoid schizophrenic. The last I heard, the police were moving him from the jail to Western State Hospital for a psychiatric evaluation. But that's all I know about him."

"What does that mean—that he's schizophrenic?"

"Literally, schizophrenia means the splitting or shattering of the mind. It can assume as many different forms as there are people. As far as I'm aware, in Ferry's case, he experiences positive symptoms of the illness—delusions, hallucinations, but no thought disorder. I don't have any experience with him, though. I don't know more than that."

"Tell me what those terms mean," Nick said. "*Delusions, hallucinations.* He sees things?"

"Yes." The director took a drag on her cigarette. "He sees things, hears things. In layman's terms, he's lost touch with reality. He isn't able to distinguish between his own thoughts and reality."

Nick felt himself shiver. "Was he being treated?"

Nick noticed the director's hesitation. "I wish I could offer you more help, Mr. Wilder," she said, "but I really don't know. He was another one of our residents, nothing more. There are a lot of people here just like him, Mr. Wilder."

"Capable of violence?"

"Everyone is capable of violence under the right circumstances. You know that, Mr. Wilder. In most cases, though, the person most at risk of harm is the schizophrenic himself."

"And in Ferry's case?"

The director examined Nick from behind her glasses. "From what I remember, he's a pretty big man. He was loud—that was my impression. Angry. Threatening. But is he violent? I'm not a doctor, Mr. Wilder, just a social worker. And I'm only five-two, though." She tried to smile. "So everyone's big to me."

"What about Henry Dean?" Nick pressed. "Does the name Henry Dean mean anything to you?"

"Should it?" The director considered the name. "No," she said at last. "Henry Dean, no."

"What about James Warren?"

The director pursed her lips and shook her head.

"Do you keep records of the people you serve here?" Nick asked a second time.

"That depends on what you mean by serve, I suppose. We offer a number of different services. We provide over a thousand meals a day in our dining room, and we don't keep track of the people who eat with us. We also offer counseling services and programs like vocational training and drug-dependency clinics. It would be up to the groups and individuals running those programs whether they keep track of the individuals in attendance. The people who use our facilities are transient, and often they don't carry government IDs or passports or Social Security cards. Usually they don't even have birth records. Keeping accurate track of our population can be a challenge—not to say a waste of time."

"What about the people who live here? Doesn't the shelter keep records of the people occupying its rooms?"

"We do our best," the director acknowledged.

"Can you access your files for me, then?"

"To what end, Mr. Wilder?"

"A few weeks ago, in New York City, an indigent man by the name of Henry Dean became psychotic, entered a boutique, and without motive murdered two people with a broken bottle."

The director fastened Nick with a curious stare, waiting for him to continue.

"A few months ago, in Milwaukee, a homeless man, Jimmy Warren, became psychotic, broke into a private home, and without motive killed two people in their sleep."

"You think the murders are related somehow? And related to your brother's murder as well?"

"I don't know." Nick realized how tentative he sounded. "I do have reason to believe, though, that both Dean and Warren lived in Seattle. Like Ferry."

"I see." The director took a pen and wrote the two names down on a sheet of paper. "Why don't you leave it with me? And give me your phone number. I'll look into it. If I can find anything out about either man, I'll give you a call."

A few minutes after Nick left her office, Carla Lewis picked up her phone. Holding the receiver against her ear with her shoulder, she punched in a number and lit another cigarette at the same time. "It's me," she said when a man answered. "Yeah, I'm okay." She brushed some ash from the front of her dark blue polyester shirt. "Listen, I thought I'd ask you a question. I just had an interesting visit from a man asking around about a few of our population. Hmmm?" She puckered her lips sideways and exhaled a cloud of smoke. "Nick Wilder. He's from the *Telegraph.* But that's not what brought him here. He also happens to be the brother of the man Jackson Ferry stabbed to death last week down on the waterfront. Yeah. Nick Wilder. Sam Wilder's brother." She inhaled, turning a half inch of her cigarette into ash, then again breathed a billowing cloud of smoke into the stuffy room. "What's that? Yeah." She looked down at the sheet of paper on her desk. "Henry Dean and James Warren. I thought I'd give you a call, see if you could place them. I don't think either one of them was a resident here, so I couldn't be of much use. I'll double-check, but in the meantime I thought maybe you might know them. Maybe you saw them at the clinic?" The director took another drag on the cigarette, then stubbed it out in an overflowing ashtray. "Sure," she said. "Whenever you get the chance." Then she hung up the phone.

On the other end of the line, a tall, athletic man replaced the phone into its cradle. He stood up from his expansive, teak desk and walked to the huge plate-glass window at the corner of his office. Lifting a sheer privacy curtain, he gazed down thirty stories beneath him at the façade of the Four Seasons Hotel. Cars took on the aspect of toys from this height, and he let his eyes follow a Tonka-sized city bus down the street. At last, straightening his elegant jacket, he returned to his desk.

"Who am I seeing next?" he asked, pressing an intercom button on the high-tech phone.

"You're free for another half hour, Dr. Barnes," a pleasant feminine voice replied.

"Thanks, Millicent," he said. Then he crossed his office to a cashmere upholstered daybed beside a pair of gleaming teak bookshelves and, sitting down, rested his head pensively in his hands, his elbows on his knees.

chapter 26

When Nick opened his eyes, he had the feeling that he hadn't slept. He had been dreaming, though—a dream so intense that he thought it was real. The sheets were wet with sweat, and his shoulder ached horribly. He lay still, searching the room with his eyes, then shifted onto his back. He didn't want to wake Sara. He waited, listening to her even breathing until he was satisfied that he hadn't disturbed her, then got out of bed.

Since the evening of the gala, Nick had been dogged with the sense that he had seen the man with whom Hamlin had been speaking somewhere before. As the official from the EPA responsible for awarding the Elliott Bay contract to Hamlin's company, Ralph Van Gundy had been in the news. This association alone hadn't felt right, though. Nick couldn't shake the feeling that somehow he *knew* the man.

In his dream, he had been standing in front of the massage parlor on Fourth Avenue, looking up at the red neon sign in the second-floor window. A light rain had been falling, and the sky was low and threatening. Nick was by himself on the street. The clerk inside the dingy store on the ground floor of the building had become a Doberman, and he snarled ominously at Nick from behind the plate-glass window, teeth bared. The flimsy, ragged door swung open. Yellow light spilled like water into the dark street. And then Hamlin stepped outside, dressed incongruously in the tuxedo he had worn at the gala, followed by the stout man he had led into the concert hall. The head of the Washington EPA. Ralph Van Gundy.

Nick crossed the small apartment to his desk. His laptop was buried under a pile of papers, bills he had been ignoring for the last few weeks. He pulled the computer out, then powered it up. He had long since deleted the photographs from his camera. The resolution was too high for him to store too many pictures on a single memory stick. He kept backups on his computer, though, and he opened the folder that contained the massage parlor pictures.

"What is it, darling?"

Nick hadn't heard Sara approach, and her voice made his heart jump. She put a hand on his shoulder, then leaned down against him, snuggling him from behind.

"Is there something wrong?"

"I just can't sleep," Nick said. "That's all."

"What are you doing?" She peered at the screen of the laptop. "Who's that?"

Nick shrugged. "No one."

"Tell me," she said, giving his neck a soft kiss.

"A man named Ralph Van Gundy." Nick couldn't think of any reason why Sara shouldn't know. "An associate of your father's."

"Jason's not my father," she said, pulling away from him.

"I'm sorry. Your stepfather, I mean." He glanced over his shoulder to look at her. "Hamlin was blackmailing him, I think. To win some government business."

"What?" She sounded genuinely shocked.

"I don't know. I'm not sure I should tell you."

"Tell me, Nick. Can you prove it?"

Nick shook his head, his mind starting to check off possibilities. "Not yet. Maybe." He reached forward and pulled the screen down. "I'm sorry. I shouldn't have said anything."

"Come back to bed, darling."

"I can't," Nick said. "I've got to go."

Nick parked his car outside a white shingle house set back from the street behind a lush, verdant lawn, partially hidden by a copse of giant elms. It was still dark, and from what Nick could see there was no movement inside the house yet. Nick knew that Laura Daly was an early riser. She was in the newsroom most mornings before six A.M. It was Sunday, though. Maybe Daly was sleeping in. Finally, at seven o'clock, Nick couldn't wait any longer. Lifting his laptop off the passenger seat, he opened the door and braved the cold, heading up the rain-soaked concrete path to the front door. He rang the buzzer; then, when he still didn't hear anyone moving inside, raised the knocker and gave it a few taps.

Daly looked flustered when she pulled the door open. Her hair was mussed from her pillow, her cheeks lined with a few sleep creases. She had pulled a heavy terrycloth robe over her pajamas, but she hadn't been able to find her slippers, and her feet were bare. "Nick?" Daly squinted, trying to bring the young man into focus. "Is that you? What are you doing here? It's barely seven o'clock."

"I'm sorry," Nick said. "I thought you'd be awake."

"Normally I would be. Are you okay, son?"

The raw concern in Daly's voice made Nick pause with regret, and he didn't reply.

"I couldn't find my slippers." Daly looked down at her uncovered feet, as if to prove the point. "Just give me a moment—I feel naked without them. Come inside, why don't you? There's coffee on the stove from last night. Pour yourself a cup, and I'll be right down."

A few minutes later, they were sitting across the small kitchen table in the dim light of the early morning. The kitchen's exterior wall was cased in glass, and even though the rain had stopped falling, drops of water cascaded from the trees, trickling in streams down the windowpanes. Nick had placed the laptop on the table between them, and Daly was staring at the screen, slowly shaking her head. "There's no doubt about it," she said, a hard note in her voice. Despite the situation, the editor's posture didn't reflect a suggestion of any hesitation. "No doubt at all. That's him. That's Van Gundy."

"I took these pictures outside the massage parlor."

"I remember."

"We sat at your desk and discussed them when I turned them in."

"I know, Nick. I was there. I remember."

"You paid me for them."

Daly looked up at Nick. Her frustration was palpable. "What are you suggesting?"

"What happened to the story, Laura?"

The editor's eyes blazed, then dimmed.

"I've had so much on my mind I almost didn't notice. You never printed these pictures. You didn't run the story."

Daly looked away from Nick, then, pushing her chair backward clumsily, stood up from the table, gathering her robe as if she were cold. Nick understood that his suspicions had been correct. Still, he couldn't believe it. He followed the editor with his eyes as she walked across the kitchen to the wall of windows, waiting for her to speak the truth.

"It was Hamlin," she said at last. Her voice was low, barely a whisper.

Nick waited for her to continue, stunned by the confession.

"This wasn't a piece we were going to run. It was never a story at all." The aging editor stared out into the backyard. The house was set on at least an acre, and there wasn't another structure in sight, only a carefully tended garden. "Jason came to my office and told me about the bust. The police were going to raid the massage parlor—just like I told you, just like they did. He said he wanted pictures taken. I didn't ask him why."

"You didn't want to know why Hamlin was going to all that trouble?"

The gray-haired woman shrugged her shoulders. "You took the pictures, I gave them to Jason. I didn't want anything to do with it beyond that."

Nick glanced back at the screen of his computer, trying to make sense of the situation. "I've still got the pictures," he said at last.

"Let's take him down, Nick."

Nick felt suddenly cold.

"I never should have let it go this far." The editor sounded weary. Her gaze didn't waver. At last she turned to face Nick. "What you've got right there is enough."

"You want to run these now?"

Daly shook her head. "We don't publish them. We use them. Just like Hamlin used them to coerce Van Gundy to award him that contract. Only we use them against him this time."

"What are you going to do?"

"Me? I'm not going to do anything. You are."

"What do you have in mind?"

"You take these pictures to Van Gundy, Nick. Get him to flip. He won't have a choice. You tell him we've got proof that Hamlin threatened to run a story in the *Telegraph* ruining him if the EPA didn't award him the contract to clean up Elliott Bay. It's up to him. He can be part of the story or part of the solution. Either way, the pictures are coming out, so he might as well join us."

"If he cooperates with us," Nick said, following the editor's logic, "the story will be about Hamlin. If he doesn't, it will be about him."

"Exactly."

Something was still bothering Nick. "What I don't understand," he said, thinking out loud, "is why the police let Van Gundy go that day."

The editor's eyes narrowed.

"They arrested the other two johns," Nick said, finishing his thought. "Why didn't they arrest Van Gundy?"

"Hamlin's a very rich man. He's got friends, Nick." Daly smiled weakly. "Think about it. How did Jason know about the bust in the first place? And how did he know that Van Gundy would be there? He had a lot of good help setting Van Gundy up. There's no telling where this thing will lead you once you start digging."

"What about you, Laura?"

"Me?"

"You're part of this, too. Aren't you?"

The editor clenched her jaw.

"Aren't you?"

To Nick, she looked suddenly like an old woman. "You let me worry about that. I've been waiting years for this. Years. It's time to take that bastard down."

Gathering her robe, she walked across the kitchen toward the study just opposite. "You wait here. I've got a few calls to make. It's Sunday, but I'll raise Johnnie and see if I can't get a phone number for Van Gundy."

"I need to talk to you, Sara."

Nick and Sara were walking along the water in Seward Park a few hours later, hand in hand, making a circuit of the small peninsula in a light rain. It was late afternoon already. A cold, moist wind was blowing off Lake Washington, and it was so misty there was no sky. Nick tried to make sense of the large houses lining the opposite shore, hovering without perspective in the fabric of the air.

"I'm not sure how you're going to feel about this," he said, struggling for the right words.

"You know, you can tell me anything," Sara reassured him.

"The man whose picture you saw on my computer this morning—Ralph Van Gundy—I told you I thought your stepfather was blackmailing him."

"You told me you couldn't prove it," Sara said.

"We're going to go after him." Nick faced Sara, gauging her reaction. "I'm meeting Van Gundy later today. I think he's going to testify against your stepfather, even if it means going down himself."

Sara took the information in somberly. "I see."

"It's going to be bad for your stepfather." Nick wanted

to make his point clear. "Hamlin's a wealthy man, but he's not immune. I wanted to tell you first, because I'm not sure how you'll feel."

"Are you asking my permission?"

Nick thought about the question. "I don't know. Maybe. I just don't want anything to come between us."

"Because if you are, you have it."

Despite himself, Nick was surprised by Sara's reaction. As intimidating as he was, Hamlin was Sara's stepfather. He had adopted her legally when he married Jillian. "I've never really understood your relationship," Nick said carefully. "With Hamlin, I mean."

"Are you asking me a question?"

Nick realized that he wanted to know what Sara thought of Hamlin. "Yes," he said. "I guess I am."

Sara walked in silence. Nick was wondering whether he had gone too far when she spoke. "People didn't understand why my mom got involved with Jason," she began. "There were rumors. People said that Jason wasn't in love with my mother. They said that he married her for another reason."

Nick had never liked the way Sara called her stepfather *Jason,* by his first name. It sounded so intimate. "I don't know about any of that," he admitted. "Those types of stories wouldn't mean anything to me, even if I had heard them."

Waiting for Sara to continue, he listened to the nearly still water lapping the shore, barely visible beneath the fog shrouding them. The branches of a few large trees reached toward them, suspended eerily in the swirling mist. He had the momentary sensation that he was walking through the scenery of a dream. A gigantic whirl of steam rolled past them overhead, tendrils breaking off and reaching down to caress their faces. Nick resisted the urge to duck out of the way. "If he wasn't in love with your mother," he prompted when Sara remained silent, "what other reason could he have to marry her?"

He felt Sara's fingers wrap more tightly around his bicep. A sailboat emerged from the mist, gliding soundlessly across water, its tall sails billowing out above its polished teak deck. Nick became aware of the splash of its hull slicing the bay only after it disappeared once again into another bank of fog.

"When Mother met Jason," Sara said at last with a slight tremor, "he was already engaged to someone else." She bristled at the memory. "He broke off the engagement to marry my mother."

Nick tried to piece together what she was telling him.

"He's sixty. Jillian's only forty-six. And he's a powerful man. Physically, I mean. He's very, very strong." Sara's fingers dug into Nick's muscles, constricting the flow of his blood through his arm. "A man like Jason's used to getting his way—everything he wants."

"I'm not sure I understand what you're saying." Nick's confusion was melting into an apprehension he couldn't yet define.

"A man like Jason doesn't act impulsively. He's always in control. He dominates."

Nick knew firsthand how threatening the silver-haired man could be.

"A man like Jason doesn't break off an engagement lightly."

"So he must have loved Jillian very much, then."

"People blamed *me*," Sara continued, ignoring him. "They said terrible things. They said I tricked Jason into marrying Mother. They said I seduced him."

Nick's blood turned cold all at once. The back of his neck felt strange, as if someone were tickling his skin. Each of Sara's fingers now was cutting into his arm.

"I didn't seduce him, though. He raped me."

Nick stopped walking. When he turned to face her, the thin silver chain that he had given to her glinted in the weak light, drawing his eye to Sara's neck.

"Jason raped me, Nick. Then he married Mother."

Nick took Sara in his arms. The white mist surrounding them had turned gray, and Nick held on tight. Her cheek was cold against his skin, then warm with tears. For the first time since he had met her, Sara was crying.

chapter 27

It was nearly five by the time Nick pulled his old Toyota to a stop in front of the high-rise Federal Building where the Washington state EPA had its local offices. The sky had begun to darken. Except for a few homeless people guarding a couple of shopping carts covered with black plastic garbage bags, the brick plaza in front was deserted. Nick switched off the engine, then craned forward to look up at the building. One or two lights burned high inside the 1950s tower, and the lobby at the base of the building glowed slightly orange. This late on a Sunday afternoon, though, the building was otherwise dark.

Nick raised a hand to his face, rubbing his mouth and his cheeks and his temples with his fingers, trying to fight the strange dizziness overtaking him. He became aware of the smell of Sara still on his fingers. He closed his eyes, transported back to their bedroom in a confused blur, almost as if he were being pulled through a wild, twisting tunnel on the spine of a roller coaster. She had pinned him to the bed. Angrily, he thought. *Pull my hair. Damn you, Nick.* Viciously. *Choke me.* Savagely. She had held him down by his shoulders. Dug her fingers into his throat. Her thighs had cut into his hips as she had pulled herself down on top of him. *Hit me.*

Nick opened his eyes.

Fifteen minutes had disappeared somehow since he had parked his car. Fifteen minutes. Where had the time gone? Van Gundy was waiting for him upstairs in his office on the thirtieth floor. Nick couldn't afford to be late. He didn't want to screw this up. He didn't just want to take Hamlin down. He wanted to destroy him.

I don't want to hurt you.

Slap me. Damn you, Nick. Hit me.

Nick squeezed his fingers into his eyes and rubbed his forehead, then at last pulled the latch on the door. After leaving Daly's house that morning, he had stopped to print copies of the photographs, and he lifted them off the seat next to him and climbed the stepped brick plaza. A homeless man followed Nick's progress through the dark, wet shadows. Halfway up, Nick briefly locked eyes with the man.

The guard didn't look up when Nick entered the lobby. He headed straight for the elevator bank servicing the thirtieth floor and stepped into a waiting elevator. The doors slid closed behind him, and seconds later the cab began its quick ascent three hundred feet above the plaza.

Across town on the edge of Lake Washington, inside the men's locker room at the Bellevue Tennis and Polo Club, Jason Hamlin and William Gutterson were lounging in heavy armchairs in front of a muted sixty-inch flat-panel plasma TV, thick towels pulled around their waists and draped over their shoulders. Having just finished a few games of squash, they were alone in the locker room. Except for the high-pitched trickle of a running faucet in the shower and the nearly inaudible hum of the central heating, the place was hushed, nearly silent.

Gutterson's head was propped against the plush fabric of his chair, his eyes closed. Hamlin was studying the older man. The police chief's body sickened him. The way his towel cut into his soft stomach. The pockets of fat that formed flabby breasts sagging to the sides of his torso. The long wet hair plastered to his chest. Even the pallid color of his skin.

Gutterson opened his eyes, as if he was aware of Hamlin's scrutiny. "You've got to understand," the police chief said, picking up their conversation. "I've been behind my desk for the last twenty years. I'm not as young as I used to be. I'm sixty-seven years old, for God's sake. It's time for me to step down."

The news of the police chief's imminent departure didn't come as a surprise to Hamlin. Nevertheless, he was puzzled by the timing. "There's something you're not telling me," he said.

Gutterson eyed him. He didn't trust Hamlin any more than Hamlin trusted him. The last thing he wanted was to show weakness. What the hell, though? Hamlin would know soon enough. Her hair would begin falling out. They wouldn't be able to hide it any longer. "Martha's got cancer," he said.

Hamlin turned the situation over coldly in his mind. "There are different types of cancer," he said, speaking the words without the slightest trace of sympathy. "These days the survivability rate is pretty good."

Gutterson looked away from the businessman. "This

is pretty serious, Jason." He was thinking about how white his wife's skin had become. "The doctors say it started in her pancreas. Now I don't know." Two months ago they had been planning a trip onboard a cruise ship traveling from Los Angeles to Singapore. The disease had taken them by surprise. Their lives had been thrown upside down practically overnight.

Hamlin took the information in.

"It's good that you know. We've been friends for years now, Jason. You should know this before everyone else. I'm not sure. I think I may take her down to Mexico." The night before, he had held Martha's hand while she had vomited her guts into the toilet. She had been so violently sick that she had soiled her pants, and Gutterson had had to clean her up before putting her into bed. "They say there are some practitioners down there who've had success with experimental treatments. I thought maybe I'd try. We thought maybe—" Gutterson didn't finish his thought.

Hamlin scrutinized the older man. Until this moment he had never understood how much the police chief loved his wife. He considered whether there might be any value in the knowledge.

"So that kind of begs the issue between us, doesn't it, Jason?"

Hamlin pursed his lips, ignoring his question. "Who's going to replace you, Bill? Any idea yet?"

"My guess is it's going to be Dombrowski," the old man answered. "You might want to give him a call."

"Dombrowski," Hamlin repeated. "Over in Homicide, isn't he?"

"He's not a bad guy."

"So I hear," Hamlin said. "A straight shooter, by all accounts."

"I'll sit him down before I'm gone. Have a little talk with him."

"When's this going down?"

"Hmmm? I don't know. Soon. A week? Two on the outside. I'll let the mayor know first and assess the situation with him. I'm sorry to leave him in the lurch. But I'm halfway out the door already. This won't wait. I can hear the clock ticking."

Hamlin narrowed his eyes, sucking his lips against his teeth.

Gutterson felt uncomfortable, caught in the man's predatory stare. "So what about it, Jason?" He glanced down the length of the locker room. "The time has come for our reckoning, you know what I mean?"

Hamlin understood the demand. "Relax, Bill. All I do is give you a few numbers to memorize, and the matter will be taken care of. You can stop in the Caymans on your way back from Mexico. I don't know why you think you even have to ask. You know I'm a man of my word."

Gutterson settled into his chair, once again leaning his head back and closing his eyes. "I'm glad," he said. "It would be pretty bad for both of us if you weren't."

The elevator cab was getting smaller. The fluorescent light was getting brighter. The walls were closing in. The squeal of the elevator running along its vertical tracks at high speed had crescendoed from a whisper into a loud scream, and Nick wasn't certain anymore whether he was climbing or dropping in a free fall. He raised a hand to his forehead. When he brought it away, his fingers were drenched with liquid. He stared at his hand, certain that his fingers were streaked red with blood rather than sweat.

When the elevator came shuddering to a stop on the thirtieth floor, Nick staggered from it drunkenly, trying on uncertain feet to make a straight line down the hallway. The walls were flying toward him from either side. Not more than ten steps down the corridor he reeled, fell to his knees, then hit the floor facedown. He realized he was bleeding. A small red pool was spreading underneath him. He closed his eyes, trying to remember what he was doing there, trying to figure out how he had banged his head. Confused, his mind was filled with an image of a man he didn't know. A stout man with a bushy mustache whom he didn't recognize. A scared and angry man who didn't mean anything to him. Nick's face was pressed against the floor. He wanted to scream. Then he descended into blackness.

Sometime after eight P.M. Nick regained consciousness. Three hours had passed. He raised his head, expecting to find himself in the corridor on the thirtieth floor where he had fallen. The light was too bright, though, and he wasn't able to make immediate sense of his surroundings. The walls glistened with a cheap fluorescent glow. The floor was slick beneath his hands, painted white. His clothes rustled as he pushed himself up, echoing as though he were inside a concrete chamber. Stairs rose next to him. His gaze traveled up the wall until he found a stenciled black sign. He had no idea how he had gotten there, but he had collapsed inside the Federal Building's fire stairwell, between the twenty-sixth and the twenty-seventh floors.

Nick was dizzy, but the floor wasn't reeling anymore, and he was able to stand. He took hold of the steel railing, and, clasping the manila folder containing copies of his photographs in his free hand, he pulled himself onto his feet. Breathing hard after climbing the stairs back to the thirtieth floor, he paused in the air lock on the landing to catch his breath, then pulled open the door. The corridor was empty. He stopped, listening. Except for the hum of an elevator accelerating up its shaft, the building was silent. He found his cell phone in his back pocket and looked at the time. 8:13. Van Gundy would be long gone by now, he figured. Strangely, though, Nick's phone hadn't registered any calls from him. Why hadn't Van Gundy tried to reach him when he didn't show for their appointment? Nick had given him his number when they spoke on the phone. Van Gundy had demanded it. Making his way down the corridor, Nick raised his eyes, looking for Suite 3015.

Ralph Van Gundy's name was spelled on the thick oak door in polished brass letters that seemed to glitter in the light. Nick was reaching toward the heavy doorknob before he realized that the door was already ajar. He opened his mouth to speak Van Gundy's name, then instinctively realized it would be a waste of breath. He pushed the door open with his knuckles.

The wooden floor creaked underneath him as he entered the office. He stepped onto the thick wool rug to muffle his footsteps, then crossed the swankily furnished reception room to Van Gundy's private office. Once again the door was ajar.

Nick's jaw clenched. Van Gundy's corpse, facedown in a pool of coagulating blood, lay on the other side of the doorway, a stiff leg blocking the full swing of the door.

Nick examined the body long enough to confirm that Van Gundy, like the other victims, had been stabbed to death. Then he turned and began retracing his steps.

His heart nearly stopped when, halfway across the suite, the phone on the secretary's desk rang. He knew without reflection that the person on the other end was Van Gundy's wife, wondering where her husband was. And he knew that she would already have called the police and it wouldn't be long before someone sent the security guard from the lobby up to investigate.

It was only when Nick was taking hold of his shirttail to grab the handle on the door leading back into the fire stairs that he remembered having come this way before. He reached up to his forehead, shuddering at the touch of the crusty dried blood he found there, then pushed the door open and hurried down the stairs, taking them as quickly as he could.

Nick was alone in his apartment at ten-thirty when the first report of the homicide was broadcast on the news. Sara was out with friends. She would be home, she had said, by eleven.

A pall has fallen over the city of Seattle tonight in the wake of yet another senseless, unprovoked attack by a homeless man this evening.

Nick recognized the Channel 11 reporter's voice before he saw an image of her face on the TV screen. A few seconds later, Sheila's heavily made-up face hovered above his bed, relating the details of another homicide with deceptive authority.

This is the first such attack since the police announced the arrest of the so-called Street Butcher, Jackson Ferry. Ferry is believed to be responsible for the brutal slaying of Samuel Wilder, a successful bioengineer working for Matrix Zarcon. The police also believe that Ferry may have been responsible for the mur-

der of another homeless man known simply as Dickenson, as well as the homicides of Claire and Daniel Scott. Until Ferry's arrest last week, Seattle was gripped by fear that yet another serial killer was walking our streets. Police thought Jackson Ferry's arrest put an end to that. But no more.

The body of Ralph Van Gundy was found tonight in his office in the Federal Building downtown after he failed to return home. As in the case of the other homicide victims, he had been stabbed in the chest multiple times. There is some good news tonight, though. Police credit the work of Detective Adam Stolie, who cordoned off Federal Plaza immediately upon discovery of the murder, for the capture of the alleged perpetrator of the crime. The Seattle PD found the murder weapon on the person of a homeless man camped in the plaza, as well as blood on his clothing. The Federal Building is open twenty-four hours a day, seven days a week, manned by a private security company. Police are investigating how it could be possible to enter the building without the notice of the security guard stationed in the lobby.

Nick switched off the TV to answer his cell phone.

"Did you see the news?" Daly didn't stop to identify herself. "Van Gundy's been stabbed."

"I know," Nick said. "I was there."

Daly registered the information. "You went to see him as we planned, Nick?"

"This afternoon," Nick confirmed. "This evening," he said, correcting himself, remembering the time. "He was dead when I got there."

"Jesus." Daly connected the dots. "I'm not sure I understand, Nick. If he was dead, why didn't you call the police?"

"I don't know." Nick clenched the phone. He didn't

want to tell the editor about his blackout. "I got scared. I ran."

"Jesus," Daly said again. The editor understood the severity of the situation. "What's going on?" she asked. "Sam. Daniel Scott. The other murders." She didn't remark that they were all somehow connected to Nick. She didn't have to.

"I don't know, Laura."

The editor took a deep breath. "Are you all right?"

Nick shook his head. "I can't really say. I'm pretty confused. We decide to co-opt Van Gundy to take Hamlin down, and the very same day he ends up dead. You have to admit, it's a pretty huge coincidence."

"What are you suggesting? You think Jason's behind this somehow?"

"It sure looks that way."

"The report said that the police have taken a homeless man into custody."

"I heard."

"And I just can't imagine Jason Hamlin doing something like this."

"You don't know what he's capable of," Nick said, thinking of Sara.

"You sound pretty upset, Nick. Are you sure you're okay?"

Nick didn't respond.

"Anyway," Daly continued, "even if Jason is somehow responsible, how could he have found out so quickly what we were planning? You and I only talked about it this morning. And except for Johnnie, no one else knew what we were planning to do."

After hanging up the call, Nick stood up from bed and walked to his desk. He opened his laptop and brought up a picture of Sara.

chapter 28

Standing in the pitch blackness of his windowless bathroom, Nick tried to remember if he had looked at the clock when he had dragged himself out of bed. He was in a blind daze, and he had no idea what time it was. The door was closed behind him. His heart was palpitating in his chest.

There was someone else in the bathroom with him. He was certain of it. Someone just next to him, cloaked in the impenetrable darkness. *Was it Sara?*

Nick stopped breathing, hoping to catch the intruder out, but the roar of blood coursing through his veins filled his ears, too loud for him to hear anything else. He reached a hand out next to him. The room was suddenly huge. Too huge. He took a tentative step, feeling for the toilet with his toes. *Nothing.* Maybe he wasn't in the bathroom at all. But where the hell was he, then? The light switch—he had to flip the light switch. Panting, he reached in front of him, where the sink was supposed to be, shocked when his fingers smacked into its cold, hard porcelain surface, then reflexively raised his hand to the wall to find the plastic switch.

The overhead lamp lit the room with the violence of lightning. *There was someone standing in front of him, looking directly back at him.* Nick opened his mouth to scream. His eyes were wide with terror. And then he relaxed. He was standing in front of the mirror on the old, rusty medicine cabinet. The person in front of him was no one other than himself. Relief washed over him, and he started to laugh. The cackle of his laughter echoed through the small, cramped bathroom. And then it stopped, just as soon as it began. A hand had gripped him by the throat and was strangling him.

Nick fought with the hand, trying to pry the fingers from his throat. The harder he pulled, though, the tighter the hand clamped his windpipe. He choked for air. He couldn't breathe. He kicked a foot backward, trying to push the attacker away from him. His foot struck out into the air, feebly. His vision was beginning to darken. He was losing consciousness. He couldn't seem to pry the goddamned fingers loose from his throat.

He needed to know who was attacking him. There was a sour stench in the bathroom. *It must be one of the homeless men from the shelter.* His vision had become black and white, though, and he couldn't see anything in the mirror. Nothing but his own image, and then the hand on his throat. He struggled, trying to turn himself around. Trying to get a view of his attacker. His hip banged hard against the edge of the sink, bruising him. The pain was intense, but he used the sink's leverage to twist to the side. The attacker's arm came into view in the mirror. And then, finally, the attacker's face. Nick's heart leapt into his throat. *It was Sam.* Sam was standing behind him, his fingers wrapped around his throat, strangling him to death.

"Sam, no," he managed to say. "No, please, Sam, no."

It must be a dream.

The stench in the bathroom was the smell of Sam's rotting corpse. Nick's neck was wrapped with a skeleton's fingers, razor sharp and cold and superhumanly strong.

"It must be a dream," Nick said out loud. "It must be a dream." He let go of the hand on his throat and flicked off the lights. The hand was gone. He leaned forward onto the sink in the pitch blackness that again engulfed the bathroom, gasping for air. "Somebody help me," he said, and he began to cry.

He fumbled across the bathroom in the dark, battling with his sense that the room had once again become infinitely larger than it should have been, and leaned over the bathtub and twisted the knobs to turn on the shower. A few seconds later, when the water had warmed up, he stepped into the spray, raising his face to the showerhead. The warm water rushed over him, down his body in the darkness, pummeling his head, reviving him, waking him up and bringing him to his senses. Then the stream on his forehead crescendoed into a roar, and the water got so hot that it was scalding him. He took a step backward, sliding unsteadily on the slippery surface of the tub. Sharp jets shot from the showerhead with tremendous force, threatening to pierce his skin like so many knives. His feet were slipping. He was losing his balance. Blindly, he reached out to try to steady himself, grabbing the shower curtain, narrowly avoiding a dangerous fall.

When Sara found him two hours later, Nick was leaning against the tile wall at the back of the bathtub, holding his arms around himself and shivering. The water had long since gone cold, and he was shaking so violently that he could barely stand.

"My God, Nick," she said, pulling the curtain back. "What are you doing in there?"

Nick didn't move.

"Nick? Please, Nick. You're scaring me. Nick!"

At last he turned, and when she saw his face she hardly recognized him. His lips were blue. His eyes were bleary and unfocused, so bloodshot she thought they were cut, bleeding. Sara backpedaled in shock. "Nick," she said, mouthing his name again and again. "What is it, darling? What is it?" She recovered herself and reached her hand toward him tentatively, afraid despite herself that he might leap out at her or try to hit her hand away. He allowed her to take hold of him and to lead him from the cold water. She wrapped a towel around him and took him back into the bedroom.

It was still dark. Nick looked at the clock as she tucked him in under the tangle of his dirty covers. It wasn't yet four A.M. When would this night end?

"Shhh," Sara said. "Shhhhhh." He realized he was crying. "Shhh, Nick. You sleep now. Everything will be okay. You're just exhausted, darling."

"I need help, Sara," he said.

"I know, darling. I know you do."

"I'm sorry."

"Don't say that, darling. You just go to sleep. There's a doctor I know. The best psychiatrist in Seattle. Dr. Alan Barnes. I go to him, too, sometimes. I'll take you there myself. I'll take you to see him first thing in the morning."

Oh my God. Oh my God, Sara, what is happening?

* * *

Nick sat inside the huge Mercedes, folded like a rag doll against its door, unconscious of its luxurious comfort. The city of Seattle whizzed by in a montage. The rain had stopped, and bits and pieces of sunlight were sneaking down through a thinning layer of clouds, dotting the ground and sides of buildings with a patchwork of strange, brightly lit geometric shapes. Like puzzle pieces, Nick thought, dipped in a different vat of dye from the rest of the landscape. When the small chunks of color started to take flight, twisting and leaping into the air as though sucked up into the vortex of a cyclone, Nick closed his eyes. He didn't wonder whether the world was shattering. Instead, he wondered why Sara couldn't see the colorful tornado, too.

The directional signal was blinking. When Sara pulled the car to a stop at the intersection just in front of the Four Seasons Hotel, Nick's gaze traveled listlessly to the white zone in front of the hotel. He took in the doorman dressed in black, standing at the curb with a silver whistle in his mouth, a top hat on his head, waving his hands for a taxi. Hazily he remembered watching Sara disappear into the hotel through its plate-glass doors, arm in arm with a tall man whose face he hadn't been able to glimpse.

"How do you know Barnes?" Nick heard himself ask.

"I told you already, honey," Sara said. "I see him, too."

"Why?"

Sara laughed. "That's personal. It's complicated."

"Because of your father," Nick said. He had the feeling that he wasn't able to control his own voice.

"Because of my stepfather," Sara acknowledged quietly. "Yes."

"This is the third time."

"What?" The traffic light changed, and Sara tapped the accelerator, easing the car across the intersection, toward the garage in the basement of the high-rise directly across the street from the Four Seasons. "What do you mean—the third time?"

"Did I say that?"

Sara turned to glance at him.

"This is the third time that I've heard that name," he said. "Dr. Barnes."

"Well, he's pretty well known, darling."

"In just the last few weeks. I never heard his name before."

"You're going to like him. He'll be very helpful, you'll see."

"Sam told me to come see him. Then after Sam was killed, I actually saw him. Down at the Hudson Hotel. I saw Barnes there that same night I saw Jackson Ferry."

Sara was navigating the giant car down the granite-paved ramp into the bowels of the tall building. A valet wearing a red polyester jacket was standing next to a stop sign tacked to a concrete pillar, waiting for her with a parking ticket in his hand. "Good morning, Ms. Hamlin."

"And now you," Nick said. He thought about waiting for Sara to come around to the passenger door to let him out, then realized he was capable of opening the door himself. He yanked on the latch and stood up onto shaky legs, proud of the small achievement.

chapter 29

Nick was aware of the handsome doctor scrutinizing him. It felt as if the man's eyes were able to penetrate his skull. He was convinced that the psychiatrist was able to see everything that he was seeing. The thought scared him at first, but then began to comfort him. It would be nice to have an ally, someone who understood what he had been going through since his brother's murder. Nick clung to the edge of the cashmere daybed where he was lying down, one foot on the floor, his head propped up on a comfortable cushion, his eyes wide open. The doctor had begun the session by pulling the blackout shades closed, but Nick had asked him to open them again. He wanted the daylight. He had begun to fear darkness of any kind.

"You knew my brother," Nick said. He tried to remember why he had spoken the words, then recalled the doctor's first question: *So what brings you down here to see me, Nicholas?* "People call me Nick," he said, only vaguely aware how scattered his speech sounded.

"Yes, I did know your brother," Barnes said. His voice was soft but very firm, and once again Nick found himself comforted by the doctor's presence. This man would not let him stray.

"Were you friends?"

"I wouldn't say so, no. We knew each other professionally. Your brother was developing a series of drugs based on some genetic coding his company had under patent. It's groundbreaking, really, the research he was doing. I was working with the company on the psychiatric side. As a consultant. I got to know your brother that way."

"He wanted me to come here and see you, too."

"Did he?"

"The night he was murdered, he mentioned your name to me. I don't remember much from that night. Just images. Visions."

"It's not unusual for a person to suppress the memory of a traumatic event, Nick."

"But I do remember Sam mentioning your name to me," Nick continued, as if the doctor hadn't spoken. "Telling me that I should come talk to you."

The doctor didn't try to fill the silence. He was sitting in a large leather easy chair, one leg crossed over the other, a pad of paper in his hands. With his long hair and broad, handsome face, he didn't look like a psychiatrist. He looked more like a movie star, Nick thought. When Nick at last closed his eyes, the image of the doctor reclining in his chair, entirely relaxed, waiting for him to continue, remained with him.

"And then I saw you. Down at the Hudson Hotel. Do you remember?"

"Yes, I remember you."

"In the bathroom, with those three men. You came in, and they backed off."

"I remember."

"Did you know Jackson Ferry?"

"Yes."

Nick opened his eyes. The doctor's demeanor hadn't changed. His legs were still crossed, and he was holding the pad of paper in front of him on his knee, doodling something that Nick couldn't see. "You did?"

"One of the things I do, Nick," Barnes responded, "is run a clinic for the city of Seattle, in conjunction with the emergency shelters. Basically, we offer counseling and treatment to people who can't afford psychological help themselves. Jackson was one of my patients. I saw him personally a few times, in fact, before referring him to one of the other residents."

When Nick once again closed his eyes, the image of Ferry's ravaged face emerging from the shadows leapt from the recesses of his mind. The homeless man's breathing was short, raspy. Determined. He grunted as he reached the two brothers, raising the knife in the air. Nick put himself in front of him, but Ferry wasn't coming for Nick. He stabbed the knife deliberately at Sam. Nick intercepted him, grabbing the homeless man's wrist. The stench of the man's filthy clothes filled Nick's nostrils. He wanted to vomit. The rags on the man's hands felt oily and wet, his red, puffy cheek grazed up against Nick's as Nick fought to stop him. Nick opened his eyes. For a moment the vision continued to blind him, and he twisted abruptly on the daybed, dropping his other foot to the floor.

"What is it, Nick?"

The doctor's voice yanked Nick back into the present. A thin shaft of sunlight was streaming through the sheer curtains, reaching weakly across the parquet floor. Barnes must have been aware of Nick's distress, but he remained at ease. Nick relaxed. The doctor's calm radiated from him with palpable warmth. Nick stretched his neck and tried to loosen his shoulders. He balled and then unclasped his hands. "I don't know, Dr. Barnes," he said. "I don't know what's happening to me."

"You're fighting it," the doctor said to him.

"I'm scared."

"Stop fighting it." The doctor spoke without inflection. "Whatever it is that's happening, it's something your mind wants. Something your mind needs. It's like jumping into a cold pool of water. If you fight it, it only gets worse. Once you relax and accept the cold, you'll get used to it. You'll be able to swim. You'll be able to see what it is that your subconscious mind is trying to tell you."

Nick became aware of his hands digging into the soft cashmere upholstery of the daybed.

"Relax, Nick. Relax your hands."

Once again Nick was struck with the impression that the doctor was able to see inside him.

"Why don't you start by trying to remember what happened to you that night? The night your brother was killed. Tell me what you see. Tell me what it is that's haunting you."

Nick had Jackson Ferry by the wrist. He was squeezing so hard it felt as if he would crush the homeless man's bones. Nick's eyes were fastened on the steel knife. The light from the street lamp overhead was glistening on the blade, giving it an oily sheen. Nick had caught Ferry's other arm with his free hand, but the man twisted free. He was larger than Nick, at least a few inches taller. Ferry made a strange noise in his throat. An animal sound, like a baboon's vicious growl. Everything was happening so fast. Ferry had come at them out of nowhere. Nick was losing his grip. "Get him, Sam," Nick managed to say. "Help me." A second later, the homeless man overpowered him. Nick was on the ground underneath him, and the taller, stronger man was kicking him in the ribs. He wasn't wearing shoes, but Ferry's feet felt as sharp and heavy as clumps of steel. It felt to Nick as if the man was breaking his rib cage. There was a blur of motion above him, and he raised his hands to protect his face.

"Jackson!" Sam was shouting. "Stop it, Jackson. Stop it. You'll kill him."

How was it that Sam knew the man's name?

Ferry turned, and the blade of the knife scintillated like a jewel as it arced through the black air. Nick heard it slice into his brother's stomach. Blood splattered into Nick's eyes. Sam stumbled, then fell. Nick clambered to his knees. Turning on him once again, Ferry's foot seemed frozen for a split second in front of his face. Nick had the feeling he should be able to avoid the kick. Then the foot was connecting with his forehead, splintering his skull. And Nick lost consciousness.

When he awoke, he was facedown on the asphalt of the parking lot, a few chunks of gravel stuck to his cheek. Something was caught between his lip and his teeth, and when he tried to move his mouth to speak, sharp needles of pain shot through his jaw. He became aware of a rustling sound behind him, and then the sensation of movement at his feet. When he began to turn around, the homeless man plunged an iron foot into the small of his back, shoving him down into the asphalt again, grinding his cheek against the gritty pavement. *You and I are brothers.* Nick tried one more time to twist around. He had to know whether the man was actually speaking these words to him or whether he was imagining them. *You don't know what's real and what isn't,* the voice said, and Nick became convinced that it was just a hallucination. How else would the man have known what he was thinking? The man's foot was still resting on the small of his back, and he shoved him forward again, even more violently. Nick felt the skin peel from his face.

He turned over when the man let him go, but he didn't try to stand. His ribs were bruised, and he was having difficulty breathing. He raised his head off the ground and watched the man sit down on the asphalt between Sam and him and strap on the Nikes he had yanked from Nick's feet.

Nick closed his eyes. When he opened them again, he was hunched over his brother's body. Ferry was gone. The knife was lying on the ground beside him. Sam was bleeding profusely, his head twisted to one side, a trickle of blood leaking from his mouth. Nick's hands were shaking as he reached down toward his brother's battered face, thinking to caress him, perhaps to look for a pulse. His fingers were just above his cheek. He was about to touch Sam's face when the cell phone in Sam's jacket began to ring.

And Sam opened his eyes.

"Sam was still alive," Nick said. "Ferry didn't kill him."

"Are you sure?" Barnes asked him.

Nick closed his eyes, trying to remember. "The knife was lying on the ground next to him."

"Ferry is a strong man. Maybe Sam didn't die right away. But if Ferry stabbed him, the wound was probably enough to kill your brother."

"No." Nick shook his head. "When the police arrived, the knife was in my brother's chest." Nick opened his eyes. "With my fingerprints on it."

"I'm not sure how much faith you should place in your own memory, Nick. It's possible that your mind is inventing the images you think you're remembering. Like when you dream."

The rush of images that had washed over Nick had released him from the daze he had been in, at least temporarily. "What's happening to me?"

The doctor looked down at the pad of paper in front of him, propped still on his knee. "Honestly, Nick?"

Nick waited.

"There's no way to sugarcoat this. What you have described to me sounds like the onset of schizophrenia."

Nick let the import of Barnes's words sink in. "But I'm twenty-nine years old, Dr. Barnes."

"It's not uncommon for schizophrenia to manifest itself in males in their late twenties. Normally, there are some warning signs, but not always." The doctor narrowed his eyes. "Are you telling me that you've had no forewarning? A traumatic episode in your childhood, perhaps? Some indication that you might be predisposed to a change like this in your psyche?"

For a split second Nick was standing on the frozen lake in his skates, his hockey stick in his hand. The man in black was sinking beneath the surface of the icy water. Then Sam was fishing his hockey stick from the hole and prodding the corpse, forcing the lifeless body under the slab of ice.

"I'm not saying it *is* schizophrenia," Barnes said. "Listen to me carefully. I'm saying that it sounds like the early onset of the illness, that's all. There are a series of tests and evaluations we have to do. And then, if it is schizophrenia, you'll receive treatment. In the meantime, what you need more than anything else is rest. You've been through incredible stress. You're exhausted. It's evident in your face. In your eyes." The doctor stood up and walked to his desk, where he picked up a small brown bottle with a white cap. He wrote a few words onto its label in a difficult-to-read scrawl. "These are pretty powerful tranquillizers. Take one at night before you get into bed." He smiled. "You'll be asleep in a few minutes, and you'll sleep the entire night."

Nick looked at the clock on the wall. He couldn't quite believe that two full hours had passed. "Sara will be waiting for me," he said, straightening up. He took the small bottle from the doctor's hand.

"You're lucky to have her. She's been through quite a bit herself. So she knows what it feels like to be you, Nick. Don't be afraid to trust her with your feelings. She'll take care of you."

Nick turned to leave the room.

"Millicent will make another appointment for you on your way out. I'd like to see you tomorrow."

"I don't have medical insurance."

"Forget about it. I'll see you tomorrow."

"Thanks, Doctor," Nick said. Barnes had already sat back down at his desk, though, and was shuffling through a few papers, and he didn't seem to have heard him.

Nick felt a wave of gratitude course through his body when he opened the door to the outer office and found Sara still seated there where he had left her. She could so easily have moved on. She could so easily have had anyone else she wanted. Nick knelt down in front of her and took her cool, smooth hands in his and brought them to his lips. "You make me want to be a man you can be proud of," he said.

"I am proud of you, darling," she said. Then she pulled him up off his knees and locked her arms around his neck. "I need you, too. Just as much as you need me."

chapter 30

"Pack a weekend bag," Sara said. It was ten-thirty in the morning, and she had already been out for coffee. She sat down on the side of the bed with an expectant smile on her face, waiting for Nick to open his eyes. Ever since seeing Barnes a few days before, Nick had not only been sleeping through the night, he had been waking up later and later. He was taking the tranquillizers Barnes had given him, and the doctor had put him on a couple of other medications as well. Nick was looking rested again. The insurance money had come through on Sam's life insurance policy, and Nick was feeling safer, more comfortable in his skin.

He rolled over in bed. Sara's weight on the mattress had disturbed him, and her voice was slowly penetrating his consciousness. He woke with a bewildered smile on his face, shielding his eyes from the soft sunlight streaming into the room.

"You opened the curtains," he said to her.

"It's time to get up," she said. Sara looked around

the bedroom they had been sharing for the past weeks. The sunlight revealed a huge mess. "It's time for a little change of scenery."

"What do you have in mind?"

"Pack a weekend bag," she repeated, "and you'll see."

In Sara's car half an hour later, Nick twisted around to make certain he had tossed his heavy black wool sweater onto the backseat. Sara had told him they were heading up to her parents' cabin on San Juan Island in the Puget Sound. Two weeks before Christmas, it was going to be cold. Sara slowed the huge car down. They were heading south on Highway 5 toward the private airport at Renton, the tall buildings of downtown Seattle whizzing by on either side of them. "My parents are going to be there," Sara said solemnly.

"What?"

Sara took his hand. "I want this relationship to mean something," she said, giving his fingers a gentle squeeze before letting go.

Nick was thunderstruck. The thought of seeing Jason Hamlin sent a small frisson of panic shooting through his chest, and once again he twisted around, this time to double-check that he had packed his pills. An image of the brown plastic bottle with the handwritten label filled his mind. He told himself that he had definitely packed the various medicines. It would be silly to check. Reaching backward over the seat anyway, he pulled his small suitcase from beneath his heavy wool sweater and unzipped the center pocket.

"Nick?"

He ignored her. His heart was racing. He couldn't find the black toiletry bag where he had stowed his medicines. He had been certain that he had packed it into the center pocket, on top of his running shoes.

"I thought you'd be happy," Sara said. "I thought maybe it would help if you got to know my parents better. To stabilize everything, I mean. And I'm sure they want to get to know you, too."

Nick tried to slow himself down as he searched his suitcase. He didn't want to alarm Sara any more than he already had. "I—don't worry," he said. "I am glad." He unzipped the side pocket, then pulled out a few of the T-shirts he had packed, at last unearthing the small black toiletry bag. Taking a deep breath, he twisted back around. Closing and then opening his eyes, he concentrated on his heart rate the way Barnes had counseled when he felt a panic attack approaching. "I am glad, Sara," he repeated, measuring his words. "You have no idea how much it means to me that you trust me with this—and that you want me to spend time with your family."

When Nick closed his eyes, an unbidden image filled his head. *The knife that had killed his brother, protruding from Sam's chest, his own fingers clamped around its handle.* Blood was seeping from the wound around the entry point of the long, shiny blade.

Startled, he opened his eyes. This was the first hallucination he had experienced in the last couple of days. He turned toward Sara to replace the vision with her face. Concern flashed in her eyes, but her gentle confidence reassured him. "I just don't want to make a mistake with them," he said. *You murdered your own brother.* Nick paused, gritting his teeth, trying to erase the voice echoing inside his head. *The knife was still on the ground when Ferry left.* "This is a big step, and I haven't been well. You know that. I don't know whether I'm ready."

"You've been doing so much better," Sara said. "You can do this, Nick. I know you can."

He smiled at her, watching her profile as she drove.

To some extent Nick knew she was right. If this relationship was going to go anywhere, it was now or never. He took a deep breath and turned to face the windshield again, watching the road as Sara pulled off the highway into Renton. His head was clear. Sara was absolutely correct, he would be fine.

A few minutes later, they were pulling up to the small airport on the south side of Lake Washington, where a small fleet of seaplanes was berthed along wide wooden piers, bobbing like toys in the calm waters of the bay. Nick stepped out of the car. The air was crisp and cool and salty, and he made a pledge to himself to remain calm and focused, grounded in the present.

Hamlin gripped Nick's sweaty hand in his own larger, dry hand so tightly it was uncomfortable. Nick understood that he hadn't been expecting anyone with Sara. "Nice to see you again," the silver-haired man said. Nick sensed his disdain. "We met at the gala, didn't we? Nicholas Wilder, isn't it?" Hamlin locked eyes with Nick, daring him to mention the meeting in his office.

"It's Nick," Sara said, answering for him.

"How nice of you to join us, Nick," Sara's mother said. About to climb into a small seaplane and head for a tiny island a hundred miles away on the Sound, she was dressed in Ferragamo and Chanel. Her face was perfectly made-up. "You can call me Jillian," she said, extending her hand. Her fingers were cold from the brisk weather when she offered them loosely to Nick.

"It's a beautiful day for flying," Hamlin said. He led them down the length of an old wooden pier lined with small de Havilland seaplanes. In the distance across the water, the city of Seattle rose on one side, glistening in the sun. On the other, the homes lining Lake Washington were dwarfed by the range of mountains hovering behind them. The elegantly dressed man raised his face toward the sky. "Hardly a cloud in sight. No wind today. We're going to have an easy flight."

"We do this every year this time," Jillian said. "Two weekends before Christmas, to open the house up for the winter. As far as I can remember, this is the first year we've actually had sunshine. Usually it's raining. A couple of years ago, it was sleet and snow."

Hamlin stopped at the end of the pier, where a larger, two-engine plane was waiting for them. "It's only a half-hour flight," he said. "Thirty-five minutes. But it's a lot nicer when the weather's good."

"Do you fly the plane yourself?" Nick asked.

"Jason's a good pilot," Sara said.

"I've been flying since I was a kid," Hamlin said. "I was flying before I was driving."

"Jason is from Vancouver originally," Jillian informed him. "Their family had a house on the islands up there, and they used to fly in and out all the time."

"It gets so it's in your blood," Hamlin said. "Nothing like a good takeoff and landing on the sea."

Nick excused himself to make a call while Hamlin was conducting his inspection of the plane. Shielding himself from the wind behind the wall of a small steel shack on the side of the pier, he keyed Daly's number into his cell phone. "I just thought you'd want to know," he said after the editor picked up, "I'm about to leave Seattle with Hamlin."

"What?" Daly sounded surprised. "Where are you?"

"I'm at the airport in Renton. It's okay, Laura. I'm

with Sara. We're flying together, all four of us. Sara, me, Hamlin, and Jillian. We're going up to one of their houses."

"They invited you to San Juan Island?"

"Yeah."

"You think you can handle this?"

Nick dropped his eyes, squeezing the phone against his ear. "It wasn't my idea, but I'm okay." He glanced over at Jason Hamlin. The wind picked up, whistling in the phone's mike. "I figure now that I'm here, maybe I'll press him a bit about Van Gundy."

"Take it easy, Nick." Nick was aware of the woman's distress. "Forget about the paper for a few days. Just take care of yourself."

Ten minutes later, they were ensconced in the small plane. Hamlin and his wife sat up front in the two cockpit seats, Nick and Sara in the seats behind them. The rotors turned over, and, engines buzzing, they taxied away from the dock. Despite how calm the water was, the plane bounced up and down and sideways like a boat as it cruised toward the buoy marking the beginning of the strip on the bay used as a runway. Hamlin was talking on the radio, seeking clearance from the tower. Nick took a quick look over his shoulder at the next row of seats, where they had stashed their bags, making certain one last time that he had his suitcase and the pills inside. "Are you okay, honey?" Sara asked in a loud whisper.

Nick wanted to reassure her. "I'm fine," he said, realizing as he spoke the words that he actually was. "This will be fun."

"I'm glad the weather is so good," Jillian said, turning to look at them as the plane approached the runway. Hamlin was beginning to adjust the throttle for takeoff. Nick guessed that she had overheard Sara's concern. "It will make for a nice flight. Have you flown in a small plane before, Nick?"

Nick felt Sara take his hand. "This is my first time."

"You're in for a treat on a day like today," Jillian said. "It will be beautiful. And once we're there, it will be a real pleasure to have the sun. Do you play tennis, Nick?"

They reached the beginning of the runway, and Hamlin straightened the plane, then opened the throttle. The sound of the two engines became a deafening roar, and the small cabin was filled with a sudden rush of cold wind. Forgetting her question, Jillian turned forward to look out the front window. Nick watched the water skim by on either side of them through the blur of the aircraft's rotors. The plane's movement became less choppy as it picked up speed, then its pontoons broke free from the surface, and they were airborne.

Sara squeezed Nick's hand as the city of Seattle gradually came into view. Within a few minutes they were flying at a dizzying altitude, the inlets and bays and mountains and forests of the Pacific Northwest spread out beneath them in a patchwork of blues and greens. Hamlin eased up on the throttle, and the engines quieted back down. They cut a straight line north over a mass of land that disintegrated into the small, craggy islands dotting the Puget Sound.

"Pass me that flight path, would you, Jillian?" Hamlin said to his wife, pointing at a printout on the seat next to her.

Jillian turned back to face Nick and Sara after handing the paper to her husband. "We weren't expecting anyone with Sara," she said to Nick. "Normally it's just the three of us. You're a welcome surprise."

"It's a small house," Hamlin added with false modesty, briefly facing them, too. "But there's plenty of room."

"And plenty to do," Jillian said. "The Wheelers tell us the fishing has been pretty good this year. I don't know if you like to fish or hunt, Nick. Jason is a big game hunter."

"The Wheelers are the caretakers," Sara explained. "They live there year round and do a little farming on the estate."

"I can't pry Jason away from his fishing pole," Jillian said, still looking at Nick. "He even guts his catch, which is more than I could do. But you look like a good outdoorsman yourself, Nick. You look like you could handle a gun and a knife."

Once again, the image of his hand on the handle of the knife protruding from Sam's chest erupted into Nick's mind. He was kneeling next to the body, and he could feel the knife's steel blade plunging into the flesh and bone of his brother's chest, parting his ribs, piercing his heart. A shadow shifted next to him in the darkness. *Had someone else been there, too?*

Nick became aware of Sara's soft hand on his, gently tugging him back into the present. The plane's engines were whining, but the cabin was quiet. Jillian was facing forward, looking out the front. Beneath them, the landscape had changed, dominated by the sapphire expanse of the Pacific. Nick had no idea how long he had been out.

A few minutes later, Hamlin eased off the throttle, trimming the flaps, preparing to land. "There it is," Sara said, leaning against Nick, pointing toward the largest of the islands poking through the flat surface of the water. Nick glanced at her, wondering if it were possible that she hadn't noticed his blackout. She leaned forward, excitement animating her face. "Our house is the one just there," she said. "The one with the gray roof, all the way at the top of the island, where the land juts out like a small peninsula. There, do you see it?"

The house was huge, even from this height. It consisted of three or four structures set on a gigantic emerald lawn stretching from a thick grove of trees down to a sandy beach. There was a long, narrow pool in front and then behind it a tennis court and a parking lot dotted with a few cars and a small truck.

"Jason will land the plane in the water there, just in front of the beach," Sara said. Nick noticed the long pier stretching out into the water from the craggy shore, a huge yacht berthed on one side of it.

"I was expecting a cabin," Nick said.

"Isn't it romantic?" Sara pulled him against her.

"It's beautiful."

Hamlin twisted around to say something at just that moment, and Nick saw him lower his eyes, following Sara's arms down to his thighs, where she had buried her hands. A small burst of revulsion flitted across the powerful man's face. Flustered, he jerked back around, unable to remember what he had been about to say. "We'll be down in a couple of minutes," he announced instead. "Make sure you're strapped in, Nick."

chapter 31

At dinner that evening, the Wheelers prepared freshly caught salmon, homemade bread, and winter vegetables from the Hamlins' gardens. The meal's aroma wafted pleasantly through the warm house, drawing everyone downstairs. The afternoon had been so still that they sat down to the table with the windows open. From outside, they could hear the waves lapping the edge of the beach and the call of sea birds flying in gyres over the nearby coastal cliffs.

As night fell, the weather abruptly changed. Clouds gathered above the island, and the surf crashing onto the shore swelled to a roar. A cold north wind began to blow, sporadically at first, tossing the white curtains into the dining room, then more steadily. In the center of the table, the candles flickered and burned sideways, sending small plumes of black smoke into the air. Catharine Wheeler hurried into the dining room to pull the windows shut as it began to pour.

"Well, so much for our game of tennis tomorrow," Jillian commented over the sudden downpour.

"We wouldn't have been a match for you and Jason anyway," Sara said.

Hamlin took a large sip of his wine and cleared his throat. "You're not much of a drinker, Nick," he said, nodding toward Nick's untouched glass.

Nick smiled uncomfortably. Barnes had told him to avoid mixing alcohol with the different medications he had prescribed. "No. I guess I'm not." An image of the bottle containing the tranquillizers came to mind, and Nick felt a prickly hunger for one of the pills.

"Go on, try it," Hamlin encouraged him. "I think you'll find it a pretty excellent glass of wine. It comes from a little winery I bought a few years ago down in Napa, California."

Nick picked up the glass and examined the wine.

"You don't have to," Sara said, cautioning him.

"I want to." Nick raised the glass to his lips and took a generous swallow.

"So?" Hamlin asked him.

Nick set the glass carefully back down on the table. He realized that he had hardly been able to taste the wine. It felt acidic on his lips, dangerous. "It's good."

Hamlin almost snorted. His contempt was obvious. "You hardly touched it."

"Really, Nick, you don't have to," Sara said.

Looking from Hamlin to Sara, Nick felt a lightheadedness washing over him. Still, he was lifting his glass, about to take another sip to appease his host, when a voice whispered something in his ear. *You drank vodka the night you killed Sam.* Nick looked sharply to his side, wondering who had spoken, then, recovering himself, realizing that there was no one there, set his glass back down.

"Really, darling," Sara said, disturbed, placing her hand over his. "There's no need to do anything you don't feel comfortable doing."

Hamlin raised his eyebrows. He looked first at Sara, then at Jillian. Nick understood that he had been surprised to hear his stepdaughter call him *darling*. "You know, Nick," he said, "Sara hasn't mentioned you to us once since the night of the fund-raiser. Has she, Jillian?"

Jillian returned her husband's stare with an icy gaze.

"Forgive me for being so blunt"—Hamlin said, turning on Nick again—"but why don't you tell us a little about yourself. I don't know much about you."

"Jason!" Sara objected. "You don't have to tell him anything you don't want to, darling," she said to Nick, subtly stressing the diminutive. Then she faced her stepfather. "It's not polite to grill him like that."

"That's okay," Nick said. "I don't mind answering."

"You see?" Hamlin said. "He doesn't mind. After all, he doesn't have anything to hide, does he?"

Nick felt dizzy, then all at once overcome with anger. He understood why Hamlin didn't want him to mention their meeting in his office. The man could barely conceal his unnatural interest in his stepdaughter. *But why was Nick letting him get away with it?* He tried to assess whether his sudden outrage was reasonable, but he couldn't seem to separate it in his mind from the dizziness he was feeling. He shot a look across the table at Hamlin, trying to master the chaos of his thoughts. A spurt of panic gripped him by the throat. He didn't want to lose control of himself again. Not now. Not here. "Why are we playing games?" he managed at last, trying to keep his voice calm. "You know exactly who I am. You know I work for the *Telegraph.* You've even spoken to Laura Daly about me."

"You work for the *Telegraph*?" Jillian supplied politely, trying to steer the conversation to calmer waters. "That's right. I remember you telling me that the night we met, at the gala."

"I speak to Laura two, three times a week," Hamlin said steadily over his wife, staring Nick down. "Your name has never come up." He smiled, aware that Nick was foundering. "So what's the paper got you working on? You say you're a photographer, right?"

Actually, sir, we're working on a piece right now about the Washington State EPA. About how they awarded you a contract to clean up Elliott Bay, and how coincidentally you killed a story about a man named Van Gundy. And how the police didn't arrest Van Gundy when they raided the massage parlor down on Fourth Avenue, and how now Van Gundy's conveniently dead. The only thing holding us back from running what we've got is the stranglehold you have on Laura Daly's throat.

Nick struggled to maintain his composure. As much as he wanted to stand up to this man, he wasn't capable of a confrontation. The room was spinning. "Yes, I'm a photographer. I work on assignment."

"One word from me," Hamlin pointed out, "and you'd be unemployed."

"Like I said," Nick agreed, "I work for the *Telegraph.* You own the paper."

Hamlin continued to stare at him, even after Nick's eyes had dropped to the table. "You're not Sara's usual cup of tea," he said, when Nick remained silent. "Like I said, forgive me for being blunt."

"Jason, really," Jillian said.

Sara twisted in her chair, glaring at her stepfather, opening her mouth to defend Nick.

"That's okay," Nick said again, touching Sara's hand to still her. "I don't mind. I don't know what Sara's usual cup of tea is, Jason, and I don't really care." He didn't stop to think. "I'm in love with her." The words had leapt from his mouth, and when he heard them echo in the room's sudden silence, his face flushed red. Nick had never told Sara that he loved her before.

"That's enough now," Jillian said quietly.

Next to him, Sara turned in her chair, placing one hand on Nick's shoulder, the other on his thigh. She waited for Nick to face her, and when he did their eyes connected. Sara's lips parted, but she was too overcome to speak. Her eyes fell, glistening with unexpected tears.

Hamlin picked up his glass of wine and drained the remainder of its contents, then reached across the table and poured himself another. "I don't know about *enough*. Maybe Nick here would like to hear what Sara's usual cup of tea is. Eh, Nick? There have been a few, let me tell you."

Sara raised her head and shifted in her stepfather's direction. "That's enough," she said, minting her mother's words with a note of finality.

"Enough of this conversation," Jillian concurred. "And enough of that wine, Jason."

"You think so?" Hamlin picked up his glass and swallowed a mouthful. "It's only seven-thirty, Jillian. We've got a long night ahead of us. You play cards, Nick? Bridge?"

Nick's hands were on the table. He didn't seem to hear Hamlin's question. "Excuse me." His chair scraped loudly on the floor behind his knees, nearly tipping backward as he stood up. An image of Sam lying prone on the asphalt, his own hand clasping the knife jutting out from his brother's chest, had once again overwhelmed him. *The blurry shape of another person was emerging from the blackness next to them.* Forcing himself back into the moment, Nick grasped the edge of the table, steadying himself. "I think I'll step outside for some air."

"Suit yourself." Hamlin laughed, unable to sheathe his derision. "You're my guest. The house is yours."

The dining room, lit in the romantic glow of the candlelight, reemerged in front of Nick's eyes, and he took a few halting steps toward the doorway leading to a side porch where in the summer the family sometimes took its meals.

"Wait for me, darling," Sara said. "I'll join you outside in a minute."

Nick pulled the door open and let himself outside, taking a deep breath of the cool, sea air. The rain was falling in sheets beyond the overhang of the roof, and a faint mist enveloped the porch. It was cold, and the deluge roared in his ears, but it felt good to be outside, away from Hamlin.

Sara waited until the door had closed behind Nick to speak her mind. Still, sitting down on an upholstered teak bench on the porch, Nick was able to hear her every word. "You don't know what you're saying," she said to her stepfather. "You don't know how cruel you're being."

"He's not worth the shoes on your feet, Sara," Hamlin shot back.

"That's my business, Jason. You heard what he said. He's in love with me."

"And you?"

There was a long pause.

"I don't think it's any concern of ours," Jillian said, "what Sara thinks of him."

"Yes," Sara said at last. "I do love him, if you want to know."

"He's a pussy," Hamlin said scornfully. "You're not in love with him, *darling*, and you know it."

"You don't have any right to judge him," Sara said. "You don't have any idea what he's been dealing with."

"What's a kid like that got to deal with, Sara? He's too busy making ends meet to look in a mirror, let alone to get his arms around a girl like you." Again, Hamlin's derisive laughter rattled through Nick's consciousness. Standing up from the bench, he approached one of the windows and peered back into the candlelit dining room. Jason Hamlin was holding his glass of wine over the table, leaning back in his chair to flaunt his mirth. His teeth were dazzlingly white beneath his silver mustache, his rigid shoulders square above the back of the chair.

"His brother was murdered last month," Sara said, biting the words off as venomously as she could.

Nick watched the smile fade from Hamlin's face. The man could have won an Oscar.

Jillian looked at her daughter in surprise. "Last month?"

"Wait a minute," Hamlin said. "What did you say his name was? Wilder?"

"Yes. Nick Wilder."

"His brother wasn't Sam Wilder, was he?"

"Yes, he was."

Hamlin shook his head. "I'll be damned. His brother was working for a company I'm about to take public. Matrix Zarcon. I remember the day he got killed. Stabbed to death by that bum. The Street Butcher, right?"

"So you should give him a break." The outrage was gone from Sara's voice.

"I should say so," Jillian agreed.

Hamlin took a large gulp from his glass, considering it pensively before setting it back down. "You're a fool, Sara."

"You've had enough to drink now," Jillian said.

"No," Hamlin growled. "I mean this seriously, Jillian. Sara. You're a fool to seduce a boy like that."

"I don't think this is any business of ours," Jillian said.

"You and I both know this kid's nothing more than the flavor of the week," Hamlin said. "The only difference is this time you're playing nurse to a wounded, lovesick child. Mark my words, Sara. No good will come of it."

Outside, Nick turned from the window. He left the porch, walking away from the house into the freezing rain.

Sara found Nick on the beach an hour later, after the rain had let up. The sky had emptied, and a huge round moon was hiding behind a few gigantic stray clouds, searing their edges fiery white. "I was worried about you," she said, approaching him, taking him gently by the hand. "You've been gone for a long time. You just vanished."

"I needed some time to myself," Nick said. "Time to think."

Sara looped her arm under his elbow. "You look better," she observed.

Nick realized that she was right. At least temporarily, the fresh air had cleared his head.

"Why don't you come inside? It's getting late. It's been a long day."

Nick continued walking along the beach, as though

he hadn't heard her. Hamlin's words had hit their mark, and Nick wasn't able to stifle his growing insecurity. "Why do you stay with me, Sara?"

She didn't respond. She tightened her grip on his arm, pulled him closer to her.

"Your stepfather is right," he said. "I'm a total mess."

She stopped, twisting him around to face her. Circling him with her arms, she slipped her hands beneath his shirt, caressing him. "I'm yours, Nick," she said. "No one else's." She found his lips with hers. The last thing he saw before he began to kiss her was her eyes, sparkling, radiant in the moonlight. She had the most beautiful eyes, Nick thought, that he had ever seen.

They were walking up the lawn, halfway back to the house, when they heard Hamlin and Jillian's voices, raised in anger.

You can say what you want, Jillian, but you know as well as I do that there's nothing to this. She doesn't love him. I don't even know what she sees in him.

You're a sick man, Jason.

Why, because I don't want Sara dicking around with some asshole?

Listen to yourself. You're jealous, aren't you?

She's your daughter, Jillian, I'd have thought—

Exactly. She's my daughter, Jason. My daughter.

Sara wrapped her arms around Nick once again. "I'm glad you're here," she said. "You might not understand this. But I'm really glad you're here."

The scrape of a door being unlatched echoed across the lawn, and a bright yellow light spread over the grass nearly to their feet. A large silhouette filled the door frame. "Is that you?" a male voice asked.

"Yes, Todd," Sara said.

"Catharine's got the room made up, Ms. Hamlin," Todd Wheeler said. "The third bedroom on the hallway—the one with the double bed—like you asked."

"Perfect," Sara said.

Her voice faded into silence, and Nick realized that Hamlin and Jillian had ended their argument. He became aware of the sea lapping the shore behind them.

"Mr. and Mrs. Hamlin are retiring to their bedrooms now."

"I'll see them in the morning, then," Sara said.

"Good night, Ms. Hamlin."

"Yes. Good night, Todd. Tell Catharine good night, too."

Todd Wheeler disappeared inside, taking the bright yellow light with him as he closed the door. Nick and Sara stood where they were, staring up at the moon fading in and out of the clouds, then continued toward the house.

chapter 32

The moon was red. Bathed in blood, it had fled to the horizon. When Nick opened his eyes, it seemed to be floating at the very edge of the empty sky, casting an orange, coruscating glow over the water. Nick kept his eyes trained on the shimmering disk, puzzled by its savage, gory color. It dawned on him that he had no idea where he was.

He sat up, expecting to find himself in bed next to Sara. Instead, he found himself in a narrow single bed beneath thick covers in a room he didn't recognize.

It's just a dream. The moon has never been this color before. Wake up, Nick. You're having a bad dream.

His hands felt sticky, and he rubbed them on the bedspread, then threw off the covers and set his feet onto the floor. He was surprised to find himself clothed in his jeans and socks, wearing one of the T-shirts he had packed. Hadn't he and Sara already undressed and gone to bed? His skull was throbbing where he had been bruised the night Sam had been killed, and he raised his fingers gingerly to his forehead. A wave of dizziness washed over him, so intense that he thought he might pass out, and he closed his eyes. When he opened them again, Jason Hamlin was lying next to him in the bed. Nick looked at him, becoming aware bit by bit that the man was dead. His throat was slit from ear to ear, and the bed was soaked in blood. Nick leapt from the side of the bed, stifling his own scream.

It's just a dream, Nick. You're having a dream.

When he looked back down, the corpse was gone. The bed was empty. He reached down, touching the sheets to make certain. They were dry. There wasn't any blood. He straightened up and looked around the strange room. There was a desk against one wall and a dresser against another. A knit rug on the floor. He recognized the windows belonging to the Hamlin house and the view over the lawn, stretching down to Puget Sound. This was not the same room, though, where he had gone to sleep.

An image of the brown bottle filled his mind. The last thing Nick remembered was taking a glass of water from Sara's hand and swallowing one of the pills, then lying down onto the comfortable double bed in the room that had been made up for them. He had wrapped his arms around Sara, burying his head into the cool, silken mass of her hair. He must have fallen asleep seconds after his head hit the pillow. He became aware again of the stickiness on his hands, and he wiped them on his T-shirt. Had he been walking in his sleep?

It's just a dream, Nick. You're still in bed with Sara. Wake up. Wake up, and everything will be fine again.

He took an uncertain step toward the door. It was open a crack. He could see its edge glinting in the moonlight. Its painted surface felt cold and slick as he drew it toward him. The floor creaked, startling him, as he took a step into the hall. He stopped walking, listening. The house seemed to be humming. A quiet buzz filled the air, like the steady murmur that an old electric clock makes.

It was darker in the hallway. Nick waited until his eyes had adjusted, then took a hesitant step down the corridor that ran the length of the second floor. "The third bedroom on the hallway," he said in a whisper, remembering what Todd Wheeler had said to Sara. His voice sounded so raspy and guttural he wasn't certain that it belonged to him.

Nick was ten steps down the hallway when the corridor vanished, replaced by a vision of his hand on a doorknob. He was twisting the cold, painted knob, pushing the door open, entering a large, elegantly furnished room in the Hamlin house. The curtains were drawn back from the windows, and the moon was shining into the room through a myriad of small glass panes from the very peak of its arc, at the top of the sky. Hearing a rustling sound, Nick stopped, frozen where he was. When he looked down at his hands, he saw that he was holding a kitchen knife. Its blade reflected the silver rays of the moonlight with a sinister glint. The rustling sound resolved itself into someone moving beneath blankets. The shadows directly in front of him shifted, and Jason Hamlin's silhouette became visible against the wall behind a large bed. Hamlin cleared his throat. "Sara?" he said, peering at Nick through the moonlit darkness.

Nick's foot got caught on the long Oriental runner, and the hallway reappeared in front of him. He stood where he was, trying to catch his breath. His hands were damp with sweat, and he became aware again of how sticky they were. Deliberately, he lowered them and rubbed them on the thighs of his jeans and then the sleeves of his T-shirt, trying to clean them off. He wanted to turn on a light. He wanted to see his hands. He looked down the hallway, searching for the door to the bathroom, trying to remember which one it was.

His heart began to race in his chest as he reached for the white porcelain knob of the bathroom door. An image of his hand reaching down to pull open a drawer and then lift out a knife flashed through his mind. He hesitated, then grabbed the doorknob and pushed the door open, frantically searching for the light switch. The sink, too, felt sticky, just like his hands. His fingertips stuck to its surface, as though they were tacky with glue. He found the switch on the wall next to the sink, and the room was abruptly flooded with light.

The white tiled room was smeared red. Strawberry veins streaked the walls, interrupted with handprints the color of scabs. The sink was awash with drying blood. Nick closed his eyes.

You're imagining this. This isn't real. You're still in bed. You're asleep. Hallucinating.

He opened his eyes again, barely able to recognize his own reflection in the bathroom mirror. His face, too, was covered in blood. His clothes were soaked red. He looked down at his hands. They were stained, caked with drying blood and bits and pieces of sinew and flesh and gore, as though he had plunged his hands into the carcass of a dying animal. He began to shake.

Barely able to find the strength to turn the taps, he thrust his hands underneath the faucet. The water turned bright red, swirling down toward the drain like a fountain of blood. He grabbed the soap and tried to wash his hands clean. The more he scrubbed, though, the more blood was loosened from his skin, the more red the sink became. Finally, his hands clean, Nick splashed his face with water and rinsed the stains from his cheeks and forehead as well.

You murdered Sam.

He took a white towel off the bar next to the sink and dried his face. The towel turned red, as though it had been dipped it in paint.

And now who have you murdered, Nick: Sara?

Terror welled up inside him, taking his breath away. Had he murdered Sara? Would he kill everyone he loved? His brother first, now his girlfriend, too. He let the towel drop, then, leaving the light switched on, stepped back into the hallway. The floorboards creaked underneath his feet. He tried to move stealthily but couldn't. He was panicking, certain that he had killed his lover. He had gone downstairs to the kitchen. He had taken a knife from the drawer. And he had killed her.

An image of Hamlin sitting up in his bed once again filled his mind, followed by an image of the man lying in a tangle of blood-soaked sheets, his throat slit from ear to ear. Nick stopped walking, straining to hear. The house had remained silent, but he was breathing heavily now, panting. The sound of his panic filled the corridor.

They're all dead. You've killed them all, Nick.

"Shut up," Nick heard himself say. His raspy voice echoed through the house. "Shut up, Nick," he said more firmly. Then he walked to the door of the bedroom where he had gone to sleep with Sara. She was sitting up in bed when he pushed the door open, the blankets held to her chest, looking in his direction. She squinted as the light shone into the room from the hallway.

"Nick?"

It felt to Nick as if his legs would collapse underneath him. He was filled with relief. "You're okay," he said.

"Nick, my God," she said. "What is it?"

"I think I'm having a nightmare," he said.

Sara leapt out of bed, unable to mask her terror. "What is that, Nick? What is that all over you?"

Nick looked down at his freshly scrubbed hands. Thin red streams were trickling down his arms. Dried blood at his elbows had turned to liquid again in the water from the sink. His shirt and pants were covered with dark stains. "Do you see it, too?" he asked her.

Sara rushed to Nick's side. "Have you hurt yourself? My God, Nick, what have you done? What's happened?"

"I'm okay. I don't know."

Sara was fingering the bruise on his forehead. It hurt so much that Nick pulled his head backward, away from her. "All this blood." Sara looked down at his shirt and then his jeans. "What happened, Nick? What have you done?"

Nick shook his head. "I don't know."

Sara backed away from him, her face turning white, her lips becoming two thin lines. Nick understood what she was thinking.

"I must have done it," he said.

"My God, Nick." Sara's voice was a whisper. She hesitated, then, dressed in her panties and a T-shirt, pushed past him and ran into the hallway. She screamed when she saw the blood in the bathroom, then continued to run down the hallway. "Mom!" she shouted. "Mom!" Nick was right behind her when she pushed open the door to her mother's room. Jillian sat up in bed, dazed and scared in the sudden light from the overhead lamp. "Mom!"

"What is it, Sara?" she asked. When Nick stepped into the room next to her daughter, she cried, "What's happened? What is it? What's happening?"

"Where is Jason?" Sara demanded.

Dazed, her mother pulled her blankets to her chest. "He sleeps in his own room, Sara. You know that."

Sara didn't wait for her mother to get out of bed. She pushed past Nick into the hallway and crossed to a room on the other side. The instant she switched the lights on inside, she began to howl.

"Get away from me! Get away! Don't touch me!" she screamed at Nick when he tried to stand next to her. Nick took a faltering step into Hamlin's room, then stood gaping at the corpse. Exactly as he had pictured, Hamlin's head was nearly severed from his body, and the mutilated carcass was lying in a confused tangle of bloody sheets on his antique bed.

Downstairs in the house, lights were being switched on, followed by footsteps and voices. Seconds later, Todd Wheeler, his clothes pulled on and wearing his boots, was ascending the stairs two at a time. He marched down the hallway in their direction, his shotgun in his hand. The huge house seemed to quake beneath him.

"Call the police, Catharine. Now!" he shouted when he reached the doorway into Hamlin's room. Then he took the butt of his heavy steel rifle, gripped it in one of his callused hands, and swung it across Nick's face, dropping him like a puppet.

Nick woke to the roar of a helicopter descending on the front lawn. Its landing lights flooded the house through a multitude of small-paned windows, papering the walls and floors with a brilliant checkerboard. Nick's first conscious thought was that he had been dreaming, and he imagined that he would be waking up into a better reality. Then he became aware of the rope wrapped tightly around his wrists, cutting into his skin, securing him to a large wooden chair. He tried to free himself, but his legs and arms were tied so tightly that his hands and feet were swollen. His blood could barely circulate. He heard voices behind him, and he tried to turn his head to see who it was. "Sara?" The voices behind him were silenced. "Sara, is that you?" He struggled against the ropes, tried to twist in the chair.

"He's awake," he heard Todd Wheeler say.

"The police are coming inside now." This was Sara's voice.

"Sara!" Nick shouted, helpless. Outside, he could see the helicopter touching down. Its motor began a slow, thumping decrescendo into a high-pitched whine.

Sara appeared in front of Nick. There was a look in her eyes he did not recognize. "I'm sorry, Nick," she said. "We had no choice."

"My face, Sara," Nick heard himself say. He felt an intense throbbing in his jaw where he had been struck. After that, the room became a blur. Nick was only vaguely aware of the three uniformed policemen streaming into the house, of Stolie standing in front of him, reading him his rights. Stolie leaned down, shining a small flashlight into his eyes. A man dressed in white stood next to him and measured something out in a small vial. When he stuck a syringe into Nick's arm, Nick tried to pull his arm back. He tried to scream. But he couldn't move, and he couldn't speak. He was floating, drifting away. The last thing Nick remembered was lying down on a cloud and being swept up toward a bloody moon. He didn't remember the stretcher. And he didn't remember the helicopter ride back into Seattle, buffeted by the approach of a cold front.

The chaos disappeared, and the frenzy of sounds

vanished. From time to time Nick sensed someone standing next to him, or caught glimpses of a man flicking a syringe held up to a fluorescent light or examining a clipboard and whispering secrets to his shadow. That was all he was conscious of for days, until he finally opened his eyes, awake, in an uncomfortable bed in a green tinted room that smelled like disinfectant, his arms fitted securely into the tight sleeves of a starched white straitjacket.

chapter 33

"Where am I?"

A man dressed in a white polyester uniform was holding a small Dixie cup toward him. By now Nick understood that the cup would contain three tablets. A large one that was difficult to swallow. A small one that tasted acridly bitter. And then one of the medicines Barnes had given him, a tiny daisy-yellow pill that left a strong aftertaste in his mouth. At nighttime, before he went to sleep, the cup would include a fourth tablet as well, one of the orange tranquillizers from the brown bottle with the white cap. Nick had begun craving these pills. He would wait for them in the windowless room as nighttime approached, trying to measure the hours, a growing hunger yawning inside him that could only be satisfied with the grains of the miniscule orange pill.

Nick took the Dixie cup from the man and obediently dropped the pills into his mouth, then took another cup from him and swallowed them down with the rancid-tasting water it contained. He had learned a couple of days before that it was pointless to refuse the medication. The straitjacket had come back into the room, and, unable to resist, Nick had been tied back down to the metal bed. A man with strong hands that smelled like iron had squeezed his nose while another man had force-fed him the pills like a dog. After that, he had spent twenty-four hours in restraints. It was better to take the pills voluntarily and remain free in the room. The door was locked from the outside. There was no TV, and they had left him nothing to read. There wasn't anything at all to do. Without a window, he couldn't even look outside. The pills they were giving him kept him asleep most of the day anyway, but time hardly passed when the straitjacket was on.

The orderly froze for a split second when Nick spoke, then looked at Nick with eyebrows raised. He was a short, wiry Hispanic man. These were the first words Nick had uttered since his incarceration, and it stunned the man to hear Nick's voice.

"This is Western State," he said as he took the cup back from him, answering Nick's question. He crumpled the cup in one of his silicone-clad hands. "You're inside."

"The asylum?"

"It's a psychiatric hospital, man," the orderly said.

Nick became aware of the pills he had just swallowed breaking down in his stomach. He could feel microscopic particles of the medicine beginning to circulate through his system, dulling his senses. "How long have I been here?"

"Five days."

"I want to see a lawyer," Nick heard himself say.

"I don't know nothing about that, man."

"How long are they going to keep me here?"

"From what I understand, they can only keep you

here fifteen days," the orderly said. "For a psychiatric evaluation, to make sure you can stand trial."

"Stand trial for what?"

The orderly was straightening his bed. He shook his head, deciding not to answer. "You got questions, ask the doctor."

"The doctor?"

"Dr. Barnes, man." The orderly glanced at his watch. "He told me to give you your medicine now so he can come see you in an hour."

"Barnes is here?" Nick felt a wave of relief course through his body. "Dr. Barnes is going to see me?"

"Yeah, man. Dr. Barnes is here. Dr. Barnes runs this place."

"He'll be here in an hour?" Nick's question was interrupted by the sound of happy laughter. It took seeing the startled expression on the orderly's face for Nick to realize that it belonged to him.

"Lie back down," the orderly said. "Some of this shit can make you dizzy, man. You better be lying down when it hits your blood."

Nick acquiesced. "Dr. Barnes will be here in one hour," he said, settling back onto his uncomfortable bed, repeating the words like a mantra. "Dr. Barnes will be here in one hour."

"That's right, man. Take it easy. I'll see you again at three."

Nick closed his eyes. "Dr. Barnes will be here in one hour," he said one last time as the orderly shut and locked the huge steel door behind him.

Nick was dreaming about the flight to San Juan Island. The sky was crisply blue, without a cloud in sight, and the state of Washington spread out beneath them like a gigantic diorama. The water of the Sound was a steely sapphire plane, and the mountains were covered with the growth of the Pacific Northwest rain forest. Sara turned to him and, burying her hands between his thighs, gave him a kiss. Nick's heart burst with happiness as the aircraft soared over the undulating landscape as effortlessly and gracefully as a giant eagle. Then, interrupting the gentle solace of his vision, out of nowhere Jason Hamlin's hand shoved Nick aggressively backward. *You're one hell of a lucky son of a bitch to get a taste of lips as sweet as that.*

Barnes had unlocked the door and stepped into the room. Nick's eyes were moving rapidly from side to side beneath his eyelids. The doctor shook him, yanking him from his sleep.

The orderly was looking at Nick over the doctor's shoulder. "He's been sleeping eighteen or nineteen hours a day," he said. "Sometimes I have to wake him up with a cold towel on his face to feed him the pills. I could get you a wet towel if you want."

"No, thanks," Barnes said. "His eyes are opening. He's coming out of it now." Nick became aware of the doctor's bright blue eyes—as bright, he thought, as the sky had been the day of that flight. The memory brought him back into his dream. "Nick? Can you see me? Do you recognize me?"

A smile spread across Nick's face.

"That's good," the doctor said. He turned to the orderly. "I'm going to be taking him outside for a little walk. I think he needs some air."

"That's up to you, Doc."

"We'll need a wheelchair. One of the chairs fixed with restraints."

"Sure, Doc."

Barnes turned back toward Nick. "Can you speak, Nick?"

Nick nodded.

"That's good. That's really good. I'd like to have a little talk with you."

Once again Nick's face lit with a weak smile. He was grateful for the doctor's presence, grateful for a friendly face. "I just have to close my eyes for a minute," he said. He was aware of the medicine working its way through the membrane of his brain. The room went dark. He tried to cling to the thought that Barnes was here at last, standing with him in his room, talking to him. But the pull of the medicine was too strong, and he was abruptly gone.

Nick awoke in weak sunshine. A few rays of light were filtering through the branches of a giant maple tree in the hospital gardens. Nick squinted at the fiery ball of flames peeking at him from between the tree's branches, then became aware of the doctor's face hovering above him, looking down at him curiously. Nick tried to raise one of his hands, to shield his eyes from the glare, but he couldn't move his arms. He tried harder to lift them, then began to struggle, trying to pull his legs free as well. "You can't move," the doctor said to him. "You're strapped in, Nick. It's pointless to try."

Nick stopped moving. He looked down at his arms, imprisoned by wide black Velcro straps against the steel rails of the wheelchair. His body and legs were strapped into the chair as well, too tightly. Nick looked up at the doctor, a weak appeal shadowing his eyes, but Barnes shook his head.

Gradually, Nick took in the surprising beauty of the hospital gardens. It felt good to be outside in the sun. The doctor had wheeled him to the far side of the property, to a remote area behind a chain-link fence that required a security clearance for entry. The lawn was carefully tended here, and the rolling landscape was artfully planted with shrubs and trees. "How long?" Nick heard himself say.

"Good, Nick. It's nice to hear your voice."

"How long have I been inside?" he asked the doctor, forgetting that the orderly had already told him.

"Five days, Nick."

Nick heard himself laugh. "It feels much longer," he said. "I almost don't remember—" *Being anywhere else,* he thought, finishing the sentence in his mind.

"Luis tells me that you started speaking again today."

Nick nodded his head and tried his best to smile at the doctor. He congratulated himself for figuring out that the orderly's name must have been Luis. "How is she, Doctor?" he managed to ask.

The doctor ignored his question. "I was surprised to hear it."

Nick fought to remember what the doctor was talking about.

"And I'm surprised to find you so coherent now."

"How is Sara, Dr. Barnes?" Nick repeated, unable to follow what the doctor was telling him.

"I've got you on some pretty heavy meds, Nick. I'm surprised to find you awake at all."

Nick shook his head. "I'm starting to remember things."

"I know you are," Barnes said.

"There was someone else there," Nick said. "The night Sam was killed."

"Who, Nick?"

"And in Hamlin's room." Nick's hand was on the doorknob. He was twisting the knob, pushing the door open, entering Hamlin's large, elegantly furnished room. The curtains were drawn back from the windows, and Nick looked down at the kitchen knife in his hands, shimmering in the moonlight. Next to him, a dark figure seemed to emerge from the shadows, too blurry to see. *There was someone there in the room with him.* Someone standing next to him.

The doctor smiled. "Your schizophrenia is progressing pretty aggressively, Nick. Much more dramatically than I ever would have predicted."

Nick looked up at the doctor, trying to make sense of what he was saying.

"You only think there was someone else there."

"No, Dr. Barnes."

"Yes, Nick. You know who that other person was?"

Nick's blood suddenly turned cold. He knew what the doctor's next words were going to be.

"It was you, Nick. *You.* You watched yourself kill Sam. You watched yourself kill Hamlin, too."

The image of Sam's body lying on the asphalt burst back into Nick's mind like a slow-motion explosion. His hand was on the handle of the knife, and the blade was sinking into his brother's chest. Just like the doctor said, he was watching himself murder his own brother. "I killed Sam," Nick said, shaking his head from side to side, trying to bring the doctor back into focus in front of him. "I killed him, Dr. Barnes. I killed him."

"Yes," the doctor said quietly. "You did." Hitching his trousers up on his thighs, he squatted down in front of the wheelchair so that he could look Nick in the eye. He rested his hands on the wheelchair's armrests, just in front of Nick's fingers, balancing himself. "The thing is, Nick, I wouldn't blame myself too much if I were you. You killed Sam, yes. But it wasn't really your fault. Not with all the Zarconia he was feeding you. It's kind of ironic, really. Sam pretty much brought the tragedy onto himself."

Tears sprang into Nick's eyes, blurring his vision. He wasn't able to follow what the doctor had said. He understood, though, that Sam had been poisoning him somehow, with the drug that Matrix Zarcon had been developing.

"Your brother was doing genetic research to create a drug to treat advanced forms of schizophrenia," Barnes explained. "He needed subjects to test the drug on. The FDA would never allow the kind of testing a company like Matrix Zarcon needs to perform. So where else would a man like your brother turn?"

Nick didn't want to hear more.

"He turned to me, Nick. I'm sitting on hundreds of cases of schizophrenia in the free clinic, manifested in people without families—people without a past or a future, people without friends."

Revolted, Nick pulled hard on his restraints. He torqued his arms from one side to the next, twisting them against the tight bands. The Velcro on his right arm crackled a little as it began to give. Vigorously he wriggled, struggling to get free.

"There's a lot of money in a new drug, Nick. More millions than you can conceive of. Your brother knew, though. And he knew that I would understand, too."

Nick felt the Velcro begin to loosen, and, laboring to keep his face from reflecting the effort, he twisted his wrist even harder, until it felt as if his bones would snap.

"The drug worked wonders at first. Sam and I thought we were sitting on a gold mine, and we convinced Jason Hamlin of it, too. The problem was, Nick, that a few of our test subjects began developing a proclivity for violence. You met a couple of our failures. Henry Dean in New York. James Warren, now incarcerated in Wisconsin."

You're the one who told me to do it. Aren't you, Doc? James Warren, Nick realized, had mistaken him for Sam. Just like Daniel Scott, too, had confused him for one of the doctors treating the homeless.

"We needed a control subject to test the drug on. You know what a control subject is, don't you, Nick?" The doctor looked at Nick expectantly, as if he thought Nick would answer. "A control is someone without schizophrenia. A subject whose reaction to the drug we could test and analyze apart from any mental illness. It was Sam's idea to test the drug on you, Nick. Not mine."

"No." Nick's teeth were gritted together. The Velcro made a loud scraping noise as he levered his forearm. All he had to do was get one hand free, and he would be able to tear the other restraints off as well. "No. You're lying."

The doctor was undisturbed by the rip of the Velcro. "You must be able to see the irony, Nick. Not only did the drug give you—a relatively normal subject—exacerbated schizophrenic symptoms, it brought out a very definite violent tendency in you, too. I don't know the history between your brother and you, but as a psychiatrist I'd say there wasn't too much love lost on either side, eh, Nick? Jackson Ferry—another one of our subjects—attacked Sam. It seems he didn't like being a human guinea pig. It seems he didn't like your brother any more than you did, Nick. He attacked Sam and you. You defended yourself. But then when Ferry left, you finished the job. You killed your brother yourself."

At last, with an abrupt rip, the Velcro gave under the force of his effort. Nick's arm flew up from the chair's rail. His fingers attached themselves to the doctor's throat. They dug into the doctor's flesh, rending his windpipe, ripping his arteries. But the doctor continued smiling. He didn't even move to react.

Nick looked down at his hands, realizing with a shock that he was still strapped to the chair. He hadn't busted through the Velcro at all. He began to cry, whimpering, tossing his head from side to side.

"I understand exactly how you feel, Nick."

"Please," Nick shouted. *Please!*

"You hate me so much right now you would kill me, eh? You'd strangle me to death if you could, wouldn't you? Stabbing is more your thing, though, I suppose." The doctor chuckled, then straightened his legs and stood back up. At the same time he reached a hand into his jacket pocket and pulled out a syringe and a needle wrapped in clear plastic. The needle's wrapping fluttered like a butterfly, hanging in the air for a moment before dropping to the ground. The doctor attached the needle to the plunger, then reached into his other pocket and withdrew a small vial of clear liquid. "You have so much methamphetamine in your system right now, Nick," he said, puncturing the top of the vial with the needle and drawing some of its clear fluid into the syringe, "that a small dose of an MAOI should be enough to give you a good old-fashioned heart attack." Barnes looked down at Nick, his mouth stretched into a cruel smile.

As the doctor turned his attention back to the syringe, Nick caught sight of something else behind him: *a man approaching him.*

Nick had no idea how the man had gotten there. He had no idea whether he was real or another hallucination. He simply appeared behind Barnes. Nick looked over the doctor's shoulder, trying to make sense of the man's face. His features were blurred and jumbled, and Nick had only the faintest idea who the man was.

"And if you're lucky enough to survive the heart attack, Nick," Barnes was continuing, oblivious to the man behind him, "your brain will be so badly damaged that I doubt you'll be telling anyone anything about our little conversation. I doubt you'll even remember it yourself."

The doctor finished filling the entire syringe with fluid, then, squirting a little from the needle, lowered the lethal injection toward Nick's arm. His hand was steady. The needle glinted in the sunlight. Nick felt sweat break out on his forehead.

The man behind the doctor was resolving himself into Jackson Ferry. Nick was certain as the needle punctured his bicep that he was only imagining him there. Ferry, dressed in white, his ravaged face twisted with repressed rage, was nothing more than another figment from the recesses of his mind, a memory from the night he had burst from the shadows when Sam was killed. As the apparition raised its fists into the air, however, Nick remembered that Ferry, too, had been incarcerated at Western State Hospital, pending his trial for Sam's murder.

When Ferry brought his fists down onto the back of the doctor's head, the doctor crashed forward onto Nick, plunging the syringe deep into his arm. The needle tore through his muscle and dug itself into his bone, but the doctor never pushed the plunger into the tube of the injector. The fluid inside the syringe remained where it was.

Nick watched helplessly as Ferry battered Barnes in the face with his fists. Blood splattered the white legs of his hospital-issue trousers as Ferry took his thumbs and dug them into the doctor's bright blue eyes, gouging them from the sockets, plunging his thumbs deep into the doctor's skull. When the eyeballs popped out from the doctor's head, dangling loosely from his stretched optic nerves, Ferry began to laugh.

And Nick at last began to scream.

Part 6

chapter 34

Three days before Christmas, Nick was sitting on a steel cot in the Seattle jail, his head in his hands, his fingers buried in his unwashed hair. It had been a grueling period of days since Jackson Ferry had escaped from the hospital yard and killed Barnes. Nick had been transferred to the jail the day before, but only after undergoing an extensive psychiatric evaluation at Western State. The drugs that the doctor had been feeding him inside the ward were just now receding from his system.

Nick looked up at the approach of footsteps. His eyes were ringed with dark circles, because he was still having trouble sleeping, and his vision was bleary. He was feeling much more alert than he had for some time, however, and he was able to track the blur of movement through the steel bars.

When Nick saw Stolie, a smile spread across his face, and he stood from the cot to greet him. The detective had visited him the day before, too, and he had assured

Nick that he would do everything he could to secure his quick release.

"I have some good news for you, Nick," the detective announced as he approached the cell. He turned to the guard on duty at a small steel desk just beyond the holding area and asked him to slide back the motorized outer doors. "The prisoner has made bail," he told the guard. "I have the papers here. He's to be released into my custody." Stolie set the small briefcase he was carrying down on the floor and pulled a couple of loosely folded papers from his back pocket, then tossed them on the desk. "Just a few more signatures," he said to Nick over his shoulder, "and I'll have you out of there."

Nick watched the detective sign his name onto the forms. "Who paid my bail?" he thought to ask, clinging to the steel bars that still separated them.

"No 'thanks'? Just who paid?"

Nick smiled. "You have no idea how grateful I am to you. It's just that bail was set at five hundred thousand. I don't know anyone with that kind of money."

The guard buzzed open the remaining door. Nick watched the detective grip one of its heavy bars and slide it back on its rails. He had to fight the urge to leap from his confinement. "Come on," the detective said. "Let's get out of here."

They were walking down the wide corridor when Nick realized how somber Stolie looked. "You've made yourself some real enemies in the department," the detective said, as though he were answering a question that Nick had posed.

"I imagine that means you have, too."

The detective flashed Nick a strained smile. "I suppose. But it's not my head in the noose."

"So tell me, who paid for my release?" Nick asked him again as they approached the jail's two-story lobby.

"You have an appetite for some eggs and bacon?"

Nick shook his head. "Coffee, maybe."

"You're looking pretty damned thin."

"I haven't felt like eating much."

"Okay, coffee, then." The detective's voice echoed through the tall, empty lobby as he pushed open the front doors. "Let me buy you a cup across the street before I let you go, and I'll catch you up." He looked up to measure how hard the rain was falling, then, hunching slightly, placed a hand on Nick's shoulder and guided him down the concrete staircase.

"So like I said," Stolie began as he joined Nick at the bar lining the plate-glass window, handing him a coffee in a tall white paper cup, "you've managed to collect a number of enemies in the department. You might have passed your psych tests with flying colors and impressed the doctors over at the hospital, but as far as the lieutenant is concerned, you're no less guilty today than you were last month."

"Lieutenant Dombrowski?" Nick asked.

"Yeah, Lieutenant Dombrowski. He showed up at your bail hearing himself and personally begged Judge Fong to lock you up and throw away the key." The detective smiled. "He thinks you've got us all fooled. You're a psycho serial killer, and the last thing we should be doing is letting you out on the street. He doesn't buy into any of the Dr. Barnes stuff. He's even talking about a conspiracy between you and Ferry."

"What about all the drugs in my blood?" Nick pointed out. "What does he make of that?"

The detective shrugged. "Says you could have been taking them yourself. Look, Nick, I don't mean to be freaking you out with any of this. I'm only telling you because I think you should know. With Gutterson stepping down, Dombrowski's been made the acting chief. The department is going to be watching you, making sure you keep your hands clean. I've got my orders, too. One false move and you're back behind bars without bail."

Nick nodded. "Thanks. I appreciate the heads-up."

"Yeah, well—the truth is, it looks like you've made a few friends, too."

"What's that?"

"Your bail. The five hundred thousand. It was picked up by Sara Garland."

"By Sara?" Nick remembered her standing next to him in the doorway into Jason Hamlin's room. *Don't touch me! Get away from me!* He cringed, remembering the streaks of blood covering his T-shirt and jeans, the small chunks of gore that had been stuck to his hands and arms. He chased the image from his mind.

"I haven't spoken to her myself," Stolie said.

Nick remembered the horror in her eyes.

"But she's standing with you, Nick. I think she wants to see you again." The detective took a sip of his coffee, then set the cup down and gave Nick a long, assessing stare. "Just keep in mind you're out of jail on borrowed time. You're not a free man yet. There's an evidentiary hearing scheduled for January fifteenth—three weeks from now. After that, it will be up to the DA whether to take you to trial for Jason Hamlin's murder. Your brother's, too."

"That's what the public defender told me."

"You're going to have some pretty powerful people in the department gunning for you at that hearing."

Nick took the information in. Still untouched, his coffee was growing cold in his hand.

"Myself, Nick, I'm going to do everything I can in the meantime to see that you're not only exonerated, but that you don't stand trial at all. As far as I'm concerned, we've got all the evidence we need right here." The detective lifted the small briefcase he had been carrying onto the table between them.

"My computer," Nick said.

"That's right. You remember that insurance policy Sam bought over the summer when he borrowed your computer? It turns out Sam was exchanging e-mails with Barnes over the summer, too, and your laptop here automatically made a copy of all the e-mails he sent."

"The e-mails confirm that Sam and Barnes were working together?" Nick surmised.

The detective tapped Nick lightly on the shoulder. "Your brother wasn't very discreet. Barnes himself didn't leave much of a trail, but your brother said enough so that we can pretty much piece the whole chain of events together. It's just like you said—Barnes and your brother were testing their new drug on human subjects without their knowledge, and at higher doses the drug was causing some pretty psychotic behavior."

"I still have trouble believing that Sam would poison me." The disbelief was evident in Nick's voice.

"He stood to make millions," Stolic reminded him. "And for what it's worth, as far as I'm concerned, the doctor was the ringleader anyway. You know what I discovered, Nick? It turns out the doctor had a vacation house on a certain island on the Puget Sound."

"San Juan Island?"

"That's right. Not as grand as the Hamlins', but only a couple of miles away. I don't have proof yet, but my guess is that Barnes was on the island the same time you were, the night of Hamlin's murder. I'm heading up there myself this afternoon to question the caretakers at the Hamlin estate. Barnes set you up, Nick. Our forensic tests are going to find evidence linking him to the crime scene. Or maybe we'll turn up something proving that Hamlin had found out about the doctor's conspiracy. One way or another, I'm sure we'll be able to trace the entire scheme back to the doctor."

Nick closed his eyes, considering the idea. For weeks he had been haunted by the vision of a shadowy figure standing in Jason Hamlin's room next to him, looking down at Hamlin's mutilated corpse. He tried now to bring the image into his mind, but could barely hang onto it. Was it Barnes? He wanted to believe it, but he couldn't be certain that he was remembering anything definite. As far as he knew, Barnes may well have been right. The shadowy figure he had seen in Hamlin's room might have been himself. The drugs had been splitting his identity into fragments.

"I don't know," he said, looking down at the cold cup of coffee cradled in his hands. "Sometimes I think I can remember someone there with me the night Sam was murdered. But then I can remember holding the knife that killed him myself." He glanced at the detective. "And I think maybe I can remember standing over Hamlin's body with a knife in my hand. Bits and pieces, you know? Things come back to me from those nights, but not everything. I don't know. I just can't remember."

The detective regarded him. "Maybe it will come back to you once the drugs are completely gone from your blood," he said. "I hear the doctors are weaning you off them gradually."

"Some of them are pretty powerful," Nick acknowledged. "You can't just stop taking them. I'm feeling better every day, though."

"I'm sure it will make sense soon enough, Nick. And in the meantime, like I say I'll do what I can to nail down your innocence." The detective took another large swallow of his coffee, then pushed the briefcase across the table toward Nick. "Here you go. This belongs to you. We've copied everything we need from the hard disk." He reached into his back pocket and took out his wallet, then pulled out a few twenties, setting them carefully on top of the black nylon briefcase.

"I can't possibly take that," Nick said, looking at the money.

Stolie smiled. "I can't give you a ride back to your apartment." He stood up. "Like I told you, I'm on my way back up to the island now. You're going to have to catch a cab."

Nick was broke. He hesitated, then took the money and slipped it into his pocket. He didn't know how to thank Stolie, so he didn't try.

In the taxi, Nick gave Laura Daly a call. The editor was relieved to hear from him. "I've been worried, Nick," she said. "I was going to visit you today, to see if there was something I could do. From a legal standpoint, I mean."

"Sara bailed me out," Nick informed her.

The editor took in the information. "She's more solid than I first thought," she admitted.

"I might still need your help, Laura."

"What's up?"

"Not immediately. Stolie tells me the police are still pursuing me, though. As far as Dombrowski's concerned, the case isn't closed yet."

"Barnes had his prints all over this thing," Daly insisted. "The police have got to see that."

"Dombrowski's never liked me," Nick said. "He's been dogging me from the start."

"We'll talk once you've had a chance to rest. I know some lawyers who'll love nothing more than to take Dombrowski on." The editor wanted to reassure Nick. "We'll see you through this. You can be certain of that."

"I don't know why you're doing this, Laura."

Daly ignored the implicit question. "So what's next? Where are you now?"

"On my way home." Nick shrugged. "I don't know. I thought maybe I'd try to see Sara."

"Are you sure that's a good idea?" Daly asked, too quickly. She hadn't been able to disguise her apprehension, and Nick understood from her tone that it wasn't for him that she was afraid. *She was afraid of what he might do.*

"Don't worry, Laura," Nick said dryly. "I'm feeling better. I'm not going to hurt her." He had managed to keep his voice light. He found himself wondering, though, whether he would ever be free from suspicion. In the end, if it came to a trial, his best defense might be that he wasn't responsible for whatever he had done. "I didn't kill anyone," he said into the phone. He wasn't talking to Daly anymore, he was talking to himself. "I couldn't have."

"I didn't mean—" Daly faltered. "I just meant the police will be watching to see what you do," she said, trying to recover herself. "Especially if what you say about Dombrowski is true."

"I appreciate your concern."

"Just get some rest," the editor said. "You've been through a scare."

Nick hung up the call. It had been more than a scare. Daly was right, though. What he needed now was sleep.

chapter 35

The rain had let up, and the asphalt was shimmering in weak sunlight. Reflections of the sky were trapped in puddles scattered across the pavement, as though the atmosphere had shattered, Nick thought, and lay in a million pieces on the ground.

When Nick stepped from the taxi, Sara's car was parked in the middle of the lot behind Nick's apartment building, jets of steamy exhaust billowing from its twin tailpipes. His heart leapt in his chest when he saw her profile in the driver's-side window. Sara turned to face him as he crossed the rain-soaked lot, and their eyes met through the tinted glass. Nick hesitated in midstep, nervous, anxious not to disappoint her.

Sara didn't roll down her window as he approached. Instead, she pushed the door open and flew into his arms. Her skin felt cool and soft in his hands, against his cheek. He could barely comprehend the intensity of her desire, but he didn't question it. He needed her, too. Without Sara, he would have nothing left. "I didn't expect you," Nick said. "I wasn't sure I was ever going to see you again."

Sara took a small step back from him, holding his arms in her hands and looking into his eyes, a slightly quizzical look on her face. "How can you say that, Nick?"

Nick shook his head. A rush of words came to his lips, but there was too much he wanted to say.

"I have faith in you," Sara said. "I *know* you. You didn't kill your brother, and you didn't kill Jason. You're not capable of it. I'm the one to blame. I'm the one who took you to see Dr. Barnes, and I'm the reason you trusted him. It's unspeakable, the things he did to you." She took his hands and lifted them to her lips. "I'm only glad that you're still alive, darling. I can't think what would have happened if that man—Jackson Ferry—hadn't attacked Dr. Barnes. You'd be dead, Nick. And I'd be alone."

They stared at one another without speaking.

"I'll never be able to repay you," he said at last, "for the money you posted for my bail."

Sara shrugged her shoulders. "This car's worth three times the amount I had to put up to secure the bond. I would have put up a hundred times as much to get you out a day earlier."

Nick's face was buried in her long silky hair. "I think I really do love you, Sara," he said. "And it scares me."

"I love you, too, Nick." She raised her hands to his shoulders and pushed him back from her, so that she could look into his eyes. "But it doesn't scare me. It excites me." She reassured him with a broad smile. Nick became aware, belatedly, of a rhythmic high-pitched tone emanating from the Mercedes. He turned to glance at the car, realizing that its door was still ajar and that Sara had left the engine running.

"Aren't you coming inside?" he asked her. "Aren't you going to stay?"

Sara laughed. "I didn't come here to stay with you," she said lightly. "I came here to pick you up and bring you home with me."

Nick looked at her in question. She had never once invited him to the house in Bellevue. The only time he had seen it was when he followed her there, that same morning that he had seen her disappear into the Four Seasons Hotel. Nick found himself overcome with memories of the two of them together in his small studio. Lying in bed. Waking up in the middle of the night to run downtown and find a place to eat. Sitting on the pathetic sofa reading, Sara's head heavy in his lap. As dazed as Nick had become in the last weeks, these had been some of the most powerful, most meaningful moments of his life.

"The house is mine now, Nick," Sara said. "There's no need for us to stay here in this ridiculous little apartment any longer. My mother is away, down in San Francisco with her sister. They invited me to come down, too—for Christmas—but I wanted to be here with you."

"I hadn't realized." It hadn't crossed Nick's mind that the estate would belong to Sara now that Jason Hamlin was dead. "Jason didn't have any children of his own?"

Sara frowned at the idea. "He was a bachelor until he met my mom. I told you that." She leaned forward and gave Nick another tight hug. "Wait until you see the house, darling. You're not going to believe how beautiful it is."

Nick glanced up at the windows of his apartment. "Maybe I should get a few of my things together," he said. "I don't know, some of my clothes. A toothbrush." Relaxing, realizing how lucky he was, he laughed. "Are we going to be there long?"

Sara tugged his hands. "I'll stay here with the car. But don't keep me waiting. Grab enough for a couple days. After that, we'll go shopping. I want to wipe the slate clean, Nick. I mean it. I want to start fresh in every way."

Nick stood by himself on the pier behind the Hamlin estate. The view over Lake Washington, looking back at the city of Seattle, was extraordinary. The gigantic mansion dominated this corner of the bay. From where he stood, Nick was able to see a number of the other houses along the shore, set in lavish gardens, surrounded by lush evergreen trees. A seaplane like the one Hamlin had piloted to San Juan Island was descending toward the small airport in Renton, at the southern end of the lake. In the far distance Mount Rainier was crowned with a cap of white snow, blending into the clouds as the sky emptied of color.

At his back, the grounds behind the Hamlin house stepped up from the pier on a series of terraces. A tennis court was carved so discreetly into the side of the bluff that it complemented the landscaping. A huge light blue pool could just as easily have been an elegant fountain. Nick had never experienced wealth like this before. He had never even imagined that wealth on this scale could exist. It seemed inconceivable that a single man could earn enough in a lifetime to own an estate like this one—let alone the house on San Juan Island and the vineyard in Napa, and who knew what else as well.

This was what Sam wanted to grab for himself. This was the prize Sam had had his eyes on. This was what Sam had been willing to risk the sanity of his own brother to attain: a life led in a house on the shore of a lake of sapphire water, on the edge of this rainy city, lost in the far corner of the Pacific North-

west. Nick was all at once overcome with a memory of the house he and Sam had grown up in, and a sad smile flitted across his face. As fiercely competitive as Sam had always been, it had never occurred to him back then that he didn't have everything he would ever in his life need, right there on his doorstep. The two brothers had always had everything they could conceive of in each other. *When had that comfortable happiness been lost?*

"Sam was still alive when Jackson Ferry took my shoes and left me in the parking lot," Nick recalled out loud.

Standing at the end of the pier, he closed his eyes against the seductive view and tried to remember the course of events the night that Sam was murdered. It felt like something that had happened twenty years before. Little pieces of the tragedy stuck with him in snapshots: His hand on the handle of the knife as it slid into Sam's chest. Jackson Ferry's face emerging suddenly from the pitch black shadows. Standing barefoot on the pavement in Elliott Bay Park. His memory broke down, though, when he tried to string the images together. Try as he might, there were black periods he couldn't seem to fill with any color.

"I was on the ground," Nick said under his breath, trying to give shape to the unease gnawing at the back of his mind, "lying on my stomach when Ferry took my shoes." He remembered trying to turn over. He tried to resist the homeless man, but couldn't. "He shoved his foot into my back. He took my shoes, then he left. I turned over and got up onto my knees and found Sam." Once again, Nick closed his eyes, squeezing them shut to try to recall the image to his mind. "I reached down. I was about to check his pulse. And then something happened, and Sam opened his eyes."

Sam's cell phone had rung in his jacket pocket.

Nick opened his eyes. The sun had continued to set, and the heavier clouds above him had turned into charcoal. Farther off, a patch of blue sky had become blood red. Across the water, the color was trapped in the windows of the taller buildings, glimmering as if they had caught fire. "Did I answer the phone?" he whispered.

"Yes. I took it from Sam's pocket, and I flipped it open."

It's Sam. He's been stabbed. Send an ambulance now, please. We're on the waterfront, just beneath Pike Place Market. Hurry, please. Hurry!

"Who was it?" Nick asked himself. "Who called Sam? Was it someone I knew?" He shook his head. Someone was walking toward him from the shadows. He could hear the footsteps in his mind. The person's shoes scraped on the gravel. And then nothing. "There was someone else there," Nick said. He narrowed his eyes and pursed his lips, trying to force himself to remember. "Or was it just the drugs?" he asked himself, frustrated. "No, I'm sure someone else was there. There must have been."

Nick was so wrapped up in his thoughts that he didn't hear Sara approach. She came up behind him, carrying a tall crystal flute of champagne in either hand. "Are you feeling well enough for a small celebration?"

Nick was startled by her voice. A burst of adrenaline spiked his heart, and for a second he felt himself overcome with a now familiar feeling of dizziness and disorientation. He fought to maintain control. "The doctors said I should be careful drinking any alcohol for the next few weeks," he said. He smiled, dazzled by Sara's extraordinary beauty. She had changed from her jeans into a long white dress, the fabric so sheer that he could see the outline of her body beneath. Its wide train billowed behind her in the breeze. Relaxing, he took a cold, frosty glass of champagne from her hand. He was aware of its crisp taste on his lips as she kissed him. When she leaned away from him, he got lost in her eyes.

"I heard you saying something as I came up," she said, clinking his glass with her own before taking a sip of her champagne. "Were you on the phone?"

"Hmmm? No." Nick shook his head. "Just talking to myself a little." He laughed awkwardly. "Nothing important."

Sara gave him a look of concern, then let her face soften into a smile. "To you, Nick," she said, lifting her glass.

Nick shook his head somberly. "No."

A look of confusion crossed Sara's face. "No?"

"No," he repeated. "To you." Then he raised his glass to his lips and swallowed the champagne bottoms up.

chapter 36

They were walking hand in hand along the shore beside the pier when Nick was rocked by the first hallucination he had experienced since being released from the asylum. Dwarfed by the mansion above them, they were stepping over a litter of driftwood that had been carried in by the tide in front of the last few storms. Amid the calm, blissful beauty of the moment, Nick stopped short. His eyes opened wide with terror. Sara felt it in his fingers. His hand went stiff, and she turned to look at him. "Nick?" He didn't hear her, though. He was mesmerized, transfixed by the vision seizing his consciousness.

The light was dim inside the kitchen at the Hamlin house on San Juan Island. A window was open a crack, and a gauzy curtain was fluttering above the counter. Nick could feel the cold fingers of the weak breeze on his face as he looked down at an open drawer in front of him. His eyes were drawn to the dancing curtain. Small white pieces of moonlight seemed to be sewn into its fabric, and as it twisted and floated in the air, shadows played on the white marble countertop beneath it. Nick was hypnotized by the movement. Then he remembered his mission, and he returned his attention to the drawer, once again searching for a carving knife.

The carving knife with the Japanese writing on the blade, Nick. The largest carving knife in the drawer to the left of the sink.

Nick lifted a couple of utensils from the drawer, then spotted the knife. His hand was drawn to it like a magnet. He picked it up and held it in front of his face, twisting it from side to side in the moonlight. The light seemed to get trapped inside the herringbone ripples of its lethally sharp blade.

His hand was on a doorknob. It was a heavy brass doorknob, colder to the touch than the ambient air in the long hallway stretching the length of the second floor. He was aware of the knob's weight as he turned it. The door unlatched with a satisfying click, and Nick pushed it steadily open. He paused to pass the carving knife from his left to his right hand, then took a step inside the large, elegantly furnished room.

He became aware of Jason Hamlin's regular breathing before his eyes were able to adjust to the lack of light. The moon had drifted behind a few heavy storm clouds, and Nick stopped just inside the doorway, waiting until he was able to make sense of the fuzzy shapes hidden in the black and gray shadows enveloping the room.

Hamlin moved in the bed. Nick's eyes tracked the sound just as the moon peeked out from the clouds, shedding its light through a grid of small-paned windows, revealing the splendor of the huge bedroom. Hamlin was stretched out comfortably on the bed in front of him, his sleep made heavy by wine. Bluish light flickered on the floor as the clouds parted in front of the moon.

The illusion of movement confused Nick, and he stood stock still, his grip tightening on the handle of the knife. And in that moment, he became aware of a shadowy figure standing next to him. His heart leapt. *He wasn't in Hamlin's room alone.*

Someone else was there with him. He wasn't imagining it. *Someone was standing next to him, reaching out to touch his arm.*

"Nick? What is it, darling—Nick, talk to me." Sara's voice penetrated Nick's consciousness, bringing him back into the present. A small wave tumbled over the rocky beach in a salty froth, reaching his feet and splashing his ankles with surprising force.

"I don't know," Nick said. "I'm not sure. I've been feeling so well these last few days."

Blinking, trying to remain focused on the water running over his feet, he was nevertheless blinded by an image of Jason Hamlin's corpse, lying on his bed in a thick pool of drying blood. Nick brought his hands to his ears, trying to shield them from a sudden, deafening roar.

"What's happening, Nick? Tell me."

A second later, the sounds and images vanished as abruptly as they had appeared, replaced by Sara standing in front of him in the shadow of the Hamlin mansion, peering at him with gentle concern. "It's nothing," Nick mumbled. His legs felt weak underneath him. "I'm sure it's nothing. The doctors said I'd get flashbacks—that pieces of the last few months would force themselves into my consciousness from time to time."

Sara reached out and caressed his cheek, then let

her hand rest on his shoulder. "Shall we go back to the house? It's getting dark anyway, and it's been a long day. You're tired and hungry."

Nick allowed himself to be led back toward the mansion, a half step behind Sara as she guided him over the rocky beach to the lawn, then up the bluestone steps that ascended through a series of terraces to the marble porch off the living room. The house was lit inside with the intensity of a furnace, glistening through an arcade of glass doors. Nick felt winded from the short climb. His legs hadn't yet recovered from his incarceration, and he stopped at the top of the stairs to catch his breath, gazing inside the house at the impossibly opulent collection of furniture and art and Oriental rugs that Hamlin had amassed. "It's wonderful here," Sara said, following his stare, "isn't it?"

A piece of modern sculpture caught Nick's eye. A life-size bronze depicting a modern soldier in battle, dressed in full army gear but carrying an ancient Greek sword and shield. Nick's eyes were drawn to the sword. It was sharp enough, he imagined, to slice through skin if you were to run your finger down its length. The way the steel was glinting in the light fascinated him, dragging him back into his hallucination, and for a split second he was standing in the kitchen at the Hamlin house on San Juan Island, once again in front of the open drawer. The knife with the Japanese writing on its blade was clasped in his hand. Nick struggled to stay in the present, fighting the powerful image from his mind. He became aware, though, of a distant rumble in his ears, like an approaching train, and he knew that the crescendoing roar would bring another hallucination with it.

The knife with the Japanese characters on its blade

sliced through Jason Hamlin's throat, nearly severing his head from his body. It wasn't an easy cut to make. The sinews and muscles of the man's neck were stubborn, and they resisted the blade with the tension of tiny steel cables. The knife wanted to get lodged in the spinal cord at the back of the man's neck. The larynx punctured, then ripped. It was like cutting through a piece of nylon rope. Flesh tore audibly. Blood was everywhere, sticky on Nick's hands. *The hand on the knife isn't mine.* The disembodied voice echoed through Nick's head like a clap of thunder, and with it the image abruptly disappeared.

Nick hadn't moved. He was still standing in front of the doors leading into the living room. Now, though, Sara was hanging impaled from the sword in the bronze soldier's hand. Its razor-sharp blade jutted out from her chest, covered in blood. Her head was slumped forward, her arms dangling lifelessly at her sides. Her feet were suspended over a pool of coagulating blood.

Nick shrank from the vision, then fell to his knees, his hands over his eyes, then over his ears, his chest heaving with panic. *You killed Sam, Nick. You murdered Jason Hamlin and Ralph Van Gundy. And now you're going to kill Sara, too.*

Sara knelt down next to him. Nick was aware of her hands, soft and cold on his forehead and in his hair, gently stroking him on the back. "I'm no good, Sara," he heard himself say. "I'm a murderer."

"Shhh," she whispered.

"I'm afraid, Sara. I'm afraid I'm going to hurt you, too."

Sara took Nick into her arms. "Let's go inside," she said, drawing him to his feet. The crystal champagne flute fell from his hand as he tried to find his balance, shattering into a thousand pieces on the marble floor. "The champagne was a bad idea, darling. Let's get you into bed."

Nick woke up at the Hamlin estate on San Juan Island.

Sara was lying next to him in the double bed that had been made up by the Wheelers, in the third bedroom down the hallway that ran the length of the house. Nick moved to the edge of the mattress, then dropped his feet to the floor. The bed groaned beneath his shifting weight as he stood up. Moving stealthily to the window, he peered through a crack in the heavy curtains, watching the moon slip between two huge storm clouds, then gathered his clothes. He had set his jeans and T-shirt on the back of a chair, and he slipped them on. The floorboards creaked underneath him when he stood on a single foot to slide into the legs of his pants, but Sara didn't even murmur. As far as Nick could tell, she was sound asleep.

He let himself out into the long hallway, then closed the door behind him. The latch snapped into place with a click. The household was asleep. The hum of an old electric clock in the kitchen vibrated throughout the house. Nick stood entirely still for a moment, listening. Then he made his way down the long, wide corridor to the top of the stairs, one slow step after another, the wood plank floor cold on his feet.

He crossed the dining room into the kitchen. *Sara hasn't mentioned you to us once since the night of the fundraiser. Has she, Jillian?* The moonlight was dancing on one of the curtains—a single curtain hanging loose over an open window. Nick paused halfway across the kitchen, hypnotized. Then he crossed the rest of the way to the counter, reaching for the drawer just to the left of the sink.

The carving knife with the Japanese writing on the blade, Nick. The largest carving knife in the drawer to the left of the sink.

Nick grasped the heavy knife. It was perfectly balanced. A beautiful knife with an eight-inch hardened steel blade and a handle made of mahogany. He admired it in the dazzling light of the moon. Slivers of light scintillated like strands of gems in its oily sheen. He measured its weight, twisted it slowly in the air. He wasn't sure how long he had been standing there before he realized that he wasn't in the kitchen alone.

He turned, raising his eyes in surprise. And as he turned, he realized that he wasn't at the Hamlin house on San Juan Island at all. He was standing instead in the unfamiliar kitchen of the Bellevue estate, with no recollection of how he had come there. Sara was standing next to him, peering at him curiously. A sour taste came to his mouth. He had to think before he recognized the flavor of the champagne.

"You were there in the kitchen," Nick said. "I took the knife. But you were there in the kitchen, too, Sara, the night that Jason Hamlin was killed."

Sara hovered in front of him in the dim light of the room. When a wave of dizziness nearly knocked him from his feet, a smile spread slowly across her impossibly beautiful face. Grimacing, Nick reached for the counter. He managed to remain on his feet for a few seconds longer, then at last took a drunken step away from the counter and tumbled onto the floor. His eyes closed on his way down, and the blur of his shadowy fall melted into peaceful blackness.

* * *

Nick was lying facedown on the asphalt. Chunks of gravel were stuck to his cheek, and his skin was badly scraped. His head had hit the pavement, and a lump had formed on his forehead, throbbing painfully. When he moved his mouth to speak, sharp blades of pain shot through his jaw. For a moment he was blind, his eyes were burning as though he were staring into the sun.

Jackson Ferry was tugging at his feet. When he began to twist around, Ferry plunged one of his bare feet into the small of his back, shoving him down into the asphalt, once again grinding his cheek against the pavement. "You're just as diseased as I am, you hopeless son of a bitch," Ferry said. His voice was raspy and guttural, but surprisingly clear. Nick tried one more time to twist around. "You don't know what's real and what isn't," the homeless man said to him. "I know. It's the same for me. One minute I'm in the here and now. The next I'm somewhere else." He stopped moving. "You and I are brothers," he said. Then he savagely yanked the Nikes from Nick's feet. His own foot was still resting on the small of Nick's back, and he shoved him forward again, even more violently. Nick felt the skin peel from his face.

Nick turned over when Ferry let him go, but gingerly. He didn't try to struggle to his feet. His ribs were sore, and he was having difficulty breathing. He raised his head off the ground and watched Ferry sit down between Sam and him and pull his shoes on, his straggly hair covering his face, a few oily strands caught in his purplish, festering lips. The homeless man stood up. "I feel sorry for you," he said. He looked down at Sam, sneering hatefully. "Him, no. Him, I wanted to kill. I had to kill him, man, to get him out of my head." He flashed a gruesome toothless smile. "You know what I mean, don't you? I can see it in your eyes, man. You're one of his guinea pigs, too."

Nick hunched over his brother's body, cataloging the damage that Ferry had inflicted upon him. The knife was lying on the ground next to him, its blade sharp beneath Nick's knee. The homeless man had slashed Sam's face, and part of his cheek was hanging from the bone. His mouth was a bloody pulp, nearly unrecognizable. His teeth had been kicked into his throat. He was bleeding profusely from the wounds that Ferry had left in his torso. Nick's hands shook as he reached down toward his brother's face, thinking to caress him, perhaps to look for a pulse. His fingers were just above his brother's torn cheek when the cell phone in Sam's jacket rang. And Sam opened his eyes.

"Sam," Nick said spontaneously. "My God, Sam."

Sam gazed up at his brother, but his eyes didn't focus. His head was beginning to tremble and jerk in the beginning stages of a seizure. Nick placed his hands on Sam's shoulders, trying to still him.

The phone sounded again in Sam's pocket, and Nick reached for it. It didn't matter who was calling. All that mattered was that he get help. Sam would die without medical attention. Perhaps it was already too late. Nick searched his brother's pockets for the phone. Examining it as he figured out how to take the call, he recognized the incoming number on the phone's caller ID. His first reaction was simply relief. It was Sara calling. *Sara.* She would know what to do. She would call an ambulance.

Then it registered with Nick: *Sara was calling Sam's phone.*

Nick took the call. "Sara, thank God it's you," he said into the phone, practically shouting. "It's Sam. He's been stabbed. Send an ambulance now, please. We're on the waterfront, just beneath Pike Place Market. Hurry, please. Hurry!"

Nick was sitting in the same place ten minutes later, bent over Sam's body, watching his brother bleed to death, when the scrape of footsteps on the gravelly pavement echoed across the parking lot. Beneath his hands, Sam was gasping for air, whimpering and crying as he died. Behind him, Nick became aware of the waves splashing against the waterfront and the occasional sound of boats and voices over the bay.

Nick looked up at the indistinct figure emerging from the fog and shadows encircling the parking lot.

Nick opened his eyes.

The darkness resolved itself improbably into one of the lavish bathrooms in the Hamlins' Bellevue estate. The marble floor was unforgivingly hard underneath him, and the porcelain edge of the toilet was digging into his shoulder. *What was he doing there?* His vision blurred, and the bathroom disintegrated into millions of tiny black-and-white dots.

Nick was sitting in the familiar, beaten-up front seat of his old Toyota. He opened his eyes wider, trying to figure out where he was, trying to make sense of the buildings and people surrounding the car. His eyes were drawn to the red glow of the traffic light across the intersection. Then the light became a smear as Nick's eyes focused instead on the white-faced skyscraper looming behind it: the Four Seasons Hotel. Nick leaned forward in his seat, his hands wrapped around the thin plastic steering wheel. He was trying to get a good view of Sara through the misty windshield as she stepped from her Mercedes. A tall doorman from the hotel, dressed in a long black coat and top hat, stepped smartly around her car and opened her door, then helped her to her feet. "Good morning, Ms. Hamlin," the doorman said. "Welcome back to the Four Seasons Hotel."

As the traffic moved, Nick's eyes were drawn to the unexpected figure of a man approaching Sara from where he had been hidden, beneath the canopy sheltering the hotel's carriageway. The doorman was leading Sara around her imposing car, and he blocked Nick's view just as the man stepped from the shadows to greet Sara. Nick watched as Sara's hand fell intimately to the man's waist. The man tried to find her lips with his own, but Sara pulled away from him, glancing back over her shoulder. She took his hand instead, and playfully pulled him with her toward the hotel entrance, eagerly anticipating the sex that would follow. Nick hadn't once seen the man's face. Still, Nick would have recognized the man anywhere. He knew this man better than he knew anyone else on the face of the planet.

Sara had snuck out of the apartment that morning not just to be with another man, she had slipped out to make love to Sam.

The light was switched on inside the huge bathroom at the Hamlins' Bellevue estate, blazing into Nick's retinas with the intensity of sunlight. He squinted, trying to decipher the shapes around him. The room was more than twenty feet wide, luxuriously appointed with its own fireplace. A series of recessed canister lights above the long mirror at the double sink shone down onto the floor.

Nick couldn't move his arms to shield his eyes. Sweat broke out on his forehead. A rope bound his arms and his legs, pinning them together. He tried to struggle, straining against his bonds. Finally, realizing that he couldn't free himself, he gave up.

When he laid his head back on the hard floor, he became aware of the voices. Clenching his teeth, he raised his head off the floor again and squinted in the direction of the conversation.

Nick was standing in the kitchen in the house on San Juan Island, hypnotized by the moonlight dancing on the curtain above the open drawer. "Take that one," Sara said to him. She was standing beside him, pointing toward one of the knives in the drawer. Nick turned to face her, surprised to see her next to him. "That one, darling," she said again. "The largest carving knife in the drawer to the left of the sink. The carving knife with the Japanese writing on the blade." He lifted a couple of utensils from the drawer, then grasped the knife and held it in front of his face, twisting it from side to side in the moonlight. "Follow me, Nick," Sara said. "We have an important job to do."

Nick's hand rested on a heavy brass doorknob. He was aware of its weight as he turned it. "Go on," Sara said. "Open the door." The catch unlatched with a satisfying click, and Nick pushed the door open. He paused to pass the carving knife back to his right hand, then took a step inside the large room. When Hamlin moved in the bed, Nick's eyes tracked the sound. Sara laid a hand on Nick's shoulder to reassure him. The pressure of her fingers sent shivers of pleasure radiating through his body. Sara had told him that she loved him. Jason

Hamlin was threatening her. He had raped her, and now Sara was asking Nick to protect her. Nick shifted the heavy, balanced knife from one hand to the other. He would do whatever Sara asked him to. He took a step closer to the bed. The floorboards creaked beneath his feet.

When the moon peeked from behind the clouds, the shadows directly in front of Nick shifted, and Jason Hamlin's silhouette became visible against the wall behind his large, antique bed. Hamlin cleared his throat. "Sara?" he said in confusion, peering vaguely into the moonlit darkness. "Jillian?"

Nick felt Sara's hand on his shoulder, urging him forward. Hamlin's eyes opened wide in shock. They seemed to be focused on something specific. At first Nick thought it was the knife in his hand. Hamlin was looking past him, though. Nick followed the older man's eyes. The blade of a second knife, identical to the one in his hand, glinted in the moonlight. Jillian emerged from the shadows.

"You hold on to Nick," Jillian ordered Sara. "Don't let him get in the way." She reached the bedside before her husband was able to react. Sara clamped her arms around Nick, wrenching him to the ground. Nick heard Jillian's knife plunge into Hamlin's chest. The man didn't make a sound. He fell back onto the bed in a torrent of blood. Nick watched from the floor as Jillian savagely ripped her husband's throat from ear to ear.

"Bring Nick here," Jillian instructed her daughter. "We need to get his hands wet with this blood."

Lying with his head on the marble floor, Nick tried to focus on the reflections in the large mirror above the sink. Sara and her mother were standing on the far side of the bathroom.

"We've got to be careful," Jillian was telling her daughter, "to make sure that we don't bruise his wrists and ankles with that rope. This has to look like a suicide."

"We'll do it now while he's still unconscious," Sara said. "No one is going to question this, Mom. The whole police department knows he's insane."

Nick strained to raise his head off the floor, and bit by bit he brought the two women into focus. "You poisoned me," he said. His lips were so chapped that they split as he spoke, and the rancid flavor of his own blood filled his mouth.

The bathroom fell silent. Sara and her mother exchanged a meaningful glance. Then Sara turned to her lover, and their eyes met across the huge bathroom in the house she had inherited upon her stepfather's death.

Slowly, a lurid smile spread across her face.

chapter 37

Nick became aware of his cell phone in the back pocket of his jeans. His mind was hazy, working laboriously. His hands were roped tightly together, but, struggling hard, he could move them side to side. He fought to lift his head, working to bring the huge bathroom back into focus. He must have blacked out again.

Sara had left the room, and Jillian was washing her hands at the sink, a look of concentration on her face. After toweling dry, she slipped on a pair of latex gloves, then crossed to the far end of the bathroom and dimmed the lights. Nick twisted to one side, straining to reach his phone. The rope cut sharply into his wrists, and the hard, cold floor dug into his hip. He gritted his teeth and found the edge of his back pocket with his fingers, then clamped down on his abs. At last, the phone was in his hand.

Holding it at his side to keep the light of its LCD display hidden, Nick flipped the phone open. Nick had programmed Stolie's number into the phone's memory some time back, and he brought the number up with the press of a few digits. His thumb was on the send button when Sara stepped back into the bathroom, carrying a knife from the kitchen. He was aware of the echo of her shoes on the marble floor before he saw her. He pressed the button, then kept his fingers over the phone's earpiece, muffling its sound. As Sara addressed her mother, he could hear Stolie's voice faintly on the other end of the line, and his heart leapt with relief. After a few seconds, though, Nick realized that the detective hadn't picked up the phone after all. The call had gone straight to the policeman's voice mail. A jolt of panic coursed through Nick's body as he remembered that Stolie had told him earlier that day that he was heading back up to San Juan Island.

He didn't have much time. Sara and her mother were conferring across the bathroom, preparing to kill him in cold blood, just as they had killed Jason Hamlin. His mind was reeling. His wrists were aching beneath the knotted ropes. He had to act now.

Fumbling the small phone in his hands, he used his thumb to press 9-1-1 into the keypad. His fingers were tingling. The nylon rope was beginning to tear his skin. The phone was slipping from his hand. He made one last effort to hold onto it, but it slid free, and he let it go. It dropped down next to him noiselessly, tangled in his T-shirt, just out of his reach. Nick lay back hopelessly on the floor. He didn't know whether he had hit the send button. The last thing he was aware of as he lost consciousness was the beat of Sara's footsteps approaching him, echoing against the tiled walls of the bathroom like footsteps in a crypt.

* * *

Sara was leaning over him, the knife in her left hand, her right hand gloved in latex, clasping his wrist. She had lifted his arms and was examining the damage Nick had caused himself with the nylon rope. His skin was broken, and Sara was wondering whether a forensic investigation would be able to reveal that he had been tied up. Halogen light reflected off the thin silver chain around Sara's neck, stinging Nick's eyes. "How are you doing, darling?" she asked when she realized that he was watching her.

"You poisoned me, Sara," he said.

"I know I did."

"What was in it? What did you put in my champagne?"

"What do you think, Nick? I didn't want to add a new drug to the cocktail in your system. It wouldn't do for the police to become suspicious."

"And now you're going to kill me."

"Shhh." She held an index finger dramatically to her lips. Despite himself, Nick could not believe how beautiful she was. "Soon enough, my darling," she said. "Very soon."

"Why?"

Sara laughed. She looked around the palatial bathroom. "You have to ask me why, Nick?"

"Why *me*?"

"Because you loved me," she responded. "Because you're a fool. And because you had a brother jealous enough to kill you himself. Sam was the one who suggested I pick you up at the coffee shop. Have you figured that out yet? You and I didn't meet by accident. This whole thing was Sam's idea. And he was right, Nick. You made the perfect sacrifice."

"You killed Jason Hamlin," Nick said, trying not to slur his words. "You killed your own stepfather. And now you're going to make it look like I committed suicide. That's why you bailed me out. Just to kill me. You knew I'd begin remembering."

Sara caressed her fingers through his hair as she might a sick child's. "Now, you go on back to sleep, Nick," she said. She gave his forehead a light kiss, then stood up, putting the knife down on a marble counter. "It will all be over soon."

When she turned to her mother, Nick once again felt himself lose consciousness. The drugs were heavy in his blood, and he couldn't keep his mind focused. He was reeling backward, spiraling into a bottomless black void.

The sound of heavy masculine footsteps revived him, dragging Nick from his daze. It could have been moments later, or hours. Nick's mouth tasted bitter, and he realized that he had vomited. He opened his eyes as the lights flared onto their brightest setting. Impossibly, Stolie strode into the room in a blaze of fiery whiteness. As though he were surrounded by a white-hot halo, Nick thought, flying in on Icarus's melting wings.

Nick felt a wave of relief rise in his chest. His 911 call had gone through. The precinct had gotten the call and made sense of the conversation he had been having with Sara. They had tracked Stolie down, and, unbelievably, he had made it here to the house and forced an entry just in time.

Nick struggled to raise his head off the floor. "Stolie," he managed to say. His voice cracked. He was barely able to speak above a hoarse whisper. But it didn't matter now. The detective was here, and he would rescue him and arrest Sara and her mother.

When Stolie stopped to speak to Sara and Jillian,

Nick was overcome with alarm. The detective hadn't drawn his gun. They would trick him. They would try to convince the policeman that he was delusional, and then the moment the detective turned his back on them, they would stab him. Sara was so beautiful, Jillian so refined. How could anyone believe them capable of such a brutal conspiracy? Who wouldn't believe them? But then Nick realized how foolish he was being. Stolie had seen him lying on the floor, his hands and legs bound with nylon cord. There would be no way for Sara and Jillian to explain this away.

Their voices seemed to reach Nick from a distance. Desperately clinging to his precarious consciousness, Nick tried to make sense of what they were saying.

How long has he been here like this?

Two hours.

The rope cut his wrists. They're bleeding, and bruised, I think.

I'll take a look. In the meantime, why don't you start filling the bathtub?

Nick twisted around. What was happening? Why was Stolie asking them to fill the bath? Had they somehow convinced him that they didn't intend Nick any harm after all? Nick struggled to lift his head. "You don't understand," he managed to say. "They've been planning this for years." He was desperate to make himself understood. "Sara seduced Jason Hamlin. That's why Hamlin married Jillian, he wanted Sara. They planned this from the start. To get his money."

From across the room Nick saw smiles appear on Sara's and Jillian's faces, and the look of disgust on the detective's. When Stolie crossed the floor, the cadence of his footsteps catapulted Nick abruptly back to the night that Sam was killed.

* * *

Nick was hunched over Sam's body, watching his brother bleed to death, holding him as still as he could. Minutes had passed since he had spoken to Sara on Sam's phone, and Sam was fading. The gravelly scrape of footsteps echoed hollowly across the parking lot, and Nick looked up into the shadows.

When Nick saw the uniformed cop emerge from the mist, a wave of profound relief cascaded over him. Sara had called the police, and they had made it in time. The officer's radio was buzzing, and he reached down and switched it off as he approached. His face was blank, emotionless. Even as confused as he was, Nick understood that something was very wrong. The officer wasn't reacting with the urgency that the situation demanded. And now that he looked, the officer was familiar to him, and he didn't belong in this uniform.

"Please," Nick said. "Can you do something? It's my brother. He's been stabbed. We need to do something. We need to get him to a hospital."

Beneath him, Sam's head was shaking, jerking spasmodically in his grip. Nick clamped his hands ever more tightly around his brother's face. Trying desperately to keep his brother alive.

The officer knelt down in front of Nick. "You're pretty messed up," he said. "Aren't you?"

"I don't know," Nick said. "I don't know what's happening."

The officer looked at him, then turned his attention toward Sam. "It looks like the knife missed his heart," he said. "Otherwise your brother would have been dead long ago." He noticed the knife trapped underneath Nick's knee and reached to pick it up. He held it in the light for a few seconds, examining its blade. Then Nick watched as Stolie gripped the knife and placed the point directly above his brother's heart and shoved it into his chest. The rip of the blade slicing through flesh screamed in his ears, and, instinctively, as life escaped from his brother, Nick let go of Sam's head and grabbed the knife.

"You were in on it from the beginning," Nick said.

Stolie was kneeling over him, holding Nick's hands in the air by the excruciatingly tight nylon cord. He shifted his weight at the sound of Nick's voice. A small smile lifted the corners of his mouth, but his eyes remained hard and emotionless.

"How much have they paid you?" Nick asked him. "How much does it cost to buy a homicide detective?"

Stolie placed a hand over Nick's mouth and squeezed. His grip got tighter and tighter, until Nick couldn't breathe.

Sara was standing beside them, opening the taps into the tub. "You'll kill him," she said.

The detective glanced at her. "Isn't that the point?"

"We don't want to suffocate him." Nick could hear Jillian's voice, but he couldn't see her. "Let him go, Mr. Stolie. We'll do it the way we planned."

Nick felt Stolie's grip tighten on his jaw. Over the length of his arm, the man's eyes bored holes into Nick's. Then he let go. He remained kneeling over him, watching Nick gasp for air.

"There," Sara said. "The tub's filling up."

"Let's get it over with," Jillian said. "After this, we have a lot of cleaning up to do."

Stolie leaned forward and scooped Nick into his arms. Nick felt himself being hoisted into the air. The sudden movement dislodged his phone from the fold in his T-shirt, and it clattered on the floor. "What the hell is that?" Stolie said as he set Nick down into the cold water.

Sara snatched the cell phone from the floor. "It's on," she said.

Letting go of Nick, Stolie grabbed the phone from her. He examined it for a second, then switched it off. He held it up at Sara and Jillian threateningly. "He called 911."

The color faded from Sara's cheeks.

"It was connected," Stolie said. He tossed the phone onto the counter. "Give me the goddamned knife. Let's get this done."

"It's right there." Sara pointed at the carving knife she had brought from the kitchen, lying on the counter.

Stolie slid the blade between Nick's wrists, severing the nylon cord. Then he grabbed Nick's left hand and turned it palm up. Nick tried to pull his arm away, but he was too weak to struggle. Stolie had only to tighten his grip. He placed the point of the blade down onto Nick's bared wrist, then, looking blankly into Nick's eyes, plunged the sharp steel savagely through his skin.

When Stolie let go of Nick's arm, it fell loosely into the bathtub beside him. Nick watched the blood pump from his body into the water as if it didn't belong to him. It spread quickly, like some kind of an infection, turning rusty brown against the white porcelain sides of the huge sunken tub. Sara stood next to Stolie, watching Nick die, a strange look of fascination in her eyes. Stolie lifted Nick's other arm, gripping it roughly in his strong hands, ready again to puncture his veins with the bloody blade of the knife.

The last thing that Nick was aware of as his blood

pressure dropped, before a profound coldness overcame him and he lost consciousness, was the silver chain around Sara's neck. Then the shock that branded her beautiful eyes.

Nick didn't hear Lieutenant Dombrowski as he stormed the room. He didn't hear the door slam back against the tiled wall. Nick's heart was barely beating. He was dying, and he didn't hear the blast of the gunshot from Dombrowski's service revolver. He didn't see the look of agony on Stolie's face when the first lead bullet tore a hole in his chest.

The second bullet left a circle of blood on Stolie's forehead, before exploding the back of his cranium and plastering it in bits and pieces against the bathroom wall.

chapter 38

Laura Daly was working Christmas day, as she always had. On that cloudless, sunny day, the huge, nearly empty newsroom was unusually bright with natural light. Nick wasn't certain why, but it felt like Christmas. "It's an incredible story," Daly was saying. "What a tapestry. I can't quite believe it—all of them working together. Sara, Jillian, Barnes, your brother. Detective Stolie. What a conspiracy."

"There was a lot at stake. And there were a lot of different things going on," Nick acknowledged. "Sara and her mother had been planning this for years, but they were still opportunists. Who knows? Maybe they hadn't been planning to kill Hamlin from the start. Maybe they had only been planning to set him up for raping Sara, to see how much they could extort from him. When Sara met Sam and found out about his work with Barnes, the opportunity he presented was too good to pass up. Sam and Barnes were trying to bilk money out of Hamlin, too. Why take a little, though, when you can get your hands on the whole thing?" Nick smiled ruefully at his boss before he went on. "Like Sara said, I was the perfect sacrifice. And then Jackson Ferry came along and nearly spoiled their plans. Lucky for them they had Stolie to help them pick up the pieces."

Daly shook her head. "And they murdered Van Gundy, too."

"I should have put it together earlier."

"You were drugged, Nick. Half out of your mind."

"Except for you, Sara was the only one who knew that I was going to meet him. Stolie was the triggerman, but it was Sara and Jillian who wanted Van Gundy dead. The last thing they needed was you and me breaking open that scandal. We would have brought down Hamlin's empire right before they got their hands on it."

Daly looked very satisfied. "It's going to make a damn good series of headlines."

Nick shrugged his shoulders. "I don't want anything to do with it."

"No," Daly said. "I'm sure you don't." She became pensive. "What are your plans? I suppose you'll have to stay here in Seattle for Sara and Jillian's trial. But after that?"

Nick cast his gaze down toward the floor. "I don't know," he said. "I really don't know."

Daly looked at him through the eyes of a friend. "You really shouldn't take the wrong lessons from this."

Nick waited for the woman to explain.

"It must not be easy to accept Sam's guilt. And it must hurt, everything you lost with Sara. I can't even imagine. But the thing of it is, Nick, no man can go through life alone. My father once said to me, 'You walk your destiny through a labyrinth.' I think about that sometimes, and it strikes me how difficult it is to walk that labyrinth by yourself, without a beacon." She rested a hand on Nick's back. "Whether you understand it or not, you have a family here in Seattle." Nick was unable to mask the skepticism creasing his forehead. "We don't want to lose you."

Laura Daly let her hand linger too long on Nick's back, waiting for him to meet her gaze. Their eyes connected, though only for a second. Nick looked away without returning her smile. He wasn't certain why, but he found himself thinking of the son she had lost, who had disappeared without any trace.

I don't have a family, he thought to say, but the words died inside him. *Neither do you, Laura. And I don't know anyone who does.*

Outside in the street, the sun was shining brilliantly on the huge wreath hung above the front doors of the *Seattle Telegraph* building. A homeless man walking past stopped to tie his shoe, then regarded the young man as he exited the building, a camera dangling from his bandaged arm.

"Anything you got for me, I'd be grateful," the bum said.

Nick reached automatically into his pocket for a few coins but then stopped himself. He looked the other man in the eye and shook his head. "Sorry," he said.

"It's Christmas," the homeless man said bitterly.

Nick shrugged, then turned and began walking away. The homeless man watched him, then began walking slowly down the sidewalk in the opposite direction.

ACKNOWLEDGMENTS

It has been a long trip.

I can trace the beginning all the way back to a day in Kumasi, Ghana, when at five years old I decided to sell my parents a copy of a book I had stapled together—a few pages I called *Ali & Fatima*. Next stop was the aptly titled *An Event That History Forgot*, which I wrote in the wee hours of the morning during the summer of my twelfth year. After that follow too many failed attempts to remember. I never stopped believing. What makes this journey all the more extraordinary, though, is the help I received along the way from family and friends. Belief in yourself is a graceful blindness. The belief of others is a blind grace, a precious faith.

I am not going to try to reckon that faith here. I hate books with long acknowledgments. There are a few names, though, that must be mentioned. Not to would be criminal.

To the extent that any of this story appears at all effortless, the credit belongs to the people who picked me up and carried me the last few big steps. John Paine, whom I will never be able to repay. Jaimee Garbacik (I will always remember the first call I received from you. I was standing in Miami International, about to board a plane. "Is this Craig?"). Frank Weimann ("Hey—I have some good news for you."). And Michaela Hamilton, who is all the proof I need that guardian angels do exist.

Any deficiencies are mine.